We hope you enjoy this book. Please return or renew it by the due date. *8/20*

You can renew it at www.norfolk.gov.uk/libraries or by using our free library app.

Otherwise you can phone 0344 800 8020 - please have your library card and PIN ready.

You can sign up for email reminders too.

D0524518

Also by Cath Weeks

Friends Don't Lie

Cath Weeks

piatkus

PIATKUS

First published in Great Britain in 2019 by Piatkus
This paperback edition published in 2020 by Piatkus

1 3 5 7 9 10 8 6 4 2

A CIP catalogue record for this book
is available from the British Library.

ISBN 978-0-349-41873-5

Typeset in Bembo by M Rules
Printed and bound in Great Britain by Clays Ltd, Elcograf S.p.A.

Papers used by Piatkus are from well-managed forests
and other responsible sources.

Piatkus
An imprint of
Little, Brown Book Group
Carmelite House
50 Victoria Embankment
London EC4Y 0DZ

An Hachette UK Company
www.hachette.co.uk

www.littlebrown.co.uk

To Wilfie and Alex, with love

What charm can soothe her melancholy,
What art can wash her guilt away?

Oliver Goldsmith 1728–74

PROLOGUE

Sometimes, when the light fell a certain way, she could see a child sitting in the long grass.

The child, dressed in yellow, was wearing a sunhat over her peach-blonde curls. She was so small, or the lawn so over-grown, she barely cleared the grass. Beside her, a bee hovered drowsily over a pot of lavender that was almost done flowering for the summer.

There was a thickness to the air, a stillness. A crow was cawing from above; a mirage of heat wobbled on the tarmac in the lane beyond. The telegraph wires were humming.

Everything trembled, grew heavy for a moment, like a drop of water dangling from a tap, quivering, before falling.

In the blink of an eye, it had changed. The silence grew unbearable.

A strange sound then – a horrifying sound.

And then, nothing. The child had gone, was no longer vis-ible in the grass.

Sometimes, when the light fell a certain way, she could see all that.

Other times, she could see nothing at all. On those days, it was as though none of it had ever happened.

ANGELA GOULD

Milford resident, Dorset

Angela had always wanted to be a Silkie. Had she written a bucket list — had such a thing existed back then — she would have put *be a Silkie* right at the top, ahead of having kids or getting married; and she hadn't been the only one.

These days, everyone in town knew the Silkies, even those too old or young to have been at school with them. They were everywhere, running local businesses, volunteering, being good eggs.

For all her longing, Angela had never joined their ranks. They had their original members, were watertight. That was never going to change.

So, she had settled for marriage, children and watching the comings and goings of the Silkies from behind her dining-room curtains.

She might have been bitter about it, might have hated them, had they not been so infectiously likeable. In all her years of living in Milford, she had never met a single soul who had a bad word to say about any of them.

One of these days, she would summon the courage to knock on Melissa's door. They had lived opposite each other for over a decade yet rarely said more than hello. Grasping hold of a Silkie was like trying to catch a falling leaf. Somehow, she never found the right moment to attempt it and the days stretched on, unaltered.

1

Saturday 14 April 2018

Melissa was gazing out of the window when Lee stole up behind her. 'What time's Jenny coming?' he said.

'Soon,' she replied.

'She's bound to be late,' he said, kissing the back of her neck. 'Another hour, at least. Enough time to pop upstairs . . .'

She turned to face him, poking him in the stomach. 'Is that all you think about?'

'No,' Lee said, smiling. 'But the kids are out; it's just you and me . . .' He wiggled his hips, his smile broadening.

She cast her eyes up and down his lean body. He was wearing skinny jeans that made him look gangly. Standing there, wiggling, he could have been sixteen again, trying to get her to sneak into the back room of her mother's bungalow and French kiss to Bon Jovi.

His hair was stuck on end; she reached up to smooth it flat, then gave him a kiss on the cheek – the sort of goodbye kiss that she gave the children before school.

'Guess that's a no then. But if you change your mind . . .' He slapped her bottom, before turning away, his foot skittling a pencil across the floor. 'Kids,' he said, sighing.

'She said she'd clear it up when she gets back.'

'Likely story.'

Polly, their youngest child, was nine years old and passionate about colouring in. She left little shrines of pencils on the floor around the house, reminiscent of the twig bonfires they encountered in the dunes at the beach.

'Am I picking her up from pony club?' Lee said.

'No, we'll get her on our way back later.'

'And what about Keener?'

'You really should stop calling her that.'

'She knows I'm only joking.'

'But still . . .' Their middle child, fourteen-year-old Nina, was called *Keener Nina* by her classmates. She wanted to be a doctor and was working hard at school, while the rest of them looked on in wonder.

'She won't be back from netball until teatime,' Melissa replied.

Turning to look out of the window again, she watched for Jenny's car. She couldn't see a single thing moving in the garden – not a branch, bird or blade of glass. It was very hot for April, an unexpected heatwave that was forecast to last several weeks.

'What are you ladies up to anyway?' Lee asked.

'Not much. Jenny wants to go for a walk along the beach. We're picking Rachel up on the way; she's desperate to get out of the house – something about Al being an idiot.'

Lee smirked. 'She's always calling Al an idiot.'

'Oh, you think?'

That's because Al is an idiot.

She didn't say so out loud, though.

'Well, be good,' Lee said, scooping up a pile of paperwork from the kitchen counter and tucking it under his arm. 'I'll see you later.'

'Have fun,' she said, watching him leave the room. His walk

6

was light, loose, as though his bolts weren't as tightly screwed as everyone else's. He didn't seem to be ageing much either.

Eternal youth – the illusion of it – was surely one of the advantages of marrying your childhood sweetheart, association being a powerful thing. Most people would deem early marriage a disaster, but it had worked well for her and Lee. Both forty-two now and married for twenty-two years, Lee looked the same to her, felt the same to her as the first time she had kissed him. He had tasted of blackcurrant bubble gum. To this day, she sighed when pouring Ribena.

There was comfort in that – great comfort.

She glanced at her watch, tutting. Jenny never arrived on time; it was impossible for her to do so. For someone so beautifully packaged, she was chronically disorganised. Not like Melissa, who had mastered the art of pretending to look relaxed while running a family and a business.

Somehow, miraculously, Jenny also ran a family and a business, in a bubble of chaos. Yet the bubble was very pretty and no one got hurt and everyone seemed happy, so perhaps there was nothing to worry about.

Still, for Melissa, the temptation to interfere was too great. She was always trying – delicately, covertly – to help Jenny be more efficient. Best friends from the age of four, once upon a time she had demonstrated the best way to make a castle in the sandpit: it was all about the packing of the sand.

Nowadays, she suggested tips to Jenny at opportune moments.

This new phone app brings all your to-do lists together.

Have you thought about using a filing cabinet?

Why not keep the petty cash for the hair salon in the till and not in that pair of tights at the back of the drawer?

Melissa smiled. The tights as a banking system was classic Jenny.

Withdrawing from the window, she sat down on the sofa

7

and picked up the phone just as it beeped. It was a text message from her other friend, Rachel.

It was commonly believed that three was a disastrous formula for friendship, but Melissa didn't agree with that. She, Jenny and Rachel had been close friends for years. They were similar enough to get along, whilst each bringing different qualities into the mix. What did it matter how many people were in a group, so long as you didn't step on each other's toes? Things only became awkward when you both showed up wearing the same dress, so to speak.

Rachel was the smartest one in their circle of friends, their three husbands included. With John Lennon spectacles and bobbed hair, she always spoke carefully, holding on to every word as it met the air. Just lately two prominent frown lines had appeared between her eyes, seemingly overnight.

Melissa noticed these things. As unofficial leader of the group, it was her job to do so.

I need to cut the trip short. Sorry. Al's being a muppet. Rach xox

Poor Rachel. She had been born with large hands, not literally; just that she had to carry her needy husband as well as her two slightly less needy – but give them time – sons.

Melissa put her phone down and gazed into space, wondering whether there was more to Rachel's current woes than the usual Al annoyances.

She would take her to one side later and ask if everything was all right, if there was anything she could do to help. The more serious the problem, the less likely Rachel would be to open up. She was notoriously difficult to extract information from, a fact that Melissa had learnt the hard way at primary school. Back then, Rachel had been known to eat paper if it held secrets.

Perhaps a glass of wine in the sunshine on the way home would do the trick.

⚓

Gareth was just walking back to his car, having dropped Max off at the rugby club, when his phone rang. Normally, he stayed to watch his sixteen-year-old son play. He enjoyed talking to the other dads, having a laugh and a grumble, stamping their feet on a frosty sideline to keep warm.

No chance of freezing today. It was boiling, which was why he was leaving. Hot weather always caught him out, especially in April. He didn't have sun lotion or a hat with him. There was no shelter at Milford Rugby Club, aside from a smelly changing room. Five minutes of standing on the sideline and he'd be redder than a plucked hen.

Shame to miss the match, though. Maybe he would pop home, grab what he needed and return.

He pulled his phone from his pocket. 'Yuhello.'

It was Jenny. 'Where are my car keys?' she said.

'How should I know, sweetheart?'

'Well, you had them last.'

'Did I?' he said, stopping by his car, leaning back against it. Already, just in that short walk, the back of his shirt was damp. He watched Max running on to the pitch – a skinny teenager who looked as though he would be crushed by the opposition, but who would surprise them all with his sinewy strength and speed.

Born in Wales, having moved to Dorset as a child, Gareth was proud of his heritage and proud too of his son, the rugby ace. No doubt Max would have preferred to have played football, like all his other friends, but he had been worn down by Gareth's pestering. And now look at him: team captain.

Gareth was glad that he could share these precious moments with his son. If only that were the case with his daughter, Olivia, Max's twin sister.

Poor Olivia was just as skinny as Max, if not more so. Always eating carrots: liquidised carrots, carrot sticks; and watching how-to-draw-eyebrows tutorials online.

Was that normal behaviour for a sixteen-year-old girl?

Yes, Jenny kept assuring him. Totally normal.

The carrots and eyebrow tutorials were just two of the many things that he didn't understand about Olivia. A gulf had opened up between them lately that neither of them seemed able to cross. Luckily, Jenny was there for them, bridging the gap.

It would pass, she kept telling him.

Sometimes, more often of late, the gulf that lay in the middle of his family actually made his heart hurt. Until two years ago, Olivia had been his little angel. Now she looked at him as though he were a gargoyle.

'You moved my car earlier,' Jenny said.

He turned his attention back to his phone. 'That's right, I did,' he said.

'So, where did you put the keys?'

He pictured Jenny's car. She had just bought a small custard-coloured Honda for running around town in, with a view to the twins learning to drive it next year. The interior was biscuit coloured. Sitting inside it, especially in this weather, was like being sat inside a warm apple crumble.

'I hung them back up,' Gareth said.

'Well, they're not here,' Jenny said. 'I'm late to pick up Mel ...' She paused. 'Oh ...' There was a tinkling sound. 'They were in my back pocket all along.'

He laughed. Jenny was a nightmare – always losing things, running late. How she managed to run her hair salon was an enigma. She specialised in children's cuts; never had a town had such fashionably coiffured kids.

There was a swell of cheering from the crowd then as Max tucked the ball under his arm and raced down the pitch. 'Go on, son!' Gareth roared.

'What's happening?' Jenny said.

'Damn. He nearly scored a try,' Gareth said.

'I wish I was there,' Jenny said. 'Is he . . . ?'

'Jen,' he said.

'Yep?'

'Get going.'

'Right. Yes. I'm off.'

Hanging up, he felt oddly disconcerted – a grouchy feeling poking around in his stomach. He didn't feel like hurrying home now for sun cream. He would stay and watch the match from the car.

Wincing at the heat inside the car, he swung the doors wide open. According to the gauge on the dashboard, the temperate was twenty-eight degrees.

A sudden noise made him look up. The crowd was cheering again. Max was sprinting for the line. 'That's it!' Gareth shouted, jumping out of the car.

Max had scored a try. He was looking over at his dad, his blond hair catching the light, his cheeks red with exertion. Gareth was shouting and waving and whistling, beside himself with jubilation.

A car pulled up alongside Gareth then, and a man and his daughter got out. Gareth grinned at them. 'That's my boy, that is. Just scored, he did. Bleedin' brill-yunt!'

Sometimes, he sounded more Welsh. This was one of those times.

The father smiled politely before making his way over to the sideline, his daughter holding his arm.

Holding his arm!

How old was the girl – fifteen, sixteen? She looked a similar age to Olivia.

Gareth sat back down in the car rather heavily, continuing to watch his son. But every so often, his eye flitted over to the father and daughter.

He was going to have to do something to lessen the gap between himself and Olivia. Yet he had no idea where to begin.

Jenny would know. He would talk to her about it again, impress on her how much it was getting to him. Jenny would know what to do.

2

'You can't just drop this on me, Al. It's not fair.'

'Not fair?' Al said, opening the wardrobe and running his hand along the row of shirts – shirts that she ironed every Sunday evening.

When had he last thanked her for doing so? When had he *ever* thanked her for the multitude of tasks that she did behind the scenes to keep the household ticking over?

'It's work, Rachel.' He selected a pink shirt and put it on, watching himself in the mirror. 'Fair doesn't come into it. You think that I want to go over to Portbridge on a day like this and spend it in some stuffy meeting? 'Course I don't. But I've got no choice. I'm the CEO. And someone has to pay the mortgage.'

Rachel rolled her eyes. It seemed to escape his notice that she worked too. Yes, she didn't earn anywhere near as much as him, but still ... She sat down on the bed, folded her arms. 'I was looking forward to seeing the girls.'

'And you still can ...' he said, fiddling with his cufflinks. 'Besides, you see Melissa every day at the marina. Surely that's enough?'

'No,' Rachel said. 'That's work.'

'Look, all I'm asking is that you drop Ned off at football. Then you can go to the beach.'

'Fine,' she said, not feeling fine at all.

Al fastened his tie then stood at the foot of the bed, holding his hands out to pull her to her feet. 'Come on,' he said. 'It's not so bad, is it?'

How to explain to him that in a house full of males, outnumbered as she was, being with her girlfriends – having a life of her own – mattered greatly?

She loved her two sons wholeheartedly, loved him too, but she relished spending time with her friends, when she could talk about things that they understood. Sometimes, she tried talking to Al. But he listened to the first part, then glazed over, finally looking for signs that she was coming to an end so that he could add a pertinent comment in conclusion.

You couldn't rely on a man for life-affirming conversations – not her man, anyway.

He tucked her hair behind her ears, kissed her on the lips. She caught a little waft of his aftershave and kissed him back, cursing herself, her spectacles steaming up.

If he weren't so good-looking it would all be different. How many times had she found herself thinking that in twenty years of marriage?

'You don't have to hang around after you drop Ned off,' he said.

She wasn't intending to.

'And Joel's back from hockey, when?' he asked.

She shrugged. Now that Joel was seventeen and driving, he was keeping his own hours to a certain extent. If he wanted to get a place at university, he would have to study hard. She couldn't tell him that enough. But Saturday afternoons were his to do with as he saw fit.

Ned, on the other hand, was only twelve. She wasn't in any rush to hurry him along the growth chart. He still slept with his teddy bear and called her mummy and she relished every time that he did.

'I assume that Ned will need collecting after football?' she called after Al as he bounded down the stairs.

'Er, yes . . .' he said. 'If you don't mind.' He stopped by the front door, rifling through the shoe rack for his brogues.

'So, by the time I get down to the beach, I'll have one hour with the girls?'

He smiled sheepishly. 'I'll make it up to you.' He kissed her again, longer this time.

She pulled away. 'Just go.'

He bent his knees to look into her eyes. 'Are we OK?'

He looked insecure, uncertain. For one moment, she got a kick out of seeing it there on his face. He still needed her, wanted her.

She could have answered his question differently. Things weren't OK, but she couldn't tell him that, not yet at least. She needed time to think. That was the thing with her: always thinking. Sometimes her thoughts made her rigid, stiff, where she held herself so still.

'Yes,' she said. 'Now go.'

'I'll see you later, gorgeous,' he said. 'Love you.' And he was off, the door closing behind him with a rattle of the knocker.

Rachel sighed, then went through to the lounge to find Ned, who was lying on the sofa reading *The Beano*. 'Let's get ready for footie,' she said, tapping his legs to get him to move.

'Do I have to?' he said.

'Yes. Go upstairs and get changed. And hurry.'

He couldn't have left the room more slowly.

She picked up his comic, which was lying strewn on the floor. Then she picked up a sock and a glass of water, and two used tissues, which she pincered delicately.

Sometimes, she felt as though she was just clearing up after males. Was it like this with daughters too? All mothers felt like this to a certain extent, surely, no matter who lived with them.

15

Unless you were like Jenny, who never seemed to clear up, never seemed to let it bother her.

Her tummy flipped over at the thought of Jenny.

She had wanted so badly to talk to her today. It would have been the perfect opportunity to do so. Melissa would have run down to the shoreline as soon as they got to the beach, like she always did. Rachel and Jenny always brought up the rear, watching their friend paddling in the sea, whilst the two of them linked arms, chatting.

Now there wouldn't be time for a talk, not in the way she had envisaged. It wasn't the sort of thing she could just blurt out. The timing had to be right.

She would have to rethink it.

'Come on, Ned,' she shouted up the stairs. 'We really must go.'

⚓

It was hot in Jenny's Honda on the way back to town after the beach. Melissa lowered the window, waving her arm up and down in the airstream as they sped along the country lane. There wasn't much traffic, which was surprising given the sunshine. Yet the heat was intense, the sort that almost went full circle into being bad weather. There was a smell of burning rubber in the air, of tarmac melting, of dust and dried grass.

The atmosphere inside the car was a little strange, Melissa felt: brittle, slightly strained. Perhaps it was the weather, which was freakish in itself.

Beside her, Jenny was driving, wearing huge cork-wedge sandals and oversized shades, her hair scooped into a smooth bun. At only five foot one in height, she looked tiny at the wheel. Drivers behind would think that the car was driving itself.

Sitting on the back seat, Rachel was perfectly motionless,

lips pursed. She looked very tired today, and pale in her short sleeves and shorts.

'So, our two have gone shopping today, then,' Melissa said.

'In this heat,' Jenny said. 'Crazy.'

'Wouldn't have been my first choice of activity, must admit.'

'How long have they been seeing each other now?' Rachel asked, sitting forward.

Melissa turned sideways to talk to her. 'About a year?'

'Surely longer?' Rachel pushed her spectacles further up her nose, the two frown lines between her eyes looking ever deeper. Something was definitely troubling her, but a glass of wine on the way home was apparently out of the question – too much to do today.

'They've been dating one year and five months,' Jenny said, raising her shoulders at the wheel and then dropping them again.

'That long?' Melissa said. 'Time flies . . . '

'How's Frank's revision going?' Rachel asked.

Melissa's eldest child and only son, Frank, was seventeen and about to crash his way through his A levels.

Not like Rachel's eldest son, Joel, who was on target to attend a Russell Group university, which was a big deal, according to Al.

'Put it like this,' Melissa said, 'he's currently in Topshop with Olivia picking out leggings. That's his priority. No offence.' She tapped Jenny's knee.

'None taken.'

Frank was dating Jenny's daughter. At sixteen, Olivia still had a year to go before knuckling down for exams – and knuckling down she would be; Jenny had always made that quite clear.

It was for this reason that no one really took the relationship seriously or expected it to last. They were always saying

17

amongst themselves that when their kids split up, they hoped they would do so civilly, with minimal fuss.

'Frank's just not interested in education or exams,' Melissa said. 'All he wants to do is work down the marina as soon as he can. He wants to be just like Lee.'

'Awh,' said Jenny. 'That's sweet, Mel. You're lucky that he knows what he wants to do. And he'll be good at it, too. At least you don't have the problem of wondering who to pass the family business on to. That can be a real headache for some people.'

'Hmm.' Melissa looked out of the window, her hair buffeting around her face. The topic of conversation was a regular one for them, always leaving her with the same unsettled feeling, despite knowing that nothing was glaringly wrong.

Lee, for one, was delighted about Frank's intentions. His boat yard, Silks Marina, had been in his family for several generations. He would have hated parting with it in later life, were it not for Frank. Lee and the marina had become one and the same over the years. A skilled carpenter, he smelt of sea air, glue, paint, oil – in a good way. And now Frank would too.

The marina served them well as a family, there was no denying that. Melissa worked there herself, hosting events. In the early stages of their marriage, she had run the office. But five years ago she had overseen the remodelling of one of the boat sheds into a party venue, which she now ran. At the same time, Rachel had taken over the running of the office.

Melissa had always known that she was destined to marry someone connected to water. Her own family owned the Sea Kayaking Academy three miles around the corner from the marina. She had grown up hopping about in canoes, dipping about in waves. It had only been a matter of time before she had slipped around the coastline to join Lee.

How could she expect anything different of Frank? She just

didn't want him to be hurt when everyone left him behind, including Olivia.

'Well, that's it, ladies,' Jenny said, pulling up outside Rachel's house.

'Thanks for the lift,' Rachel said. 'Sorry the plans got messed up.'

On the pavement, with two imposing lion-topped gateposts looming over her, Rachel waved at them. Then she put her neat leather rucksack on her shoulder and started down her driveway.

'One sec ... ' Melissa said to Jenny, unbuckling her seat belt and getting out of the car. 'Wait!' she called out.

Rachel stopped, turned in surprise.

Melissa hung her thumbs on the edges of her shorts pockets. 'Is everything OK?'

Rachel smiled, but it quickly vanished. 'Yes, why?'

'You seem down.'

'I'm fine. It's the heat making me tired.'

Melissa nodded. 'Well, you know where I am ... '

No sense pushing it. Maybe it really was just the heat. She went to walk away, but Rachel was still standing there.

She hadn't ever seen Rachel dithering before. The effect was unsettling, as though they were wobbling each other on an ice rink. Behind them, Jenny's Honda was still running. 'Take My Breath Away' was drifting out from the car stereo.

'Can I ring you later?' Rachel said. 'There's something I'd like to ask you.'

''Course,' Melissa said. 'I'll be in all night.'

'Thanks.'

They kissed goodbye, parted company, Melissa feeling a wave of satisfaction at having reached her friend, but also of curiosity as to what the problem was.

'What was that all about?' Jenny said, as Melissa got back into the car.

'Nothing much. Just checking she's OK. She seemed a bit quiet.'

'She's always a bit quiet.'

'True.'

They left it at that. Jenny tended to take things at face value. She gave a shrug, pressed her ludicrously large cork heel down on the accelerator, her silver bangles jangling, and they took off into the sunshine, heading for home.

3

The landline rang at eight o'clock that night, just as Melissa was cleaning Polly's teeth. 'Mel!' Lee shouted up the stairs. 'Phone!'

'Carry on brushing by yourself, Pols,' Melissa said, leaving the bathroom. 'Do it carefully.'

Hurrying downstairs, she took the cordless phone into the utility room, pushing the door shut behind her.

As expected, it was Rachel on the line. 'I can't be very long,' Rachel said. 'Al's around.'

Did that mean that this was about him? Intrigued, Melissa pressed the phone closer to her ear. 'How can I help?'

Rachel paused. 'I wondered whether we could go kayaking?'

'Down at Mum's?'

'Yes.'

'Well, of course. But why is that such a—' She was going to say *big deal*, but Rachel cut her off.

'Do I need to book it up?' Rachel said.

'Yes. Speak to Mum or David. When are you thinking of going?'

'Next Saturday.'

Melissa was confused; going kayaking wasn't a big thing. The six of them did it from time to time and had done so ever since they were teenagers. With her mother's academy being so near to town, it made sense to take the kayaks out every so often, free of charge to boot.

'Would you mind not coming?' Rachel said.

Melissa cocked her head in surprise. 'What?'

'Maybe you and Lee could sit this one out. It'll be just the four us – me, Al, Jenny and Gareth. Is that all right?'

Melissa didn't know how to answer that, didn't know whether she thought it was all right or not. Nowhere was it written that she had to accompany her friends everywhere they went. Yet it was her mother's academy and Melissa was the best kayaker by far and had always gone with them before.

That said, Al was proficient enough to lead a simple trip.

'I do have my reasons,' Rachel said.

'Which are?'

Rachel paused. 'I want to talk to Jenny. We can walk along the beach, leave the men for a while.'

'So why can't I come?'

Again, Rachel paused. She was speaking in her slow, considered style, but there was something else in her tone that wasn't usually there – something that Melissa couldn't quite identify.

'Because I don't want it to look obvious. If you're there, the men will wonder why you're not walking with us. And I need time alone with her.'

'Why?'

'Please, Mel,' Rachel said. 'Don't make me explain. Not yet.'

Melissa frowned. She didn't like the sound of that. 'Are you going to tell me eventually?'

'Yes.'

'You swear?'

'I swear,' Rachel said.

Melissa couldn't imagine what it was that Rachel would need to talk to Jenny about so privately. Since when had they kept secrets from each other? That wasn't the way things worked between them.

'Why kayaking?' she asked. 'Why not go for a walk around town or have a coffee?'

'Because it's not as simple as that. I need something that we can all enjoy together – something fun and ... bonding. Something that she can't just get up and walk away from.'

'I see.'

She didn't see. Nothing about this was clear.

'Please, bear with me,' Rachel said softly, her voice wavering.

What else could Melissa do?

'OK,' she said. 'But give me a clue what it's about. I mean, is it serious? Are you dying? Is—'

'No one's dying,' Rachel said. 'We just need to ... smooth something out.'

'Like ironing?'

'Sort of.' Rachel laughed nervously. 'It's not something for you to worry about. I promise. Please, let's not escalate this.'

Melissa had no intention of doing so. She didn't even know what it was that she would be escalating. There was no chance whatsoever of escalation.

'When you find out what it is, you'll understand.'

'Well, then I can't wait,' Melissa said drily. 'Have fun. Send me a postcard.'

'Don't be like that, Mel. It's not about you. This is just something that I have to deal with and then all will be well.'

'Fine.' Melissa sniffed touchily. Beyond the door, Polly was running up and down the hallway – playing with Nina, by the sounds of things. Polly was laughing her head off, in the way that children under ten tend to do.

Would any part of this matter in the long run? Melissa thought. It was only a kayaking trip.

'Go ahead,' she said. 'Make sure Al plans it all, like I always do.'

'Will do. Thank you. I really appreciate it.'

'Bye for now, then,' she said, hanging up and leaning back against the washing machine. While she trusted Rachel implicitly, their conversation had thrown her. She didn't own the rights to Jenny's friendship, or to any of the Silkies', yet she was used to being in the centre of the group, all paths leading to her. Being left out didn't sit well with her at all. However, hopefully it would only be a temporary affliction.

There was nothing she could do about it for now. Fretting wouldn't help. Pushing the matter from her mind, she opened the door on to her loud family.

Lee had joined the girls and was charging about, shouting something about ninjas. Frank was sitting on the stairs, shaking his head at them, doing the loser sign with his thumb and forefinger. He was far too cool and old to be playing with them.

This was one of Melissa's favourite things: seeing her family gathered in one place, in one camera shot.

And then Lee barged past her and she lost her footing and went flying on to the floor and everyone laughed and came over to help her up; even Frank.

⚓

Rachel hung up and gazed around her, at the cobwebs lining the garage doors and the thick sticky dust on the jam jars and paint tins on the shelves – shelves that were slightly wonky because Al wasn't the best of handymen but was too proud to admit it. Their house was full of wobbly fittings and fixtures that Al had assembled, only for her to go around and secretly tighten them afterwards. If that was a metaphor for something, she didn't know what it was.

She looked at the phone in her hands, wondering what Mel would make of their conversation. Although they were a firm three, it had always been the case that Melissa and Jenny were closer to each other than she was to either of them.

It wasn't an obvious dynamic; it didn't bother her. She accepted that Mel and Jenny were sister-like, intensely close, and enjoyed the friendship that she shared with them both.

At least, that was the way things had gone until recently. But now everything had been turned upside down and she was having to fix things and put them back up the right way again.

And in doing so, she was having to break ranks. It wasn't her place to have secret conversations with Jenny at the exclusion of Melissa. She was well aware of that. Melissa wouldn't like it one bit, but was also kind-hearted and always wanted to do the right thing. Melissa would sit back and wait on this one, Rachel knew so.

She had always been rather in awe of Melissa, looking up to her, even though they were the same age and height. Melissa wasn't pretty in an obvious way, not like Jenny. During their school years, she had been immensely popular because of her supreme levels of self-confidence. She had never seemed to act as though anyone were watching her, yet they always had been, all of them.

Now, as adults, mothers, Melissa's confidence was even more of a marvel. With green eyes and tousled hair, she barely wore make-up – just a dab of lip balm. Somehow, she still pulled off the natural look, whilst the rest of them were buying anti-ageing creams and gazing fretfully into the mirror at wrinkles and enlarged pores; at least, Rachel was.

'Ah, there you are.' The side door to the garage had opened and Al was standing there in a pool of light. 'What are you doing out here?'

She stood up, slipping the phone into her pocket. 'Trying to find the bathroom paint,' she said.

'The what?'

'The paint – I'm redoing the bathroom.'

'On a Saturday night?' he said. 'I thought we said we'd get Ned off to bed early and watch a film?'

'I was just . . . Never mind. I'll leave it.'

'Good,' he said, holding out his hand to her.

She followed him inside the house but couldn't settle that night to watch the television. Her mind kept straying to next Saturday, to the deed that lay ahead.

Every so often Al took a sip of wine and squeezed her knee, checking that she was enjoying the film as much as he was, and she nodded and smiled to assure him that she was. Why wouldn't she be?

26

4

Saturday 21 April 2018

They all met in the car park at the Sea Kayaking Academy, Al having driven like a maniac because he was intent on getting there first. He was taking ownership of the outing and had planned it carefully, as you had to do with kayaking trips, however small, so he had told Rachel several times.

It was a glorious day, the heatwave still running amok. Inside the academy's reception area, it was very warm with flies buzzing against the window panes. Rachel rang the desk bell and Melissa's brother appeared instantly from the back office.

'Good morning,' he said formally.

'Hi, David,' Rachel said. 'We're here to take the kayaks out.'

He looked at her blankly, his cheeks reddening.

'Is there a problem?' Al said. Rachel glanced at him, hoping that he wouldn't be too officious. He was wearing a polo shirt, his collar turned up against the sun, a strip of sunblock on his nose as though he were a lifeguard.

'Is your mum here?' Rachel asked.

David shook his head. 'We don't have any customers booked in today. I'm here to do ad-min-is-tra-tive work.' He was frowning, concentrating on making sure he said the word correctly.

Rachel felt her heart sink in pity for him, despite the fact that Melissa had always made it clear that no one was to feel sorry for her younger brother. He just needed a little longer to organise himself, as she always put it.

'We could just have a picnic?' Rachel said, turning to look at Jenny and Gareth, who were lingering diplomatically amongst the pamphlet stands.

Jenny, holding a cool bag in her arms, said, 'Fine by me.'

But Gareth groaned. 'I was looking forward to kayaking,' he said. 'It'll be bleedin' boiling sitting on the beach.'

'Surely, you don't mind us taking the boats out, David?' Al said. 'You booked it up, didn't you, Rachel?' He turned to her.

'Yes,' Rachel said. 'I spoke to David.'

They all digested this, reaching the same conclusion: that David had stuffed up the booking.

'Well, I vote we take the boats and be done with it,' Al said.

'Um . . . ' David said.

'That settles it, then,' Gareth said, clapping his hands. 'Let's go.'

David didn't seem very happy about the situation, but wasn't equipped with the vocabulary or the gumption to argue. He stepped dutifully from the foyer and led them down the path to the boating sheds.

Rachel hung back, adjusting the handle of her cool bag, which was digging into her arm. She rubbed the red mark on her skin, watching David pull the four kayaks out of the shed one by one, carrying them on his shoulder, setting them down on the grass.

'We can take it from here,' Al said, slapping David on the back. 'Cheers, bud. You're a class act.'

Rachel winced. Next, Al would be fist-bumping him.

David turned to go. 'Thank you,' Rachel said, smiling.

He smiled back politely, but Rachel saw the reticence on his face. He rarely did anything without his mother's say-so. Hiring out kayaks without a booking would be tantamount to a crime in his eyes.

David returned to the office and they set off along the sandy boardwalk, each of them dragging a kayak. Jenny was looking pretty, coquettish in sparkly flip-flops and a Hawaiian-print shorts jumpsuit. Rachel didn't covet the look, however – preferred being practical in sea-proof rubber shoes and clothes with UV filters.

'What are the boys up to today then, Rach?' Gareth said.

'Joel's revising,' she said, 'and Ned's at a birthday party with a sleepover.'

'Nice ... Olivia's at the cinema with Frank, in this heat, can you believe?' he said.

Rachel laughed. 'I remember that – sixteen years old, with all the time in the world, back in the days when sunshine was there to waste.'

'Max is wasting it plenty too,' Gareth replied. 'Stuck indoors gaming all day over at his mate's. We should have dragged them along for some fresh air.' He turned to Jenny. 'Might have helped me bond with Olivia. Ever thought of that?'

'No, not really,' Jenny said. 'Can't see her getting in a kayak.'

'Why not?' he said.

'Because she's sixteen?'

'Fair enough,' he said.

'What's that?' said Al. 'Family bonding? I can recommend paintballing.'

Jenny scoffed with laughter. 'Maybe for your two boys, Al. But for Livvie? Really?'

'Sounds like you're going to have to take her shopping then, Gareth,' said Al. 'Or to a nail saloon.'

'It's not a saloon, you numpty,' said Jenny. 'It's a salon.

29

And besides, they're called nail bars nowadays. Get with the programme.'

'Oh, I'm with it all right,' said Al, pulling his shorts down a notch and trying to do a gangster walk.

'Stop it, Al,' said Rachel. 'It's embarrassing.'

Jenny was laughing, her white teeth glowing in the sunshine.

'Yeah, you're embarrassing,' Gareth said, nudging Al with his kayak so that he toppled off the boardwalk and on to the sand, where he teetered unsteadily before regaining his balance.

'For Pete's sake,' Al said, half-joking, half-vexed. 'We've got a schedule. We can't be mucking about.'

'You were the one walking like you've soiled yourself,' Gareth said.

More laughter from Jenny. One of the reasons why she had married Gareth was because he made her laugh; she often said so.

'Seriously,' Al said, 'we need to keep an eye on the time.'

'Yes, sir,' Gareth said, saluting.

Rachel drew alongside Jenny, bumping kayaks. 'Fancy a stroll after lunch, before we go on to the water?' she said.

'What's that?' Al said. 'A stroll? You'll have to do it afterwards. No time before.'

'Oh,' Rachel said.

That was a shame, but not the end of the world. So long as they talked before the day was out, it wouldn't have been a wasted trip.

'Shame Mel has a migraine,' Jenny said. 'Hope Lee's looking after her.'

''Course he is,' Gareth said. 'Poor sod. He does whatever she tells him to.'

'That's not true,' Jenny said. 'Mel isn't bossy.'

It was Gareth's turn to laugh. 'Mel isn't bossy? Ha! Pull the other one.'

Rachel went quiet, feeling uncomfortable discussing Melissa and the lie they had told their friends. Melissa had pulled out of the trip at the last minute with the migraine excuse. Rachel was touched, grateful; she would make it up to her as soon as she could. She just hoped that it was all going to be worth it.

⚓

Melissa was trying to shelter underneath a tree but it was a puny shrub providing little shade. She leant against Lee, wilting against him, wondering how the girls were managing to play netball in the midday sun.

'Is it nearly over?' Polly said, tugging on Melissa's arm. 'I'm boilllling.'

'Not long now, poppet,' Melissa replied. 'Ten minutes, max.'

'That's ages,' said Polly, flopping about dramatically. 'I'll be *dead* by then.'

'Hang on in there, Pols,' said Lee. 'Try not to die. It's bad for team morale.'

Normally Polly was at pony club at this time, but it had been cancelled because of the heat and the risk of sunstroke for the young children. Evidently, fourteen-year-olds were exempt from such protective measures. The girls on the netball court, Nina included, all looked very red and sweaty. One girl kept stopping play to take her inhaler. On the drinks table that Melissa had arrived early to set up, the segments of oranges were limp, the trays glinting harshly in the sunlight, the cups of water growing tepid.

'Go on, Milford!' Melissa shouted, as Nina's team moved towards the net. They were fast, these girls, and tall – so tall. 'That's it. Shoot! *Yes!*'

She jumped up and down, clapping. 'Another goal! Our girls have got this!'

31

After the final whistle blew, after they had led a depleted Nina from the court, Melissa began to pack up the refreshments table.

'Thanks, Mel,' one of the mums called out as they passed by, leading her daughter to their car. 'You're a star.'

'Ever wondered,' Lee said, dropping his voice, waiting for the family to pass out of earshot, 'why it's always you doing this and no one else?'

Melissa shrugged, dropping a box of dirty cups into the back of the boot. 'Because I volunteer,' she said. 'I like helping out. It's what I do.'

'Yes, but why don't they help sometimes? It stinks of oranges in our car.'

'That's the price you pay for being a good egg,' she said.

'Stinky oranges?' said Polly.

'Yep.'

'Well, I think it's a lovely smell, Mummy. It's like you have your own perfume.'

On the back seat of the car, Nina was lying lifeless, her face hidden in a towel. 'Well done, Nina,' Lee said. 'You were great. Best wing attack on the team, in my opinion.'

'I was the only wing attack on the team,' Nina said drolly.

As they took off, Melissa gazed in the direction of Hope Cove, wondering how the others were getting on. They would be setting up the picnic about now, she reckoned.

Lee read her mind. 'How you holding up?' he said quietly so that the girls wouldn't hear. They were already talking in the back, or Polly was at least, with Nina listening unresponsively from underneath the towel.

'About what?' Melissa said.

'Come on,' Lee said, glancing at her, smiling. 'It must be killing you. The Silkies going kayaking without you?'

'What's wrong with that?' she said. 'They're perfectly

entitled to. I'm fine about it.' She reached forward, put the radio on, tapped her hand to the tune.

He didn't say any more, just reached for her hand and held it.

She didn't move away, liked it there – always did.

⚓

The journey out to the little island of South Rocks was just the way Al had said it would be: easy, idyllic. 'Enjoying yourself, gorgeous?' he said to Rachel over his shoulder.

He always called her that. At some point, she was going to have to ask him not to. It always sounded ironic. She was a lot of things – empathetic, companionable, comely even – but gorgeous was not one of them.

'Yes, thanks,' she said.

'Everyone all right?' he shouted.

'Yankee Doodle Day OK,' was Gareth's reply.

At South Rocks, they came to a halt. Rachel gazed at a crop of grass that was growing high amongst the rocks, like a tuft of hair sprouting on a bald head. 'What now?' she said. 'Go back?'

'Yep,' Al said, wiping sweat from his forehead and dipping his hand into the sea.

'Actually . . .' Jenny said. 'I have a surprise.'

'A surprise? What, here?' Gareth said, looking about him as though expecting to see a three-tier cake in the water.

'Can we go around the back of the island quickly?' Jenny said.

Al shrugged with his mouth. 'Could do.'

'I'm happy either way,' Rachel said.

'You go ahead then,' Gareth said. 'I'll wait here and catch you on your way back.'

'No, you won't,' said Al. 'We all go, or no one goes.'

'Please, sweetheart,' Jenny said. 'Trust me. It'll be fun.'

'Fine,' Gareth said huffily.

Al was gazing up at the sky, hand to brow. The sunblock on his nose was starting to glisten and smear.

'What is it?' Rachel asked.

'Just looking at that grey cloud.'

'Is it a problem?'

'Well, it could mean that the weather's changing.'

'You worried about it, mate?' Gareth asked.

Al continued to look at the sky. 'It'll be all right. But if we're going around the island then we should get on with it. It'll take a while for the clouds to reach us, if they're even coming this way.'

'Let's get going then,' Rachel said.

And they set off, paddling along the front of the island, following its periphery at a safe distance from the rocks.

It wasn't until they were turning the corner and heading out to sea, with the island on their right, that the wind appeared. It was gentle at first. Rachel felt it lifting her hair, cooling her skin. Al was alongside her; behind them, Jenny and Gareth were chatting, laughing about something.

A wave slopped against the side of Rachel's kayak, icy water splashing her legs. 'Ugh! I'm soaked!'

'Don't worry,' Al said. 'Bound to get a bit wet.'

'I'm soaked too,' Jenny called. 'My kayak's full of water. It's like sitting in a bath tub.'

'Well, you wanted to do this,' Al called back. 'Do you want to turn around?'

'No,' Jenny said. 'Keep going.'

They reached the end of the island, turning the corner to paddle along the back.

And that was when the wind hit them.

It was strong, attacking them head-on. Rachel gasped, her hair flailing up and around her. She thought for a moment that she couldn't advance; the wind was blowing her backwards. 'What the heck . . . ?'

'It'll be worse here,' Al said. 'Once we turn the corner, it'll be easy again. You'll see.'

'What's that?' Gareth shouted.

'Keep going!'

Rachel fixed her eye on the end of the island, about two hundred metres away, paddling as hard as she could. It was exhilarating, using all her strength to move forward with the force of the wind against them.

A large wave hit the bow of her kayak, splashing her face. Glancing upwards, she noticed the dark sky, the clouds gathering. 'Look up, Al!' she said.

'What?'

'Look at the sky. It's a storm. We're in a storm! We shouldn't have come this way!'

'Don't look up there,' he said. 'Concentrate on paddling. We just need to get around the corner.'

'You all right?' she shouted behind her.

'Hey?' Gareth said.

'Are you all right?'

'Just about!'

'Jenny?' she said. 'What about you?' Another large wave hit the front of her boat, spraying her.

'Nearly there,' Al called from ahead.

'Jenny?' she said again, shivering. 'You OK?'

Gareth was calling to her too. 'All right, Jen?'

Rachel was trying to look behind her, but couldn't without swerving. Large drops of rain or the sea – she couldn't tell which – were hitting her face. There was water everywhere – cold waves, grey spray, heavy clouds of moisture overhead.

She wasn't enjoying this now, was beginning to feel frightened. 'Jenny?' she called.

It was a while before they heard her reply. She sounded some way off. 'We need to stop, Al,' Rachel said. 'Jenny's behind.'

Al eased off paddling; Rachel copied.

'Keep going, Jen,' Al said, glancing over his shoulder, his kayak tipping unstably. 'Catch us up.'

Now that they had stopped paddling, the wind was blowing them backwards. Jenny was approaching them. She wasn't as far behind as Rachel had feared.

'I'm here,' Jenny said. 'But I'm getting tired.'

'Keep going,' Al said. 'We're nearly there ... Look.'

They were only a couple of metres from the corner. They got their heads down, battled it out.

'We're there!' Al shouted triumphantly.

This elevated Rachel, the excitement in his voice. They rounded the corner one by one and were now heading in the direction of the beach. Just the sight of sand – of land, home – heartened her.

But to her dismay, they hadn't lost the wind at all. It was now on their left. And it was even stronger, pushing them closer to South Rocks.

Al dropped back alongside her. 'I thought you said—' she began.

'Do a strong paddle on the right,' he said. 'Then a light stroke on the left. Then repeat.'

'What's that?' Gareth said.

'Strong paddle on right, light stroke on left,' Al shouted.

Rachel tried to do as instructed but was starting to tire.

What about Jenny?

'Jen?' she called.

'She's with me,' Gareth said.

'I'll try to get to the back,' Al said. 'I can watch her from there.'

Even as he said it, he must have known that it was impossible. The current was dragging them out to sea. And there were rocks underneath; Rachel's paddle had just struck one.

'I thought it was high tide,' she said.

'It is,' Al said. 'At least, I thought it—'

A gust of wind rattled them, sending Al veering to the left, out to sea. 'Al!' Rachel shouted, just as a wave reached high above her in a sheet of spray, filling her kayak with water.

Gareth was shouting something behind her, but she couldn't look back, couldn't hear him clearly. They were being driven too close to the rocks. She wouldn't be able to keep going for much longer – would surely capsize.

Another wave hit her and she swallowed a mouthful of water, feared that she might choke. Her hair was wrapping itself around her neck; her fingers and toes were numb.

Momentarily, everything went quiet, her ears blocked with water.

There was an almighty gust of wind, a swell of waves, and suddenly she was moving at speed. 'Al!' she shouted, as she was swept forward, away from the others.

Petrified, she closed her eyes, screamed.

And then everything slowed down. Disorientated, she looked about her. There, on South Rocks, was the clump of grass she had spotted earlier. She was at the front of the island again. Somehow, she had made it.

The wind began to push her forward again. She caught sight of Al, a dozen metres away, his back to her. 'Jenny?' she shouted. 'Gareth?'

Gareth responded. It sounded as though he was behind her. 'Jenny?' she shouted again. There was no reply. She paddled as hard as she could, trying to turn her kayak enough to look backwards.

And then she caught sight of her. Jenny hadn't made it on to the open waters like the rest of them. She hadn't made it around the corner of the island, but was being pulled backwards, the way they had just come.

'Al!' Rachel shouted. 'Do something!'

He was further away from her now, struggling to stay afloat. 'Gareth!' she shouted.

Gareth was saying something incoherent. The wind was howling in Rachel's ears, whipping her hair viciously around her face.

She panicked. 'Jenny! Jenny!' She tried to turn around fully, but the wind was pushing her too forcefully. The more she tried to turn, the more her kayak was swinging from side to side, out of control. '*Jenny!*' she screamed.

For one moment, she was facing her friend. Jenny was hysterical, begging for help.

Rachel paddled frantically. She could no longer see or hear Gareth or Al. The wind paused, long enough for Jenny's plea to reach her. 'Rachel! Help! *Help!*'

And then a huge wave rose, engulfing Jenny.

Rachel cried out, swallowing mouthfuls of water. When her eyes cleared, she was just in time to see her friend capsizing against the rocks before being dragged around the corner, out to sea, out of sight.

5

'Go on then,' Lee said, picking up a slice of pizza and biting into it. 'Call them. I know you're dying to.'

'Don't speak with your mouth full,' Melissa said.

'Call who, Mummy?' said Polly, pulling a string of mozzarella from her pizza to see how long it would stretch; quite a long way, as it happened.

'Stop that, Polly,' Melissa said. 'And don't listen to Daddy. He's talking nonsense.'

'Her friends,' Frank said, also speaking with his mouth full. 'The ones she's obsessed with controlling.'

Melissa smiled; Frank knew how to tug her chain. 'Yeah, right, obsessed . . . That's me.'

'Shame *you're* not obsessed with anything but Olivia,' Nina said. 'You might actually be able to do something with your life.'

'Oh, shut up, Keener,' Frank said.

Melissa raised an eyebrow at Lee. 'See? Your son copies you. In every respect.'

Nina dropped her pizza slice on to her plate. 'Oh, so what are you saying? Dad calls me Keener too?'

''Course not,' Lee said.

''Course he does,' said Frank. 'Everyone calls you Keener.'

Nina thought about that for a moment, then shrugged and picked up her pizza again. 'That's Dr Keener to you.'

Melissa laughed. She was proud of her daughter. Nina would need that kind of attitude to get through medical school, if that was where she was going.

'Turn that up, please,' Polly said, pointing to the radio. 'I love this toon.'

'It's *tune*,' Frank said.

'Well, I say toon, like *Looney Toons*.'

'It's *Looney Tunes*, actually, Polly,' Nina said. 'Everyone thinks it's *Looney Toons*, but that's a mistake. It was always *Looney Tunes*.'

'Whatevs,' said Frank. 'You're all loonies IMO.'

'What's IMO?' said Polly.

'Text-speak for In My Opinion,' said Nina, tossing her hair over her shoulders. 'Frank can only speak in abbreviations. Long words are too much for him.'

'Shut it, geek.'

Nina's cheeks flushed. Every now and then, someone hit the target and wounded her. 'Mum?' she said.

'Cut it out, Frank. Be nice to your sister.'

All weapons set down, peace reigned for several minutes. Melissa gazed at her phone on the sideboard, wondering when would be an appropriate time to call Rachel. It had just gone six o'clock. She didn't want to seem as though she was checking up on them. She simply wanted to know how they'd got on and was hoping that Rachel would be able to tell her what the secret was now. She had been a good girl and had done as asked, waiting patiently all week. There was only so much suspense a person could take.

This was what she was thinking when the landline rang from the hallway. 'Excuse me,' she said, jumping up, leaving the table.

She picked up the phone eagerly, hoping it would be Rachel. Instead, it was a voice that she didn't recognise. For several seconds, she couldn't place the conversation at all.

It reminded her of the times the school had rung over the years to tell her something mundane about a form to return or a cake sale to organise, but how her first thought – always at the sound of the unknown voice – was that something had happened to the children.

She did the same thing now, despite knowing that all three children were alive and well, six feet away, eating pizza.

'. . . Apologies . . . phoning on behalf of Rachel Beckinsale . . .'

'I'm sorry?' Melissa held herself still. It was gloomy in the hallway, with evening creeping in through the frosted glass panel of the front door. 'Where are you ringing from, again?'

'Portbridge General Hospital. Rachel was hoping you could collect her belongings from Hope Cove. The police can do it, if you prefer, but she asked for you.'

'What? Why? What's going on?'

'I'm afraid I can't discuss details over the phone.'

'But why is she there?' Melissa said. 'Are the others with her?'

'Like I said, I can't discuss that. Would you prefer the police to deal with this?'

'No, it's fine. I'll do it.'

'Thank you.'

She was about to ask where precisely at the hospital she should go, when she realised that the woman had already hung up.

'What was that about?' Lee said, appearing in the doorway, chewing.

'Rachel's in hospital. I need to go down to the beach and collect her bag.'

'You what?' said Lee, rubbing his hands free of crumbs, swallowing hastily.

'I don't know what's happening. The woman wouldn't give

me any information.' She gazed about her, at her denim jacket hanging up, her shoes on the rack.

'I'll drive you – we can all go.'

'No. You stay with the kids.' She grabbed her keys. 'I don't know how long I'll be needed for. I'll call you as soon as I get there.'

'I'll try ringing the others,' Lee said.

'OK,' she said. 'Text me if you hear anything.' Poking her head through the kitchen door, she called to the children. 'Back in a minute. I've got to do something for Auntie Rachel.'

At the front door, she stopped to take a breath, thinking about the quickest route to the hospital from the beach.

Lee walked her out to the car. 'Don't hang around at the beach. If you can't find what you're looking for, just go. It'll be dark soon.'

As she started the engine and reversed, he made a phone sign with his thumb and little finger. 'Call me,' he shouted.

⚓

Down at the cove, the atmosphere was ghostly; or maybe that was just her imagination. The hawthorn trees lining the beach looked crabby, crooked, outlined against the sky. Not yet in bloom, the trees' buds were glowing in the twilight like the whites of eyes fixed on her.

Untying her jacket from her waist, Melissa slipped it on as she started down the boardwalk. Behind her, her mother's kayaking academy was in darkness. Sometimes, a cat or sudden wind set off the security lights, but tonight all was still.

She could see the cool bags and rucksacks on the picnic rug halfway down the beach. Hurrying to them, she knelt down, reaching into Al's bag for his rolled towel. It was still dry; inside the towel, she found his phone. She did the same for the others; all their phones were there and their towels dry.

They had taken the boats out and hadn't returned here. Not far away was the dock that they would have departed from. The waves were slopping against the wooden structure nonchalantly, telling her nothing.

Packing up the bags, she carried them back up the beach. Evidently, they had eaten their picnic. The cool bags were light, beer cans twanging about inside.

She was just about to step back on to the boardwalk when something caught her eye: three tracks in the sand, leading from the shore to the hawthorn trees. Her heart racing, she stared at the three kayaks lying in a line in the gloom of the trees.

She dropped the bags and approached. Even in the failing light, she could see that two of the kayaks were pale spearmint blue: Al and Gareth's. The other one was red, so faded in colour after years of use that it looked like the tip of an ice lolly that had been sucked white.

They always took the same kayaks out, the ones they had carved their initials in years ago as teenagers. It was a ritual, a tradition of sorts.

Crouching down, she peered at the side of the red boat. RBA. Rachel's old pre-married initials.

Jenny's kayak was the missing one.

She sat back on the sand with a bump, looking about her, dumbstruck. What was going on?

She couldn't sit here. She had to get going. Returning to the bags, she picked them up and carried them up to the academy.

Telling herself to remain calm, she loaded the bags into the boot and drove steadily out of the car park, turning on to the country lane, heading in the direction of Portbridge, just as darkness took another step forward.

6

Gareth opened his eyes. Something above him was very bright. The sun? It didn't feel warm in here, though. He was shivering, his teeth chattering incessantly.

What the—

He tried to move, but a sharp pain in his head made him reconsider. His right knee was throbbing as though it had been whacked with a mallet. He eased himself up to look about him and saw that he was attached to an intravenous drip.

Then he saw the nurse at the end of his bed; she was writing on a clipboard.

'Oh, good,' she said. 'You're awake.'

She rounded the bed and came towards him, undoing the crackly Velcro on a blood pressure monitor before fitting it to his arm. She pumped up the band and waited.

Then the band released and the nurse exhaled. 'Perfect,' she said. 'Getting better. That's what we like to see.' She was writing on her clipboard again. 'Fancy a cuppa?' She hung the chart on the end of his bed.

He looked at her in bewilderment, unclear on details such as his name and what he was doing here. It hardly seemed the time for tea.

'I'd recommend a hot drink,' she said, 'if you can manage

44

it. I'd like to see your temperature up a smidgen. But you're certainly out of the woods.' She smiled.

He examined the identification tag on his wrist, just to be sure: DAVIES 18–07–1975.

Struggling to sit upright, he pushed away the blankets that were weighing heavily on his body, tucked right underneath his neck as they were.

'What's happening?' he said, his voice croaky; he barely recognised himself.

The nurse perched on the arm of the chair alongside his bed. 'Don't you remember?'

'I . . .' He tried to think. Every part of his body seemed to be hurting, but mostly his knee and his head.

'You were in an accident,' she said. 'You were admitted earlier with bruising and moderate hypothermia.'

'What time is it now?' he said, looking at his bare wrist. His watch was gone. Come to think of it, he didn't seem to have anything with him at all. There was nothing on the nightstand beside him. All he had was his foggy brain. Was this some kind of hell?

'Six o'clock,' the nurse said.

Far later than he had expected.

'Why don't I remember anything?' he said.

'You will. As your body warms up, everything will begin to regulate and you'll feel less confused. I promise.'

Something flashed across her face then – a sudden doubt or unease. Even in his current state, he saw it but couldn't decipher what it was and didn't want to ask. He sensed that it was something personal relating to him: a nasty problem lying underneath the surface, yet to reveal itself.

'How about that cuppa?' she asked.

He nodded resignedly. 'Where am I?'

'Portbridge General,' she said. 'Critical Care. Just rest there a minute and I'll be right back.'

He watched her leave the room, her rubber shoes creaking.

Looking around the room, he saw that there was a curtain separating him from the next patient, possibly from dozens of them. He couldn't hear anything, though. 'Hello?' he called. 'Anyone there?'

He wanted it to be his friends, his family, the people he loved. He could picture them all as clearly as though they were standing before him, in a strange hospitalised version of *This is Your Life*.

But then he felt it again: the sensation of something dark, disturbing, hidden from view. He forced himself upright, closed his eyes, tried to focus on what it was that his mind was running from.

He could see the ugly swirl of the sea, could hear Al shouting instructions and Jenny calling out behind him that she was tired. He could taste salt, felt the sting in his nose and throat as he swallowed water.

Wave after wave came, scaring them. He, for one, was scared. Al didn't seem to be – at least, he wasn't letting on that he was. He was roaring instructions at them as though on one of his Scouts excursions. Al hadn't been a Cub Scout leader for years, yet some locals still greeted him with the traditional name of the leader: Akela.

Yet even Akela was tiring.

Gareth opened his eyes, rubbed his face. He couldn't do this with his eyes shut. It was too claustrophobic, too frightening.

He gazed at the window. He could hear Jenny crying out for him. He was trying to turn around to look at her, but couldn't do so without smashing into the rocks. In front of him, Rachel was thrashing about, the bow of her kayak jerking from side to side. Al had disappeared from view.

Rachel was shouting. He couldn't hear what she was

saying; the wind was making too much noise. Jenny was screaming now, calling out for help.

Then there was an intense pain in the side of his head, as he lurched on to his side, and a blow to his knee.

He realised that he had stopped shivering.

Everything was quiet.

He could hear the nurse's footsteps creaking down the corridor as she returned to the room, carrying a tray of tea.

'I brought you a couple of bickies,' she said. 'Bit of sugar to perk you up.' She glanced at Gareth as she set the tray down. 'Are you all right?'

'Nurse,' he said, 'where's my wife?'

⚓

Rachel reached for Al's hand. He was worryingly still. She watched the monitor, not understanding what the numbers meant – not needing to know, so long as Al's heart was beating, his lungs working.

He had severe hypothermia. Found in the water some distance from his kayak, he had been airlifted to hospital. And now they were monitoring him closely. If things didn't improve soon, they would remove his blood, warm it and return it. She was praying that it wouldn't come to that.

For now, they were warming him with intravenous fluids, heated blankets and warmed oxygen, which he was inhaling by mask. The consultants had been in several times in the last few minutes – in and out, conferring in hushed voices.

They were here again now, amassing at the foot of Al's bed to read his chart.

She gazed fearfully at her husband's grey face. Why had he stayed in the water so long?

Because he hadn't been able to admit defeat, not even when

his opposition was the sea. The last she had seen of him, he had been fighting to turn around and save Jenny. And then he had been carried from view.

She blinked away tears, feeling guilty for having got off lightly with mild hypothermia. She hadn't stayed in the water as long as Al. The coastguard rescue service had picked her up at the next bay, where she had managed to swim to shore after capsizing.

She didn't know what had happened to Jenny and Gareth, hadn't had the courage to ask after them yet. For now, worrying about Al felt like enough to deal with.

She hoped that her boys were all right. Thankfully, Ned was at the sleepover party – safely tucked away at his friend's house. And Joel, well, he was seventeen. Absorbed by his studies and his own needs, he would relish the silence at home, not realising that anything might be strange about it until far later.

Pressing Al's hand, tears pooled in her eyes. Her skin felt tight all over, crisp like parchment. She couldn't imagine what had gone so badly wrong.

Was Jenny all right? What if she wasn't?

Rachel moaned, squeezing Al's hand. If only she hadn't suggested the trip. If only she hadn't asked Melissa not to go with them.

She gave a start at the sudden sound of a woman's voice. It was a consultant calling out for the nurse to take Al's temperature again.

'He's strong and fit,' the consultant said, smiling reassuringly at Rachel. 'He's got every chance of making a full recovery.'

Rachel nodded mutely. Out of her depth, she found herself even less vocal than usual. As if to compensate, however, her mind hadn't stopped talking. She wondered whether the reverse was true – whether chatty people had quiet minds.

They waited whilst the nurse took Al's temperature. 'You

must be Jenny?' the consultant said, looking with curiosity at Rachel.

'No, I'm his wife, Rachel.'

'Oh. I'm sorry. I didn't . . .'

'Jenny's our friend,' Rachel said. 'Al was in the water so long because he was trying to help her.'

'Well, that makes sense. He was calling for her when he first arrived.'

Rachel tried not to react to that, gazed down at her feet, her cheeks burning. Thankfully, the doctor's attention had moved elsewhere: the thermometer reading was ready.

The consultants gathered, murmuring again. Then they turned to her. 'Good news. He's on the up and up . . . We'll be back again shortly.'

Rachel nodded a thank-you.

After they had left, she looked down at herself. She was sitting in the chair beside Al's bed, wearing a patient's gown and hospital pants. With Al out of danger, now was the perfect time to summon the strength to enquire after Jenny and Gareth. Yet she was utterly out of energy. So, she remained where she was, watching Al's pulse rate oscillate on the monitor, his oxygen mask whispering as he breathed in and out.

ANGELA GOULD

Milford resident, Dorset

Angela knew that something was up when she saw Melissa dashing out of the house not long after the pizza delivery boy had arrived. Angela didn't like to pry, but theirs was a quiet road with more or less the same patterns day after day. When things happened differently, they tended to stick out.

She was standing at her kitchen sink, washing up, when she had heard the *pop pop pop* of the scooter coming along the lane and saw Lee Silk at the door, receiving the stack of pizza cartons.

But then, shortly afterwards, Melissa had taken off in the car with a worried look on her face.

A sudden recollection of a moment several hours before came back to Angela then. She had been loading groceries into the boot of her car at the supermarket when the air had filled with the sound of a passing helicopter. The sun had been in her eyes, but she had just been able to make out the red and white colours of the coastal rescue helicopter.

Peeling off her washing-up gloves, she picked up her phone and dialled Nessa.

Nessa's husband was a member of the coastguard rescue team. If anything had happened, she would be sure to know.

7

Melissa went through the main doors of Portbridge General, looking about her for a clue as to where to go. The atrium was huge, with a sea life mural on the walls and ceilings that were giddily high with fans circling noiselessly.

A doctor in scrubs was coming towards her. 'Excuse me,' Melissa asked him. 'Is there an enquiry desk?'

He pointed over his shoulder. 'Down there, on the left.'

'Thank you.'

At the desk, a lady who didn't stop typing told her that Rachel Beckinsale was in ward E, a minor injury unit. 'Go back out the main doors, turn left, left again, then right and you're there.'

Melissa couldn't have found her way there had she tried. 'What about Jennifer Davies?'

'One moment ... I'm afraid no one's been admitted by that name.'

That was good, then. Was that good?

'And Gareth Davies?'

The receptionist paused typing, casting an inquisitive eye over Melissa and the bundle of bags hanging from her shoulders, before turning to her keyboard again. 'He's in Critical Care.'

'Critical Care ...' Melissa said. 'Is that—'

'It used to be called Intensive Care.'

'Oh God,' she said. She would go there first. 'How do I get there, please?'

'Carry on down the corridor, take a right and it's signposted. But you'd better be quick. Visiting hours end at eight o'clock.'

Melissa was already off, pushing the handles of the bags firmly on to her shoulders. As she walked, she could hear the muffled sounds of phones ringing from within the towels – strange vibrating noises as though being held under water. The sound was haunting, disquieting.

The Critical Care unit was indeed signposted, but only because it was like walking to another town. On arrival, her shoulders were throbbing, her back damp with perspiration. The nurses pointed her to a room opposite the main desk, saying that she could go in for a short while.

She knocked on the door, but then wished that she hadn't because no one heeded her whatsoever.

Gareth was sitting up in bed, looking pasty-faced, numb. A nurse was talking to him soothingly, squeezing his hand.

Melissa stopped, setting the bags down beside the wall, absorbing the scene.

Nothing about it was reassuring. Rather, a nasty sensation was creeping over her. She kept her gaze on Gareth.

Look up, Gareth. Notice me.

But the nurse was helping him to lie down. He closed his eyes, lay still.

The nurse turned to look at her. 'Hello,' she said, approaching, scanning Melissa cautiously. 'Can I help?'

'I just wondered how Gareth is. I'm a friend.' She gestured to the bags at her feet. 'I brought his stuff. Is he all right?'

'He's not too bad. He just needs to rest. I've given him a mild sedative.'

'Oh. Is . . . ? Well, can you tell me what happened? His wife

Jenny is my best friend. I'd just like to know where she is — where Jenny is—'

She broke off, disconcerted by the look on the nurse's face.

The nurse touched Melissa's elbow lightly. 'Perhaps we could talk about this outside ...'

Standing in the corridor was hardly private, opposite the nurses' desk as they were. Yet the point was that they were away from Gareth, Melissa suspected. The nurse led her to a row of orange chairs that were attached to the wall, each with a puffy cushion like the segments of a caterpillar. 'Take a seat.'

The cushions whooshed as they sat down. Melissa felt as though she were sinking fast, the air rushing from her.

'I'm so sorry to tell you that your friend, Jenny, didn't make it.' The nurse spoke rapidly, a little frown on her otherwise smooth young forehead. 'I don't know the details, I'm afraid.'

Melissa's mouth was so dry, it was difficult to speak. She opened her mouth, closed it again. All she could think of was Jenny as a child, bouncing on the space hopper, her crimped blonde hair going up and down, blowing a huge bubble of gum.

'What?' she said.

The nurse placed her hand on Melissa's. 'You're not going to be able to take this in – not here. And I don't have enough information. Would you like me to call someone to collect you?'

Melissa shook her head.

'How about a drink of water?'

She didn't reply. The nurse stood up. Melissa looked down at her hands, which had gone mottled and speckly like Spam. They'd had a teacher at school nicknamed Spam because of his bald pink head. Jenny had always found it hilarious.

The nurse returned, handing Melissa a plastic cup of water, which felt so cold in her hands. She sipped it slowly, thinking

53

about Jenny's twins, Max and Olivia – about where they were, what they were doing.

'Do her children know?' she asked.

'I'm not sure. But the police and social services will be involved by now.' The nurse glanced at the watch on her chest. 'I'm afraid I have to get on. But ask at the desk if you need anything, OK?' And the nurse set off down the corridor.

Melissa gazed at the painting on the wall opposite – a senseless confusion of swirls and stripes.

Her phone was ringing. She pulled it out from her jacket pocket and saw that it was her mum.

'Melissa? The police said there's been a serious incident at the academy. I just spoke to Lee and he said that you're at the hospital with Rachel. What's going on?'

She shook her head in response.

'Melissa?'

Her throat was swelling. She bent her head, squeezed the corners of her eyes, rocking on the heels of her feet.

'Where are you now?' her mother said.

She gulped as she began to cry. 'I'm still at the hospital.'

'Have you heard anything? How's Rachel?'

'It's ... it's Jenny ...' Melissa said. 'I don't know what happened. No one's told me. But Jenny didn't make it. That's all I know.' She began to cry harder, stifling the sobs so that she wouldn't disturb the nurses at the desk, the patients on the ward. This was the worst place to be crying, the worst place to be alone.

'What ...? Jenny?' her mother said. 'Oh goodness, no. Melis—'

'I can't do this here. There are people everywhere.'

'Then we need to get you home. Would you like me to come and pick you up?'

'I've got the car. I can drive myself.'

'Are you sure?'

'Yes,' she said, wiping her tears.

'Well, don't hang around then. Go home to Lee and the children before it gets dark. Are you leaving now?'

She nodded.

'Melissa?'

'Yes, Mum. I'm going.'

'OK. I'll call you first thing tomorrow. And Melissa?'

'Yes?'

'I'm so sorry about Jenny.'

And the call ended.

She stared at her feet – at her white espadrilles, which she lived in during the warmer months. The straw soles were coated in sand. Rubbing them together, she left a little trail of sand on the floor like a pepper mill.

What about Al? Where was he?

She went to the desk. 'Is Alistair Beckinsale a patient on this ward?' she asked.

'Yes. He's in room three. But you don't have long. Visiting hours are over soon.'

She began to walk down the corridor before remembering the bags. Returning to Gareth's room, she placed his rucksack carefully inside his bedside cabinet. He was in a deep sleep, his face pinched with pain. Medication couldn't erase that look from him; maybe nothing ever would.

She would have liked to have kissed him on the cheek, but didn't trust herself to do so with the lightness of touch required. So she withdrew and went to find room three.

⚓

Rachel was sitting in a chair next to Al's bed. Looking crumpled, reduced, her skin had taken on the greenish hue of her hospital gown.

Dropping the bags, Melissa hurried forward. 'Oh, my goodness,' she said, crouching down, placing her hand on Rachel's knee. 'Are you OK?'

'I think so,' Rachel said. 'I've been watching him.' They both turned to look at Al.

'How is he?' Melissa asked.

'Not good,' Rachel said. 'He stayed in the water too long. He has hypothermia, but they said he's getting better.'

'And what about you? Have they checked you out properly?'

'Yes. There's nothing wrong with me,' she said.

Melissa went back over to the bags. 'I brought your things. Would you like to wear this?' she said, pulling a sweater from Rachel's bag.

'Please,' Rachel said. Standing up, she put the sweater on, her movements laboured.

Melissa waited, wondering how much Rachel knew. It was impossible to tell by looking at her. She looked so different without her glasses on; her eyes appeared sunken, small. The salt water on her face had left her skin dry-looking, her eyelids crêpey.

And then Rachel spoke and Melissa realised that the task of messenger was hers. 'Where's Jenny?' she asked.

'Let's sit down,' Melissa said.

'I don't want to sit. Just tell me where she is.'

'I . . . I don't know how to . . . '

Rachel was staring at her in horror.

'She didn't make it,' Melissa said, her eyes filling with tears.

Rachel turned her back to Melissa, shaking her head.

'Say something,' Melissa said. 'Please. Tell me what happened today.'

What Rachel said next confused her.

'He was calling for her when he arrived.'

'Who was?' Melissa said. 'What do you mean?'

A loud knock on the door made them both jump and they turned to see two policemen in uniform. 'Sorry to barge in on you,' one of the officers said. 'But could we have a word?'

8

Sinking lower into her chair, Rachel bowed her head, trying to block out what was happening. She could hear Melissa talking quietly.

'What do you need from her?' Melissa was saying.

One of the policemen didn't want to play the game and kept his voice at booming level. 'We're carrying out inquiries into the death of Jennifer Davies . . . That's Rachel Beckinsale, over there, I take it?'

'Yes.'

'Are you a relative?'

'A close friend.'

The voices drew closer. Rachel kept her head bowed. She felt a hand cupping her shoulder as Melissa stood behind her.

The loud voice spoke, startling her, right above her as it was. 'Mrs Beckinsale, can you confirm that you were on the kayaking trip today that resulted in the death of Jennifer Davies?'

The death of Jennifer Davies. She wished they wouldn't keep saying that.

'Mis-sus Beck-in-sale,' the officer repeated.

'It's OK,' Melissa said, squeezing her shoulder. 'I'm here.'

Rachel felt tears forming. 'Yes,' was all she said.

'Can you tell us what happened?'

'I . . .' she began.

'Does she have to do this now?' Melissa asked. 'She's in shock.'

'I'm afraid so. We appreciate how difficult it is, though, so take your time.'

Everyone was waiting for her to speak. She couldn't remember what the question was.

'Mrs Beckinsale, how long were you in the water for?'

She gazed up at the policeman, a tear tickling her nose. The harsh voice didn't match his face, which looked squishy, malleable. 'I don't know,' she said.

'What time did you enter the water?'

'Two o'clock?' she said uncertainly.

'I rang Alistair last night,' Melissa said. 'He said they'd be setting off at high tide. Easy enough to work out what time it was if you look at a tide table.'

'Yes,' Rachel said, another tear tickling her nose. She brushed it away. 'It was high tide.'

The shorter officer with the squishy face pulled a notepad from his jacket and flicked it open. 'The coastguard was notified just after three o'clock, meaning that you'd probably been on the water for over an hour, although most of that time you were in the kayaks, nice and dry. Is that right?'

'Yes,' Rachel said. 'It was nice, until we reached South Rocks.'

'I see . . . So, what happened?'

Rachel gazed ahead of her, recalling the glassy surface of the sea – how beautiful and inviting it had looked at first. 'A storm came out of nowhere.'

'Why didn't you turn back?' the other officer asked.

She thought about that, recollecting the thrill of battling the wind and waves. 'Because it was fun.'

'So, what changed?'

She scowled at him. 'The weather.'

The shorter officer took over. 'Can you tell us what happened when the storm hit?'

'We got into trouble around the back of the island,' she said.

She heard it clearly: the sudden intake of breath that Melissa took.

'What?' Melissa said, staring down at her. 'You went around the back of South Rocks?'

Rachel hesitated before speaking again. It felt like a very loaded question. She glanced at Al, wishing that he could help her.

'Mrs Beckinsale,' the officer said, 'please answer the question.'

'Yes,' she said. 'We did.'

As she spoke, she felt the little tug as her friend pulled away from her – releasing her grasp on her shoulder, moving from her side.

Rachel looked down at the floor in shame, following the smears of cleaning agents that were showing up in the glare of the fluorescent lighting.

'Why did you do that?' Melissa asked.

Rachel couldn't answer, couldn't remember why they had gone around the island when the plan had been simply to go there and back.

'I'm confused,' the tall officer said, looking at Melissa. 'Why shouldn't they have done that?'

'Because it's dangerous,' Melissa said. 'Jenny wasn't confident enough to go around the back of there with a storm rolling in.'

'Did you tell Al that last night?' Rachel asked her. 'Did he know?'

Melissa frowned, opened her mouth to reply. 'I . . .'

'I'm not saying that you should have,' Rachel said. 'I'm just . . .'

'It didn't come up,' Melissa replied. 'He said he was just going

60

there and back. Everyone knows that once you've planned a route, you don't deviate from it.'

There was a horrible silence.

The shorter policeman turned to Melissa. 'I'm sorry, but who are you, again? Are you some sort of canoeing expert?'

'Not exactly,' Melissa said. 'My mum owns the kayaking academy – the one they went from.'

'You must know a thing or two, then?'

'My kayaking skills are advanced, yes. And I'm a fully trained lifeguard. But that's about it.'

'Sounds pretty good to me. Why weren't you with your friends today?'

It felt at that moment as though everything had been unplugged, drained – the machinery keeping Al alive, the air they were breathing.

'I had a migraine.'

Rachel couldn't believe that Melissa had just said that. Was there any need to keep up the pretence?

She couldn't think quickly enough, couldn't decide what was best. Perhaps Melissa had concluded this too and had bought them some time.

As the policemen turned to their notes, consulting with each other, she gazed at Melissa, her cheeks flushing with gratitude.

⚓

Melissa had never been any good at lying. Her only hope was to speak quickly and get on with it.

Saying that she had a migraine was probably stupid, but she had thought it best to stick to the story that they had told everyone else, until Rachel said otherwise.

The shorter officer closed his notepad. 'I think that's

everything for now,' he said. 'Thank you for your time. We'll be in touch if we need anything else.'

As the men left the room, Melissa gazed after them, not wanting them to leave, taking all the information with them.

On impulse, she hurried after them. 'Officers!' she called out.

The men came to a halt adjacent to the nurses' desk. Gareth's nice nurse was sitting at the desk, head bent over paperwork.

Melissa kept her voice down. 'I was wondering if you could tell me where Jenny is?'

The tall officer narrowed his eyes at her, his interest piqued. 'In the hospital mortuary, so I believe. Why do you ask?'

'I just wondered if there was anything that I could do ... to help?'

The officer shook his head. 'Not that I can think of right now.'

'She ...' A trolley bearing a patient was heading towards them. Melissa stepped aside, bumping into the wall. 'Her parents are dead and she didn't have brothers or sisters. Her husband's under sedation ... So ...' She shrugged. 'I'm here, if you need anyone.'

'Good to know. Thank you.' The officer smiled sympathetically.

'Do you know where her children are?' she asked.

'No. But one of our colleagues will, for sure. They'll be in safe hands.'

She played with her twine bracelets. 'Can you tell me what happened?'

'Not as yet, I'm afraid. First we have to wait for the coroner's decision on whether there'll be a post-mortem.'

'Oh. But why would they do that?' she said.

'Standard practice. Even with accidents, we still have to establish what happened.'

She nodded, knowing that she had other questions, but not knowing then what they were.

'We'd best get on. You take care now. We'll see you later.' And the officers made their way down the corridor to the double doors, where they waited to be beeped out.

Melissa stood watching the nurse at the desk, before walking slowly back to the room.

Rachel was seeing to Al, adjusting his bed covers, tucking them in. 'What did you want to speak to them about?' Rachel asked.

'Just where Jenny is. They said she's in the mortuary. They might do a post-mortem.'

Rachel stopped what she was doing and looked at Melissa in alarm. 'I can't believe this is happening.'

Melissa drew closer to her, adopting a tone of intimacy that she hoped her friend was ready to replicate. 'Tell me what happened out there today, Rach,' she said. 'What went wrong?'

To her disappointment, Rachel seemed unreachable, closed off.

'I don't know,' she said.

'But why didn't you want me to go with you? When are you going to tell me that?'

'I . . .'

'Rach, please.' She tried to look into Rachel's eyes, but Rachel was avoiding her gaze, looking away, looking anywhere but at Melissa. 'Why are you being so secretive? This isn't like you.'

'That's because I've not been in this situation before.'

'So, tell me. Let me help."

There was a noise behind them and Gareth's nurse appeared. 'Hello again,' she said, smiling kindly at Melissa. 'It's well past visiting hours, I'm afraid, ladies.'

'Can I stay the night?' Rachel said. 'I'm his wife.'

'Well, there's a fold-out bed along that wall over there, if you're desperate.'

'I am,' Rachel said.

The nurse looked at Melissa.

'It's OK,' Melissa said. 'I'm going.'

Melissa picked up the bags, placing them near Al's bed, realising that there was only one bag remaining: Jenny's.

'Thanks for coming,' Rachel said.

They were both being polite, unnatural, with the nurse in the room.

'It was the least I could do,' Melissa said. 'Where are the boys?'

'Ned's at his friend's house for the night; Joel's at home. I'll call them in a minute. Thank you for bringing my phone.'

'That's OK.' Melissa felt that there were other things that needed sorting, but her head was throbbing, distracting her from thought.

'Do you think the twins will be all right?' Rachel asked.

'Not sure. I'm going to check on them now.'

'They'll be pleased to see you.'

Small talk. What else was there to say when there was so much that couldn't be said, not with the nurse in the room, tending to Al's drip, filling in his charts?

'Good luck,' Melissa said, and left it at that.

It would have been impossible to feel more alone as she walked along that corridor, holding her deceased friend's bag in her arms, even knowing that her husband and children were waiting for her at home. They felt so far away. All she could feel was the unbearable sadness of loss – the loneliness of knowing that, even though everyone experienced it at some point, no one ever felt it in quite the same way.

No one could possibly know how she felt about losing Jenny. She held the beach bag tightly, knowing that it contained some of the last things that her friend had ever seen or touched. If she was allowed to, she would keep this bag for ever – underneath her bed, hidden away.

Outside, darkness had fallen. She couldn't think where she had left the car. She looked about her in a stupor. And then remembered: it was zone J. J for Jenny.

As she went to the car, she rang Lee. There were three missed calls from him on her phone, as well as a voicemail from an unknown caller.

She listened to the message. It was social services; her details had been given to them as an overnight guardian for Olivia and Maximilian Davies, subject to CRB checks, as a temporary measure until their grandparents arrived from Wales. Melissa was to return the call to make the necessary arrangements.

She wanted to speak to Lee first, so rang home.

'It's me,' she said.

'Mel . . .'

She closed her eyes. She had wanted so badly to hear his voice, yet now she couldn't bear to hear a tender word from him.

'Please,' she said. 'Don't say anything. I can't handle it.'

He hesitated. 'How are you?'

'I'm . . .' She couldn't answer that honestly, not without worrying him. 'I'm just leaving.'

'Are you all right to drive?'

'Yes,' she said. 'I'm fine.'

'You don't have to do this alone.'

She bit her lip. 'I know. But I just want to go home.'

'Then we'll hang up now,' he said. 'You just concentrate on driving. There's no rush. We're all here, waiting for you.'

She hung up, pressing her hands to her face to cool her cheeks down. She felt hot and cold and dazed.

As she drove back to Milford, she cried, the street lights

blurring. With the beach bag beside her, she kept her hand on it, feeling the softness of the sweater that was poking out of the top.

When she pulled into the driveway at home, Lee, Frank, Nina and Polly were standing on the front step.

She got out of the car, her legs heavy. Carrying the beach bag, she set it down on the step. 'You should be in bed, Pols,' she said. It sounded more of a reprimand than she had intended.

Polly's bottom lip trembled. She was wearing a polyester nightie that crackled with static as she reached for her daddy's hand. 'I couldn't sleep, Mummy. I was too upset about Auntie Jenny.'

Melissa gazed at her friend's sweater in the beach bag and began to cry. Nina began to cry too, hiding her face in her hands. Frank coughed awkwardly. Polly hopped from foot to foot. Lee put his arms around Melissa and held her, drawing her hair away from her tears, before leading her into the house and closing the door on all that the day had brought.

Warm feet; that was all she could think that she wanted.

9

Sunday 22 April 2018

Gareth heard his parents' voices before he saw them. He perched on the edge of his bed, hands clasped to his knees, trying to set his mouth to a welcoming smile but it kept flickering like a dodgy connection.

And then there they were, little and large, all the way from Pembrokeshire, standing in the doorway and looking at him with such pity that he felt cold with fear. It was real; it really was happening.

'Oh, Gareth,' his mother said, beginning to cry as she hugged him. 'My poor, poor boy.'

Gareth's father was a good four inches taller than him, even at eighty years old. Gareth couldn't remember a time in his life when he hadn't looked up to this Welsh giant of a man.

'Son,' his father said, pulling him into his arms and slapping his back. 'I'm so very sorry. Jenny was … well, you know what she was to us.'

A daughter; she had been like a daughter.

Gareth looked then for his own children, gazing beyond his parents to the two diminished teenagers who were standing in the doorway, already bearing the marks of grief.

Max was wearing a sweater with his hood up and was avoiding eye contact. Olivia, however, was looking right at him. Her hair unbrushed, with charcoal shadows under her eyes, she was searching for the good, trying to find something hopeful in this abject misery. He knew so because it was exactly what Jenny would have done.

'Livvie, Max,' Gareth said in a splutter, holding his arms out to them.

Olivia went to him, tucking her face into his shirt to weep. Max hesitated and then his face creased with upset and he lurched forward to join them.

They stood like that for a short while, hiding their faces in each other.

Max broke away first, looking up at Gareth. 'How did it happen, Dad? I don't get it. You were only kayaking. It was a sunny day. How—'

'It's all right, Max,' Gareth's father said, stepping forward, placing his hand on his grandson's shoulder. 'We all want answers. I've every intention of finding out what happened.'

'What does that mean?' Gareth said, wiping his face with the freshly pressed handkerchief that his mother had discreetly handed him. She was wonderful in a crisis, the magician's assistant of tragedy.

'Exactly what I said,' his father said. 'I intend to make sure that we get all the facts.'

'The facts?' Gareth said. 'She drowned, Dad. It was an accident. We got caught out. The only thing I don't know is how it got so bad so quickly. One minute it was beautiful and the next—' He broke off, blew his nose, stamping his feet to prevent another crying attack.

Olivia crossed the room to sit on the bed with her grandmother, the two of them holding hands. 'I agree with Grandpa,' Olivia said. 'We need to know exactly what happened. Uncle

Al was in a charge, right? So, he obviously, like, cocked up.'

Gareth went to the door and pushed it shut. 'Hush, Olivia. You can't go saying things like that. Al's a patient here.'

'At least he's alive,' Max muttered.

Gareth looked fretfully at his son and then at his father, who was standing with his arms clasped behind his back – a classic look that said he had all the time in the world to wait for his son to accept his will.

'Have the police spoken to you?' his father said.

'They were here earlier, yes.'

'And what did they say?'

Gareth sat down on the edge of the bed and rubbed his face. The sedative that the nurse had given him last night felt very much like a hangover today. His knee and his head were still sore, but he was well enough to be discharged and was waiting for the paperwork to be completed.

'I . . . uh . . . Well, not much. They had a bereavement officer or something with them. She wanted to know whether I was up to identifying the body.'

There was a silence.

Gareth held his head in his hands. How could his head feel so heavy? It felt impossibly unstable, like a bowling ball resting on a flower stem.

'I can do it,' his father said.

'No, Dad. It's OK. I just a need a day or so.'

His father pursed his lips solemnly. 'Why put yourself through it, when I can step in for you?'

'I agree,' his mother said. 'Let us do something to take the load off. That's what we're here for.'

He wasn't going to fight, was in no fit state to.

'Did you give a statement?' his father asked.

'Did you, Dad?' Max said, pulling his hood down and gazing at him intently.

'Of sorts. I was still in bed – could barely open my eyes.'

'Are they going to do a post-mortem?' his father asked.

'A post-mortem?' Max looked horrified. Olivia made a little choking sound and her grandmother put her arm around her.

Gareth nodded. 'I think they might.'

'And you're all right with that?' his father asked.

''Course not. But I've signed the consent form. I didn't have much choice.'

Olivia moaned and began to cry again.

'It's unpleasant,' his father said, 'but it must be necessary or they wouldn't be doing it.' And then his father rubbed his hands briskly together to herald a change of subject. 'Maybe we should try to get a cup of tea from somewhere?'

Gareth stood up, his knees creaking. 'Yes, give yourselves a break before you set off again.'

'Set off? Where to?' his father said.

'Well, home, of course.'

'Home?' his mother said. 'We're here to stay, son. For as long as you need us. You'd like that, wouldn't you?' she asked Olivia.

'Yes,' Olivia said, trying to smile, a tear trickling down her cheek.

'It's all right, my darling. We'll get through this,' his mother said, stroking Olivia's hair. 'We're all here for each other. That's what family does.'

There was a pause as they took in this statement. And then Max began to cry and they gathered round him, telling him that it was going to be all right; that things would get a little worse and then a lot better.

Gareth waited alone in his room while his family went in search of refreshments. He wanted to be there, ready, when the nurse came to tell him he could go. The way the hospital ran reminded him of a cathedral clock he had visited in Wales as a boy; the bells had rung and little men on horses blowing trumpets had appeared. Those children who arrived moments later had to wait a full hour before the little men appeared again.

Fragments of memories. They had been coming to him all morning. He had been dreaming of his late grandmother in the early hours, the only person he had ever grieved until now. It felt safe remembering her, rather than dealing with his present loss.

How to deal with losing Jenny?

He didn't know.

He thought about what his father had said about getting all the facts. The police had made it clear that any sudden death warranted examination, especially when the person's health was sound. But Gareth already knew that the only thing that had gone wrong out there on the waves was the weather.

He had asked after Al earlier. No longer on the same ward, Gareth having been removed from Critical Care, his nurse hadn't been sure how Al was, had said she would get back to him, and then hadn't.

He hadn't asked again, would wait until he got home and then he would be able to start dealing with everything properly, cohesively.

Alone, he allowed himself to cry again.

As he lost himself in grief, he could see Jenny smiling at him in her red kayak. *Please, sweetheart . . . Trust me . . . It'll be fun.*

He stopped crying, clasping his hand to his forehead in sudden realisation.

Jenny had suggested going around the back of the island. Somehow, in all the confusion, he had forgotten that.

Picking up his phone, he went over to the window, dialled Melissa. She answered after several rings, her voice sounding small, stifled.

'It's me,' he said.

They both went quiet right away, allowing the gaps to speak for them – to say all the things that neither of them was prepared or able to take a stab at.

'Thanks for having the twins last night,' he said.

'No problem.'

There was a pause whilst she cried a little. He listened, willing himself not to break down again. If he kept crying, he wouldn't be able to see straight.

'Mel . . . ' he said. 'Did you know that we went around the back of the island?'

'Yes. Rachel said.'

'It was Jen's idea.'

'Jenny's?'

'Yes. She said she had a surprise for us. Do you know what she meant?'

'No. I haven't a clue.'

'Me neither. I can't think why she'd have wanted to go around there.'

'It's dangerous,' Melissa said. 'Although everywhere is, in a storm. But that particular bit can be tricky. I wouldn't have taken you round there if I'd have been with you.'

The line went very quiet then.

'Mel?'

'I'm still here,' she said.

'Thanks for helping out,' he said. 'You've always been there for us.' His voice wavered.

'And I always will be,' Melissa said. 'This doesn't change anything.'

He felt his Adam's apple tightening. He looked out of the window at a mother and child who were hurrying away from the hospital, holding hands, the child skipping along.

People took moments of happiness for granted, all day, every day.

'Have you told the police about this?' Melissa asked.

'No. I was too out of it earlier when they were here.'

'Well, perhaps you should.'

'Will do.'

'What are you doing now?' she said.

'Going home hopefully. Mum and Dad are here. The kids are ... well, you know how they are. They're sixteen. This is going to hit them hard.'

'But you're not alone, Gareth. You have us. We're the Silkies.' She laughed – such a terrible nickname – even though she was crying. 'We stick together.'

'Yep.'

'I'll call you later.'

'OK, Mel.'

They ended the call just as footsteps sounded behind him. It was the nurse. She smiled at him. 'You're free to go,' she said.

He didn't feel free.

He picked up his bag and went to find his family.

10

At three o'clock in the afternoon, Melissa sat down on the sofa with a cup of tea. She had just finished clearing up the lunch things; she still had to get the beds ready, plus organise dinner for seven people.

Rachel's boys were staying the night – even Joel, surprisingly, independent young man that he was. It seemed that everyone wanted to stay together. That was the way they always operated: in and out of each other's houses, mucking in when needed.

Joel and Ned were currently up the garden treehouse with Nina, playing music. Every now and then, Melissa heard the soft thump of a distant bass. Were it not for Polly, colouring in on the floor by Melissa's feet, she would have felt sufficiently relinquished of her duties to doze off.

She hadn't slept last night. Everyone had been too upset so they had sat up in sleeping bags, like a strange funereal campout, only indoors.

Frank had been so attentive to Olivia, asking if she needed anything. Out of his depth, all he could do was keep offering his girlfriend sugary tea. He would be shattered today, yet had just gone with Lee to the marina to see to a difficult customer who was demanding urgent boat repairs.

Melissa sipped her tea, trying to make sense of the last twenty-four hours. Every time she thought of the accident, her stomach lurched. She couldn't bring herself to imagine what Jenny must have suffered. She had been having the same thought over and over: that it shouldn't have happened in the first place, that there was something about it that didn't seem right.

Everything was too up in the air for logical thought, however. They would have to wait until things had settled down, falling into place.

She thought of what Gareth had said over the phone earlier about Jenny's surprise around the back of the island.

What surprise?

Setting her tea down anxiously, she picked up her phone. There wouldn't be enough time to visit Rachel in hospital today, not with everyone here to look after. She would call her instead.

'Can you hear that?' Polly said.

'What?'

'Listen, Mummy.'

There came the sound of tyres crunching on gravel, followed by car doors slamming. Melissa was about to peer out of the window, when the doorbell rang.

Polly jumped up. 'I'll go,' she said, disappearing from the room.

Melissa followed her down the hallway. At the door were two men: one with a face full of freckles, the other older, with large brown eyes.

'Melissa Silk?' the older man said, flashing a badge at her.

'Yes?'

'Sorry to bother you on a Sunday. I'm Detective Sergeant Lloyd and this is Detective Constable Wilson. Could we speak with you, please?'

'Of course,' Melissa said, standing aside for them. 'Come on in.'

'I'll show you where to go,' Polly said, always eager to play hostess, darting ahead of the men.

They gathered in the lounge, the breeze from the French doors lifting the edges of the curtains. It was a warm day, the heatwave not having abated. Both the men's foreheads were glistening; they looked overdressed in suits and ties.

'Could we have a word in private?' the sergeant said, glancing at Polly.

'Absolutely,' Melissa said. She stepped one foot out of the patio doors and called up the garden. 'Nina?'

They all waited, a polite silence descending.

'Shall I pack up my pens?' Polly asked.

'No, leave them, poppet,' Melissa said.

Nina appeared, stepping through the doors, face red with surprise at the sight of the strange men. She had recently had a brace fitted on her teeth, which she was still getting used to. Slurping on it, she raised her eyebrows at Melissa for an explanation.

'These men are detectives, Nina. They just want to talk about yesterday. Could you please look after Polly for five minutes?'

Nina looked at the men and then held her hand out to her little sister. 'Come on, Pols.' And the girls traipsed out into the garden, sliding the patio door shut behind them.

Melissa turned to the detectives. 'Please, take a seat.' She pointed to the sofa.

'Thanks. We won't keep you long,' the sergeant said, sitting down. 'We're making inquiries into the accident at Hope Cove. We understand Jennifer Davies was a close friend of yours?'

'Yes.' Melissa sat down on the armchair opposite them, glancing down at herself abashedly. She was wearing an old broderie anglaise dress, the first thing she had grabbed that morning.

'There'll be an autopsy,' the sergeant said. 'Drowning nearly always concludes in death by misadventure, though.'

Death by misadventure. It sounded so civil compared to the ghastly fate that Jenny must have suffered. 'What does that mean exactly?' she asked.

'Basically, that the deceased took a risk voluntarily, entering into an activity with known dangers.'

Melissa had to agree with that. There was always an element of danger with kayaking, which was why she had told Al to check everything thoroughly.

'We were wondering if there was anything you could tell us – anything that might have seemed odd or out of place about yesterday?' The sergeant gazed at her with his soulful brown eyes. His eyelashes were so dark and thick; they looked wet, clumped together.

'I . . . ' Melissa said.

Did they mean the fact that Rachel had asked her not to go with them, or the fact that she had been weirdly secretive in the run-up to the trip?

'Mrs Silk,' the constable said, 'can you think of any reason why someone may have wished to harm Jennifer?'

'Harm her?' Melissa said in surprise. 'Why would you say that?'

Neither of the men answered the question. They simply waited for her to answer theirs.

'No,' Melissa said. 'She was popular. Everyone was fond of her.'

The sergeant nodded. 'Yourself included.'

'Very much so,' she said, welling up. 'I'm sorry . . . I haven't slept . . . '

'It's all right. Take your time. We know how distressing this must be.'

She pressed the corners of her eyes. 'It's fine,' she said. 'Carry on.'

77

'We understand you're in a tight-knit circle of friends that have been together a long time. The Silkies, so the locals call you. Is that right?'

'Yes.'

'And you all get along?'

'Definitely.' The music out in the treehouse was suddenly turned up and then abruptly turned down again. She smiled apologetically at the two men.

'What are your thoughts on this so-called surprise of Jennifer's during the kayaking trip?' the sergeant asked.

'I don't know what to think about that,' Melissa replied. 'It doesn't make a lot of sense to me.'

He sat forward in his seat to address her, looking at her attentively. She knew what was coming next, felt the hairs on her arms stand on end.

'Can I ask why you didn't go with them? We hear you're good at kayaking and that your mother owns the academy.'

'I had a migraine,' she said, poking her finger through a hole in the embroidery on her dress, avoiding looking at them.

It was a silly lie. They weren't idiots.

'Yet you phoned Alistair Beckinsale on Friday night to give him some advice about the trip, which suggests that perhaps you weren't ever intending to go?'

Melissa blushed. 'The migraine came on Friday night. Sometimes they can knock me out for the following day, especially in this heat.'

'Nasty stuff,' the sergeant said, sitting back in his seat. 'So, what advice did you give Alistair?'

'The usual: make sure he checked the weather, and that he planned the trip and stuck to it.'

'Yet he didn't, did he? Because they went around the back of the island.'

It felt terribly hot in the room with the patio door shut. She

78

shifted uncomfortably in her chair again then scooped her hair up into a knot, patting it to check that it was secure.

'It seems that your brother, David, forgot to enter your friends' booking into the system down at the academy,' the sergeant said. 'Does that sound likely?'

'I'm afraid so. He has learning difficulties.'

'And does your mother often leave him on his own to run the office?'

'He wasn't running the office. There weren't any customers. It's not high season yet. Sometimes he does a bit of admin work to keep himself occupied.'

'But is that safe practice? If he forgets to book people in then surely anyone could show up at any time?'

'Yes, but they'd be refused,' she said. 'He doesn't let the kayaks go without a booking.'

'Yet on this occasion . . .'

She gazed at him, her head foggy with tiredness. She couldn't think what he was getting at.

'Look, all I know is that David's capable of doing a job,' she said. 'But Al can be very persuasive. I expect David felt press-ganged. They're my friends. He probably didn't want to argue with them.'

The sergeant nodded. 'Your mother said much the same thing.'

'You've spoken to her?'

'Yes. She showed us around the academy last night.'

'Oh.' She looked at her lap uneasily, imagining her mother leading them down to the beach in the dark, the sea shifting malevolently. She hoped that David wasn't blaming himself. He had a strong sense of right and wrong, and felt guilt keenly.

'She said that your friends were always particular about taking their own personalised kayaks out,' the constable said.

'Yes,' Melissa said. 'They're initialled.'

'So, they'd have stuck to their own boats again this time?'

'Almost definitely, yes.' Something occurred to her then. 'Have they found Jenny's kayak?'

'Yes,' the sergeant said.

'Can I . . . can you tell me where it was?' She bit her lip, waiting for the response, hoping she could handle it.

'Both the kayak and Jennifer were found some way out to sea. I understand it took the rescue team quite a while to locate her.'

Melissa closed her eyes momentarily, clasped her hands on her lap.

'I'm sorry,' the sergeant said. 'We're nearly done.'

'There's just one more thing, if you don't mind,' the constable said. 'I don't know much about kayaks, but apparently there are plugs in the bottom that you undo to release water?'

'Yes,' Melissa said, nodding limply.

'When the team uncovered Jennifer's kayak, they noted that both plugs were undone.'

She looked at the constable, not understanding the point, wishing he would be clearer. 'None of the other kayaks were unplugged,' he said. 'Just hers.'

Both men were watching her closely.

'That doesn't mean as much as you might think,' she said. 'People unplug them all the time. Any kayaker will tell you so.'

'Yes. We've already spoken to a few experts.'

'Then you know it's true.'

'But surely it must have compromised her ability to control the boat? She would have been sinking faster than the others?'

'Not necessarily,' Melissa said. 'Some people keep the plugs open all the time to let out water.'

'But they let water in too?'

'Yes.'

'So, how do you prefer to kayak? Plugs open or shut?'

She hesitated, not because she didn't know the answer well enough, but because she wasn't sure what it was that she was supposed to be saying and why.

'I prefer them shut,' she said.

The sergeant stood up then. 'Well, I think that's all for now, Mrs Silk. Sorry to have caused you any distress. You've been very helpful.'

She saw the men to the door, said goodbye and closed the door firmly behind them, standing with her back to it, going back over the conversation that had just taken place.

She had answered their questions to the best of her ability to assist their inquiries, whilst still protecting Rachel; at least, she hoped she had.

But what was all that about the plugs?

Returning to the lounge, she picked up her phone, sent a text.

Rachel, we need to talk. Call me as soon as you can. Mel xxx

NESSA MERRY

Milford resident, Dorset

Nessa set the iron down on the ironing board to answer the phone. 'Hello?'

'Nessa, it's me again.'

It was Angela Gould. She sounded stirred up.

'What's wrong?' Nessa asked, watching as her son came into the kitchen, his lanky arms extending to reach up to a shelf.

'You won't believe it.'

'Hey?' Nessa said, putting a finger to her ear to block out the sound of cupboard doors slamming, cutlery rattling. No one could storm a kitchen like a teenage boy.

'The police just left Melissa's,' Angela said.

'The police?'

Her son stopped what he was doing and gazed at her, intrigued. She flapped him away and he left the room.

'Yes. I'm sure that's who they were: two smart men in suits with identity badges. Do you think they were detectives?'

'Sounds like it,' Nessa said. 'Must be because of yesterday.'

'Oh, it's just awful. I can't stop thinking about poor Jenny. It's so tragic. I can't take it in, can you?'

'No,' Nessa said, narrowing her eyes. 'But that's because we don't know anything yet. The more information that comes out about what happened, the easier it'll be to process.'

'Well, I'll definitely let you know if I hear anything.'

'Me too,' Nessa said. 'Anyhow, I'd best get on … Are you still going to Zumba tomorrow?'

'I was going to, yes. It'll be a nice distraction from all this.'

'I'll see you there then,' Nessa said, hanging up. She picked up the iron, ran it along the sleeve of a blouse, lost in thought.

According to her husband, who had been part of the rescue team that had taken Rachel Beckinsale to hospital, the Silks hadn't been anywhere near the kayaking accident.

So why would detectives be talking to them about it?

11

Monday 23 April 2018

The school was fine about Joel and Ned staying home. The receptionist, Gilly Green, who was known more for her gossiping than her administrative skills, told Rachel over the phone that the boys could take as long as they needed.

Rachel hung up quickly before she could be interrogated. She felt certain that there would be a polite pause, after which everyone would weigh in. The fact that Al had organised the trip and had somehow misjudged things was bound to be the subject of discussion. She was determined to shield him from any thoughtless comments.

She felt hollow, dried out, yet still the tears came. She had cried all night in the hospital at Al's bedside, only to well up again on waking, so much so that her eyes were horribly puffy and sore.

She couldn't help but feel responsible for what had happened. The trip had taken place at her instigation. Had she taken Melissa's advice and gone for a stroll or a coffee, Jenny would still be here.

She began to cry again, despite the fact that Ned was sitting next to her on the sofa. The boys had only just walked back from Melissa's. Joel had darted straight upstairs to start revising, but Ned had remained in the lounge, his eyes flitting between parents.

Al had been sitting motionless in the armchair for the past half an hour, since arriving home from hospital.

'Did you see it happen, Mummy?' Ned asked. His eyes were red-rimmed with tiredness, his hair messy.

She couldn't keep crying like this in front of him. It wasn't fair; he was only twelve.

'Not really,' she said. 'It happened so quickly.'

'Is Daddy going to die too?'

'What? No, Ned. He's getting better, aren't you, Daddy?'

Al didn't look at them, didn't move.

'Do you want to play something, Ned?' she asked him.

'Fortnite?' he said, eyes brightening.

'I was thinking Cluedo or Scrabble.'

'Oh.' His shoulders slumped.

'Choose something else then. Go and have a look in the games cupboard.' He stood up, sighed, left the room. Rachel looked at Al in concern.

On the table beside her, her phone glowed and beeped as a text arrived.

How's Al? Are you home yet? Need to talk. Mel xxx

Her stomach churned. Melissa had sent several messages last night, to which Rachel had given vague replies. She knew that she had to sit down and talk to her properly. It was just that she wanted to delay the moment when Melissa concluded that she was to blame.

She welled up again, her eyes stinging.

Dammit! *Stop crying!*

She picked up her phone, replied to Melissa.

Just got home. I promise we'll talk the first opportunity I get. Rach xox

The doorbell rang then, causing her to drop the phone. She glanced at Al for guidance as to whether he wanted guests, but he didn't appear to have heard. For a second, she contemplated not answering, before reasoning that their cars were in the driveway. It would be obvious that they were home.

The doorbell rang again. 'Are you gonna get that, Mum?' Joel shouted from upstairs.

'Yes,' she called back, going out to the hallway, stopping to check her appearance in the mirror: hideous.

She opened the front door to two men in suits. Her first incongruous thought was that they had come to arrest her for manslaughter.

'Mrs Beckinsale?' one of the men said with a quick smile. 'No need to look so worried. We're here for a chat, if we may? I'm Detective Sergeant Lloyd, and this is Detective Constable Wilson.'

'Hello,' she said. 'Come in.' And she opened the door wider for them, her mind racing.

Why were they here? What did they want?

Leading them back to the lounge, she motioned for the men to sit on the sofa while she went to stand behind Al's chair.

'Sorry to pounce on you the moment you get home,' the sergeant said. 'But we have a few questions, if that's all right?'

Al stirred then, came to life. 'Go ahead,' he said.

Rachel wasn't sure that she had heard him speak since the accident. His voice sounded exactly the same. But then why wouldn't it? Not everything had changed out there on Saturday. She couldn't think of anything else at that moment that was normal, though. Everything around her seemed murky, altered, like petrol on a puddle.

'We understand, Mr Beckinsale, that you planned the trip. Could you tell us what that involved?'

'I was thorough,' Al said.

'Could you expand on that, please?'

'I checked the weather, the tides – everything you're supposed to do.'

'And you also took advice from Melissa Silk over the phone the night before the trip?'

'Yes.'

'She seems to know what she's doing,' the sergeant said.

There was a pause. Rachel watched a fly enter the open window and head straight for the ceiling, bumping itself up and down, before circling the room crazily.

'Can I ask what you do for a living, Mr Beckinsale?' the sergeant asked.

'I'm CEO of EMS, the insurance company.'

The sergeant nodded, turning his mouth down as though impressed.

'I'm perfectly capable of organising a kayaking trip,' Al continued. 'I was also . . .'

No, don't say it, Al.

' . . . leader of the Cub Scouts for many years.'

Rachel closed her eyes momentarily.

'I was Akela.'

'Akela?' the sergeant said.

'The traditional name for a Cub Scout leader.'

'Oh, I see.'

Rachel gazed at the carpet. He was bright, her husband – ambitious, forceful at work. Yet socially, he never seemed able to judge how much to say. He struck gold, impressed, and then threw it all away by adding something else. He was like a child adding more paint, more glitter to an art project to garner praise.

'Yet someone died,' the sergeant said. 'And we need to understand why. I think that's what stands out the most: how strikingly bad the conditions were.'

The sun came in through the window then, lighting the top of her husband's blond hair in a glorious glow.

Someone had told her once – a mother at school – that Al looked Dutch. She hadn't been sure what that meant, didn't know anyone Dutch to compare him to, but assumed it meant that he had strong features: blue eyes, a sharp, straight nose, a thick head of blond hair. He was certainly striking, and he was hers. And at that moment she wanted to tell him so. Instead, she gazed at the back of his head, willing him not to blame himself.

'I did all I could,' he said.

Rachel pulled a crumpled tissue from her pocket, held it to her nose.

'No one's doubting that. But we need some details. Could you tell us when you last checked the weather?'

'First thing Saturday,' Al replied. 'We also looked at the weather at the academy and it was fine.'

'However, apparently the academy website hadn't been updated for twenty-four hours. David Reeve was completely unaware that a storm was imminent.'

'The print-out on the wall looked good.'

'The print-out was from the day before. And besides, it wouldn't have given you enough details to base a safety check on. Apparently, it's more like a token gesture for tourists.'

'So, what's the point of it?' Al said testily.

Rachel moved closer to him, placing her hand on his shoulder. 'It's all right, Al,' she said. She looked at the detectives reproachfully. 'He's been very poorly.'

'We're aware of that and we're trying to make this as painless as possible,' the sergeant said. 'We've nearly finished.'

'Another contributing factor was the tide,' the constable

said. 'Your wife told us that you left during high tide, which was, when?'

'Two o'clock,' Al said.

'Should have been plain sailing,' the constable said. 'Yet according to Gareth Davies, it didn't feel comfortable by the time you got around the back of the island, but as though there was a strong current that you were fighting against. Would you agree with that?'

Rachel looked at Al, at the back of his hair, which was still set ablaze.

'Mr Beckinsale?'

'Yes,' Al said.

'Having spoken to the local coastguard,' the constable continued, 'it would appear that high tide was at one o'clock.'

'No, it wasn't,' Al said, shaking his head.

The sergeant gazed at Al thoughtfully. 'OK, let's park this for now,' he said. He glanced at his colleague. 'We'll make a move. But if you think of anything else, please let us know.'

Rachel showed the men out. As she was opening the front door, the sergeant turned to speak to her. 'I don't suppose you have your husband's tide table to hand?'

'Maybe,' she said. 'I'll check.'

She went to the utility room, reached into the compartment in Al's rucksack where he kept his maps and guidebooks. Sure enough, there was the tide table. She returned to the detectives, handing the booklet to the sergeant, who flicked through it.

'Thought as much,' he said. Then he drew her out of the front door, where he spoke quietly. 'This isn't adjusted for summer time. Apparently, yachtsmen prefer them that way, so some versions are printed without the time difference.' He held the booklet up, flapped it. 'Mind if I keep this?'

'Take it,' she said. 'But I don't understand why it matters?'

He looked at her regrettably, his brown eyes softening. 'Because you were an hour out.'

'Oh.' She pushed her spectacles on to her nose, trying to absorb the information. 'So ... we ...?'

His colleague stepped in. Younger, he spoke frankly, without apparent empathy. 'With the hour lost, plus the extra time that it took you to go around the island, you arrived at the dangerous spot two hours after high tide. According to the coastguard, the current runs strongest at that time. It couldn't have been worse.'

Rachel gazed at the booklet in the sergeant's hands. 'Oh no,' she said. Then she glanced back at the house. 'He mustn't find this out. He'll be devastated.'

'We'll try our best. But it's a police investigation and these things tend to come out.'

Her mouth trembled. 'He'll never forgive himself.'

'I doubt anyone would be cruel enough to blame him,' the sergeant said. 'His error was only one of a number of mishaps.'

'Oh?' she said, grasping at this hopefully. 'What else ...?'

'Well,' he said, tapping the booklet on his open palm, 'David Reeve forgot to enter the booking; the academy website wasn't updated with the weather change; and Jennifer wanted to go around that dangerous section, which no one seems able to explain.'

'Don't forget the plugs,' the constable added.

'What plugs?' Rachel said.

'The plugs in Jennifer's kayak were open. None of the others were. Only hers.'

They both looked at her, watching her response.

She thought back to the minutes, moments, before the last time she had seen Jenny. 'She said she felt as though she was sitting in a bath tub,' she said.

'Yep, would have been, with holes in the bottom of the boat.'

'Why were her plugs open? I don't understand.'

'You and me both,' the sergeant said. 'To be honest, it's a wonder any of you made it back to shore at all, given that set of circumstances.' He turned away, taking off his suit jacket. 'You take care now, Mrs Beckinsale. And try to reassure your husband that this was not the work of one cock-up.'

She closed the door behind the officers. Ned was coming down the stairs with a tower of board games wobbling in his arms. 'Monopoly?' he said.

It was the last thing she wanted to do. 'Yes, Ned. Set it up in the playroom. I'll be right there.'

She was about to go into the kitchen to make a cup of tea, but changed her mind, deciding to check on Al first.

Noiselessly, she entered the lounge. Al was standing with his back to her, looking out of the window, saying something very faintly. She stopped, listened, her head to one side.

She caught it then.

'Jenny. Oh, Jen.'

12

They decided to close the marina as a mark of respect. Only Lee was going in to work today, behind the scenes, continuing with the urgent boat repairs.

Melissa printed a sign to post on the office door so that no one would bother him. *Closed until further notice due to bereavement.* She was also going to put a sign on the door of Mon Petit Hair, Jenny's salon.

'Do you want me to put those up for you?' Lee asked, as he clipped on his cycle helmet. 'Save you a job?'

'No, it's all right,' she said. 'It'll give me something to do.'

Lee lifted his leg over his bike. 'After that, make sure you rest. You've had the house full all weekend. You haven't stopped.'

'I need to go and see Rachel, though, and check on Gareth.'

'Are they ready for visitors?'

She frowned. 'I'm not just any old visitor.'

'Yes, but look what they're going through. Let them contact you when they're ready.'

'What if they think I don't care?'

'Mel,' he said, 'they'll never think that.'

Polly, who was sitting in the back seat of the car, banged on the window, then pointed at her Disney princess watch. 'Uh, hello?' she shouted.

Nina wound the other window down. 'Come on, Mum,' she said. 'We'll be late.'

'Shut up, Keener,' Frank said, from the front passenger seat.

'You shut up, butt face.'

'Charming,' Melissa said, kissing Lee goodbye. 'I'd better go. I'll see you later.'

As she reversed down the driveway, she almost backed into their neighbour, Angela Gould, who was setting out at the same time, dropping her children to school.

Melissa waited to see who would give way, all the while knowing that Angela would be the one to do so. She had known Angela on a cursory, sketchy basis since childhood, yet from the glimpses she had seen of her, Angela was a people pleaser.

Sure enough, Angela smiled and waved at her to go right ahead. Melissa waved a thank-you, before driving off.

The journey to senior school was two miles. It felt longer that morning, given that the children were conversation-less. Still warm out, Polly was in her summer dress, and Nina and Frank had ditched their jumpers.

'Have you heard from Olivia today?' she asked Frank, glancing sideways at him.

'No,' he said. 'Should I have?'

He sounded defensive. He was tired; they all were.

'I just wondered how she was doing. This is a lot for her to deal with.'

'Yep,' he said flatly.

She pulled into the lay-by opposite school and put her window down in anticipation of goodbye kisses.

Nina was the first to oblige, bending her head through the window. 'Bye, Mum,' she said, swinging her book-laden rucksack on to her shoulder. 'You're going to be all right, aren't you?'

Melissa tried her best to smile reassuringly. 'Don't you worry about me. You just go and be awesome.'

It sounded fake, but it was the best she could do.

Frank poked his head in next, tentative, twitchy, as was his style now that he had a girlfriend and his mother was no longer the sole recipient of his affections. 'Laters, Ma.'

'You know I hate *Ma*,' she called after him.

He smirked over his shoulder. 'Sorry, Ma.'

She sighed, watching her two teenagers go through the gates to school, trying to walk as far away from each other as possible. Then she turned to Polly, patting the empty seat beside her. 'Want to climb up front, Polly Pops?'

'Yep,' Polly said, skirt rising as she clambered forward.

They drove home again, ditched the car and then walked to primary school – Melissa's favourite part of the day: a peaceful ten-minute walk in nature with her little girl.

That morning, they walked in silence. Polly didn't seem to mind; she skipped along, stopping to poke spiders' webs and pick up snail shells. The morning sun was already strong, yet Melissa couldn't celebrate in that fact. She wondered whether life would always feel like this now, like broken skin. She felt the urge to try to patch things up, yet there was nothing to fix. Jenny was gone, irreparably.

At the school gates, she came to a halt, gazing in dismay at the throng of parents in the playground, each one a potential catalyst for an emotional outburst from her.

I'm so sorry. Poor, poor Jenny. Such a lovely woman. How are you holding up?

Faces were starting to turn her way – faces full of concern and sympathy. A small unchanging community, most of the residents in Milford had grown up together, seeing their children grow up together in turn. The news would have rocked the town's foundations, unsettling everyone.

'It's all right, Mummy,' Polly said, tugging on her hand. 'You can come in. Everyone knows about Auntie Jenny. If they don't, I'll tell them and then they'll understand why you're saddy.'

Polly always called it *saddy*, a small relic from early childhood that she had chosen to keep.

'Actually, I think I'll leave you here, if that's OK?'

'That's fine.' Polly said, going on tiptoes to kiss her goodbye. Parents and children were flowing past them, in and out of the school gates, stepping out of their way. 'Look after yourself, Mummy. I don't want you to die.'

'What?' She pulled Polly to one side, away from the main flow, and crouched down to speak to her. 'Listen, what happened to Auntie Jenny was a one-off. Things like that don't happen every day. Do you understand?'

'So, it won't happen to you?' Polly said.

'No,' Melissa said.

'Promise?'

'Promise.' She tapped her daughter's nose then stood up. 'Now you go and play with your friends and try to forget all about this.'

They kissed goodbye again and then Polly sped off into the playground, pigtails bouncing.

'I'm so sorry,' a voice said, close by Melissa's side.

It was Nessa Merry, PTA Powerhouse. Distracted by Polly, Melissa hadn't noticed the woman advancing until it was too late.

'You must be devastated,' Nessa said. 'What an awful thing to have happened. So hard to take in.'

'Yes,' Melissa replied. It was hardly adequate, but what else could she say? She placed one foot out of the gate, indicating her intention to leave.

'How's Gareth doing, poor man?'

'I . . . I think he's all right.'

Other parents were looking over with interest. If Nessa Merry could talk to Melissa Silk then surely they could express their deepest regrets also?

It seemed to her that more people were beginning to edge towards her. She would be trapped here, awash with their condolences. She glanced at her watch. 'I'm sorry. I have to go.'

'Of course,' said Nessa, touching Melissa's arm. 'There must be so much to do, so much to process. Do let me know if—'

'Will do,' Melissa said, turning away.

It was a bit abrupt, but it was the only way to release herself.

⚓

At home, the house seemed unbearably quiet. She had been hoping that at least one of the children would have wanted to stay home, but they were keen to get back to normal as best they could. Nothing said normal to them like school.

She couldn't stay here, skulking around. She changed into a sundress, scooped her hair into a butterfly clip, grabbed her bag and left.

It took her five minutes to drive across Milford, to the sleepy east side where nobody went unless they lived there or were visiting someone who did.

Pulling into a potholed driveway that was threatened to be overtaken by the giant plum tree on its border, she stopped the car and got out, a magpie clacking above her.

She smelt the air. It was so familiar: a whiff of petrol, sea salt. Modern life hadn't touched this part of town. The bungalows had pebbledash walls and rusty gates with curly ironwork, beyond which tyres hung from worn ropes on apple trees.

She went up the pathway and on to the porch where she knocked and waited.

Her mother came to the door, wearing coral lipstick and a snakeskin belt around her waist to clip in her shirtdress. She had black curly hair, frazzled with streaks of grey, and dark eyes that shone from her tanned face like wet blueberries.

They couldn't have looked more different, Melissa had always thought.

'Are you going out?' Melissa asked.

'Only shopping,' her mother said. 'But it can wait. Come on in ...' She held the door open for her. 'You don't have to knock, you know.'

It was true, she didn't; she used to live here, after all. Yet, somehow, she always did.

'I'll put the kettle on. Cup of tea?' her mother called as she went down the hallway to the kitchen. Melissa followed her halfway, before turning into the lounge. The door was open; she could see the top of her brother's head above the sofa.

'Yes, please,' she called back.

She sat down beside David, who was watching one of his favourite ocean documentaries. 'How are you?' she said.

'Very well, thank you,' he replied.

There was a spot of milk on his cheek. She wiped it off. He didn't register the touch.

She folded her arms, gazed around the room. Nothing had changed; nothing ever did here. It was a shame, the sadness that she always felt the moment she entered the bungalow, as though it were a basement flat that you descended into, leaving joy with your shoes at the door.

Her parents had split up when she was only seven years old. Perhaps that had been the start of the unhappiness that had set up camp here. It certainly wasn't David's doing: he sent hoots of laughter around the place on a regular basis, albeit while watching TV. Their father had died not long after moving out – a sudden heart attack. The news should have been painful, but

Melissa didn't remember it as such, having barely known her father even when he had lived here.

'There you go,' her mother said, entering the room and handing her a mug of tea before sitting down. 'How are you feeling?'

Melissa shrugged. 'Awful.'

'I'm sorry. It's a horrible business, especially when it comes out of the blue like that. The shock is half of it – trying to take it in,' her mother said, folding her legs at her heels. 'Are the children at school?'

'Yes. They wanted to go.'

David whooped with laughter then, throwing his head back, clapping his hands. It was his favourite part: the huge shoal of fish swarming through the ocean, up and up.

'I've closed the academy temporarily,' her mother said. 'There's tape everywhere.'

'What, like a crime scene?'

'Sort of,' her mother said. 'The kayaks are cordoned off, anyway. People can't go traipsing about down there. Even in an accident, they still have to account for everything.'

David laughed again, loudly.

'I'm sorry,' her mother said, 'but I have to say that I feel this is my fault. If I'd have been there, none of this would have happened. Poor Jenny. When you think of all the times she played here as a child . . . '

'Mum,' Melissa said. 'You can't think like that. You weren't to know. And besides, if anyone was to blame for not being there, it was me.'

Her mother frowned at her. 'You can't go blaming yourself, Melissa. Lots of things contributed to what happened. It was a disaster all round.'

It was quiet then, but for the soothing voice of the documentary narrator and the tinkling music accompanying a bobbing seahorse.

Melissa glanced around the room, her eye resting on a photograph in a silver frame on the mantelpiece. Sometimes, she could look at it; other times, she couldn't. Today, however, she wanted a closer look.

Setting down her mug, she approached the mantelpiece and picked up the photograph. Behind her, she could sense that her mother was sitting very still, watching her. If there was a protocol in the bungalow, this was most definitely breaking with it.

She touched the glass, wiping a film of dust from it to see the child within: a little girl sitting in the grass, a daisy chain on her head, her face so blanched by light that some of her features were lost, edgeless.

Putting the picture back, she went to the window overlooking the garden. A ginger cat was picking its way across the lawn, its tail raised above the long grass like a snorkel above water.

With a deep breath, she allowed herself to look at the area near the laurel hedge. She could almost see a yellow dress, peach-blonde curls of hair.

And then David clapped his hands, dispelling her thoughts.

'I should get going,' she said, turning to face her mother again. 'I've got a lot to do, and you need to go shopping. Thanks for the tea.'

'You're welcome. Any time, Melissa. You know where we are.'

So formal, so proper. And so dependent on Melissa's initiation.

You know where I am too, Mum, she always wanted to say. But what was the use? Her mother was sixty-two years old and had the academy and David to look after. She had long since deduced that Melissa was a self-contained entity who could look after herself. Whether that was true or not didn't come into it. Her mother had enough to deal with at her time of life.

'Love you, David,' Melissa said, stooping to press a kiss on to her brother's head.

'I love you, Melissa,' he replied.

She headed down the hallway, stopping by the front door to put on her espadrilles. 'It was nice to see you,' her mother said. 'Don't be too hard on yourself. Things will get easier, you'll see.'

Melissa, sitting on the floor, kept her head down.

You have no idea how I feel – not about Jenny or about anything. You never did.

I came here because I thought that just once you might make me feel better, but once again I am disappointed.

'I'll see you soon, Mum,' she said.

And she walked away and got into her car, putting her sunglasses on the moment that she reached the main road where she could cry.

She hadn't gone very far when she realised that she didn't want to cry any more. She was done with crying. Jenny would have hated this, everyone sitting around sobbing and despairing.

Instead, she was beginning to feel angry. She didn't know what the source of the anger was, yet she was prepared to go with it anyway. It was better than misery, for sure. It felt more productive.

Crossing town, she turned on to a smart avenue of large red-brick houses, before driving through two lion-topped gateposts and coming to a stop behind Al's BMW.

13

Rachel pulled the front door open, expecting it to be the detectives again, having just shown them out, only to see Melissa standing there.

She thought she had made it clear that she wasn't available to talk yet. 'Hello, Mel,' she said, looking at her friend warily.

Melissa seemed on edge. She was jangling her car keys, her mouth taut.

'Would you like to come in?' Rachel said, hoping that she wouldn't.

'Thanks,' Melissa said, stepping into the house. 'How's Al?'

'Fragile,' she said quietly. 'Two police detectives just came around. I don't think that helped ... Let's go in here,' she said, leading them into the kitchen.

'What did they want?' Melissa said. She was wearing a white sundress with capped sleeves that made her arms seem girlishly thin and her face colourless.

'Just crossing Ts.'

'Crossing Ts?' Melissa said. 'That's putting it lightly.'

'What do you mean?' Rachel said.

Melissa threw her car keys down on to the counter; she looked irritated. 'Why are detectives involved in this, Rachel? Have you thought about that at all?'

'I ... not yet. I—'

There was a tap on the door then and Ned entered furtively. Rachel, transfixed by what Melissa had just said, didn't heed him at first.

'Hello, Ned,' Melissa said, recovering quickly and shooting him a smile.

'Hi, Auntie Mel,' he replied, then looked at his mum. 'When are we playing Monopoly?'

'In a minute,' Rachel said.

''Cos the board's set up.'

'Then go ahead and choose your playing piece,' she said, slightly testily.

'I already have. I'm the hat, you're the boot.'

That sounded about right.

'Sorry, Ned. I won't keep your mum long,' Melissa said. 'Just five minutes, OK?'

He nodded solemnly and then retreated, closing the door behind him.

Melissa waited a moment before turning to Rachel. 'Just tell me why you didn't want me to go with you, and then I'll leave you in peace.'

'Not now. You can see that my hands are full.'

Melissa held her hands out either side of her. 'No one else here that I can see. So, go ahead.'

'It's not that easy,' Rachel said.

'Why isn't it? Why can't you tell me?'

'Because I can't. I need more time.'

'I've already given you time. I've been more than patient. But you can't keep giving me the run-around. It's not fair. I'm beginning to imagine the worst.'

'What's that supposed to mean?'

Melissa pulled a stool out from under the counter and sat down. 'It doesn't mean anything,' she said. 'I'm just struggling to understand what happened. I mean, one minute you're acting all secretive and the next thing, Jenny's dead. What would you think, if it were you?'

Rachel inhaled sharply, feeling the sting of her friend's words. This was the moment that she had tried to postpone: the moment of blame. It was no easier for having delayed it.

'Tell me.' Melissa set her eyes on her – green eyes that were just like her brother's.

Rachel pictured poor David down at the academy on Saturday, watching them walk away, taking the kayaks against his will. Whatever he had been thinking at that time, she wished they had heeded him and had turned back.

'The longer this goes on,' Melissa said, 'the more I'm blaming myself.'

'You?' Rachel looked at her in surprise. 'You weren't even there! How can—'

'Exactly! If I *had* been there I'd have noticed the storm coming. And I wouldn't have taken you around the back of the island, that's for sure.'

'Oh, Mel. This is nothing to do with you.' She placed her hand on Melissa's; it was surprisingly cold. 'We're all blaming ourselves. But it was a tragic accident. The detectives are no doubt involved because the circumstances were unusual. We—'

'Just tell me!' Melissa said heatedly, pulling her hand away.

The door opened then and Al entered the room. 'Tell her what?' he said.

Melissa jumped down from the bar stool, her espadrilles slapping on the lino floor. Her dress was creased. Her hair had toppled down from its bun into a ringleted mane. Rachel wanted to straighten her friend – to smooth her dress and fix her hair – as well as clap her hand around Melissa's mouth to prevent her from saying what she was about to say.

'Why she didn't want me to go on the trip,' Melissa said.

'The kayaking trip?' Al said.

'Yes, the kayaking trip,' Melissa said impatiently. 'What else would we be talking about? Did you know that I didn't have a migraine, that that was a lie?'

'A lie?' Al said, scratching his head.

'Don't worry,' Rachel said. 'I can—'

'Explain?' Melissa said. 'Please do. I expect Al would like to hear this too.'

'I'm not sure that I understand . . .' he said.

'That's because it's nonsense,' Rachel said.

It was a daft thing to say. It was precisely why she hadn't wanted to do this yet, before she had had sufficient time to gather her thoughts.

Melissa stared at her, her cheeks flushing. 'Nonsense?' she said. 'All I wanted was an explanation. I thought I deserved that, but obviously I was wrong.' She snatched her keys from the counter. 'This is a waste of time. I'll let myself out.' And she strode from the kitchen, Al stepping dutifully aside for her like a polite butler.

Rachel followed her. 'Mel, don't go. You don't understand.'

Melissa opened the front door. 'That's because you won't tell me anything,' she said.

Rachel hurried past her friend, rounding on her. 'Stop. Wait.' She pushed her glasses on to her nose, trying to think of the right words to say. But Melissa was walking away again. 'Don't leave like this. Come back inside.'

'There's no point,' Melissa said, opening her car door. 'You're just upsetting me.'

'I don't mean to. You know I don't.'

'Do I?' Melissa started the engine and lowered the window. 'Because I don't know anything any more.' She wrenched the car into reverse, placing one arm over the back of the seat to look behind her.

'Please, Mel,' Rachel said, hurrying alongside the car as it backed down the driveway. 'We're friends.'

'No, we're not. Friends don't lie to each other.'

'I'm not lying. I'm—'

Melissa hit the brake. 'You're what?' she asked. 'What are you?' She opened her eyes wide.

Rachel tried to think quickly, her heart racing, but she was no match for Melissa – never had been. She couldn't reply.

Melissa reversed again, and then she was gone.

Rachel stood in the driveway, stunned. What had just happened?

She should have explained everything to her, but how could she have with Al standing there so helplessly and Ned waiting to play Monopoly?

She saw something out of the corner of her eye then and noticed that Nessa Merry, her nosy neighbour, was standing in her garden opposite, pretending to polish the brass on her front gate.

Oh, for goodness' sake.

Rachel turned on her heel and went back inside. Ned was waiting for her at the bottom of the stairs. 'I rolled for you, Mummy. You got a one.'

Of course she did.

Al was hovering in the kitchen doorway, looking lost.

'What was that all about, Mum?' Joel said, coming down the stairs, holding a pile of revision papers.

'Nothing,' she said. 'Melissa's just upset.'

'About Jenny?'

'Yes, about Jenny!' she snapped. And she pushed past Al into the kitchen, slamming the door behind her as loudly as she could.

'What the hell?' she heard Joel say.

Ugh!

She stamped her foot. They were all so useless, expecting her to do everything. Well, she couldn't do everything, so she had just proven. Sometimes, she was just as useless as they were.

She glared at a plate full of crumbs that Joel had left on the counter for her to put in the dishwasher. Snatching it up, she threw the plate down. It hit the floor with a satisfying smack, shattering, the crumbs scattering.

Then she left the kitchen, pushing past Al again. '*You'll* have to clear that up!' she said, and then hurried upstairs to her bedroom, fully intending to slam the door even harder. Yet by the time she had got there, she was crying – full of remorse at taking things out on her boys, wishing that she hadn't smashed the plate, which was one of her favourites.

This, she told herself, was what happened when she didn't have time to think.

NESSA MERRY

Milford resident, Dorset

'She wasn't rude to me in the playground exactly,' Nessa said to Angela at the end of their Zumba class. 'Just abrupt. Mind you, she's always been a bit like that, don't you think? A bit up herself?'

'Maybe. But then look what she's going through, poor woman.'

'Hmm,' Nessa said sceptically. Angela was always too soft, in her opinion – too ready to see the good in everyone.

Nessa picked up her gym bag, set it on her shoulder. 'Anyhow, the next thing I knew, she was over at Rachel's having a fight with her.'

'A fight?' Angela said. 'What sort of fight?'

'Well, not a punch-up,' she said wryly, 'just an argument. Rachel ran after Melissa's car, pleading with her not to leave. It was quite pathetic.'

'Crikey,' Angela said. 'I wonder what that was all about.'

They started walking towards the door of the studio, smiling goodbyes to the instructor.

'Who knows?' Nessa said. 'I might ask Gilly in the school office. She always seems to know what's going on.'

'Good thinking,' Angela said.

They went along the corridor of the sports centre, Nessa deep in thought.

She had always admired the Silkies, especially Melissa. Working at King's, the solicitor's in town, she had been exposed to juicy Silkie information over the years that she hadn't told a soul about. While she might have been a little loose tongued where others were concerned, when it came to Melissa, she had adhered to the confidentiality code.

And this was the thanks she got: a dismissive brush-off at the school gates.

Still, for once, Angela was right. Melissa was grieving. Nessa would cut her some slack.

And as for the juicy information, she was sure that it would come out of its own accord. She knew from experience at King's that when someone died, all the files were opened, the drawers unlocked, tatty moths flying out of cabinets like sepia-toned secrets being released into daylight.

14

The house had existed for forty-eight hours without Jenny and it felt to Gareth as though it were sagging, the walls having taken on a porous quality meaning that were there to be a sudden rainstorm, they would take off and float away like a giant bath sponge.

Everything felt rootless without her. For someone so scatty, Jenny had provided them with an enormous amount of stability. Not using a calendar or diary like most normal people, she had relied on memory and spontaneity and by some fluke it had worked. Once, in the Nineties, he had bought her a bulky Filofax but she had used it as a door stop.

Now, somehow, he had to find a way to nail the house down again and fast before everything came adrift. Modern children's schedules were complicated, he knew that much. He would never be able to wing it like Jenny had.

She had also known the complex combination code to unlock their daughter's mind. Without it, he would be reliant on trial and error, making haphazard attempts to reach her until he found the one that worked.

It felt unbearably sad to him that he had been about to talk to Jenny about Olivia, in the hope of understanding their daughter better.

Feeling a wave of sorrow surge, he put his hand against the wall to steady himself, hoping that it wouldn't give way.

There was no use being full of remorse and what-ifs. Somehow, he was going to have to get through the coming months, setting an example for the twins. How he dealt with this loss now would stay with them for the rest of their lives.

Maybe these were broad terms, too futuristic and speculative to be of any real use, but these were his thoughts nonetheless as he stood outside his daughter's bedroom, summoning the courage to venture forth.

He had been standing here for four minutes now.

Clearing his throat, he gave a light rap on the door, stepping forward to listen to the response.

Come in? Did she just say 'come in'?

It could also have been 'go away'.

He hesitated and then decided to proceed, trying the handle, but it was locked. Whose idea had it been to put a lock on the door?

Ah; his, after he had walked in on her getting changed last year.

'Liv?' he called, knocking again.

There was a kerfuffle going on inside the room: the sound of the curtains being pulled, a rustle of bedding, then footsteps padding to the door.

And then Olivia was standing there, her face pallid, her hair lank. 'What?' she said.

'Can I come in for a minute?'

She stood aside for him, pulling her sweater sleeves down over her hands. Wordlessly, she climbed on to her bed, sitting cross-legged, her eyes nowhere.

'How you doing?' he said, picking up a pile of clothes from the tub chair so that he could sit down.

She lifted one shoulder in a shrug.

'I know this is really tough, Olivia. It's tough on me, too. I'm not afraid to admit that this is scary stuff.'

He looked at her, trying to gauge her reaction. Did she want to hear this? Was it helping?

'I haven't a clue what to do without your mum. She was—' His voice cracked. He stamped his feet. He was fairly sure an emotional meltdown wasn't going to be of use to her. 'Well, let's just say that she was everything to me.'

He sniffed, picking up a toy penguin that was lying on the floor. Olivia had loved cuddly toys at one stage, had had dozens of them in bed with her. Glancing about the room, he realised that the toys were still there, on top of her wardrobe. Somehow, the penguin had been permitted to occupy a place on the floor, in the main domain.

If the penguin was allowed to do so, maybe there was hope for him.

He set the penguin down beside him in the chair, patted its head.

'I was wondering if you could help me, Livvie?' he said.

Again, the one-shoulder shrug.

'I thought we could sit down together – you, me and Max – and come up with some kind of a routine. You're at that age where exams are—'

'Next year,' she said, setting her eyes on him.

Bingo. She cared about exams, even now, perhaps even more so. She was looking at him very intently.

'So, let's try to work out what would suit us best. Maybe we need a whiteboard or something. I know you have a lot of clubs and commitments. I don't want that to stop. It shouldn't have to stop.'

She nodded.

'Good. So ...' He rubbed his hands together. 'Shall we sit down after lunch?'

'OK.'

He stood up. 'Thanks, Liv.'

She looked away, into space.

'And if you need to talk, come and find me, any time. I'm here for you. I know it's not the same as having your mum—' Again, his voice cracked.

Just stop talking now.

He smiled then left the room, glancing at the penguin on his way out.

Good luck, mate.

⚓

Downstairs, in the kitchen, his mother was peeling potatoes, insistent on preparing two hot meals a day, despite their lack of appetites. 'How is she?' she asked, peering over her spectacles at him.

'Really sad,' Gareth said.

'Poor little darling,' she said.

'I don't know what to say.'

'Just be there for her. You're probably doing better than you realise.'

'Where's Dad?' he asked.

'He popped down the police station in Portbridge.'

'Oh? Why's that?'

She continued to peel the potatoes. 'Just his way of helping. He wants to ask them what they're doing – whether there's anything he can do. You know,' she lowered her voice, 'sometimes you can wait a long time for the . . . for the body to be released. He's just trying to avoid that.'

'I see.' Gareth felt himself sag, the energy slumping in the walls around him, at the thought of Jenny's body in the mortuary. He was glad that his father was willing to shield him from some of the harsher clinical details.

'Yes!' Max shouted then. He was sitting on a beanbag in the adjacent dining room, wearing a headset, his thumbs going up and down on his phone.

Gareth went to join him, lowering himself what felt like a very long way to sit on the edge of the beanbag. Max took off his headphones, set down his phone. He was good like that, knowing when to stop, when to listen to the adult. Gareth had always taken that for granted. Now it seemed like the boy should have a Nobel Prize for it.

'All right?' Gareth said. Max nodded. 'What you playing there?'

'Clash Royale.'

'Is it good?'

'Not really. Just something to do.'

There was a pause. Gareth placed his hand on his son's knee. 'I know your mum was the talker – that you went to her with everything. But I want you to know that I'm here for you. I'll do my very best to do what she would have done.'

Max's eyes misted over. He blinked rapidly. 'OK, Dad,' he said, twitching his nose.

'Do you want to talk about anything right now?'

'No.' Max shook his head.

'Well, any time . . . And I was thinking that maybe if you're up for it, you could play rugby on Saturday? If it's too soon, just say. But it might help. It's your call.'

'Maybe. See how I feel.'

'Good lad.' Gareth groaned as he struggled to his feet. 'Love you,' he said, when he was standing upright.

Max sniffed, twitched his nose again. 'Love you too, Dad.' He set his headphones back on his ears and picked up his phone.

Gareth heard the sound of a car outside then and looked out of the window to see a silver Audi Allroad pulling into their driveway.

'Is that Melissa?' his mother said.

'Looks like it,' he said. 'I'll go.'

He hadn't seen Melissa since the accident. There was a moment's hesitation at the front door, after which they embraced. Maybe they were both at the same point in the grieving process, both in limbo, between tears, for neither of them cried. Instead, they looked at each other with regret and disbelief.

'I can't take it in,' Melissa said. She was fiddling with her sunglasses, shifting her feet.

'Me neither,' he said, putting his hands in his pockets. The smell of onions frying wafted from the kitchen. It prompted him to remember hospitality and basic social niceties. 'Do you want to come in?'

'No, if you don't mind ... I just wanted to see you.' She pushed her sunglasses on to her forehead, into her hair, and then proceeded to play with her car keys, winding them round her fingers. 'I'll come and see the twins sometime this week. I don't want them to think I'm not thinking of them, because I am. It's just ... '

'It's OK, Mel. They're not really up to visitors at the moment anyway.'

'I can imagine ... How are they doing?'

'Not great,' he said. 'I'm starting to realise how much Jen did, what she was to them. How do I fill the gap?'

'You don't. I mean, you will eventually, but not yet. And you mustn't try to. If there are gaps, then you must say. That's what I'm here for.'

'Thanks ... You were always good to Jenny, and to me – to all of us.' He swallowed awkwardly, looked upwards, watching a passing cloud.

'I don't know about that any more,' she said, kicking at the gravel with her shoes.

'About what?'

'Friends.' She looked at him uncertainly. 'I thought I knew who they were and what that meant, but now I'm not so sure.'

'Oh?' He felt his face flush. 'You mean Jen?'

'No,' she said hurriedly. 'Not at all. I meant ... ' She trailed off, scuffing the stones again. 'Ignore me. I'm not making any sense.' She smiled briefly. 'I haven't slept. I'm sure you haven't either. We're all just fumbling about, bouncing off the walls. It's like being in one of those bouncy castles.'

He smiled too; doing so felt odd, strained.

'You could always try a grief counsellor for the twins?' she suggested.

'They have those?'

'They do. You never know – it might help. Just a thought.'

'I'll bear it in mind.'

'Well, I'll leave you to it,' she said, reaching up to brush a kiss on to his cheek. 'I'll call you tomorrow. But if you need me before then, just say.'

'Will do,' he said.

He watched her get into her car. Something wasn't right about her.

Still, he couldn't worry about her. He had enough to deal with just trying to stop the house from losing too much air. Funny that she should have mentioned a bouncy castle. He couldn't have said it better himself. Going back down the hallway to the kitchen, he was surprised that the floor wasn't giving a little under his weight.

15

'Where are you?' Rachel said quietly into her phone. She was standing in the back garden, underneath the silver birch tree. Her feet felt cool in flip-flops on the grass. An aeroplane was crossing the sky in a magnificent puff of white, wings gleaming.

'At the marina,' Melissa replied.

She could see Al moving around inside the kitchen, making himself an after-lunch coffee. 'I thought it was closed.'

'It is.'

'Oh ... Actually, that's perfect. I can be there in ten minutes.'

'Why?'

'So we can talk in private.'

'Lee's here.'

Rachel considered that. 'That's OK.'

'But I thought it was top secret.'

Rachel put her hand to her temples, breathed, trying not to get riled. This wasn't primary school, truth or dare. 'It's not top secret, Melissa. It's ... delicate. Lee will hear sooner or later. May as well be now.'

She watched Al, who was leaving the kitchen, moving beyond view. She would tell him she was going to the supermarket. 'I'll be with you shortly,' Rachel said.

Melissa had already hung up. Rachel glanced down at herself. She was wearing a pair of creased linen shorts and a tatty T-shirt, but it would have to do.

Inside the house, she grabbed her keys and called out, 'Back in five. Just getting some groceries.'

No one replied. She closed the door behind her and hurried to the car.

⚓

It was colder down at the marina. She wished she had brought her cardigan. She glanced at Melissa's Audi, which was parked skew-whiff outside the Portakabin office. From within, she could hear the radio playing. They wouldn't know that she was here yet. She could afford to give herself a minute to gather her thoughts.

Walking towards the waterside, she rested her hands on one of the wooden stumps that formed a fence of sorts between the car park and the water. She had always loved this view. Tranquil, remote, the marina was set in the sheltered waters of the estuary. The open waters of the sea were three miles away, near Hope Cove.

She slipped her keys into her pocket, gazing at four yachts that were moored to her left, their masts reflected underneath, making them seem uncannily long. There was a familiar scent in the air: glue, diesel, paint. It was the smell that started and ended her every working day, but today it seemed stagnant, overpowering in the still, warm afternoon.

To her right was the elegant venue that Melissa had wanted built and now oversaw the running of. She was good at it, too, a natural networker and promoter. The marina held wedding receptions, birthday parties – anything that the community required. Rachel ran the office, ensuring that Lee had enough

117

supplies for repair work, as well as preparing the invoices, filing – anything that needed doing.

It all worked well. Melissa and Lee were the fairest employers she'd ever had. It was never awkward, being close friends with them too. They all got along and it wasn't the sort of working environment that was stressful.

It was just that sometimes she found herself caught out by them, her chest compressing a little.

It was mostly when they didn't know she was watching them – when Lee gave Melissa a kiss on the tip of her nose for bringing him a biscuit, or when Melissa ruffled his hair, or when they glanced at each other when a certain song came on the radio.

It wasn't like that all the time. In fact, these intimacies were rare. Yet they troubled her all the same, and she didn't even know why.

She sighed, turned away from the water and started up the creaky steps to the Portakabin. Opening the door, she saw that Melissa and Lee were sitting side by side eating a salad from the same bowl with two forks. It was one of those moments that would have unsettled her, except that they were looking rather solemn.

'Rach,' Lee said. 'Come in. Excuse us. Just grabbing a bite to eat.'

Melissa stretched out her arm slowly to turn the radio off.

Rachel sat down in her usual place, behind her desk. 'I'm sorry about earlier,' she said.

Melissa unscrewed the top of a small bottle of water and took a sip.

'I was wrong to be secretive, but I didn't know what else to do.'

'Why don't you just tell us what you've come to say?' Melissa said impassively.

'OK . . .' Rachel said, gazing down at her wrinkled shorts, her mottled legs.

And it was then that she realised that the reason she felt unsettled by her friends' intimacy was because she was always the onlooker. Even in her own home, she took her lead from Al and the boys, pivoting around their needs and demands.

When had she become a witness to her own life?

Even this – what she was about to tell them – was a moment of observation, seeing something that she shouldn't have.

She picked at the hem of her shorts. 'I saw ... Jenny ... and ... Al ...'

Melissa looked at her blankly. 'Saw them what?'

'Oh, this is difficult.' She looked about her for something to help her feel less exposed and vulnerable, but there was nothing. Melissa and Lee were looking at her, waiting. She took a deep breath. 'Kissing,' she said. 'They were kissing.'

'What do you mean?' Melissa said. 'When?'

'At the barbecue the other week.'

'For Jenny's birthday?' Melissa asked.

Rachel nodded.

Melissa gazed at Lee and then back at Rachel. 'Tell me what happened.'

'Nothing, really. It was over in a second. Jenny was at the bottom of the garden, showing Al where the new summerhouse was going. I wasn't going with them originally, but then I changed my mind and I followed them.'

'And?' Melissa said.

'They stumbled into each other in the dark, laughed, kissed, then broke away.'

'Blimey,' Lee said, whistling softly.

'I don't get it,' Melissa said. 'Were they, what, having an affair or something?'

'No. Nothing like that. It was a bit of a joke. Everyone was drunk.'

Melissa stared at her. 'A joke?'

Lee cleared his throat. 'Rach, they dated back when we were kids. Do you think they got a bit carried away and forgot what they were doing because they'd had too much to drink?'

'Yes. That's exactly what I thought. I still do. And if I were to ask Al, I'm sure he—'

'Wait a minute,' Melissa said, standing up. '*If* you were to ask him? Are you saying that you haven't talked to him about this?'

Rachel felt herself blush. 'No. Because I knew how he'd react. Or over-react. He would have begged my forgiveness and then would have insisted on avoiding Jenny.'

'So, your plan was . . . ?' Melissa said.

'To speak to her first. That's why I wanted to go kayaking, so we could talk it through before taking the boats out. I didn't want her to get awkward with me and avoid me. I didn't want to lose her.'

'Yet you did,' Melissa said.

The room fell silent.

'I'm sorry,' Rachel said. 'If you're holding me accountable for what happened, then I accept the part I played in it. I shouldn't have—'

'Rachel,' Lee said, holding up his hand. 'No one's saying that. No one's blaming you. Are they, Mel?'

Melissa had her back to them, was facing the window, overlooking the estuary. She didn't answer the question.

Rachel pushed back her chair. 'The boys will be wondering where I am,' she said. She pulled her keys from her pocket, trying to sound and act stable, whereas in fact she was doing well to remain upright. 'I'd better be off.' She headed towards the door.

'Stop,' Melissa said. 'Wait.'

Rachel turned to face them. This was it: the apology, the tears, the hug.

'When are you going to tell Al?' Melissa asked.

'I . . .'

Melissa approached, halting before her, hands on hips. 'Please tell me that you *are* going to tell him?'

'Mel,' Lee said, coming up behind his wife, touching her lightly on the arm. 'Perhaps we should—'

Melissa brushed him off. 'And what about Gareth?' she said.

'He doesn't need to know,' Rachel said. 'What's the point? It'll only hurt him.'

'I agree,' Lee said.

Melissa wrinkled her nose in dissent. 'Of course he should know! He deserves the truth. I mean, if you'd done the right thing in the first place, Rachel, and had told everyone about this and had it all out in the open, then . . .' She hesitated.

'Then what?' Rachel said. 'Jenny would still be alive?'

Melissa looked away.

'She's not saying that, are you, love?' Lee said gently. 'Come on. Let's stop this before someone says something they regret. It's no one's fault what happened.'

Rachel gazed at Melissa. 'It's all right for you,' she said. 'You always know what to do and what to say. But the rest of us don't find it so easy.'

'That's rubbish,' Melissa said. 'You're the smart one – always were.'

'Maybe,' she replied. 'If that means that I think before I speak and I weigh things up, then, yes. But I'm not always quick to act. Nowhere near as quick as you. Perhaps you would have got it all out in the open, as you say. But I didn't. And I guess I'm just going to have to live with that.'

She pulled open the office door and hurried down the steps on wobbly legs, her ears ringing with upset.

'Rach,' Lee called after her. 'Come on. Let's not argue. Let's—'

'Leave her,' Melissa said. 'If she wants to go, let her go.'

Getting into her car, Rachel fumbled the keys in the ignition, her feet feeling jelly-like on the pedals.

As she drove out of the marina, she kept hearing her friend's words – so cold and dismissive. *Let her go.*

⚓

At home, she went straight into the kitchen, intending to take a cup of tea upstairs to the bedroom and seek solace, but Al came in and stood there, looking about him. 'Where's the stuff?' he said.

'What stuff?'

'The shopping. I came to help you put it away.'

'There is no shopping,' she snapped.

'What?' he said. 'Then why . . . ?'

'I was out sorting out your mess,' she said. 'Because that's what I always do. I sort your mess. I go around the house picking up after you and straightening shelves.'

'Hey?' He swayed unsteadily, still pallid, poorly-looking. 'Is this about the accident? Because I've—'

'No!' she shouted. 'It's not about the accident!' She lowered her voice, lest the boys should hear. 'It's about you and Jenny. It's about you kissing her! I saw it, Al.' She stamped her foot. 'I saw you!'

The colour – the little that had been in Al's face – drained and he clutched the counter for support. 'Why didn't you say something before now?' he said.

She stared at him in anger and frustration. 'You think this is about what *I* have or haven't done?'

When he didn't reply, she turned her back to him and made a cup of tea, which she took upstairs.

Al just watched her leave.

16

'I don't understand why she didn't tell me,' Melissa said. She and Lee were sitting at the dining table, drinking tea. Across from them in the kitchen, Frank was making a sandwich, wearing headphones, singing to himself. The girls were watching TV in the lounge. Melissa could hear the canned laughter of a sit-com.

'Who? Rachel?' Lee said, slurping his tea.

'No. Jenny. I thought we told each other everything. Why wouldn't she have told me about this?'

He shrugged. 'Because she'd had too much to drink and was embarrassed? She probably wanted to forget all about it. Sounds like it was a stupid mistake.'

'Hmm,' she said.

'What? You don't think so?'

'I don't know,' she said. 'I'm confused about it. And upset. She should have told me. As it is, I'm always going to wonder if there was a part of her that I didn't know about.'

'Ah,' Lee said, reaching for her hand. 'That's why you were hard on Rachel.'

'I wasn't hard on her.'

'You were a bit,' he said. 'But she'll get over it. You can give her a ring in the morning and explain.'

'No, I won't. I didn't do anything wrong.'

'OK, then don't.' He patted her hand, pushed back his chair. 'Where are you going?'

He rinsed his mug at the sink, spoke over his shoulder. 'To get Polly to bed. She'll be exhausted.'

Melissa looked at her watch: half past eight already. The evening had vanished. 'I'll be up in a minute,' she called to Lee as he left the room.

She finished her tea dejectedly. Talking to Rachel hadn't cleared things up like she had hoped, but had just made it worse. And now the niggling feeling that something was wrong was undeniably strong.

Going through to the kitchen, she motioned for Frank to remove his headphones. 'Are you all right?' she asked.

'Yep.'

'Have you spoken to Olivia today?'

He was concentrating on cutting the sandwich evenly, the headphones making a *tsk tsk tsk* noise around his neck. 'She's not answering her phone.'

'Well, I saw Gareth earlier and he said she's struggling.'

Frank stopped what he was doing. 'You think?' he said sarcastically, with a touch of anger.

She gazed up at him, taken aback. 'Have I done something wrong?'

At seventeen, Frank could be abrupt, terse, but generally he was nice to her – was becoming more so as he grew beyond adolescence. But it was apparent that he was wrestling with something, his jaw bone grinding, his cheeks reddening. Was he angry with her?

'What's the matter?' she asked.

'Nothing,' he said. 'Maybe if you were to butt out and mind your own business for a change then . . . '

She stared at him. 'What? How have I . . . ?'

'Forget it,' he said, pushing the bread board away. He put his headphones back on and left the room.

'What about your sandwich?' she called after him.

⚓

Melissa was sitting at her dressing table, brushing her hair, when there was a knock on the door and Frank entered. It was late; the girls were asleep and Lee was downstairs watching TV until the early hours, as was his nightly routine.

She watched Frank in the mirror. Evidently, he had changed his mind about the sandwich. He was chewing, a morsel of bread stuck to his chin. That one little crumb reminded her that he was young, vulnerable. Her mood softened. They met in the middle of the room, their slippered toes touching.

'I'm sorry, Mum,' he said. 'I don't know why I said that.'

'It's OK,' she said, reaching up to his face to remove the crumb. 'We're all saying things we don't mean. No one's thinking straight.'

'I don't think you need to butt out ... much.' He smiled.

'Thanks,' she said. 'So, is everything all right at school?'

'Yeah. It's fine.'

'Good. And earlier ... it was about Olivia? And Auntie Jenny?' He nodded.

'There's nothing else wrong?' she said, reaching for his hand. 'No.'

'You'd tell me if there was?'

'Yes.' And he blushed deeply, eyes flitting away from hers.

What did that mean, if anything?

Perhaps he was just frustrated at not being able to reach his girlfriend or make things better for her.

'She'll come back to you. She just needs time. But she'll come around. I know she will.'

'Yep,' Frank said. 'Night, then.'

'Goodnight,' she said.

He started to leave the room. 'Frank?' she called after him. He turned slowly, the shadows under his eyes looking darker in the dim lighting. 'I love you. I'm always here for you. Don't forget that.'

'OK, Mum,' he said. 'Love you too.'

⚓

Normally, by the time Lee came to bed, she was asleep. But tonight, when he crept into the bedroom, she told him not to worry about making a noise because she was still awake.

'Everything OK?' he said, climbing into bed and nestling into her back, kissing her neck so gently that she shivered.

She turned over to look at him, at the outline of his features in the dark. 'I don't know what I'd do without you,' she said.

'Well, that's nice to hear,' he said, leaning forward to kiss her on the lips. Then he withdrew, leaning his head on his elbow. 'What's brought this on?'

'All that talk about Jenny and Al. I mean, is it OK to be doing that? I'd be devastated if it was you – if you'd kissed Jenny.'

'What you don't know won't harm you,' he said.

She thumped him lightly on the arm. 'Seriously, though, I'd be so upset.'

'Well, luckily for you that would never happen because I've got all I need right here,' he said, moving forward to kiss her again. She kissed him back, but then found herself tensing up.

She pulled away, sat up in bed, drawing her knees to her chest. 'Do you think it means anything?' she said.

'What, Jenny and Al?'

'Yes,' she said. 'I can't help thinking that it could be

126

important. I mean, one minute she's alive and well. And the next she's . . .'

'What are you getting at?'

'I think Gareth should know.'

He shook his head. 'I disagree. I'm with Rachel on this one. I can't see what the point of that is. It'll just upset him, poor bloke.'

'But he deserves the truth.'

'What truth? It could have been a full-blown affair for all we know, or absolutely nothing. Which is why we should let it go.'

'And what about the police?'

'What about them?'

'Shouldn't they know? They've been asking questions. What if they think it wasn't an accident? Why else would detectives be involved?'

'Oh no you don't,' Lee said, rolling over to turn on the bed-side lamp. He knelt on the bed in his boxer shorts, folding his arms. 'We're not telling them, Mel. I mean it. We could make things ten times worse.'

'But something feels off. Right from the start, it's felt that way.'

'That's because you're grieving and you're looking for some-one to blame. The police are just doing their job. It's part of procedure to ask questions.'

'So, they need all the facts. I lied to them about the migraine and I need to explain why.'

'Why do you need to?'

'Because they asked me if I knew why anyone would want to hurt Jenny, and I said no. But that's not true now. Because someone did have a motive.'

'You what? Because of a drunken kiss?'

She knelt up, clutched his forearm, appealing to him. 'What if it wasn't? You said yourself that they could have been having an affair.'

127

He looked at her in surprise. 'I was joking, Mel.'

'But what if they were? They used to date.'

'Yep, years ago. And for about five minutes, from what I remember.'

'Four months, actually.'

'So?' Lee said. 'I think we'd have noticed if they were in love. We spent enough time together.'

She sat back again, leaning against the headrest. 'So, you really think this is nothing?'

He joined her, resting his hand on her knee. 'I think you're upset about Jenny. I get it, I really do. But don't go to the police. Think of the twins and Rachel's boys. Imagine how they'll feel. And Gareth ... Let's just drop it, hey, before we all go nuts.'

And he turned the light out again and they settled down to rest.

Within a short while, he was snoring softly. Melissa lay listening to the rhythmical sound, thinking about Jenny.

She could remember the night of the barbecue on Jenny's birthday very clearly. They had left the kids indoors playing Twister and had gathered outside on the patio to sample Jenny's homemade sloe gin, before opening the Pinot Noir. The gin had been thick, syrupy, reminiscent of cough medicine. It had been a cold night. Gareth had lit the fire pit and they had all huddled around it in the back garden, watching the flames, the solar lights blinking in the bushes. She couldn't remember Jenny or Al acting strangely, or even Rachel. It had all felt reassuringly normal, Silkie-like.

Finally, with Lee muttering in his sleep beside her, just past two o'clock, Melissa fell asleep – her head full of sloes, kisses, flames, and within the heart of the fire, a yellow dress that twirled up and up into the night sky.

⚓

She sat up in bed, dragging the covers with her. Lee was groaning, trying to grab the sheets back.

She put her hand to her face. Her cheeks and forehead were coated in perspiration. She knelt up, pulling her damp clothes away from her skin.

What had woken her?

She listened, but the house was still. She felt for her alarm clock, pressing a button to illuminate the face. It was four thirty in the morning.

Lee reached for the bedside lamp. 'What's going on?' he said groggily.

'I don't know,' she said. 'Something woke me.'

'You were calling out,' he said. 'I think you were having a nightmare.'

'Oh.' She shivered.

He felt her back. 'You're soaked.'

She got out of bed, went to the chest of drawers for spare pyjamas. As she got changed, Lee sat upright, watching her. 'What?' she asked.

'Nothing.'

She climbed back into bed. 'You can turn off the lamp,' she said, settling down again.

He didn't move – remained sitting up, looking at her. 'Mel,' he said, 'you were calling someone's name in your sleep.'

'Hey?' she said. 'Who?'

He hesitated. 'Hannah.'

She rolled over, away from him. 'Please turn out the light.'

'If you need to talk . . . '

'I don't,' she said.

'OK. But if you—'

'I won't,' she said. 'Let's just try to get some sleep.'

He sighed, clicked off the lamp, puffed up his pillow and then was still. Outside, the dawn chorus had just begun. She resigned herself to staying awake and lay there, eyes wide open.

17

Wednesday 25 April 2018

Gareth's head was in such a haze, he didn't register that the phone was ringing. He was aware of an irritating noise coming from somewhere in the house, but just wanted it to stop. Next to him, on the table that his elbow was resting on, was a half-empty bottle of whisky with its screw cap set at a jaunty angle.

Last night was a blur. He could remember pouring himself a snifter before bed and that was it. Obviously, he had fallen asleep in his chair and now he had a cricked neck to prove it.

He shifted position in his chair, leather upholstery creaking, and gazed around the study. They called it a study, but it wasn't one really. There were no encyclopedias or files, just a signed Iron Maiden poster on the wall and dog-eared copies of *Focus* magazine piled on the shelves. Jenny used to refer to it as his man cave. It had seemed like the appropriate place for him to crawl into last night and mope.

There was a tap on the door and his father appeared, frowning at him. 'Have you been drinking?'

'Not yet. But I was just thinking about starting.'

His father shook his head. 'Come on, son. I know this is a very difficult time, but that's not the way forward.'

'It was just a one-off, Dad, to blow off a bit of steam. If I don't do that now and then, I'll explode. You know?'

He expected his father, conservative, old school, to disapprove and confiscate the bottle, but to Gareth's surprise, he nodded. 'I do know, yes. But don't make it a habit if you can help it.'

'OK, Dad.'

His father screwed the top tightly on the whisky and pushed it away so that he could sit on the edge of the desk. 'I have something to tell you.'

Gareth's stomach turned over. 'I don't like the sound of that.'

'That was the coroner's liaison officer on the phone. The preliminary results are available. I'm glad they haven't hung around. They'd like you to phone them when you're ready.'

'The coroner's liaison officer?' Gareth said. 'So that's the ...?'

'Autopsy results.'

Gareth gazed at the whisky bottle, feeling thirsty.

'I can call them, if you want me to?' his father said.

'No, it's all right. I need to do this.'

'Good chap,' his father said, standing up. 'Maybe freshen up before you tackle it. A quick shower might do the trick.'

Gareth glanced down at his dishevelled state and ran his hands through his hair. 'Yes. Will do. Thanks, Dad.'

They left the room together, his father heading to the kitchen to join his mother, who was preparing a fry-up by the smell of things.

'It'll be ready soon,' his mother called out. 'Don't go far.'

Go far. As if he could. As if his legs would take him anywhere but up and down the house, in and out of the rooms like Max's old electric train set. Sometimes, when the twins were little, they used to find a train derailed, stuck against a chair leg on the floor, its back rising, engine humming. He felt like that train – automated, running low on energy, stuck against the barrier that was his wife's death.

Wearily, he pulled open the airing cupboard to find a towel. Across the landing, Olivia's music was booming beyond her bedroom door. On the one hand, he felt gratified that she was perking up, loud music being preferable to vegetative silence. But on the other hand, her grandparents were here and weren't into hip hop before breakfast.

He would have to have a word. Knocking on the door, he called to Olivia to turn the music down.

No response. He knocked again, louder.

Still nothing. He tried the handle tentatively. It wasn't locked; she didn't lock it overnight, at Jenny's ruling.

The light was dim in the room, the curtains only open a fraction. 'Liv, can you turn that down a bit?'

She was sitting on her bed, doing something. He peered forward to see what she was up to. And then she noticed him standing there and shrieked, tossing something across the room before diving underneath the bed covers.

He snapped the light on, squinting about him. It was impossible to think with the music going. Going to the speaker, he hit the off button. Silence reigned, buzzing in his ears. Olivia's phone was on her bed, glowing. He stared at it, at his daughter's shape underneath the duvet. 'What are you doing?'

Then he remembered the object she had thrown and he looked about for it, catching sight of it underneath her desk.

He bent down, picked it up. It was a maths compass.

'Olivia,' he said, setting the compass down on her desk. 'What's going on?'

She didn't respond.

There was a knock on the door behind him. 'Everything all right?' his mother said, poking her head into the room.

'It's fine,' he said.

'Only, I thought I heard shouting . . .'

133

'It's nothing, Mum,' he said. 'Just me yelling at Olivia to turn the music down.'

'Well, don't be long. The bacon's ready.' And she withdrew.

He closed the door, approached Olivia's bed. 'Livvie,' he said, shaking the mound of bedding. 'Talk to me.'

Nothing.

He picked up her phone, which was still glowing, and read the most recent text:

Also #cutting

And the one before:

#selfharm is blocked. Try #selfharmmm

'What the ...? Olivia, if you don't talk to me right this second then I'm taking this to the authorities.'

What authorities? School? The police? He didn't know. But it worked. She was stirring, poking her head out from the duvet.

She looked petrified, her eyes wide and staring. 'Don't be angry, Dad. Please don't tell—'

'What were you doing when I came in? What were you doing with that compass?'

She looked away.

'I mean it, Olivia. If you don't tell me, I'll ...' He trailed off, unable to continue, struck dumb. Slowly, she pulled her arm out from under the bedding and held it out on display for him. A long streak of blood was congealing on her forearm, like a strawberry lace sweet.

'Oh, Liv,' he said. He stared at his daughter's sad, frightened face. 'Why?'

She covered herself back up again, slipping her arm out of sight, pulling the duvet up and around her.

He sat down heavily on the bed. This was too much. His head was reeling.

'Is this about Mum?' he said quietly.

'Dunno,' she said.

'But it's recent, though? I mean, did Mum know?'

'No.'

Well, that was a relief, wasn't it? He wasn't sure whether it was or not.

He thought of the new whiteboard downstairs that they had installed as part of their resolution to get organised, and the large diary that the twins had chosen. He had felt temporarily lifted, relieved by the thought that half the battle of parenting was getting organised.

This was the other half: the ugly, chaotic bit that stationery couldn't touch.

'Who was that text from?'

'Annabelle,' she replied.

'Annabelle Rogers, that nice girl you were in the Brownies with?'

'Yes.'

'So, what's she doing sending you stuff like that? Do her parents know?' He picked up the phone, but it had blacked out and he didn't know the PIN. Olivia snatched it from him, hid it away under the sheets.

'It's nothing.'

'Hashtag self-harm? Doesn't sound like nothing to me.'

'Just leave it, Dad.'

'Leave it? How can I, when you're hurting yourself? How am I supposed to sleep at night, knowing what you might be doing?' He gazed at her soft skin, her unmade-up face – so much nicer than when she had all that make-up on. It wasn't so long ago that she had been a baby in his arms, with her podgy limbs and downy hair. How had they gone from that to this so soon?

He thought then of what Melissa had said about a grief counsellor. At the time, he hadn't thought that it would come to
that. Now, however, things were looking very different.

'Can I see your arm again?' he said.

She shook her head.

'But it needs looking at.'

'It's not a big deal,' she said. 'Loads of people do it.'

He stared at her. 'Like who? Annabelle bleedin' Rogers?'

She shrugged. 'And others.'

'What others? Your friends?'

Again, the shrug.

'Well, I've never heard of anything so stupid in all my life.
Do you have any idea how dangerous that is? You could cut an
artery for starters. Or you could use something that's infected
and give yourself blood poisoning. Bloody hell, Olivia,' he said.
'I thought you wanted to go to uni.'

'I do,' she said.

'Well, that's not the way to go about it, is it? What would
your mum say? She'd be devastated.'

She looked down at the floor, beginning to cry. 'You're not
going to tell anyone, are you?' she said. 'Please, Dad. Don't tell
Grandma or Grandpa.'

The last thing he wanted to do was upset her.

'Come on, Liv,' he said. 'Don't cry.' He pulled her into
his arms. She fell forward, a bundle of bedding, and he held
her while she cried. 'It's all right. Shush. We'll sort this out.
We'll come up with something. I've already got an idea that
might work.'

She broke away, her breath juddery, her nose red. 'What is
it?' she said.

'A deal.'

'What deal?' she said, wiping her face, her eyes shrinking
with suspicion.

'I won't tell anyone about this – I won't go pounding on Annabelle Roger's door, nor will I march down to the school – if you'll do two things for me.'

'Go on,' she said, hiccupping.

'One: you have to see to that arm of yours right away. Put some Germolene on it and a plaster ... and promise me you'll never do anything like that again.'

She nodded. 'Promise ...' She waited, staring at him, eyebrows raised. 'So, like, do you wanna leave so that I can get dressed?'

'But I haven't told you the second thing yet.'

'Yes, you have,' she said. 'Germolene. Don't do it again.'

'That was all part of the first one.'

'Oh.' She hiccupped again.

'The second one is that you'll see a grief counsellor.'

She stared at him as though he had just changed into a Minotaur. *'A what?'*

'Sorry, Liv. Those are the conditions. If you're not happy with it, I'll go and discuss it with Grand—'

'Fine!' she said.

'So, we have a deal?'

'Whatever.'

'Good.' He stood up, straightened his shirt, recalling that he was looking rather a state and that he still had to phone the autopsy people, and eat his mother's fry-up.

Leaving the room, he looked back at his daughter. She looked terrible, but better than when he had first walked in.

There had to be some consolation in that – had to be.

⚓

He was getting ready to go for a family walk along the lane and was sitting on the front-porch step scraping mud from his wellington boots, when Melissa's Audi appeared in the driveway.

He remained sitting down, enjoying the sunshine on his face. It was early afternoon. Sleeping all night in a chair with more than the recommended amount of whisky in his stomach was beginning to take its toll. Yawning, he watched Melissa getting out of her car and walking towards him.

She didn't say anything, merely joined him on the step. Picking up the other boot, she matched what he was doing – using a stick to flick mud from the sole to the nearby bushes.

'How you doing?' she said at length.

'I've been better,' he said. 'We got the autopsy results today.'

They both stopped what they were doing. 'Oh?'

'There was no doubt about the cause of death. It was drowning.'

'I'm really sorry,' she said.

'Me too.'

They resumed cleaning the boots. 'Got any others that need doing?' she asked.

'Be my guest,' he said, pointing to the boot rack on the porch. 'Olivia's look pretty mucky.'

Melissa picked up the glittery boots then joined him again, handing one of them to him.

'They're opening an inquest,' he said.

She looked sideways at him. 'Really?'

'I was surprised too, but it's nothing sinister. It's because the cause of death wasn't disease or old age. It's supposed to give us accurate facts so we can come to terms with things.'

'Oh. So when will it be?'

'Well, there's a hearing in three months and then the final hearing about three months after that. Should be over with before the year's out, all being well, so they said.'

'And what about the funeral?'

138

He sighed. 'No idea. Dad's been brilliant. He's been on the phone to them, asking them to release ... the body ... but there's nothing we can do until the coroner gives the go-ahead.'

'And are the police still involved?'

'As far as I know. They came to see us yesterday, asking questions again.'

'What sort of questions?'

He glanced at her. 'Just going back through the details – something about Al's tide table being wrong and whether I'd noticed anything strange about that or about him at the time. I mean, if I'm honest, I just want it over with. I really can't see what Al's tide table has to do with anything.'

Melissa didn't reply, fell quiet, setting the boot to one side, resting her elbow on her knee and supporting her chin on her fist.

'You OK?' he said.

He noticed then how pale she looked, a watered-down version of herself. She seemed frail, haunted almost. He would have asked her about it, but was frightened what her reply would be. And so he left it, letting all the doubts and worries hang in the air between them.

'What you just said about accurate facts ...' she said. 'Things will come out in an inquest, won't they?'

'I suppose. What sorts of things?'

'Gareth,' she said, looking at him sombrely, 'you and I have known each other a long time ... If there was something about Jenny ... would you want to know?'

'What sort of thing?' he asked.

She hesitated. 'Something bad.'

'Oh, crikey. I'm not so sure, Mel.' He rubbed his face, tapped his feet. 'Oh, bloody hell. Come on, then. Out with it.'

'Look, I promised Lee and Rachel I wouldn't tell you,' she said. 'But it's better that you hear it from me.'

He gazed at the mud on Max's wellingtons. They hadn't done Max's boots yet, he was thinking. They had to do them next.

'Jenny kissed Al at her birthday barbecue. Rachel saw them. Apparently, it was a drunken mistake . . .' She prodded him in the ribs. 'Gareth . . . ?'

He stared at the paving stone underneath his feet.

Jenny and Al?

Kissing?

His ears began to overheat as though they were pressed against a radiator. His head was throbbing. He opened his mouth to say something, but what? What could he say? Closing his eyes, he saw the strawberry-lace trail of blood on Olivia's arm.

Jenny and Al?

There was a creaking noise behind them then as the front door open wider. It had been slightly ajar the whole time, he realised, with a crushing sensation in his chest.

His father had been in the hallway all along, sitting in the chair, lacing up his walking boots.

'What did you hope to achieve with this?' his father said, standing there wearing his khaki hat and gilet, his deep voice startling them both.

Melissa jumped up to attention. 'Mr Davies, I had no idea you—'

'Jenny was a wonderful, loving woman – like a daughter to me and my wife. I don't believe this cock and bull story. She would never have cheated.'

Gareth looked at Melissa. She was floored. Had he seen her look like that before? Normally so poised, she was opening and closing her mouth, her arms almost flapping.

'I know she was wonderful. She was my best friend. I didn't say that she cheated. It didn't mean anything. It—'

'Then why come here with this? Isn't Gareth suffering enough? Why bring vicious gossip here at a time like this?'

'Vicious?' She looked aghast and began to cry noiselessly. 'I didn't mean to hurt him. I was trying to help. I didn't know what else to do.'

Her distress, seeing her so reduced, stirred Gareth to action. He stood up, putting his arm around her. 'Don't cry, Mel,' he said. 'It took guts to do what you just did. No one else would have done it, but you.' He gave his father a warning look, trying to signal to him to go easy on her. 'This isn't easy for any of us.'

His father looked regretful and indignant at once. 'I'm sorry if I spoke out of turn.'

Melissa broke away from Gareth, straightening her denim jacket. 'It's me who's sorry. I shouldn't have come. I'm sorry, Gareth. I'll see you soon.' And she started off down the driveway.

'Mel!' Gareth called after her.

She didn't respond, but simply got into her car without a backwards glance.

He felt ghastly.

Jenny and Al.

Strawberry-lace blood.

Their house would surely fall down now.

The wheels were spinning on the gravel, such was Melissa's hurry to get away from them.

'We haven't heard the last of this,' Gareth said to his father, as they gazed at the dust that Melissa's car had left behind, like a teeny tornado. 'I can just feel it.' And he picked up Max's wellington boots and began to clean them for the walk, his hands shaking.

GILLY GREEN

Office Administrator, Milford Senior School, Dorset

Gilly was updating the attendance record when she looked up to see Nessa Merry.

'Consent form for drama,' Nessa said, dropping a form into Gilly's in-tray.

Drama, indeed! That was apt.

'Thank you,' Gilly said coolly. Nessa could have sent the form in with her daughter. There was no need to call in to the school office in person.

Nessa was lingering hopefully. 'I've not seen much of the Silkies,' she said. 'Are they in school?'

Gilly remained gazing at her screen. Nessa liked to gossip – didn't everyone in Milford? – but didn't know when to stop. It was obvious that Gilly couldn't discuss pupils' attendance, not if she wanted to keep her job.

The biggest irony was that Nessa worked at King's, the local solicitor's, so was often the first to know who had filed for divorce – the school mums being the next to know. It was outrageous, really, what she got away with.

Luckily for Gilly, the phone was ringing. She mouthed an apology to Nessa, who reluctantly retreated.

It was Rachel Beckinsale on the line. Thank goodness that Nessa had gone.

'I'm afraid we can't come to the awards night tonight,' Rachel was saying.

'Oh,' said Gilly. 'That's a shame. Is everything all right?'

She winced as she said it. Of course everything wasn't all right. It was all over town that Rachel and Melissa had argued, right outside Rachel's house. Until now, the Silkies hadn't ever fallen out, to her knowledge. They were like the sticky little burs that grew in the hedgerows, stuck together by good will and camaraderie.

Gilly realised then that Rachel had already hung up the phone. How rude!

That was typical of the Silkies. They thought they could do whatever they liked . . . including killing people.

That was the latest rumour: that Jenny Davies' death was now a murder investigation.

Gilly resumed typing, shuddering.

The police were everywhere, asking questions – and not just local officers but grim-faced men in suits who wouldn't be wasting their time on a simple kayaking accident.

The whole town was whispering, speculating about the Silkies. Maybe they'd had this coming to them. Some people, Gilly included, had often suspected that their picture-perfect friendships were just an elaborate show, designed to make the rest of them feel left out.

18

Crying too much to drive properly, Melissa drove for a hundred yards before turning into a narrow lane that led to an isolated farm. She stopped the car and turned off the ignition, pulling a packet of tissues from the glove compartment.

She hadn't intended to tell Gareth. It had just seemed like the right thing to do, given that there was going to be an inquest. Far better that he had heard the truth from her, rather than from a stranger in a courtroom.

She squeezed the tissue in her hand, listening to the ticking noise as the car metals cooled. Feeling warm, she lowered the window and closed her eyes, the sun amber on her eyelids.

Poor Gareth. She would have done anything not to have added to his suffering. She would never forget the look on his fiercely protective father's face.

Opening her eyes, she took a deep breath and gazed at the view ahead of her. The lane that she was parked on was lined with a row of blackthorn trees on her left. The trees were thick with white blossom at this time of year; from a distance it would look as though the hedges were laden with snow. To her right, unusually, there was no hedge or barbed-wire fence. Instead, the field began at the roadside and kept running down-hill until it met the sea.

That afternoon, the sea was turquoise, glistening, but Melissa wasn't captivated by it. Just around the corner was Hope Cove. She couldn't bring herself to look in that direction.

Pulling a business card from her pocket, she picked up her phone and dialled.

Detective Sergeant Lloyd answered but was still talking to someone else. She waited until she had his full attention.

'It's Melissa Silk,' she said.

'Hello, Melissa,' he said. 'What can I do for you?'

'I want to tell you something. I don't know if it's relevant. But if I don't tell you, no one else will.'

'Go on . . .'

'Rachel asked me not to go on the kayaking trip.'

'So you didn't have a migraine?'

She flinched. 'No.'

He paused. 'Is that it?'

'No. Rachel organised the trip because she saw Jenny kissing Al and wanted to talk it through with her. Everyone thinks it was a drunken kiss, nothing more.'

'And you . . . ?'

'I don't know. I just wanted to let you know.'

'We'll look into it,' the sergeant said. 'Thank you.'

There was a click as the line cut off.

That was that, then. It was done.

She glanced at the clock on the dashboard. It was time to pick Polly up from school.

She left the window down as she drove, enjoying the breeze, wondering what else there was about her friend that she hadn't known. To her, Jenny had always seemed transparently simplistic. Nothing had been tucked away, beyond view. She had cartwheeled through her days, loose change and lipstick spilling from her pockets as she went.

Mr Davies Senior had been right about his daughter-in-law,

whom he had doted on: Jenny had been wonderful and loving. He had taken Jenny under his wing as soon as she had married Gareth, replacing her awful biological parents. That was all that Melissa could really remember of Jenny's family: the awfulness, the wealth, the intimidatingly tall gates at the front of their property. Their money had taken care of Jenny far more than they had, their continual absence being the reason why Jenny had spent most of her childhood over at Melissa's.

Yet Jenny had never been drawn into saying a word against them.

Melissa had always admired this virtue in her friend, yet was incapable of emulating it. When it came to her own mother, she had always held up an ideal of the perfect matriarch, which her emotionally retentive mother fell a long way short of.

Arriving at the primary school, she parked and walked to the gates. There was the usual gathering of parents, but Melissa wasn't up to offering anyone anything other than a tense smile.

As luck would have it, Polly was one of the first children out. She ran to Melissa, her ribbons dangling loosely from her pigtails. 'Hello, Polly Pops,' Melissa said, hugging her.

They held hands as they went to the car, Polly in high spirits, chattering animatedly.

'Did you have a good day?' Melissa said, as they pulled away.

'Yes,' Polly said. 'Did you know that carrots can be purple?'

Melissa smiled. 'Yes, I did know that.'

'And that sprouts can be red?'

'No. I did not.'

'Well, they can. And, Mummy?'

'Yes?'

'Sophia's mum thinks you're a live wire.' Melissa's smile vanished. 'What's a live wire, Mummy?'

'It's . . . it means . . .'

At the senior school, it was more congested than usual, a coach load of pupils having just returned from a trip.

Melissa handed Polly her phone. 'Can you ring them and say that we're up at the trading estate?'

She drove on, past the school.

'There's no reply,' Polly said, as Melissa pulled into the estate.

'Try again, please.' She stopped the car. 'Any luck?' The sky had gone very dark, a thick grey cloud having rolled in. It looked as though the heatwave was over.

'No,' Polly said.

'Right,' Melissa said, unbuckling her belt. 'I'll have to go on foot. Are you coming with me or staying here?'

'Staying here. It's raining.'

Yes, it was. And Melissa didn't have a coat.

Great.

'I'll be two minutes. Sit tight. I'm locking you in.'

As she set off along the road, it began to pour with spiteful spikes of rain – the hedgerows tossing and churning in the wind. Her progress was slow; cars kept appearing and she had to stand in the grass verge to let them pass, all the while getting drenched.

At the gates, feeling self-conscious about her bedraggled appearance, she hung back. Over the melee of parents and pupils and cars, she could just make out Frank and Nina running down the main path from school, holding their blazers over their heads.

She was trying to shelter underneath a row of marshmallow-coloured blossom trees, when a car pulled up beside her, doing a fast, jerky three-point turn. Turning to look, she saw that the driver of the car was Rachel.

Rachel had spotted her at the same time. They locked eyes and Melissa realised that she didn't know how she felt about her friend now. Yet she couldn't ignore her. They needed each other, now more than ever.

Stepping forward, she rapped on the window for Rachel to lower it, offering her a shaky smile. 'Hi,' she said.

'Hi,' Rachel said.

She looked past Rachel to Al. 'It's good to see you up and about,' she said. 'Are you feeling any better?'

In response, he nodded. He didn't look so great – gaunt, his blond hair peppered with sudden grey. Glancing behind her, she saw that Frank and Nina had arrived and were waiting for her underneath the blossom trees.

'I'm sorry,' she said, leaning forward into the car to speak discreetly, 'but I told Gareth. And I told the police. I thought it was the right thing to do.'

Rachel stared at her, mouth open. 'What?'

'We can't withhold information. There's going to be an inquest.'

'For heaven's sake, Melissa,' Rachel said, her spectacles steaming up. She plucked them off, rubbed them on her shirt. Putting her glasses back on, she glared at Melissa. 'What's wrong with you? How does this help anyone?'

'It helps Jenny,' Melissa said. 'And that's all I care about right now.'

'More than your friends who are still alive? Did you stop to think how this might affect us? And what about the children?'

Rachel lowered her voice and glanced around her, in case anyone was listening in. Al, for one, wasn't, or didn't seem to be. He looked catatonic, barely breathing.

'This,' Rachel said, pointing at Melissa, 'is *exactly* why Jenny didn't tell you.'

'What do you mean?'

'You're impulsive,' Rachel said. 'Hot-headed. Obsessed with interfering. Well, this time you've overstepped *way* too far. If this blows up in your face, you've only got yourself to blame. Don't say I didn't warn you!'

Melissa stared at Rachel in mortification. There was a crunch of gears as Rachel wrenched the car into reverse, backing away.

The rain had stopped, Melissa realised. The sun had come out and was lighting up the puddles. It seemed very quiet. She looked about her. Frank and Nina were watching her in embarrassment.

And next to them, observing it all with barely disguised nosiness, were Nessa Merry and Gilly Green.

She held her hand out to Nina, who stepped forward, followed by Frank, and with as much dignity as she could muster, led her children away.

'What the—' said Frank.

'Just walk,' Melissa said.

19

Rachel waited for the boys to be upstairs doing their homework before tackling Al. He was sitting at the kitchen counter, stirring sugar into his coffee mug for longer than was necessary.

She put her hand on his to still it. 'I need to know,' she said. 'Was it or wasn't it a silly kiss – a one-off that meant nothing?'

He continued stirring. She grabbed the spoon, tossed it across the room. He stared at her in indignation. 'What are you doing?'

'Establishing the truth,' she said, 'so that I don't look like a fool.'

'You know the truth. The fact that you're even asking makes me wonder how much faith you have in me and in our marriage.'

'How much faith *I* have?' she said.

'Keep your voice down,' he said. 'We don't want the boys hearing. It's hard enough for Joel as it is, trying to revise with all this going on.'

She looked at him in exasperation. He had no idea – had been stagnating since Saturday, oblivious to how difficult it was for her to move on through her grief and keep going. Joel and Ned had gone back to school today and there were rugby kits to wash and lunch boxes to pack and drop-offs to do. And now he was lecturing her about their well-being? He had barely looked at the boys all week.

'This is Melissa's doing,' Al said. 'If that woman didn't feel the constant urge to be the centre of attention, controlling everything, none of this would have happened.'

'But it has happened,' she said. 'So now we have to deal with it. You've got nothing to hide, and you can tell the police that when they come here.'

'Why will they do that?' Al said.

'Because you kissed your friend's wife and now she's dead! Don't you see how it looks?'

'I don't care how it looks. We'll just tell the truth.'

'Which is?'

'Damn you, Rachel,' he said, pushing his stool back to stand up. 'If you ask me that one more time . . . '

'You'll what?'

He shook his head. 'I don't have to stand here and listen to this. I'm going back to work tomorrow to get some peace.'

'You can't,' she said. 'You're not well enough.'

'Watch me,' he said, and left the room.

She tried to hate him at that moment, yet couldn't. And that, so she realised, had been the problem all along. Even when faced with the idea of his having cheated on her, her first instinct had been to patch it up, scurrying behind him with a dustpan and brush, scooping up his mistakes.

She had always loved him more than he had loved her. She hadn't minded all that much, even if it were true that he had harboured a little crush on Jenny, having dated her in sixth form. Ultimately, he had chosen Rachel, had married her, and she had been so in love with him – still was – that she would have taken any condition of marriage, no matter how slighting it might have been. Love wasn't about balance. Everyone knew that there was nothing remotely balanced about it.

151

She retrieved the spoon from the floor and dropped it into the dishwasher. Turning the machine on, she stood with her back to it, listening to the swishing and gushing of water coming from within.

She hadn't been greatly upset about the kiss, not nearly as much as people might have thought, especially Melissa. Appearances mattered to Melissa – the outward show of being in control, the one everyone looked up to. But Rachel had always been happy to sit in Al's shadow, knowing that wherever they went people would wonder how she had snagged him.

The truth was that Al hadn't wanted a pretty Jenny for a wife, but a mother, a pragmatist. In Rachel, he had gained stability, and she had got a man who was way out of her league, complete with ego and insecurities.

It was all very well Al saying that he was going back to work, but what about her? Did she still have a job at the marina? Wouldn't things be awkward between her and the Silks now?

Everything was falling apart, slipping from her grasp.

Al had been right about one thing, though: this was Melissa's doing. Too upset to see clearly, she hadn't thought things through. Over the years, she and the others had teased Rachel for being logical, plodding, calling her Velma from *Scooby-Doo*. It was true: Rachel had never done anything rash in her life. Errors and misjudgements occurred when you were rash.

And now Melissa had asked them not to withhold information for the sake of their late friend. It was a simple enough request, and honourable too, and quite possibly the silliest thing she had ever done.

⚓

It was dark when the detectives arrived. Rachel was sitting on the sofa trying to absorb a home improvements TV show with the sound down, since Joel was in the corner of the room revising on his iPad. She glanced at Al, who was absorbed in paperwork in preparation for his return to work. Ned was playing Fortnite on his phone, wearing headphones and saying things like, 'There's a chest above you. Switch to golden scar. Quick, the storm's coming.'

She had no idea what he was talking about.

It was times like this that she would have phoned Melissa or Jenny to talk about something that mattered, like new summer sandals or eye shadow that didn't make her eyelids look crinkly. But there was no one to call. Over the years, their circle had been so tight, so self-reliant, they hadn't needed anyone else.

Had their group felt non-inclusive, elitist, to on-lookers and newcomers? Perhaps. However, there were no newcomers to town that she knew of. Milford was the sort of place where people only left, with one-way tickets.

Why had she stayed here all her life, then, not making any other friends, settling for the Silkies under Melissa's dubious leadership? She had been so under her influence, she would have followed her to a cliff edge and over.

That was exactly what she was doing: she had followed Melissa to the cliff edge and now she was falling – dragging her whole life, house and all, pots and pans and ironing board, with her, like a character from a nursery rhyme or a cautionary tale. In years to come, children would be singing about her.

The doorbell rang. Everyone looked at each other, aside from Ned who jumped up, shouting into his headset, 'Kill him. *Kill him!*'

Rachel went down the hallway, ignoring the pit of fear that was pooling in her stomach.

It's all right. It's all right.

Pulling open the door, she saw the two detectives standing there, their eyes narrowed against the downpour of rain smattering their jackets. 'Detective Sergeant Lloyd, so you may recall,' the older man said. 'And this is Detective Constable Wilson. Sorry to interrupt you after hours, but could we have a word?'

'Come on in,' she said, stepping aside for them.

'Is your husband home?'

Her heart skipped a beat. 'Yes. Perhaps we can all go in the kitchen, away from the boys, if you don't mind.'

'Actually,' the sergeant said, halting outside the lounge door, the raindrops wobbling on his coat, 'we'd like to speak to your husband on his own.'

Al appeared from the lounge, closing the door behind him. 'Fine by me,' he said, and showed the men to his study at the back of the house.

'Tea, coffee?' Rachel called after them.

'No, ta,' the constable said, before disappearing into the study.

Rachel went into the lounge to check on the boys, who made no show of having noticed that the police were here. 'Can I get either of you a drink?' Joel shook his head; Ned didn't appear to have heard.

Going through to the kitchen, she made a cup of tea and sat down at the counter jadedly. She hadn't allowed herself to feel self-pity since the accident, but she did so now. She felt unutterably sad, bereft.

Who could she call for comfort? Who could she cry to? Certainly not Al, who wasn't gifted at empathy. Besides, that wasn't the basis of their marriage. The deal was that she nursed him, not vice versa. Brutal as it sounded, she couldn't count on him for emotional support. Perhaps that was why the kiss with Jenny hadn't been as crushing as it might have been. Her self-esteem had never been left up to him.

If anyone had been entrusted with her well-being, other than

154

herself, it was her two best friends. Had she not realised this over the years, it had certainly become apparent the night that she had witnessed the kiss.

The betrayal had felt stronger for involving Jenny, rather than Al. She hadn't even told him what she had seen. Rather, she had tried to approach Jenny first.

She took a sip of tea, closing her eyes as tears formed. Without the Silkies she had no one. Her parents lived twenty miles away; she had never felt close to them. She was fond of her brothers, but they had fled town years ago. She had Joel and Ned, yet they had their own lives. She couldn't burden them with her problems.

So, who did that leave?

It occurred to her then that none of the Silkies, with the exception of Gareth, came from close families. Yet even Gareth's parents had moved back to Wales on their retirement, as was their right. But still . . . None of them had parents who looked after the grandchildren, helping with the school runs. And there were plenty who did in Milford. Rachel had looked at them enough times with envious eyes: children being led out of school by Grandma and Grandpops.

Perhaps, all along, others had been looking enviously back at them, coveting their close, unbreakable friendships.

In each other they had found replacements – intentionally or not – for family. But now they were discovering that there were no ties like blood ties. Nothing bound the Silkies together, not now that one of them was dead.

Rachel wiped her eyes. She could hear voices out in the hallway. The men were returning. She braced herself for the kitchen door to open, but it didn't. Hurrying to the hallway, she caught the detectives just as Al was about to open the front door. 'Don't you need to speak to me?' she asked.

'Not at the moment,' the sergeant replied.

'Oh,' she said. 'Then could I have a word . . . in private?'

''Course,' the sergeant said.

Al looked uneasy. 'You don't want me with you?'

'No. Stay with the boys,' she said. Then she turned to the detectives. 'Let's go in here.' And she led them to the kitchen, closing the door behind them.

Her heart was racing so fast, she would have liked a moment to clarify her thoughts. The sergeant wanted to get on with it, however. 'What's this about?' he said wearily, bearing the look of a man who wanted to put an end to a long day.

'I need to give you some information.'

'Oh, right?' the constable said, reaching into his jacket for his notebook.

'I . . . ' She eyed the notebook, the hand poised on paper, the detectives' sombre faces. 'It's about Melissa . . . She seems keen to apportion blame, drawing attention to the kiss between Al and Jenny. And I just wondered if you . . . whether you've questioned that at all?'

The men looked at her blankly.

'Obviously you think that Jenny's death may not have been an accident or you wouldn't be here now.'

The sergeant afforded her a slight nod.

'So . . . ' she began.

'Mrs Beckinsale,' the constable said, 'what is it you're trying to say?'

The room fell silent. Outside, the world beyond was black, reflecting back the contents of her kitchen. She could hear voices from the lounge – Ned shouting instructions through his headset.

'Mrs Beckinsale?'

She had to protect her boys, all three of them. She desperately wanted Joel to do well in his A levels and escape this town. The police couldn't keep coming around, questioning

Al, unsettling them. The boys would pick up on it, especially the further it went.

And who knew how far it would go? If the police really were considering all possibilities, then the situation could get very nasty indeed.

She looked at the detectives decisively. 'Melissa had a venue built five years ago at the marina.'

The men nodded.

'It cost over half a million pounds.'

'OK . . . ' the sergeant said, waiting for her to say more.

She looked at the black world outside again. At that a moment she could see Jenny crying to her for help before being dragged around South Rocks.

She looked back at the detectives. 'Ask her where she got the money from.'

157

20

Thursday 26 April 2018

Melissa called in to Mon Petit Hair early that morning to see how everything was going. Jenny's assistant, Sue, was already sitting at the counter, preparing hair foils. As the doorbell rang, she smiled warily at Melissa.

The wariness was mutual. Sue was close friends with Gilly Green, the gossiper who ran the school office, who had witnessed Melissa's run-in with Rachel outside the school only the day before. Still, awkwardness wasn't Melissa's default setting in situations such as this. She had lived in Milford long enough to know that if you acted as though nothing were the matter then most people would assume that were the case.

She came to a halt on the welcome mat, looking around her in surprise. 'Oh, my goodness!'

'Amazing, isn't it?' Sue said. Everywhere – on the windowsills, workstations, on the floor and counter – were flowers: tulips, bluebells, lilacs, snowdrops, crocuses. The fragrance was intoxicating.

Melissa stepped forward to touch a snowdrop; Jenny's favourite. She would have loved this, seeing her salon awash with bouquets in her honour.

'I didn't know what to do with them,' Sue said. 'I've been ringing Gareth, but he never picks up. I expect he doesn't want to talk business, but people keep asking me where to send the flowers. I never know what to say, since there's not going to be a funeral yet, not until the inquest is—'

'You know about that?' Melissa asked.

Sue blushed. 'I thought it was common knowledge. Gilly's husband works at Portbridge police station ...'

Ah.

'Anyhow,' Sue continued, 'there didn't seem to be anywhere to send the flowers. We couldn't put them down at the cove because it's all cordoned off. So, in the end, I said to send them here. That was all right, wasn't it?'

'Sounds sensible to me.'

Not that it was Melissa's decision to make. Over the years, she had taken the lead so many times, it was natural that people would turn to her now. But suddenly she didn't want the responsibility. She hadn't slept well again last night, Rachel's cryptic words going around her head.

If this blows up in your face, you've only got yourself to blame.

'Are you OK?' Sue said. 'You look a bit pale.'

'I'm fine, thanks,' Melissa said. 'Anyhow, I'd better get going. If you need anything, call Gareth. I'm sure he'll answer eventually.'

'Will do,' Sue said.

Melissa, giving her best impression of capability and calm, left the salon and walked to her Audi, knowing that Sue would be watching her every step.

Inside the car, she sat holding the steering wheel but not driving away. Through the large windows of Mon Petit Hair, she could see Sue still fiddling with hair foils.

Sighing, Melissa looked away, taking in the view of the high street. It was just beginning to rain, drops specking the

159

surface of the river that ran through the middle of town, down to the sea.

Her phone began to ring then and she pulled it from her bag. It was her mother.

'How are you?' her mother asked.

'Not so good.' Melissa pulled at a loose thread hanging from the steering wheel.

'You sound tired. It's going to be tough for a while, you know.'

She nodded. 'So, what have you been up to?'

'Not much. It's quiet, with the academy closed.'

'How's David?'

'He's fine,' her mother said. 'It'll do him good to be back at work. He's getting bored.'

Melissa smiled. She knew what David getting bored looked like. He rocked in his seat, chanting *boring* until they found him something to do.

'I was wondering whether you'd like to come to lunch on Sunday?' her mother asked. 'The five of you.'

Melissa raised her eyebrows. 'Why?'

'Do I need a reason?'

Yes.

'No.'

'Then come,' her mother said. 'I thought it would give you a break from cooking. Does one o'clock suit you?'

'That's fine. Shall I bring wine?' Melissa asked.

'Why not?'

'See you Sunday then.'

She hung up. *A break from cooking?* Her mother had never given her a break from anything, not even when the children were babies. Still, she wouldn't knock the offer of help, however late it was in coming.

She left the high street then, heading for the marina, thinking again of what Rachel had said yesterday.

Don't say I didn't warn you.

What had she meant by that? It didn't make sense.

The logical thing to do would be to ring her and ask, but Melissa wasn't about to do that – was still reeling from being humiliated outside the school of all places, in front of the local gossip crows.

Pulling into the marina car park, she got out of the car. Lee's bike was leaning against the office wall, but he was nowhere to be seen. However, she could hear the echoing sound of a hammer on fibreglass that told her he was working somewhere nearby.

She paused for a moment to absorb the view. There was a beautiful stillness to the early morning that begged appreciation. It had rained first thing. Festive drops of rain adorned the trees and the grass, catching the light.

Lee had stopped hammering and a silence fell, stretching out across the water, which was silver-blue as though made of pewter.

She unlocked the office door and was switching on the coffee machine when she heard the sound of a car pulling up outside. Going to the window, she was startled to see that it was the detectives.

Pulling her cardigan around her, she went to stand on the Portakabin steps to greet them. 'Hello,' she said, trying to look friendly as the two men approached. 'I wasn't expecting to see you.'

'Morning, Melissa. Mind if we take a quick look around?'

'No. That's—'

'Back in a sec.'

She watched them leave, their polished shoes crunching along the gravel in the direction of the venue. 'Would you like me to show you around?' she called after them.

But the sergeant just waved his hand. 'No need,' he said, before rounding the corner.

What did they want with the marina?

There was a hiss as the coffee maker stopped. Pouring two mugs of coffee, she took one of them outside to Lee, following the tinny hammering noise for directions.

Lee was lying underneath the hull of a boat. 'All right?' he said.

'Coffee,' she said.

'Good timing.' He put down his bronze hammer and stood up, taking the mug from her.

'Those detectives are here,' she said.

'Really?' he said. 'Just turned up, have they?'

'Yes. What do you think they want?'

'Beats me,' he said.

'Do you think it's because of what I told them?'

He shrugged, setting his mouth into a tight line of non-disclosure.

'Please, Lee. Tell me what you're thinking.'

'That it might have been easier if you hadn't said any-thing, yes.'

'But I had to.'

''Course you did,' he said.

She put her hands on her hips. 'This isn't helping.'

'What?' he said. 'I'm not doing anything – just drinking my coffee. I'm sure you've got nothing to worry about. They're just being thorough ... ' There came the sound of footsteps then. 'And here they are ... ' Lee raised his mug in greeting as the men appeared around the corner of the boat. 'Morning all.'

The detectives approached. 'Morning, Mr Silk. Nice place you have here.'

'Thanks,' Lee said. 'We like it.'

'This is a real beauty,' the sergeant said, running his hand along the side of the boat that Lee was working on. 'Yours?'

'No. Just repairing it.'

'Must be satisfying, working out here in the fresh air, by the water.'

'It's the best,' Lee agreed.

'And what about you, Melissa?' the sergeant said. 'You work mostly in that impressive-looking venue over there, I take it?'

'Yes. But it's not all that impressive really,' she said, slipping her hands into the back pockets of her jeans and smiling.

'Well, we won't keep you long ... There's just one small matter we'd like to discuss with you both?'

'Go ahead,' Lee said.

'It's about the money that you used to pay for the venue.'

'What about it?'

'Apparently, you were given it. Six hundred grand. Correct?'

'That's right, yes.'

Melissa kept her eyes on Lee. He was leaning casually against the boat, sipping coffee, as though discussing the weather.

'I understand that the person who gave you the money was Jennifer Davies?'

'Yes,' Lee said.

'You see,' the constable said, 'her husband didn't know anything about it until we talked to him just now.' He looked at them both in turn. 'We find that a bit strange.'

Melissa gazed at the boat that Lee was working on. *A real beauty?* That was how the sergeant had just described it.

It was nothing of the sort. Propped up on chunks of wood and crates, its exterior was streaked with rust stains that were oozing from the anchor and from metal bolts.

He was distracting them with compliments, trying to blindside them. She wondered whether Lee should be looking so amenable and laid-back. Didn't he realise where they were going with this?

She was going to have to take hold of the conversation and steer it the right way.

'There was nothing strange about it,' she said. 'Jenny inherited money when her parents died and she didn't know what to do with it. At the time, I was trying to get a loan for the marina. So, she decided to invest in it, as a sort of silent partner. She specifically asked that no one knew about it, except the three of us.'

'Not even her husband?' the sergeant said.

'No.'

'And that doesn't seem odd to you? As a married couple, surely you can see that's a dangerous premise – keeping financial secrets of that size?'

'Not really. I understood the reason why,' Melissa said.

'Which was?'

'She thought Gareth would try to talk her out of it.'

'And why would she think that?'

She shrugged. 'Some people are funny about mixing money with friendship.'

'And rightly so, when there's over half a million involved, I'd have thought.'

She looked at the sergeant assuredly. 'Not in this case. Jenny and I were like family. And besides, she had a funny attitude towards money. Her parents used to give her cash instead of attention, so she didn't like it very much – saw it as something to throw around.'

'I see,' the sergeant said, as though chances would be a fine thing.

'Can I just ask,' Lee said, 'how you know about this, given that Jenny wanted it kept confidential?'

'Anonymous tip-off,' the constable said.

Melissa gazed at the office, her skin goose-bumping. The paperwork was in there, filed away. It was possible that Rachel had seen it at some point while carrying out her work.

Rachel had told the police about the money because Melissa had told about the kiss.

And now the police had told Gareth about Jenny's investment – yet another blow for him to handle. Somehow, she didn't think he would be defending her to his father now, or to anyone.

'I take it that you're happy for us to examine the paperwork?' the sergeant asked.

'Yes,' Melissa said. 'You can look at it here, or you can speak to Jenny's solicitor about it at King's, in town. You won't find anything dodgy, I can assure you.'

'Right,' the constable said, almost sarcastically. 'So, the money was never an issue between you?'

'No,' she said.

'She never regretted the investment?'

'Not at all ...' She went to say something else then, but decided against it.

'What was that?' the sergeant said. 'You hesitated.'

She glanced at Lee. He nodded encouragingly.

'She did ask for the money,' she said.

'What?' Lee said, staring at her.

'She asked me whether it could be released.'

'Why didn't you tell me?' Lee said, his voice hushed as though addressing her in private and not in front of two detectives.

'Because it wasn't a big thing. She just mentioned it in passing. And I explained that the money was tied up in the business. She didn't seem all that bothered about it to me.'

'And when did this conversation take place?' the sergeant asked.

Melissa turned to look at the estuary. A puffin was sitting

on a rock by the water's edge, a cluster of silvery fish hanging from its beak.

'Two weeks ago,' she said.

There was a splash as one of the fishes flopped from the puffin's beak back into the water. The puffin took off then, soon becoming a black-and-white football in the sky as it grew smaller.

'Is there anything else you need from us?' Lee said. 'Because we should be getting back to work.'

'No, that's it for now,' the sergeant replied. 'We'll be in touch.' And then he turned to leave, the constable following after him with a backwards glance at Melissa.

Lee waited for the sound of the car doors slamming and the engine starting before he spoke. 'You should have told me.'

'I'm sorry,' Melissa said. 'I didn't think it was a big deal. I'd forgotten all about it until they mentioned it just now.'

'Even so ...' he said, looking about him for somewhere to put his empty coffee cup.

'Give it here,' she said, taking the mug from him. 'Please don't be cross. I can't handle anyone else being angry at me, especially not you.'

'I'm not cross. I just didn't appreciate what they were suggesting.' He picked up his hammer and crouched down, ready to go back underneath the old boat. 'Still, there's nothing to worry about because we've done nothing wrong.'

'No,' she said.

Lee disappeared. And then the sound of his hammer, the marina's heartbeat, rang out around the yard, echoing around the sheds and boats.

Melissa returned to the office, heading straight for the filing cabinet. She was surprised that the detectives hadn't wanted to see the paperwork right away, although they were probably more interested in the contracts kept under lock and key at King's.

So this, she thought as she pulled open the cabinet drawer and gazed at the rows of green hanging files, was what Rachel's warning had meant.

21

Friday 27 April 2018

The Lighthouse Centre in Portbridge was really something. The glass doors swooshed open to reveal the reception with its plush carpet that air-sprang visitors to take a seat on a red cube chair.

Gareth had driven by the building many times but hadn't taken any notice of it. Why would he have? No one ever thought that they would need a children's bereavement centre, keeping a pamphlet handy amongst the takeaway menus and flyers for gutter cleaning.

Yet here he was, waiting for Olivia, who had disappeared behind a door almost an hour ago. The counsellor – a red-haired lady with a sizeable smile – had asked Olivia whether she preferred to be *with Dad* or *without Dad*.

He could have answered that one himself.

'Are you sure you don't want a coffee?' the receptionist said. 'It's no trouble.'

'No, thanks,' he said. 'We'll probably be going in a minute.'

He sat up straight, gazing at the posters and flyers on the noticeboard opposite.

A letter to my ten-year-old self.

Remembering someone you've lost.

Can social media help me?

His eyes lingered on *Remembering someone you've lost*. It was hard to know how to remember Jenny at the moment. Each day, something else distorted his vision of her: first, the horrendous revelation that she had kissed Al. And then the police telling him that she had invested in the Silks' marina behind his back.

The two detectives had shown up first thing yesterday morning. Something about the look on their faces had told Gareth to take them straight through to the study, where they had spoken in low voices, out of earshot of the twins.

The marina investment had come as a huge shock to him. It hadn't sounded like something that either Jenny or Melissa would have done.

It was hard to weigh up whether it was a bigger betrayal than the kiss with Al. It felt bigger because of the sheer amount of money involved. But the Al situation sickened him because it involved his heart, his marriage and one of his best friends.

He hadn't summoned the courage to speak to Al yet. How could he, without punching him? It wasn't something that could be done by phone, text or email. He wanted to actually see the look on Al's face and gauge for himself whether it looked like embarrassment or guilt.

He was hoping for everyone's sake that it would be embarrassment. He could just about cope with a stupid drunken kiss; anything more than that was a no-go.

Surely he would have noticed if there had been a problem in his marriage? Wouldn't he?

Feeling nauseous, his stomach growled unhappily. He hadn't managed to eat very much over the past couple of days, despite his mother's sterling efforts in the kitchen.

The door of the counsellor's room was now opening, so he stood in anticipation. Olivia appeared, looking slightly smaller than an hour ago, to his mind.

The red-haired counsellor smiled at him. 'Could I have a word?'

''Course,' Gareth said. 'Wait here, Liv, OK?' Olivia nodded, pulling the sleeves down on her sweater in long twists, stretching the material.

'Let's go in here,' the counsellor said, leading him to her consulting room.

Inside, Gareth gazed about him. There were the same red-cubed chairs, but also a fish tank and lava lamps, toy cars and doll's houses.

'Please, take a seat,' the counsellor said. Gareth perched on a red cube. 'Olivia's obviously been through a great deal this past week. How's Max?'

He was a little thrown by that – the casual intimacy. 'He, uh . . . he's all right.'

The counsellor smiled. 'Did you think about bringing him today?'

'Yes. We discussed it, but he's not ready and I didn't want to push it. To him, the idea of coming here is a bit like having teeth pulled.'

'Well, everyone responds differently and you'll know better than anyone what suits your son. But if I could make a suggestion, I'd advise asking him again in a few weeks and seeing how he feels.'

'Will do . . . And Olivia? Did she mention the . . . uh . . . ?'

'Self-harm?'

His cheeks coloured. He nodded.

'Yes. She did. Obviously, we can't solve anything in one session, but it's a good sign that she opened up. You did the right thing, responding like you did. Things could quickly spiral out of control, given the situation. However, there's something else I'm concerned about.'

'Oh?' he said, his stomach doing a little flip.

'I had the impression there was something she wasn't telling me. Her focus was very much on the self-harm and her grief, and rightly so, but I sensed that she was holding something back. I speak to a lot of young people. My instincts are normally right.'

He looked at the stuffed toys scattered about the room and thought of the penguin in Olivia's room, wondering if it had managed to hold on to its floor space.

'I don't know what to say,' he said. 'If I'm completely honest ...' He clasped his hands together. 'I was struggling before all of this to connect with my daughter.'

The counsellor smiled kindly. 'Don't think of this as a test that you'll pass or fail. Think of it as a process – a lifetime's work. If you can understand the mind of a sixteen-year-old girl then you can understand anyone, including yourself. And you're not on your own. I'm here. And I'm sure you have family and friends who can help.'

Friends?

Ha!

'I've got a very supportive family,' he said.

'Good. So, draw strength from them. And in the meantime, spend as much time as you can with Olivia, without suffocating her. Try to find out what's bothering her, aside from the obvious.' She stood up. 'We'll regroup next week ... Does that sound like a plan?'

'It does,' he said. 'Thank you. I really appreciate it.'

He felt like crying. Was he going to cry? He hurried to the door.

By the time they had joined Olivia, he was over his emotional flush. 'See you next week,' the counsellor said.

As they left, making their way out of the swishy doors, he rested his hand on Olivia's shoulder, but within an instant she had wriggled away.

He couldn't keep comparing himself to a stuffed penguin; that was daft. But still, the comparison was there.

⚓

On the car journey home, Olivia sat beside him in the passenger seat, turning her body at a rigid angle away from him, the hood pulled up on her sweater.

So, there was something else that she wasn't telling him?

His head began to pulsate with complications: the kiss, the marina money, the thing that Olivia was hiding . . . His neck felt hot, itchy, too close to his collar. Putting the window down, he told himself that he couldn't think like this, trying to deal with everything at once. He had to take it one step at a time.

'Do you think that went well?' he asked.

'Yep,' she said.

'The counsellor seems nice. Are you OK to go again next week?'

'Yep.'

'Good,' he said. 'Because I think it could really help.'

She grunted a response.

'Do you fancy popping in the café before home? Break the day up a bit?'

'Whatev,' she said.

'Is that a yes?'

'It's not a no.'

Sighing quietly, he put the radio on. Ironically, 'I Can See Clearly Now' was playing.

It was only as they passed the welcome sign for Milford that Olivia turned to speak to him, pulling down her hood. 'Did Auntie Mel take money from Mum?'

'What? No, not really. Mum gave her the money as an

investment. It was a business deal . . . How do you know about that anyway?'

She looked away. 'Heard you and Grandpa talking about it after the police came around.'

'Oh. Then you know that it was all above board.'

'Where did Mum get the money from in the first place?' she asked.

'It was an inheritance, from her parents. You didn't know them. None of us did. They were as odd as they were rich.'

'But didn't she want us to have it?'

'Yes, she did, Liv. She gave you and Max six hundred thousand each.'

Olivia swivelled in her seat, straining on her belt. 'You what?'

He smiled. 'We did tell you at the time, but you were only eleven. Probably went in one ear and out the other.'

Olivia sat back with a bump. 'So where is it?'

'Locked away in a trust until you're twenty-five.'

'Oh, yay,' she said mockingly. 'So, I'm guessing you didn't know about the marina money?'

He tightened his grasp on the steering wheel. 'No. I didn't.'

'That's not cool,' she said. 'Where did you think the money was?'

'I thought all of it had gone into your trusts.'

'Oh,' she said. 'Are we going to get it back?'

He glanced at her in surprise. 'No,' he said. Then, 'Actually, I'm not sure how it works. I've not had a chance to look at it yet . . . Why?'

She shrugged. 'Just wondered.'

'Do you need money? Is there something you need?'

'It's nothing,' she said abruptly, pulling up her hood again.

What if it was drugs, Olivia's secret? She was withdrawn, moody, but then so were lots of teenagers. That didn't make them drug addicts.

173

Once again, he told himself to stick to the basics. There was no use catastrophising about every little hitch. He pulled up outside the café in the high street. 'Fancy a milkshake?'

'What am I, like, five?' she said.

'Come on.' He unbuckled his seat belt, but Olivia was sitting still, pressing her hands together as though seeing which one was stronger.

'Do you still like Auntie Mel?' she asked.

'If I tell you, will you let me buy you a milkshake?'

'OK.'

'Well,' he said, 'it's complicated.'

'That's not an answer.'

'That's because I don't have one. I don't know how I feel about her.'

'Why?'

'Because she's caused a lot of upset. Not intentionally, maybe. But still . . . She kept things from me.'

'So?' she said. 'Mum did, too.'

He couldn't argue with that. Getting out of the car, he blinked at the bright light, even though it was an overcast day. He had been spending a lot of time indoors.

Olivia slammed her door shut and rounded the car to talk to him. 'Seems to me like Mum's the one we should be angry with,' she said. And then she stomped off into the café, the Open sign rattling on the door.

An old lady was tottering along the pavement towards him, dragging an old-fashioned trolley, wheels whining. 'Afternoon,' Gareth said.

In response, the old lady grunted at him. It seemed that grunts were catching.

Wearily, he followed his daughter into the café, where she was nowhere to be seen. He looked about him in astonishment. There were only a few tables. What had

174

she done – slipped out of a window, vanished through a back door?

The woman at the counter – Angela Gould, the odd woman who lived opposite Melissa – was smiling at him. 'She's in the *Ladies*,' she mouthed discreetly, as though it were the most inappropriate word to use in daylight. 'So, what can I get you?' she said.

'I . . . uh . . .' Gareth said, surveying the counter, which was crammed with baps, pastries, cakes.

As he stood there, overwhelmed by the smell of buttery sugar, he thought of what the detectives had said yesterday morning.

Throughout the conversation, he had the feeling that they weren't just there to tell him about the money. They didn't reveal their hand at first, though. In fact, they waited until Gareth was about to close the front door on them.

Each day – they had said, just before leaving – they unearthed some strange coincidence or secret connected with Jennifer's death. And yet the accident still appeared to be precisely that: accidental.

Gareth hadn't really known what to say to that. There had only been four of them on the trip. What were these men saying: that one of them had unplugged Jenny's kayak, sending her to her death?

And yet . . . Al had kissed her; Rachel knew about that betrayal; Melissa had a secret deal with Jenny, involving an awful lot of money.

What if Jenny had asked for the money back?

'Have you made up your mind?' someone said.

Gareth came to. Angela Gould was still waiting for his order. Olivia was coming towards him, hood up, scowling. 'What's wrong with you?' she asked him. 'You look like you've seen a ghost.'

GILLY GREEN

Office Administrator, Milford Senior School, Dorset

'So ...' Gilly said, glancing about her before proceeding. It was quiet in The Lamb and Lion tonight. 'You know that Hubby got that new job down at Portbridge police station? Well, he said that it's looking more likely each day that Jenny's death wasn't an accident.'

'What?' Sue said, looking shocked.

'Surely you've heard the rumours?'

'Yeah, but I thought that was all they were. I mean, the Silkies are lovely people. I can't see any of them hurting Jenny, can you?'

'Not really. But apparently, it's something to do with money. Large amounts of cash can turn even the nicest person into a psycho.'

'For sure,' Sue said, crunching loudly on an ice cube. 'Did I tell you that Melissa came into the salon yesterday?'

'No. What was she like?'

'Barely said a word. Quiet as a mouse.'

'Interesting ... Maybe she's got a guilty conscience about something.' Gilly watched as Sue forked another ice cube out of her glass to crunch it again.

'Or maybe she's just devastated about Jenny,' Sue said. 'You should see all the flowers at the salon. She was a bit like Lady Di, really.'

Gilly thought about that. Jenny was nothing like Lady Di, but she would let it go.

'I do feel sorry for Melissa,' she said. 'But to be honest, I always found her hard to talk to. Do you know what I mean?'

'Totally,' Sue said. 'Really friendly and yet untouchable at the same time. But then, it's not surprising, really.'

'No, I suppose not ...' Gilly agreed vaguely. 'Wait, what do you mean?'

'Well, you know – after what happened to her as a child.'

'Oh, yeah,' Gilly said, sipping her wine. 'Forgot about that ... Maybe it affected her.'

'Bound to,' Sue said, fishing for another ice cube from her glass.

22

The five of them waited on the doorstep, listening to the rain splatting on to the jungle-like potted palms that were gathered on the front porch with them like additional guests. 'Can't we go in, Mummy?' Polly said, tugging Melissa's hand.

'No. Just wait a minute,' she said. 'I always wait for Grandma to let me in.'

'Come on,' Lee said. 'This is daft. It's cold out here.' And he was about to open the door, when it swung open and David was standing there, blushing coyly.

'Hello,' David said.

'Hi, David,' Melissa said, going on tiptoes to kiss his cheek.

He wiped the kiss away and then looked at the children. 'Hello, Frank. Hello, Nina. Hello, Polly,' he chanted. And then he held his hand out to Lee. 'Hello, Lee.'

Melissa smiled to herself. Her brother was wearing a polo-neck jumper with corduroy trousers, reminiscent of a 1970s children's TV presenter. 'Come in,' he said.

In the hallway, came the unmistakeable aroma of a roast lunch in its final moments of preparation.

'I'll take your coats,' David said, extending his arm out like a towel rail.

'Go through to the lounge everyone,' Melissa said. 'I'll see if Mum needs any help.'

'What shall I do with the wine?' Lee said.

'I'll take it,' Melissa said.

They were all a bit nervous, fumbling around. Nina kept sucking on her tooth brace. Frank was looking about him, examining the pictures on the walls with sudden interest. Polly was the only one who didn't appear to see what the big deal was in having lunch at Grandma's.

'Perfect timing,' her mother said, as Melissa entered the kitchen. 'You can stir.' She motioned to the glass jug on the counter.

Melissa set the wine down and began to stir the gravy mechanically.

'Everyone well?' her mother said, spooning roast potatoes into a serving dish.

'Yes, thanks,' Melissa said.

'And what about you?'

'Well, things couldn't get much worse.'

'Oh? Has something else happened?'

Melissa hesitated, unsure how much to share with her mother, who would probably find out soon enough from another source. It was best to control the manner in which the news was relayed.

'The police are making a big deal of the fact that Jenny gave me the money for the marina.'

Her mother stopped what she was doing. 'I beg your pardon?'

'The money for the venue . . . It was from Jenny's inheritance.'

'What?'

Melissa laughed. 'It was a business agreement. I needed the money.'

179

Her mother set down the large spoon she was holding. 'So why didn't you ask me?'

'Because you don't have that kind of money?'

'Even so, couldn't you have asked me, or mentioned it, at least? I might have been able to help in some way.'

Melissa looked at the gravy in the jug, at the little whirlpool she had created. She felt suddenly that this was not the right conversation to be having before a family lunch. 'Don't start, please, Mum,' she said.

But it was too late. Her mother was untying her apron, dropping it on to a stool. 'Why is it,' she said, 'that I always get the distinct impression that you'd rather ask the postman or the next-door neighbour's cat for help before coming to me?'

Again, Melissa laughed, but this time it was more of a nervous titter. 'Our neighbour's cat is Siamese. He doesn't speak English,' she said.

It was an attempt to lighten the mood, but her mother was having none of it. She snatched up the serving bowl of potatoes and headed for the door. 'Please bring the carrots and the beans,' she said icily.

Melissa stood alone, watching the steam rising from the gravy jug. She had only been with her mother for two minutes and already lunch was spoilt. How was that possible?

She was about to carry the vegetables through when her mother reappeared.

Melissa had a choice then, one that she was presented with whenever these spats broke out: to either ignore it or attempt a repair. The latter was almost impossible to pull off, but she was feeling unstable enough today to attempt it.

Her mother was lifting the chicken out of the oven, fat bubbling. 'Can we talk about this?' Melissa said, joining her.

'Not if you want your children to eat.'

'They can wait.' She tugged her mother's sleeve. 'Please.'

Her mother turned to look at her inquisitively. Then she sighed, setting the chicken to one side. 'Five minutes,' she said.

'Thank you.' Melissa cleared her throat and then wondered exactly what she was going to say. A good minute passed in silence.

'I don't see the point in just standing here while the chicken gets cold,' her mother said.

'I'm sorry that I haven't felt able to come to you in the past,' Melissa said. 'I didn't think we were close enough to—'

'I'm your mother!'

'Yes, but . . .'

'But what?'

She gazed at her mother and was struck once more by how different they were. It was supposed to be difficult to navigate family relationships with those you were most similar to, but in her experience being completely different was just as bad. How were they ever to understand each other? How could she begin to explain who she was, if for the past forty-two years her mother had failed to see it for herself?

Moments like this were agony: the realisation that she had come here once again hoping to find something different, only to discover that everything was the same.

'Why did you and Dad split up?' she said.

'What?'

This was one of the questions that she wasn't supposed to ask, not if she wanted to make it to dessert.

'You always said that it was because you were arguing,' Melissa said. 'But why were you fighting in the first place?'

Her mother turned away, lifting the chicken from its metal tray to a serving platter. 'He didn't want to be around us.'

Melissa drew closer. 'Us? Or you?'

'All of us. He didn't want the responsibility. He found it difficult, having a son like David. His heart wasn't in it.'

'And what about me?'

Her mother turned to look at her, her mouth twisting slightly. 'You were collateral damage.'

Melissa gazed at her mother, impressed that she knew such a term, but then she did have Netflix.

She seemed unsettled, rattling the cutlery drawer in search of the carving knife.

'Here,' Melissa said, spotting it on the counter and handing it to her. 'So ... you split up, he moved away, and not long after you heard that he'd had a massive heart attack, and that was that?'

'Something like that.'

'Why did he find David difficult?'

'Why do you think?'

'I dunno. Tell me.'

Her mother sighed. 'He was embarrassed of him, said he was an idiot. I thought David deserved better.'

'Too right,' Melissa said. 'Crikey. I didn't realise.'

'Well,' her mother said, laying the knife on the serving tray, 'it's not the sort of thing you tell a child. I didn't want you looking at David that way too. He had enough challenges without his own family treating him like an imbecile.'

'I'd never feel that way about him.'

Her mother paused, looking at her in contemplation. 'No, I don't suppose you would,' she said. 'You've always been good with him.'

Melissa flushed at the rare compliment. 'I hate Dad for thinking like that,' she said. 'What a loser.'

'It wasn't his fault. He just wasn't cut out to have a son like David. Some people aren't.'

'That's generous of you to say.'

'Well, he's dead now. We can afford a little generosity.' And her mother smiled conspiratorially at her.

It made Melissa feel good, that smile, as though they were sharing a secret in the kitchen, like a normal family.

'So, it was mostly because of David that you divorced,' she said, feeling emboldened. 'But wasn't it also because of . . . you know . . . ?'

'What?'

'Well, Hannah.'

Her mother looked at her with harsh disapproval, the progress that they had just made now seeping wastefully away. It was like pouring water on sand, their relationship, in the hope of building a moat for a castle.

'Mum,' Melissa said, touching her arm, 'we need to talk about her sometimes. We can't—'

'Yes, we can,' her mother said. 'We can carry on doing what we've always done. It's worked so far.'

'But it's not working!' Melissa said. 'Nothing about us is working. We barely ever speak to each other!'

There was a noise then, as Lee poked his head around the kitchen door. 'Everything under control?' he said, looking cautiously from one of them to the other.

'Oh, good, Lee. You're here,' Melissa's mother said, as though they had been sat there waiting for him. 'You can take the chicken through.' She handed him the platter. 'Maybe you could start carving it, if you wouldn't mind?'

'No worries,' he said, leaving the room, chicken in hand.

'We should join them,' her mother said. 'They'll be wondering what's going on.'

Melissa noticed the bottle of wine standing unopened on the middle of the table. Reluctant at first to come here for lunch, the idea had grown on her, gathering momentum until she had found herself choosing the most expensive Pinot Noir in the shop and had had to stop herself from buying a deluxe bouquet of flowers.

What was wrong with her?

Gazing at the wine, she began to cry. She couldn't remember the last time she had cried in front of her mother. Possibly when she was twelve and had scorched her finger trying to earn her outdoor cooking badge at Brownies.

'Whatever's wrong?' her mother said in wonder, as though Jenny hadn't just died, as though they hadn't just wasted another bucket of water on sand.

Their relationship was completely hopeless.

'You always liked Jenny, didn't you?' Melissa said.

Her mother nodded. 'She was a nice girl ... Here ...' She handed Melissa a piece of kitchen roll. 'Dry your eyes.'

'More than me,' she said.

Her mother stared at her. 'More than you what?'

'You liked her more than me.'

'What? Why would you say such a thing?'

Melissa dabbed her eyes. 'I dunno. You were always a lot nicer to her than you were to me.'

Her mother looked amazed. 'That's because she wasn't my child and she was a guest in our home! I was nice to her because her parents were never around. Poor girl. All that money and no family to speak of ... Really, Melissa, you do come out with some strange things.'

Yep, that's me, Melissa thought.

I'm the strange one.

There was a noise at the door and Lee reappeared. 'Chicken's carved,' he said. 'Ready?'

They were halfway down the hallway when Melissa remembered the wine and returned for it. She was on her way back to the dining room when her phone rang. It was a withheld number.

'Melissa? It's Sergeant Lloyd.'

She halted at the sound of his voice, just as she opened the dining-room door. Her family were all gathered at the table.

184

'Who's that?' Lee said, with the look of a man who couldn't wait any longer to eat.

She didn't reply, was too busy listening to the sergeant – to the instructions he was giving her.

'OK,' she said at length. 'I can do that.'

She hung up, remained standing at the door, holding the doomed bottle of wine. 'I can't stay.'

'What?' Lee said. 'Why not?'

'That was the police,' she said.

Lee threw down his napkin, giving her a look that said *not in front of the kids*, motioning for them to talk away from the table.

Her mother joined them in the corner of the room. 'What's going on?' she said.

'The police have new information and want to talk to me as soon as possible,' Melissa said. 'I'm going there now.'

'But can they ask you to do that? Do you have to?' Lee said.

'I don't have to, no. But they said it would be helpful.'

'For who? Them? Then don't go,' Lee said. 'Stay here and have your lunch.'

'No,' she said. 'I told them that I'm going now. I want to get it out of the way. I won't be able to eat with this hanging over me.'

'Then I'm going with you. You're not doing this on your own.'

'No, Lee. You stay with the kids,' she said. 'They need you more.'

Her mother stepped forward, touched Melissa's arm.

Melissa stared at her mother's sun-spotted hand, transfixed by the fact that she had broken the distance between them.

'I'll stay with the children, Lee,' her mother said. 'You go with Melissa. Take care of her.'

For a moment, it almost sounded as though her mother were being sentimental. But then she clapped her hands, went to the table and said, 'Right, kids, *let's eat!*' And the spell was broken.

23

It was so cold in the room that Melissa was sure that the sergeant's lips had acquired a shade of purple they didn't normally have. He was a nice-looking man; not handsome, just kindly with his soft brown eyes. It was a wonder that he still looked like that in his line of work. He could easily have slipped on a clerical collar and would have looked at home standing in a pulpit.

His subordinate, Wilson, looked similarly unscathed, with a heavily-freckled face that spoke of youth and sunshine. Yet his mouth was mean-looking and when he smiled, she noticed that his teeth were tiny, square.

'This is one of the most frustrating cases I've ever worked on, Melissa,' Sergeant Lloyd was saying. 'Everything about it says accident. But it doesn't feel like that. No one can account for the unplugging of the kayak. No one can explain to any real satisfaction why the trip went ahead in the eye of a storm. And no one seems to know why Jennifer suggested a change of plan resulting in her own death.'

He took a pen from his pocket, tapped it on the table top. 'And now to add to our problems, we're not sure about the one person whose word seemed reliable.' He set his eyes on her. 'Hence our confusion.'

She glanced about her at the beige carpet, the beige walls, wishing that Lee could have come in with her. The police had asked him to wait in the lobby, telling him to get a coffee and that she wouldn't be long. Going through the heavy metal doors to the interview room, she hadn't looked back at him for fear that she would panic and make a dash for it.

She didn't know much about the law, but was fairly certain that making a dash for it always looked like guilt.

It was not only cold in this interview room, but the air felt rationed. She was sitting on a plastic chair that bounced as she shifted position. 'I'm sorry,' she said, 'but I don't understand why you're doubting me.'

'Then let me explain . . .' the sergeant said. 'We checked everything out at King's, the solicitors. The paperwork was all in order, like you said it would be. But then the contents of the will were made known to us.'

She nodded. 'And?'

'You don't know what I'm about to say?'

'No,' she said, looking at him and then at Wilson. 'Really. I haven't a clue.'

Wilson, who had seemed disinterested moments before, became animated then. 'Jennifer Davies changed her will at the time of the business deal between you,' he said. 'In the event of her death, the six hundred thousand pounds investment was to remain with you, to be absorbed by the business.'

There was a silence. Melissa gazed at Wilson, looking at the multitude of freckles on his face, even on his ears.

'I don't understand,' she said. She looked about the bare room. 'Could I have a drink of water?'

'No,' Wilson said.

The sergeant glanced at him.

Wilson pushed back his chair, left the room without another word. There was a click behind them as the door closed.

'Melissa,' the sergeant said, 'in the event of your friend's death, you stood to gain over half a million pounds. Are you trying to have us believe that you didn't know that?'

'I'm not trying to have you believe anything. But if you want the truth, then no, I didn't know.'

'Despite your tell-all relationship with Jennifer?'

'Yes,' she said.

'So, how do you feel about it now that you do know?'

'Well, I'm surprised. But I'm not collapsing on the floor in shock either.'

'Oh? And why is that?'

'Because I told you before: Jenny was funny about money – careless. And she was generous to a fault. I always thought she'd do something like leave it all to the homeless shelter or something.'

'But what about her children? Was she careless with their money too?'

'I can't answer that. That's more of a Gareth question. We were close, but I don't know how they managed their finances, especially when it came to the twins. But I know that she wouldn't have wanted to shower them with money instead of love.'

'I see ... And how is business, down at the marina?' the sergeant asked.

'Good, thanks.'

'So, if we were to go through the company accounts and all your correspondence, we wouldn't find any references to financial difficulties?'

'No,' she said.

'Yet your office manager, Rachel Beckinsale, seems to think differently. She showed me an email that you sent her two weeks ago in which you stated that you desperately needed more bookings if the venue were to stay afloat.'

Melissa shrugged. 'That was an exaggeration. I was just saying that it would be good to be busier.'

'Good or imperative?'

'Look, what is this?' she said. 'I thought I was here to help. I didn't have to come.'

'Then why did you?'

She opened her mouth, frowned, stalling. It was a good question.

'I'm here for Jenny,' she said. 'She was like a sister to me.'

'Yes, you've told us several times now how close you were.'

The door opened and Wilson returned with a plastic cup and a jug of water. She poured herself a cup of water, sipping it nervously.

'But you had a sister, didn't you?' the sergeant said.

The room seemed to stop. Everything stopped.

Melissa set the cup down.

'Why don't you tell us about her, Melissa?'

She was so cold her teeth began to chatter. 'It's freezing in here,' she said. 'Could we have some heating on?'

Wilson laughed, and there were the tiny teeth. 'Freezing? Hardly!' he said. 'We're in shirtsleeves.'

She realised then that the two men were sitting with their jackets on the backs of their chairs and that Wilson had his sleeves rolled up.

'Am I in some sort of trouble?' she asked.

'You can leave any time,' the sergeant replied. 'But like you just said, you came here to help. And I think you want to be here. I think you want to speak to us.'

She couldn't deny it. She wasn't pushing the chair back and bolting for the door. But he was wrong about speaking; she didn't want to say anything else. So why not go? Why not find Lee out in the lobby and go home and enjoy what was left of the weekend?

Because whatever it was that she was sensing in this room – the reason for the bone-biting cold – would be going with her. This wasn't a place that she could walk away from.

She found herself perversely attracted to what they were going to say, unable to look away.

'Her name was Hannah,' the sergeant said.

She stared at the cup in her hands, the way it buckled when she pressed it.

'Hannah Reeve,' he added.

She pressed the cup a little more, seeing how much it would give.

'She was only three years old,' Wilson said. 'Tragic.'

She looked at the young constable. What did he know of tragedy? Even doing his job, he wouldn't carry tragedy in his heart, wouldn't be familiar with the shape and touch of it. He had no right to use that word, sitting there, with his jagged little teeth and baby freckles.

'Do you want to tell us what happened, Melissa?'

She shook her head. Then she set the empty cup down, pushed the jug away. 'Should I have a lawyer here or something?' she said.

Wilson smiled. 'We made it clear earlier that you're entitled to legal advice whenever you talk to us. But if we wait for that to happen, we'll all be here a lot longer. And I'm sure you want to get home to the family.'

'Yes,' she said.

Wilson nodded, smiled again.

'Melissa,' the sergeant said, 'when your sister died, you were with Jennifer Davies, weren't you?'

She didn't reply. They had told her before sitting down that she didn't have to answer their questions, was free to terminate at any time – that the conversation was being recorded, as per standard procedure. She gazed at the little machine on the table top, the tapes slowly circling around. She hadn't minded it ear-lier, hadn't taken any notice of it. But now it seemed sinister, logging her every word.

'Must have been hard for you both, growing up together, after a thing like that. Not the sort of thing you bounce back from in a hurry. No wonder you were close, the two of you.'

Melissa pulled at a wisp of wool that was hanging from her cardigan, watching it float to the ground.

'One source mentioned that there were rumours at the time that Jennifer was to blame. Not that anyone was to blame, as such. You were just kids.' The sergeant paused, thoughtfully. Melissa could feel his brown eyes on her without look-ing at him.

'However,' he continued, 'it would have been understandable if you'd held a grudge all these years.'

'Did you ask her for the money as payback?' Wilson said.

'For what?' she said.

He raised both eyebrows. 'Your sister's death.'

She glared at him and then stood up, accidentally knocking over her chair.

'Interview terminated,' Wilson said, picking up the cassette player. 'Time: fourteen twenty-eight.' He stopped the tape.

'I don't have to take this,' she said, heading for the door. 'I've been trying to help you. And now you're keeping me here in this freezing room, making accusations and—'

'No one's making accusations,' the sergeant said, holding his hand up to pacify her. 'And no one's keeping you here. We're just trying to establish the facts.'

'But I don't see what I've got to do with any of this.'

'Really?' he said, standing up and joining her. Wilson remained seated, watching them. 'Well, let me explain it the way we're currently seeing it, Melissa. We know that the plugs on Jennifer's kayak were the only ones that were open, and that you hold keys to the boat shed. You lied about your reason for not going on the trip and—'

'I told you why that was.'

He held up his hand again, raising his voice to talk over her. 'We also know that you had a strong motive as a beneficiary of the will, plus a possible motive of revenge. So . . . do you see what this has to do with you now?'

Her heart was pounding, overpoweringly so, preventing her from replying.

'We won't keep you any longer,' he said, opening the door and stepping aside for her. 'Thanks for coming in and giving up your Sunday.'

Without another word, she hurried out into the corridor and along the floor that was so shiny she could see her blurred reflection in it. Making for the heavy door at the end, she pushed it open and looked about the lobby for Lee.

He was sitting alone on a row of metal chairs. On seeing her, he jumped up. 'Did it go all right?' he said.

'No,' she said, beginning to cry. 'It didn't. They wanted to know about Hannah.'

'What? Why?'

'And there's worse . . . ' She lowered her voice to a whisper. 'Jenny left us the money in her will – six hundred thousand. It's ours, Lee . . . This all looks really, really bad.' She glanced about her. The lobby was empty, except for the officer behind the counter who was working at a computer.

'Listen, Mel,' Lee said. 'They can't do anything if you've nothing to hide.' He kissed her distractedly on the forehead. 'Come on. Let's get out of here.'

On their way out, the officer at the counter nodded farewell and the automatic doors slid open. Down the red-brick steps they went, Melissa's legs feeling weak, unsteady.

Crossing the car park to the back row underneath the fir

trees, she took in all the familiar details of their car as they got inside: Polly's sweater, Frank's headphones, Nina's coursework, Lee's bike helmet; small things that reminded her of home.

'I thought I was helping them,' she said as they drove away. She was holding Polly's sweater, stroking the velour.

He reached for her hand. 'We were naïve. But we'll be better prepared next time. You won't be talking to them again without someone with you.'

'You mean a lawyer?'

'Yes. We'll get someone on stand-by, in case we need them.'

She gripped his hand anxiously. 'I can't believe we're having this conversation. First, Jenny dies ... and now this. What are they saying? That I killed her? Why would I do that? I loved her.'

'They're just trying to pin this on someone so they can close the case,' he said. 'So you're just going to have to hang on in there until they move on to someone else.'

'But what if they don't?' she said. 'What if they keep focusing on me, trying to break me?'

'They can't break you, love. They need proof.'

'What about circumstantial evidence? Isn't that a thing? They seem to be building quite a convincing case against me.'

'Then we'll fight back,' he said. 'We'll find someone who can help.'

She looked out of the window, falling silent for a moment. 'I'm frightened, Lee,' she said. 'Really frightened.'

He glanced at her. 'I know you are. Let's just get you home.'

24

Tuesday 1 May 2018

Late in the afternoon, during a sudden heavy rainstorm, Gareth's father took the call that they had been waiting for.

Gareth was sitting at the dinner table, playing cards with Max. Over by the French windows, his mother and Olivia were kneeling together on the floor, working on a jigsaw puzzle. Every time the rain lashed against the windows, Gareth looked up fretfully. He wasn't sleeping well at night, was on edge during the day, his nerves fractured.

He was trying to listen into his father's muted phone conversation out in the hallway while teaching Max the rules of their card game. He couldn't even make out who his father was talking to.

'Take one from the top of the pile, Max,' Gareth said.

No one ever rang to tell them good news any more. Such things were long gone.

Only that morning, the solicitor had rung to tell him that Melissa had stood to gain six hundred thousand pounds in the event of Jenny's death.

That conversation had been a real hoot.

'Is that right, Dad?' Max asked him, showing him his deck.

'Yep. That's it. You should still have seven cards if—'

'Sorry to interrupt,' his father said, appearing in the doorway, taking off his glasses and rubbing his eyes. 'That was the coroner's office.'

Gareth and Max set their cards down sombrely. Olivia got up from her knees, helping her grandmother up in turn.

Everyone waited for Grandpa to speak.

'We can go ahead with the funeral.'

No one seemed to know how to react. Max broke the silence by beginning to whimper – the strange sound of a teenage boy who didn't want to cry in front of his family.

Gareth reached out to put his arm around Max. 'It's not fair,' Max was saying. 'I don't want to go to her funeral. I want her to be alive.'

'I know,' Gareth said. 'I feel the exact same way.' And then he stroked his son's hair as gently as though Max had just been born. And in some ways, he had, because grief this powerful redefined your life, changing it into something else.

'I think we need to work a few things out,' his father said stoically, sitting down at the table, picking up a notepad and pen. 'It might help us see clearly.'

Max broke away from Gareth, wiping his eyes brusquely. 'If you don't mind, Dad, I'd like to leave cards. I don't feel like it now. Is it OK if I go to my room?'

''Course,' Gareth said.

'Wait,' Olivia said, following her brother. 'I'll come with you.' And together they left the room.

'Poor mites,' his mother said. 'They don't deserve this, that's for sure.'

Gareth sat down at the table, eyeing the list that his father was making.

'Are you all right to do this now?' his father asked.

'Yes,' Gareth said. 'Let's just get on with it.'

'Well, we've already discussed most of the basics. Perhaps you'd like Mum to see to the catering?' he said, lowering his spectacles to look over the top of them.

'Catering?' Gareth said.

His father gazed at him. 'It's the done thing, Gareth. People will want to pay their respects. You won't have to do anything. Your mother and I will see to it.'

'But you've already done so much. I can't ask you to do all that.'

'Nonsense.' His father nudged his spectacles back into place. 'So, where would you like to hold the wake? This place won't be big enough.'

'Not big enough? It's plenty big!'

'But you've got to allow for at least a hundred people.'

'A hundred?' Gareth said, puffing out his cheeks.

'Stop echoing everything I say.' He turned to look at Gareth's mother. 'Don't suppose you want to cater for the entire town, do you? Probably best to order that sort of stuff in. Sausage rolls and what not.'

'Well,' she said, joining them at the table, 'you know who'd be the best person to ask?'

'Don't say—' Gareth said.

'Melissa.'

'No, Mum.'

She ignored him. 'We could hold the wake at the marina. I'm sure Melissa would—'

Gareth stood up abruptly. 'No! Definitely not the marina.'

She looked at him in surprise. 'Why not? Jenny paid for it, after all!'

'That's exactly why not,' he said. 'I'm not having people stomping around there, gossiping about the money and everything else.'

'What else would they be gossiping about?' his mother said.

Gareth glanced at his father. His father frowned at him in

warning. His mother didn't know about the kiss, nor about Jenny's will.

He sat back down, holding his head in his hands. 'Sorry, Mum. I'm an idiot.'

'No, you're not,' she said. 'You've just got a lot on your plate. It's too much.'

'Maybe you're right,' his father said, pushing the notepad away. 'This is all too much. This isn't what Gareth wants, and it isn't what the twins want either. You heard Max: he doesn't even want to go to the funeral.'

'He didn't mean that,' Gareth said.

'Even still, it was his first reaction. No one wants a fuss.'

'So, what are you suggesting?' Gareth's mother said.

'Let's do the wake here and limit numbers. We can cater it ourselves. What do you say?'

To Gareth's surprise, instead of answering, he began to cry, partly in relief, partly at the thought of his humble, decent parents making sandwiches and setting out chairs.

'I'm sorry,' he said. 'I'm a mess.'

'No, you're not,' his mother said, handing him a clean handkerchief. Gareth pressed it to his eyes; the cotton smelt faintly of peppermints. 'Don't be so hard on yourself.'

Gareth blew his nose, inhaled deeply, pulling himself back together.

'After this, Mum ... Dad ... ' he said, looking at them in turn, 'you must go home and get back on with your life.'

'Son ... ' his father said, placing his hand on top of Gareth's hand. 'You are our life.'

Gareth's bottom lip trembled. But he was rescued then from another emotional attack by the sound of the windows rattling, as a gust of wind howled, rain lashing against the panes.

He would never hear the wind howling again without thinking of that horrific journey around South Rocks.

Staring at the rain on the glass, he pictured the last time he had ever seen Jenny: a small helpless figure, swallowed up by the sea.

He had been going over the facts at night until the early hours, tossing and turning, thinking about what the police had told him and going over what he knew for sure. If someone had harmed her intentionally, then it had to have been one of the Silkies. And yet the very idea was ludicrous.

But in light of the solicitor's phone call earlier, it seemed that one of them was coming to the forefront more than the others.

Shuddering, he gazed at his mother's aged, innocent, kindly face, feeling guilty at what he was thinking – at the maggoty thoughts that were disturbing his nights, haunting his days.

He was truly starting to believe that Melissa might have done something insane.

Everyone else seemed to have their secrets.

Well, that was his.

25

Rachel sipped a glass of wine, holding herself very still in the armchair, limbs tense. She had been sitting like that for half an hour, deep in thought about Melissa. A week had gone by since their run-in outside the school and they hadn't spoken since. Such a thing was unprecedented for them – not only the argument, but the ensuing silence. It was too early to predict how much damage had been done to their relationship. For now, it was safe to say that things would be very strained between them were they to meet face to face, which Rachel had no intention of doing yet.

Melissa would be furious with her for going to the police, but Rachel had had her reasons, all of them good. She still cared about Melissa deeply, didn't wish her any harm. But the fact was that when you were in the ring, head to head, with pressure and high stakes, you fought whomever was opposite you, best friend or not.

That was an incredibly depressing thought. She took a long drink of wine, gazing at the shadows on the walls behind the boys. Both her sons were watching television on the sofa; Al was reading in the corner – a chunky thriller. She had noticed that he hadn't turned the page for a while, though.

Tucking her legs underneath her, she felt guilt standing behind her again, hovering. It had been there all week, tapping her on the shoulder, turning her head. She had managed to assuage it by repeatedly reminding herself that she had only told about the marina investment and the work emails. She hadn't mentioned what else had happened, because that would have looked too bad. But it was wriggling about inside of her, a secret that wanted to get out.

For now, she was keeping it under control. Self-restraint had never been an issue for her. Yet with the police all over town, asking questions, if they were to interview her more closely, she wasn't sure that she would be able to stay quiet.

The phone began to ring then, out in the hallway, none of the males acknowledging that fact. Only the elderly phoned the landline, was the boys' take on it. As for Al, he hadn't married Rachel so that he would have to answer the phone of an evening.

Her resentment towards him and her role as housemaid had grown stronger not only since the kiss but since the accident. Every time she had to pick up a used tissue or a dirty sock, it felt like a monumental thing to have to do. She was beginning to feel like one of the coin-pusher arcade games that her boys loved playing, the mechanism shifting backwards and forwards, with each small coin added to the pile nudging it closer to a huge fall-out.

'*I'll* answer it then,' she muttered, setting her glass down and stomping from the room.

It was cold in the hallway. She didn't put the light on. There was just enough light coming from the kitchen to see what she was doing and the darkness suited her mood.

She picked up the phone. It was Gareth. She sat down on the hallway chair. 'How's it going?' she asked him.

'Not brilliant.'

He would know everything by now: the kiss, the money. What would be going on in his mind?

She wished that she had brought her wine with her.

'How are you?' he asked.

It was nice of him to consider her. 'I'm all right.'

'Truthfully?'

She smiled sadly. 'Don't you worry about me. I'll be OK. Just concentrate on yourself and the twins.'

He paused. 'Well, the reason I'm calling is ... we can go ahead with the funeral.'

She had known that it was going to happen – of course it was going to happen. However, it had felt like a dim future prospect, forever out of reach, happening some other day but not yet.

'It's on Friday ... Rach, you there?'

'Yes,' she said. She couldn't sound horrified or even unenthusiastic. To do so would be deeply insensitive. 'This Friday? As in ... ?'

'The end of the week. Friday the fourth.'

'Oh, gosh. That's soon.'

'Yes, well, Dad already had everything on stand-by. The service will be at St John's, eleven o'clock. We're not doing a big wake – just keeping it low key, over at our place, close friends and family.'

Close friends ...

Her heart bounced uncomfortably. 'Have you invited Melissa?' she asked.

'Had to,' he replied. 'Jenny would have wanted me to.'

'But isn't it ... ?' She didn't finish the sentence, wasn't sure how to.

'Going to be difficult and awkward?' Gareth suggested. 'What with her taking money behind my back? Yeah, probably, Rachel. But no more difficult than facing Al.'

He was angry. He had every right to be.

She wished that she hadn't asked about Melissa. That was

stupid. Of course Melissa would be invited. To have excluded her would have been spiteful, which Gareth was incapable of being, not even now.

What had happened to her thinking before speaking?

'Look, you don't have to come for long,' he said. 'We just have to get through it as best we can. Believe you me, if I could get out of it, I would. But surely, we can all get together for half an hour over a bleedin' pork pie to remember Jen without killing each other, can't we?'

Was he joking?

It was sometimes hard to tell with him.

'Yes,' she said. 'We can do that, I'm sure.'

'Good. Then I'll see you Friday.'

He was hanging up. 'Gareth?' she said.

She thought she was too late, but then he spoke. 'Yep?'

'I . . . I'm sorry.'

'What about?'

My stupid husband.

Setting up the kayaking trip.

Not saving Jenny.

Telling the police about the money.

'Everything,' she said. 'All of it.'

He exhaled. 'It's all right, Rach,' he said. 'Sorry I lost my rag. I'm a bit of a mess, truth told.'

She welled up. 'You take care of yourself.'

'OK.' And this time he was gone.

She placed the phone back on to its charger and remained sitting in the dark.

Friday would be truly awful. The very public funeral followed by the very private wake.

She was making her way back to the lounge when something caught her foot and she plunged forward, landing on her elbow with a smack. 'Ow!' she called out in pain.

'Mum? Are you all right?'

The hallway light clicked on. Al and the boys were standing in the doorway, Joel with one eye still on the TV. 'What's going on?' Al said.

She stared at the object that had tripped her and which she was now lying on top of, as though to stop it from running away: Al's business suitcase.

Joel, sensing that nothing much was happening, disappeared back into the lounge. But Ned remained, watching them both. 'Are you OK, Mummy?' he asked, helping her up.

'Yes, Ned,' she said. 'I'm fine, thanks. I just tripped.' She ruffled his hair, kissed his cheek. 'Go back and enjoy your programme.'

He returned to the lounge, leaving her and Al standing across the way from each other, the silence heavy between them. Al had been noticeably quiet since appearing, not even moving to help her.

She knew why. The suitcase had been carefully placed in the shadows of the telephone table, safe in the knowledge that no one put the hallway light on of an evening and that the landline rarely rang.

'Are you going somewhere?' she asked.

He pulled the lounge door shut behind him. 'Let's not make a big deal out of this.'

'Out of what?'

He put his hands in his pockets. 'I'm moving out for a while.'

She stared at him. 'What?'

'I'm sorry, but I need to sort myself out. I'm not moving on from the accident. I can't think straight at work. And it doesn't help being here with you attacking me every five minutes about what I've done or haven't done. And—'

'Attacking you?' she said, incredulous.

'You're doing it now,' he said. 'When did you become so angry, Rachel?'

203

It was true; she was so angry, she couldn't form the words to tell him how much. Instead, she kicked the skirting board and wrung her hands. 'Arghhh!!'

'What the heck are you doing?' he said.

'You want to know why I'm angry?' she said. 'Maybe it's because you kissed my best friend. Or maybe it's because—'

'Enough about the kiss!' he said. 'This is exactly why I'm going. You can't keep doing this. You can't keep punishing me. I said sorry.'

'Did you?' she said. 'Because I don't think you did.'

'Oh, I did and you know it. And I thought you were OK with it.'

'Well, maybe I'm not. It may have escaped your notice, Al, but I'm a human being too. I have feelings. I'm not just here to serve you and clear up your mess. And at the end of the day, this *is* your mess. All of this happened because you kissed Jenny. Did you think for one minute how it would affect me? *Did* you?'

She was shouting at the top of her voice.

The lounge door had opened, and Joel and Ned were standing there. 'You kissed Jenny?' Joel said.

'Did you, Daddy?' Ned said.

Al turned to her. 'Now look what you've done,' he said.

Rachel stared at her sons in abhorrence and then at the suitcase on the floor. She thought of the moment in the arcade game when the balance tipped and the coins showered down.

This was it. She had finally had enough.

And this time, she wasn't going to clear up the fall-out.

'I'm sorry you had to hear that, boys,' she said. Then she turned to Al and spoke resignedly. 'Just do what you want, Al. You normally do.'

Ned began to cry. Rachel went to him, drawing him into her arms, holding him tightly. 'What's going on?' Joel said.

'I ... uh ... I'm sorry, boys,' Al said, 'but I'm moving out for a short while. It's not because I don't love you. I love you very—'

'Piss off, Dad. You're such a twat,' Joel said, disappearing up the stairs three at a time.

Rachel wanted to laugh at the surprise and outrage on Al's face. Yet he could hardly tell Joel off, given the circumstances. He had to take the insult.

'I'll sleep in the spare room tonight,' Al said.

'I think you should go now,' she said.

He blinked several times, mouth open.

'Saves us going through this again in the morning,' she added. 'It's not fair on the boys.'

'Will we see Daddy again?' Ned asked, twisting in her arms to look up at her. He still looked so little, only reaching her shoulders in height.

'Yes, of course. He's only going to ... ' She turned to Al. 'Where are you going?'

'The Royal Hotel, near work.'

She turned back to Ned. 'See? Not far at all.'

Ned nodded glumly. 'Do they have Wi-Fi?'

'Do they?' she asked Al.

'Yes,' Al said.

'Then we'll be fine,' Rachel said.

Al gazed at her for a moment. He was thinking about the accident, about Jenny, about the Silkies, about how close the six of them had been.

All this she could tell in a glance. That was how well she knew him.

And then he turned away, pulled up the suitcase handle, took his coat down from the rack, picked up his car keys and left. At the door, he paused. 'I'll give you a ring,' he said.

She didn't reply, simply closed the door behind him. Ned was watching the scene mournfully.

'Hot chocolate with cream and marshmallows?' she asked him.

'What, now?' Ned said.

'Yes. Why not?'

'Because Daddy's just gone. Aren't you sad?'

'I'm a mother, Ned,' she said firmly. 'This is what we do. We keep the world turning on its axis.' And she went into the kitchen to find the chocolate powder.

But the first thing she saw on opening the cupboard was Al's expensive coconut kefir probiotic drinks, fastidiously arranged as usual. And she broke down, sliding down the cupboard doors to the floor, where she hid her face and wept.

If she was responsible for turning the world on its axis, then it was just going to have to wait for five minutes.

26

Wednesday 13 August 1986

It was the middle of summer; the air was clotted with silence. Days like this were hard to fill, but somehow, they passed the time. Sometimes, they borrowed David's wooden dagger and pretended they were Injuns, rescuing Princess Hannah, who had been captured by pirates. Jenny always starting laughing and gave their position away, but Melissa was really good at creeping through the grass, surprising her baby sister.

David used to watch them from the porch. They let him join in from time to time, but usually he got too excited and wet himself or dived into the nettle patch. Normally, when it was Injuns, they told him to watch.

He was poorly that day and was lying on a camp bed in the lounge, where their mother could keep an eye on him. They had been in to see him several times. He had a bucket beside him and a towel on his pillow. He was a good patient, did whatever their mum told him to do. When they had last checked on him, he was asleep and Jenny said he looked like a cherub. *Melissa had never heard that word before.*

Jenny knew words like that. She also had a new silver necklace with an apple pendant the size of a small bouncy ball, which her parents had brought her back from New York. It's the Big Apple, Jenny had told her, and Melissa had nodded meaningfully, failing to see the connection.

They were sitting on the porch step, heads together, watching the apple pendant glinting in the sunshine. At their feet, sitting on her plastic rocking giraffe, was Hannah. She was dressed in yellow and was wearing a sunhat over her curls. Jenny always said that Hannah had peach-blonde hair, but it looked plain blonde to Melissa.

It was too hot to do very much. They didn't fancy the paddling pool; it was full of dead insects. Maybe Injuns would be all right, playing in the cool long grass. Neither of them could be bothered to get David's dagger out of the shed, so they made do with what they had.

Come on, *Melissa said, taking her little sister's hand and leading her to a suitable spot in the grass for a princess to hide in.* You wait there and then we'll come and rescue you.

Wednesday 2 May 2018

'Why are you yawning so much, Mummy?' Polly asked at breakfast, climbing on to Melissa's lap.

'I didn't sleep very well,' she said, rubbing her eyes.

She had been struggling to sleep since the police interview on Sunday, too on edge to settle. Despite Lee's assurances that the innocent had nothing to be afraid of, she was frightened that the detectives would be coming back for her. Every time a car passed by in the lane or the door knocker rattled in the wind, she jumped. In bed at night, she saw their sombre faces in the beige interview room, felt the cold air around her, saw the cassette tape slowly whirling round.

She couldn't face going through that again, although if she had to then she would have someone with her the next time. They had found decent legal representation, so far as they could tell: Sebastian Smith, an award-winning criminal defence lawyer. That was all that they could do for now, other than wait.

'Have you tried counting sheep?' Polly asked her.

'That doesn't work,' said Nina. 'It just makes you obsessive.'

'No, that's just you, Keener,' said Frank.

'Put a sock in it, butt face.'

'Come on, kids,' Lee said. 'Let's be nice, shall we? You'll find plenty of people out there in the world who'll bring you down. Our home should be a place away from all that. A safe haven. Isn't that right, Mummy?'

'Really? Safe haven?' Frank said, rolling his eyes.

'Yes,' Melissa said, yawning again. 'That's right.'

'Good,' Lee said, taking a drink of milk. 'So, who wants to tell me what they're up to today?'

'We're learning to do a pole dance,' Polly said cheerfully.

Lee nearly showered the milk across the table. 'You what?'

Frank was laughing. Melissa nudged him. 'Hush. Don't be mean.'

'What do you have to wear for that then, sis?' Frank said.

Polly folded her arms. 'PE kit, of *course*.'

'That's enough,' Melissa said. 'Do you mean a maypole dance, poppet?'

'Yes. That's what I said.'

'It's not precisely what you said,' Nina said into her bowl.

'That's it, I've had enough of you lot,' Lee said, rising from the table and dropping his glass into the washing-up bowl. 'I'm off to work.'

After the pole dance bungle, there was no more laughter. No one said very much as they shuffled about, gathering bags and lunch boxes, before going out into the early-morning light. Lee waved at them, before cycling down the driveway, turning out of sight.

There was a thin fog hanging over the shrubs, an eerie red tinge to the clouds. A large crow was standing on the lawn like a creepy omen, twitching its head watchfully.

Nina banged on the window from inside the car. 'Come on, Mum! We'll be late.'

Frank hadn't appeared yet. She would have to go back into the house and hurry him along.

In the hallway, Frank was talking on his phone while trying to put his coat on. 'Come on,' Melissa said. 'You're holding everyone up.'

On seeing her, he quickly turned away, murmuring a few words to end the call.

'Everything all right?' she said, ushering him to the front door.

'Yep.'

'Was that Olivia?'

'Uh huh.'

'How is she?'

'How do you think she is?' He was already out of the door, suddenly in a rush.

'Why are you being funny with me?' she called, locking the door.

'It's nothing.'

She ran after him, grabbing his arm before he climbed into the car.

He frowned at her. 'What?' he said.

She looked up at him. Not so long ago she had had to look down, crouching to wipe his milk moustache, to brush mud from his school trousers, to kiss him tenderly. No other relationship had to endure as much transition as mother and son. Who else did you first meet as a miniature, delicate being in your arms, only for them to rapidly outgrow you, becoming stronger, hairier?

'I just want to know that you're OK,' she said.

'I thought we were in a hurry.'

'We are.' Right on cue, Nina banged on the window again. 'We'll talk about this later,' Melissa said.

'No point,' he said gruffly, getting into the car.

On the journey to school, as Frank changed radio channel every two minutes, so Melissa's thoughts flitted about, trying to remember if there had been anything odd about Frank over the past few weeks. There was only one thing that stood out: the moment during the conversation with him in her bedroom when he had seemed cagey, evasive.

Yet, looking at him now, he seemed like the same old Frank – reluctant to go to sixth form, impatient with the songs on the radio, a bit of toothpaste on his chin. He was bound to be unsettled, given what Olivia was going through. Perhaps he was worried that her grief would be powerful enough to split them up.

Melissa would sit him down and talk to him tonight, whether he wanted her to or not.

Outside the school, Nina was already off in a blur of uniform, rucksack and hair, dipping her head in the window to kiss Melissa before running up the path and away.

Frank was slower, unbuckling lethargically. 'Laters,' he said.

'Wait,' Melissa said, leaning over to wipe the toothpaste from his face. He tutted then climbed out of the car. As he rounded the front of the car, she called to him. 'Where's my kiss?'

He stuck his head through the window. 'Love you,' she said, looking at him earnestly.

He held her gaze for an instant and she knew then that something was wrong. 'Frank ...' she said, but he was walking away, up the path, rucksack slung on one shoulder.

Maybe she shouldn't have let him go. What if he were in serious trouble? But were that the case, wouldn't he have told her? They were close, always had been. What he lacked in conversational skills, he made up for by being uncomplicated, easy to read.

And it had been there on his face: fear and upset, as though he needed help but couldn't ask for it.

A car beeped behind her; she glanced in her rear-view mirror. She was blocking the drop-off area. Waving an apology, she drove off, telling herself not to blow things out of proportion but to wait until the evening when she could talk to Frank properly. Preoccupied with the police inquiry, there was every chance that she was making more of this than was necessary.

⚓

Melissa sat at Rachel's desk in the Portakabin office, moving her phone round in a circle on the table top. When had they ever gone a week before without contact?

She wanted to speak to her but wasn't sure that she could do so without losing her temper. The last thing they needed was another bust-up. Yet she was keen to know why Rachel had told the police about the money, as well as showing them her private work emails.

Her guess was that Rachel – who had won several junior chess championships during the Eighties – had made a move in order to deflect the police's attention away from Al. In doing so, she had chosen her family over her friends. That much was plain and simple.

Yet why hadn't she been in touch to explain, or at least to enquire how Melissa was? She would realise, surely, that Melissa had been questioned by the police as a direct result of her actions? Since when, in their group of friends, was everything so hostile, so divisive?

She felt heated with anger now and was pushing the phone away, telling herself that there was no way that she was going to make the first move, that Rachel owed her an apology, when there was a sharp knocking on the door.

When they entered the office, the detectives looked different

212

somehow. It was their black trench coats, making them harder-looking, bigger. They were advancing towards her, coats flapping, the floor bouncing beneath their weight. Following them were two uniformed policemen. A blue light was flashing outside, hitting the glossy paintwork on the Portakabin door.

'What's happening?' Melissa said.

The four men surrounded her. One of the officers placed his hand heavily on her shoulder. 'Melissa Silk, I'm arresting you on suspicion of the murder of Jennifer Davies. You do not have to say anything—'

'Murder?' Melissa said. 'This is a mistake!'

Lee appeared then, hurrying into the room, hammer in hand. 'What do you think you're doing?' he said, staring at the detectives. 'You can't do this!' The police ignored him, were handcuffing her, ushering her towards the door.

She felt light-headed with fear. As she drew parallel with Lee, she began to cry. 'Lee!'

Outside, it was drizzling with rain. She wriggled underneath the policemen's grips, trying to twist around to look at the sergeant. 'Why are you doing this?' she said. 'Listen to me. You've got this all wrong!'

She began to pull on the officers' arms, sticking her feet into the gravel, but she barely halted their progress.

She was being pushed down into the back seat of the police car. She couldn't see Lee now, but called to him. 'Lee, do something!'

'Why are you doing this?' she heard him say.

'We have new information,' the sergeant told him.

'What information?'

The sergeant didn't answer that. 'Try to cooperate,' he said. 'It'll be a lot easier on everyone.' The door slammed shut then, muffling their voices.

The police car began to reverse. Melissa looked at Lee in

panic. He was shouting something to her through the closed window. She couldn't hear him.

The wheels were turning sharply on the sandy driveway. They were heading at speed out of the marina now, the detectives following behind them. Through the back window, she watched Lee growing smaller, her eyes hot with tears.

He was standing in the middle of the driveway with his hands to his head, the water still and calm beyond him.

'You can't do this,' she told the policemen. 'I haven't done anything wrong. You've got the wrong person.'

But they were too busy driving and speaking into their radios, getting on with their jobs, their bodies broad, authoritative. There was a strange smell in the car – musty, plastic, as though everything were new and untouched.

She was trembling all over. She was handcuffed, being taken alone in the back of a police car. She was cold, petrified, had no idea what lay ahead.

Of everything she had imagined during her sleepless nights of late, the reality was far worse.

She began to whimper, thinking of Frank, Nina and Polly, and of Lee standing there in the marina, distraught.

What was going to happen to her? How was she going to get out of this?

SUE ANDREWS

Senior Stylist, Mon Petit Hair, Milford, Dorset

Sue stifled a yawn. It was almost five o'clock and the salon had been desperately quiet all day. A few people had popped by to ask how things were going with the funeral preparations – like *she* knew – but no one was booking any appointments.

It didn't help that Gareth wasn't answering his phone. She didn't even know whether she still had a job. It sounded callous to be thinking about that, but she couldn't help but worry about the practicalities.

She was also concerned about the cash that was surely lying about the place. Jenny had been very blasé about money. It hadn't been unusual to find wads of notes stuffed inside envelopes or change for the till inside hair nets.

Before closing the salon for the day, she went out to Jenny's little office.

Sitting down at the desk, she felt as though she were snooping. On the desk top there was a photograph of the twins in school uniform, a hair band with blonde hair still entrapped within and a mug half full of coffee.

The mug was the worst. There was even a lipstick mark on its rim.

With a heavy heart, she opened the drawer. It was crammed full, so much so that it would barely budge to open. She poked about, between tights, mascara wands, hairclips, feeling for something that could be cash.

Right at the back, a plastic bag rustled. She pulled it out of the drawer. Peering inside the bag, she gave a gasp. Then she put it back, shoved the drawer to a close and sat gazing ahead of her in astonishment.

27

The cell was silent, but for the high-pitched ringing of panic in her ears. Everything in the small space was white and blue – blue bed, white walls. On the wall in stencilled text it said: *Would you damage your own home? Damage the cell = a charge and a court visit!*

Melissa was standing in the middle of the room, hugging her arms around her, when the door jangled open and in stepped a young man wearing a shiny suit, with the blackest hair she had ever seen.

'Sebastian Smith,' he said, extending his hand to her. 'From Coates and Carey, Portbridge. I'm your legal representation.'

She had been hoping that she would never have cause to meet him.

She shook his hand numbly. 'Melissa,' she said.

He smiled. 'It's OK. I know exactly who you are. Your husband just rang and asked me to get down here as soon as possible.' He glanced at his watch. 'Six minutes from when we hung up. Not bad, eh?'

She gazed at him, not sure what to make of him. He spoke very quickly, as though over-caffeinated.

He peered at her. 'Are you shivering . . . ? Be right back.' And he slipped out of the door and spoke to the custody manager who was hovering outside, an ID badge hanging around his thickset neck.

She sat down on the bed, wishing that she knew what time it was. Lee would have to pick the children up from school. What would he tell them about where she was?

Mummy's been arrested.

No, she didn't do it. Of course, she didn't do it. It's a terrible mistake. She'll be home again soon.

The young lawyer reappeared holding a scratchy-looking blanket which he draped over her shoulders. It felt as though she were being wrapped in hay. With him was the custody manager, who handed her a cup of tea before withdrawing, leaving the door open an inch.

'How long will I be here for?' she asked. 'I have three children.'

'It's impossible to say,' Sebastian said, standing opposite her with one leg up behind him, against the wall. 'But if you cooperate, it could be just a couple of hours.'

'And how do I do that?'

'Well, you do as you're told, answer their questions and don't cause any trouble. Does that sound achievable?'

'Yes,' she said, feeling very small, child-like all of a sudden.

'Don't get your hopes up, though.' He pushed away from the wall, squatted down before her, balancing on the tips of his feet; he didn't appear to be able to keep still. 'Nothing's definite in this game.'

It didn't feel like a game.

'Your husband told me that you've already been in for questioning without representation?'

'Yes. Is that bad?'

'Could be,' he said. 'Sometimes, they get people in on the pretext of it just being a chat. Was it something along those lines?'

'That sort of thing, yes,' she said.

'Have a drink,' he said. 'Your lips are blue.'

She looked down at the cup of tea that she was holding, as

though surprised to see it there. Slowly, she sipped the tea, barely noticing the taste. 'Do you think they tricked me?'

'Not a trick, per se,' he said. 'You went there voluntarily. But I'm guessing they were hoping you'd let your guard down and make a mistake.' He stood up again, tucking his shirt into his trousers more tightly. 'There's no such thing as chats in this business. They're looking for a conviction, not a BFF.'

She took another sip of tea. 'So, what happens now?'

'Well,' he said, straightening his tie with a jerk of his chin, 'I need to talk to them to ascertain the details about the allegations.'

'And then?'

He was already heading for the door. 'They'll allow us to talk in private first, and then they'll interview you.'

'Oh, God, no,' she said. 'I can't cope with another interview.'

'Well, what else were you expecting them to do?' he said. 'Of course they'll have to interview you. But I'll be there this time. Don't worry.' He smiled at her reassuringly and then departed. There was a dragging sound, followed by the clang of metal as the door closed behind him.

Alone, she panicked. She set her tea down and rocked back and forth. 'What am I going to do?' she said. 'How did this happen?'

She heard a small whirr then and became aware of the security camera set high above the door.

She couldn't rock and whimper. They could be watching her.

She picked up her tea, straightened the prickly blanket on her shoulders and told herself that whatever happened, she would hold it all together. She loved her family more than anything. She would hold it together for them.

⚓

Rachel was outside in the rain, rescuing the washing, when she heard the landline ringing indoors. She would let it go to answer message. Clenching a peg between her teeth, she ripped the clothes from the line, aware that if a neighbour were looking out of their window, they would see a feral woman wearing a wet T-shirt and no bra.

Indoors, holding the washing basket in her arms, she kicked the back door shut and plonked the laundry down on the counter, eyeing the red light on the answer machine.

She approached tentatively, clicking the message on.

Hello, Rachel. It's Lee. Call me back.

No 'please', no niceties, no 'how are you?'

She wondered what he wanted. She would return the call right away, rather than allow herself to speculate too outrageously.

But then the phone began to ring again.

'Hello?' she said, taking the cordless phone over to the window. She had left the rotary washing-line up. It was quivering in the wind, raindrops wobbling on its web of lines.

'Rachel? It's Lee. Where are you?'

'At home,' she said. 'You rang the landline.'

'Oh yeah.' He tutted to himself. 'I'm just around the corner. Can I stop by for a minute?'

She glanced down at her wet T-shirt and then at the basket of sopping laundry. 'OK.'

'I'm on my way.'

She put the phone down, then ran from the room and up the stairs to her bedroom, pulling off her damp clothes as she went. Outside, she could hear a car coming up the driveway already. Going to the window, she yanked a jumper over her head then watched Lee striding up the path.

She dashed downstairs, ran to the front door and then paused. What was she doing, tearing around the house?

This had to stop. The Silks weren't senior to her. She wasn't their subordinate.

She waited for the doorbell to ring. When it did, she stepped forward placidly, telling herself that there was nothing to be in a flap about.

'What were you thinking?' Lee said, before he was even through the door.

'About what?' she said.

He was wearing his trademark boat-yard checked shirt and jeans. There was a smudge of blue paint on his cheek and he was breathing quickly, his face drawn with worry.

'What's wrong?' she said.

He stared at her accusingly. 'Melissa's been arrested.'

'What?' she said. 'When?'

'This morning. I've hired the best solicitor I could find. But . . .' He trailed off, looking about him for something that evidently wasn't there. He looked back at her instead. 'I don't think there's anything else I can do.'

To her angst, he was welling up. 'If anything happens to her . . .' His voice was breaking. 'She's everything to me.'

'I know she is.' Rachel reached for his arm, touching his elbow gently. 'Come through here. Sit down.'

He followed her into the kitchen but remained standing, shifting his feet as though working up to saying something.

'Would you like a coffee?' she asked.

He shook his head. 'I want to know why you did this.'

'Me?' she said, taken aback. 'I just told the truth. I thought that was what Melissa wanted. She said that she didn't want us to withhold information, didn't she?'

'Don't get smart,' Lee said bitterly. 'It doesn't suit you.'

She fell quiet, stung by the comment. Turning her back to him, she began to pull the laundry out of the basket for want of something to do with her hands, sorting it into piles, her thoughts whirring.

It felt worse being out of favour with Lee than with any of the others. He had always been the non-judgemental one

221

whose good nature they could count on. At school, Gareth had made them laugh; Al's surface charms had been obvious. But Lee was the one they had all fancied – the skinny boy with a little dent in the end of his nose that announced that he wasn't perfect. So laid-back, it had been easy for them to mistake his friendliness for romantic interest.

Yet it had been obvious all along that he had only ever wanted Melissa, a fact that had merely elevated him all the more. For there, right before them, in their classroom, had stood the mythical one-woman man.

Holding a wet work shirt of Al's, she turned to look at Lee. 'Please don't blame me,' she said.

'You shouldn't have told the police about the money,' he said, his chin jutting angrily. 'You had no right to. It was confidential.'

'I'm sorry,' she said. 'I didn't mean to cause any harm, especially not to Melissa. You must know that.'

'But she could go to prison for murder, Rachel. That's how serious this is … I mean, what's got into you? Mel's been a good friend to you over the years.'

She put the shirt down. 'I was protecting my family. Joel's got his A levels and—'

Lee looked incredulous. 'This was about his A levels? Are you serious?'

She drew closer, stopping with a decent distance between them. 'It wasn't just that.'

'Then what?'

She hesitated. 'It was because I've got doubts.'

'About what?' he said.

'Melissa,' she said.

He looked stunned. He swallowed hard, then stepped towards her. For one moment, she thought he was going to strike her.

That was stupid, though. This was Lee.

'What does that mean?' he said.

She didn't break his gaze, looked him in the eye as she spoke. 'I think there's a slim possibility that she could be guilty. But it's a possibility, nonetheless.'

A silence fell.

She watched him. His chest was shifting up and down; there was sweat along his hairline. She was sorry to be doing this to him, but he was blinded by his love for Melissa. He had to see what might lie on the other side of his abject certainty of her innocence.

'Have you gone insane?' Lee said. 'This is Mel we're talking about. My wife.' He gestured with his thumb to his chest.

'I know,' she said, 'which is why you have to think about this, even if it's the worst thing in the world. She could have done it, Lee. You have to realise that.'

He shook his head. 'I can't believe what I'm hearing. Why would she have hurt Jenny? They were best friends.'

Rachel looked away, down at the floor. 'Because of Hannah,' she said. 'And because of the money. Think about it. She may have loved Jenny, but she loves you more. If Jenny had demanded the money back, as was her right, it would have ruined you.'

There was another silence. Lee was looking horrified. She touched his arm. 'I'm not doing this to cause trouble. You know me – I analyse everything, and it seems to me that if this really wasn't an accident, then someone must have done it and Melissa's the only one with a motive.'

'Motive?' Lee said in disgust, pulling his arm free and stepping backwards, away from her.

'Listen to me,' she said. 'She's been acting unhinged ever since Jenny died; even you have to admit that.'

'She's grieving!'

'But it's not just that. She was determined to tell everyone about the kiss, shifting the blame. Didn't you question that at all? Because I did.'

'That's because you're defending Al. How do I know that you're not just trying to shift the blame right back? Because that's how this looks to me.'

'Oh, come on. You know me better than that.'

'Do I?' Wrenching his car keys from his jeans pocket, he began to leave. 'I don't know what's happened to you, but I'm not staying here to listen to this.'

'Jenny's death,' she called after him. 'That's what happened to me. It was the worst day of my life. It was horrendous and I want answers. And if you were thinking straight, you'd realise that what I'm saying could be true ... Lee, wait!' She hurried after him. 'There's something else you don't know – something that happened before Jenny died.'

He was at the front door now. He rounded angrily on her. 'What, Rachel? What don't I know?'

She looked up at him. 'Jenny asked for the money back, about a week before she died.'

'So?' he said. 'I already know that.' He turned away again, pulling the door open in a gust of wind and rain, his hair standing on end.

'They argued,' she said. 'I heard them, at the marina. I didn't mean to pry but they were arguing right outside the office window. I heard Jenny saying that she wanted the money back and Melissa telling her that she couldn't have it.'

'That's *enough*!' Lee shouted, waving his arms and stamping his foot. 'If any of this is true, why haven't you said anything before now? Sounds like you're manipulating things, selecting which bits to say and when to say them.'

'That's not fair,' she said. 'Do you know how difficult this has been, keeping this to myself? I didn't say anything to the police or to anyone because it sounded too ...'

'Too what?' he said, scowling.

She lowered her eyes. 'Incriminating.'

This caught Lee's breath. He took a moment to gather himself. When he next spoke, his voice was steeped in self-control. 'If you breathe a word of this, I'll never forgive you.' He pointed at her. 'And if anything happens to Mel, I'll be holding you personally responsible.'

And he strode off down the path.

'Lee,' she called after him. 'Come back. *Please!*'

But he was already gone, starting the car, pulling away.

She stood there on the doorstep for some time, watching the rain falling heavily on to the potted plants, splattering on to the gravel.

All she had wanted him to do was entertain the possibility that Melissa could be guilty, for his own preservation. Yet all she had done in actuality was lose another friend.

28

'The allegation,' Sergeant Lloyd said, 'is that you premeditated the murder of Jennifer Davies, using a series of small actions intended to make her death look accidental.'

They were sitting in an interview room with a table between them. It was a different room from the previous one, but just as unappealing. There was a jug of water and four empty glasses on the table, and a tape recorder. Sebastian Smith sat beside her, rotating his pen between his fingers like a wonky wind turbine.

'You have full access to the kayaking academy, Melissa. You deleted the booking, so that it wasn't subject to the usual safety regulations. You knew that your friends would overrule your brother and take the boats out regardless. You also ensured that the systems weren't updated with the change in weather and—'

'And what,' Sebastian interjected, 'ordered the storm online?'

Constable Wilson smirked, folded his arms, but the sergeant showed no reaction and continued speaking. 'You unplugged Jennifer's kayak, knowing that the excess water would cause her to panic and tire. The only thing I don't know is how you got her to go around that dangerous corner. But I'm hoping you'll tell us that before the day is out.'

Sebastian put his hands in his pockets, setting his legs astride. 'Sounds like a lot of speculation to me,' he said. 'And how about that storm? How did my client know that it would come on that specific day, if she'd been planning this for weeks?'

'No one mentioned weeks,' Sergeant Lloyd said, setting his eyes on Sebastian as though taking him in for the first time. His expression very much said that the lawyer was speaking too much by speaking at all. 'It was all simple enough. It could have been thought of and carried out at the very last minute.'

'Even so, she's not Mystic Meg. How did she know that a storm was coming?'

'Apparently, that's easy enough to predict, if you know what to look for, which Melissa does. Before a storm, the normal wind patterns change. To her friends, it would have looked calm out there. But Melissa knew differently.'

Sebastian snorted a laugh, shook his head. 'You got proof of any of this?'

'We've now got a witness, placing Melissa at the academy the night before the incident.'

'What witness?' Sebastian said. 'And so what? It's her mother's place. She could have been dropping in teabags or laundry.'

'Hair oil,' Melissa murmured.

'Hair what?' Sebastian said.

'Oil. My mother's hair gets dry from the sea air. I order it for her specially and drop it—'

'Forget the hair oil,' Wilson said. 'No one cares about the hair oil. We care about the witness placing your car at the academy the night before your friend died. It gave you the perfect opportunity to tamper with the boat and the systems.'

'It wasn't night. It was four o'clock. And I had my children with me, after school. They'll testify that—'

'That what? Mummy's innocent?' Wilson rolled his eyes. 'At the end of the day, you've lied to us twice.'

Sebastian glanced at her.

'Lies look very bad in court,' Wilson added.

'You lied to us about the migraine, Melissa,' the sergeant said. 'And then about the marina's financial situation.'

She shifted in her chair, feeling a shiver of fear creeping up her spine. She reached for a glass of water.

'We checked out the accounts,' Wilson said. 'And we know your venue's not making any money.'

She held the glass to her lips, taking a sip before speaking. 'It's not losing money, though.'

Sebastian drew closer to her, his voice low. 'You don't have to say anything. I'd advise you not to.'

She nodded, set the glass back down.

'We also know,' Wilson continued, with a flash of his stubby little teeth, 'that in the contract between you and Jennifer it stated that she could ask for the money back at any time.'

'So, when she came to ask you for the money, you panicked,' the sergeant said. 'You told us that it was just a casual chat, but I'm willing to bet that it was more than that. Did you argue, Melissa? Did she get angry or upset with you?'

Sebastian turned towards her, whispering again for her not to answer.

'You were legally obliged to release the money,' the sergeant said. 'But you didn't have that sort of cash to give her, did you? It had all been absorbed into the business – into the venue that hadn't made any money to speak of.' He softened his tone. 'Add to that the tragic death of your sister, which Jennifer was blamed for in some quarters, and that's quite a motive.'

Sebastian was gazing at her. Most of what the sergeant had just said appeared to be news to him. He was shaking his head again.

'It'll be a lot easier on everyone if you talk to us, Melissa,' the sergeant said, 'no matter what Mr Smith is advising you to do.'

At that, Sebastian leant towards her, cupping his hand to her ear to whisper. 'They don't have any evidence. They're hoping to make you say something to allow them to charge you.' He broke off, moved away, before drawing close to her again. 'Say *no comment.*'

'Where were you on the afternoon of Saturday the twenty-first of April?' the sergeant asked. 'You've always maintained that you were at home with your husband after going to your daughter's netball match. Will your husband testify to that effect on the stand? Would he lie for you?'

'No comment,' Melissa said.

It felt obnoxious, obstructive, but Sebastian was nodding in approval and he was the only person in the room whom she was inclined to trust.

'How did you get Jennifer to go around South Rocks?'

'No comment,' she said again.

The sergeant sighed, pulled his hands away from the table, set them behind his head. 'Stop the tape,' he said to Wilson.

⚓

Melissa lay underneath the blanket, curled up on the bed. The custody manager had offered her a choice of ready meals, but she had told him that she wasn't hungry. Still, he had brought her what looked like lasagne with a tiny salad garnish on a tray, which she had left at the end of the bed, untouched. Every now and then, she caught a whiff of meat and it made her stomach churn unhappily. She kept thinking of Lee and the children, wondering where they were, what time it was, what they would be doing.

Sebastian had left hours ago and the station was eerily quiet. If it weren't for the occasional face at the small window of her door, checking up on her, she would have surmised that she was the only person still alive in her corner of the world.

It was possible that she would be kept here for twenty-four

hours, Sebastian had said. It could even be up to thirty-six hours, if someone senior authorised it. And maybe – because it was a serious offence – seventy-two, if the magistrates' court deemed it necessary, while the police sought evidence.

Were that to be the case – a prolonged detention, as Sebastian called it – she would miss the funeral. Yet the thought of missing it didn't seem to matter as much the longer she stayed here. Being in the blue and white cell had the effect of anaesthetising the mind, with the world outside becoming ever smaller and more remote.

Eventually, she grew heavy-eyed. There were no pillows. Her bed was a mattress with a padded headboard. She had been granted the blanket since she was so cold, but was to keep her arms outside of it and in full view of the door, which defeated the object.

The lights had been dimmed and the face looking through the window had transformed into someone else's, so she was guessing that the night shift had begun.

After what felt like several hours, she could no longer make out the face at the window when it peered in. Instead, there was bright torchlight beaming on to her and around the room.

She thought back to her conversation with Sebastian in the private room earlier, shortly before the interview with the detectives. He had been standing with his foot up on his chair, chewing on his pen, when he asked her the vital question. No one could hear. It was just the two of them.

Did you do it?

She had paused, distracted by the sudden recollection of her last ever conversation with Jenny. It had taken place over the phone, the day before the accident. The last thing she had said to her friend was: *Have fun out there.*

So she was thinking; and all the while Sebastian was gazing at her, eyebrows raised, waiting for her response.

No, she had said finally. *I didn't.*

He had simply nodded. He must have been used to hearing this. Did he ever believe any of them?

There was a movement at the window then and Melissa looked up to see the torch shining on her and around the room, before all fell still and dark again.

29

'You what? She's been arrested?' Gareth said, a little too loudly. His parents, in the middle of watching a whodunnit, paused the TV to listen in. He lowered his voice, took his phone out to the hallway, but his parents didn't resume watching the programme. It had gone very quiet in the lounge. 'On what grounds?'

'I'm not one hundred per cent sure,' Lee said. 'But she's been there since yesterday so they must have something on her. I'm worried sick.'

'You must be,' Gareth said. 'Why didn't you tell me sooner?'

He listened to the silence on the line; Lee wasn't going to respond. The answer was simple, as well as unspeakably awkward.

Because she's been arrested on suspicion of the murder of your wife.

There were also things that Gareth couldn't say. He couldn't tell Lee that he had begun to suspect Melissa the moment he had found out about Jenny's will.

'You'll get through this,' he said.

'I'm not so sure,' Lee said. 'I don't know where all this is headed. But I've got a really bad feeling about it. It's like they're

232

trapping her, stacking everything against her. I don't know if she's going to be able to get out of it.'

There was another pause as Lee sniffed. Was he crying? Gareth hoped not.

'Listen, it'll be all right,' Gareth said. 'You just hang on in there. And let me know what happens, and if I can help . . . '

He couldn't help, though, not only because he had too much to cope with already but because it would be too strange. Still, he felt for Lee, who was a good man – the best, really.

'I'll speak to you soon,' he said, hanging up quickly.

He stood gazing at the shoe rack – at Jenny's devilishly high cork heels.

If Melissa really had lost the plot and had caused Jenny's death, then she would have to pay for it, even if that meant bringing the Silkies – the whole marquee, with streamers, wine bottles, trestle tables – crashing down.

The party would be well and truly over. He would never speak to any of them ever again.

⚓

Three hours later, he was sitting in the reception of the Lighthouse Centre, trying to focus on the matter in hand: his daughter's mental health. Yet it was difficult to think of anything other than Melissa.

What evidence did the police have? Even given the apparent financial motive, they surely had to have something on her in order to make an arrest? Wasn't that how it worked?

And what were the police saying in essence – that she had murdered Jenny? Was that actually conceivable, despite his own personal fears? Hadn't the two of them been the very best of friends, incurably close?

He didn't know what to think. Even now, his father was down

the road at the police station in Portbridge, trying to get information about the arrest so that they could try to make sense of it.

Accidental death's one thing, his father had said grimly; *murder's another.*

Groaning, Gareth shook his head. The situation had taken a seriously nasty turn.

Olivia, sitting beside him, glanced his way, but didn't ask him what was wrong. Since Jenny's death, they were perpetually groaning, as memories nipped them. Grief was like putting your hand in a rock pool; you would wince at the cold water and then relax as your hand brushed against soft fronds and interesting corners, until something stung or pinched you and you recoiled, howling.

The door of the counsellor's room opened then and the red-haired lady appeared. She had kindly changed their Friday appointment to Thursday because of the funeral.

The funeral was tomorrow! He had barely had a chance to think about it, consumed as he was by speculation about Melissa.

What if she was released? Would she come to the funeral? Would Lee? And what about Frank? Would Olivia still want him there, as her boyfriend, if she knew that his mother had been arrested on suspicion of her mother's murder?

He was fairly sure that Olivia didn't know about Melissa yet. He would keep it that way as long as possible.

'Nice to see you again,' the counsellor said, approaching, embracing them with her huge smile. She turned to Olivia. 'Shall we?' And the two of them went off into the small room.

Gareth sat back down, drumming his hands on his knees, looking about him.

'Fancy a coffee this time?' the receptionist said.

'Please,' he said.

⚓

In the car going home, Olivia said very little as usual, other than that the session had been helpful. Yet the counsellor had taken him to one side again, insisting that Olivia was still holding out on them. She didn't think that it was about the self-harm; she was of the opinion that that had stopped. There wasn't time to discuss it further, however, for the lights were being turned out around them as they spoke. They had agreed to take it up at the next session.

Good luck with the funeral, she had said as she saw them out.

'Tomorrow's going to be very difficult,' Gareth said now, as they drove on to the lane leading to their house. 'I won't be expecting you to be sociable. Just do whatever makes it easier for you. OK? Also, I'm hoping to go back to work at the end of next week. How's that sound?'

He looked at Olivia, who was nodding her head. It wasn't in response to what he had just said, though, he realised: she was wearing tiny earphones. 'Hey,' he said. 'Did you hear any of that?'

Olivia pulled out one earpiece. 'What?'

'About tomorrow.'

'Yep.' She put the earpiece back in.

'Olivia, can you take that out a minute, please? I'd like to talk to you.'

With a long sigh, she pulled the earphones off, folded her arms.

'That's better,' he said, as they pulled into the driveway. She was already gathering her things, scrabbling to get away. 'Wait. Didn't I just say I wanted to talk to you?'

Why was it so difficult? Why, even before Jenny's death, had it been so difficult?

He felt exhausted then, looking at her angry face – irritated because he had dared to try to communicate. He considered giving up, letting her get out of the car and go. Yet the thought of doing so made him immeasurably sad.

'Olivia,' he said, 'if there was something wrong, you would tell me, wouldn't you?'

'Something other than my mother, like, drowning?' she said. 'And Auntie Mel being arrested for her murder?'

He gazed at her. 'Other than that, yes,' he said, trying to sound calm. 'I didn't realise you knew about that.'

'Frank told me.'

'It's a mess, isn't it?' he said. 'I'm struggling to get my head around it. But it doesn't affect anything between you and Frank, does it?'

'Well, *duh*,' she said argumentatively. 'It's nothing to do with him. He hasn't done anything wrong.'

'No, of course not. It's just that, well, if there was something else bothering you, then—'

'Back off, Dad,' she snapped. And she grabbed her bag and jumped out of the car, slamming the door behind her.

He watched her hurrying to the front door, practically falling over in her haste to get away from him. There was a hole in the back of her black tights. He would have to remember to throw them out.

She had no idea how much there was to do, to worry about, to fix, to ask, to notice. So much, and only one of him to do it all now.

Getting out of the car, he stood looking up at the twilight sky, watching a large arrow of birds passing by, as though showing him which way to run. Tomorrow was going to be a nightmare, no two ways about it.

He would take his own advice and do whatever it took to get through the day, which meant that he would need his hip flask. Feeling boosted by the prospect of this, he went to the garage in search of his golf bag.

It was cold in the garage, as though the last time the door had been opened it had been a cold winter's day and the season had remained, trapped within. There was a window at the back, beyond which he used to be able to see Jenny moving about in the kitchen. She had been a wonderful cook, chucking things together and seeing whether it worked; it always had.

He was reaching into his golf bag when he heard a noise out in the lane: a car pulling up close by. Then the sound of footsteps, heading his way.

It was a woman wearing some kind of fluffy mohair dress. It took him a moment to place her and then he had it. It was Sue, the woman who worked for Jenny.

'Evening,' he said. 'What can I do for you?'

'I'm sorry to trouble you right before the fune— . . . the funeral . . . But, well, you haven't been answering my calls and . . . ' She trailed off, looked down at the dusty floor.

'I don't know the first thing about running a salon. I need to sit down properly to look at it. If you can just bear with me, whilst I get sorted . . . '

'Of course,' she said.

'Your job will be safe, if that's what you're worried about,' he said.

'It's not,' she said. 'I'm not . . . ' She smiled nervously. 'Thank you. But there's something else I wanted to talk to you about actually.'

'Oh?'

'I had a look through some of Jenny's things at the salon to check for cash,' she said. 'She always used to leave money lying around, so I wanted to make sure that it was safe. And I was checking in her drawer yesterday, when . . . ' She reached into her handbag and pulled out a plastic bag, which she offered to him. 'I found this.'

He didn't take it from her. 'What is it?'

'I think you'd better look.'

He took the bag with a sinking feeling. Nothing good was going to be inside, it felt safe to say.

'I'm so sorry to bring this to you,' she said. 'But I've been worried sick. I didn't know whether the police should be told or—'

Gareth stared at the contents of the bag. And then he handed it back to her. 'Thanks for coming,' he said.

She held the bag in mid-air. 'But what do I do with it?'

'I don't really care,' he said. 'Put it back where you found it. Or shove it in the bin. It's nothing. Just forget all about it.'

'OK,' she said, not sounding OK in the slightest. 'I'll do that.'

'I'll see you then,' he said, hoping that she would turn around and walk away. Yet she didn't. She was standing there motionless in her fluffy dress with her over-made-up face, looking like one of the toilet-paper doily dolls his mother used to knit years ago.

'I hope tomorrow goes well,' she said at last.

'Thanks,' he said.

'I'll be off then,' she said. And she walked out of the garage, holding the plastic bag at arm's length as though it contained a soiled nappy or worse.

He listened to the sound of her car pulling away and then he reached into the side panel of the golf bag, pulled out the hip flask, sat down on a crate and took a long drink, telling himself to focus purely on getting through tomorrow.

30

Friday 4 May 2018

There was a noise outside in the corridor. Melissa raised her head from the mattress to listen. There came the clunking sound of the door being unlocked and then two men were standing in the doorway in a halo of light: the custody manager and Sebastian Smith.

She sat up, the blanket draped around her shoulders, her head fuzzy. Sebastian came towards her, squatting on his hind legs to talk to her. 'How you doing?'

'OK,' she said.

'Manage to get any sleep?'

'Not really.'

'Hopefully my news will cheer you up then.'

She looked at him, taking in the smoothness of his young skin, the brightness of his eyes.

'You can go home.'

'Why?' she said.

'Why?' he said, surprised. 'Because they've not been able to gather the evidence that they need. They're going to have to let the Crown Prosecution Service decide whether or not to charge you.'

239

'So they could still charge me and bring me back here?'

'Well, possibly, yes.'

'Thought so,' she said, her shoulders slumping.

'But the fact that they haven't found any evidence so far gives us reason to be hopeful.' He smiled. 'It's certainly not a done deal. So, let's get you out of here. Your husband's waiting outside.'

The thought of Lee made her summon the energy to stand up. She glanced down at herself, taking in her crumpled clothes. Smoothing her hair with her hands, she took one last look at the blue and white cell before walking out.

⚓

Lee was waiting for her by the front desk in the lobby.

She sensed the change in him right away. Maybe it was because in all the years she had known him, he had only ever looked at her with admiration and love. Even when irritated by her, the love had still been there somewhere – in the turn of his mouth, in the patient tone of his voice.

But now, something else was on his face, making his gait uncommonly taut. She didn't have time to determine what it was for she was too taken with the soothing scent of his freshly laundered shirt, the bristles on his chin prickling her cheek as he kissed her. 'Come on,' he said. 'Let's not hang around here.'

They were just about to go through the main entrance when Sebastian caught up with them. 'Mr Silk, could I have a word?'

The two men walked a few paces away, stopping near the row of empty chairs. Melissa remained where she was, staring at a noticeboard, not taking in any of the information. She could hear snippets of the men's conversation. *Crown Prosecution . . . Ordeal . . . Remain positive.*

They were coming back towards her now. Before departing,

Sebastian shook their hands, assuring them that he would be in touch very soon.

'What did he say?' she asked as they made their way to the car.

'That he thinks things are beginning to go our way.'

'What does that mean?'

'That he's hoping the case will be dropped due to lack of evidence.'

'Oh,' she said. She couldn't think of anything else to say.

Inside the car, everything smelt familiar, yet different. So tired, her senses felt heightened as well as deadened, with noises sounding sharper, more intense. She stared out of the window at the countryside, barely registering the passing scenes.

Was it possible that she had imagined the change in Lee just now? Perhaps he was merely feeling the strain. The last few days would have been impossible for him too.

'Where are the children?' she asked.

'In school,' Lee replied. 'Well, the girls are, at least.'

'What about Frank?'

'He's going to the funeral. He wants to be there for Olivia. You know that's today, right?'

'Yes,' she said. 'So, the girls aren't going?'

'No. They were too upset about you. I thought it best to keep them in their usual routine.'

'And what have you told them about me?'

He glanced at her. 'What do you think I told them? That it's a mistake and that things will get back to normal soon. What else could I say?'

'I don't know,' she said, gazing out of the window again. 'What time is the funeral?'

'Eleven. You're not seriously thinking of going?'

She looked at the dashboard clock; it was just past ten. 'I'm not sure.'

'You shouldn't even be considering it,' he said. 'Not after what you've just been through.'

'I feel like I should make the effort, though.'

'For who?'

'Jenny.'

'But you do realise that the whole town will be there?'

'So?'

'So, they'll stare at you! Everyone knows what's happened, Mel. It's not worth it.'

'Let them stare.' She folded her arms. 'I've got nothing to hide.'

'But it's not just you that you need to think about. There's Gareth too. He might not want you there.'

She felt her cheeks flush. 'Why not?'

'Do I have to spell this out? You've just been arrested for Jenny's murder. Rumours are flying around. No one knows what to think.'

Something in the way he said this made her heart begin to thump. She turned in her seat to look at him. 'What's happening?'

'What do you mean?' he said.

'You're different. Something's different. You've changed since I last saw you.'

'No I haven't,' he said. 'You're just tired and emotional.'

'I'm not emotional,' she said. 'I know what I'm seeing and what I'm feeling. Tell me, Lee. Stop the car.'

He kept on driving, his eyes on the road.

'I mean it,' she said, raising her voice. 'Pull over now!'

He stopped abruptly, pulling into a lay-by. Undoing her seat belt, she twisted in her seat to look at him face-on. 'What's going on?'

He didn't reply, but she could tell by the look on his face that she was right: there was a marked change in him. He was chewing his lip, running his finger around the steering wheel. Gone was the happy-go-lucky man; in his place was someone haggard, who held himself rigid in her presence.

'You can't even look at me, can you?' she said.

Again, no reply.

She felt sick. Her heart thumped even harder. 'I know what this is,' she said. 'You think I did it.'

She waited for him to scoff at this, to call her a fool, to laugh or shrug it off like the Lee she knew. But when he didn't say a word, she stared at him in alarm. 'You think I'm *guilty*,' she said.

He reacted then, snapping his seat belt off, turning to look at her. He hadn't shaved. His eyes were bloodshot, scared looking. The sunshine streaming in through the windscreen lit the stubble on his chin, highlighting its greyness.

'What do you expect?' he said. 'You told me that Jenny mentioned the money casually – that it was no big deal. But Rachel heard you arguing with her! She heard you, Mel!'

To her surprise, he clenched his hands into fists and hit the steering wheel. 'I trusted you, dammit!' he said. 'My whole life, I've never doubted you. Not once. And now, imagine how I feel . . . hearing that you've not only been lying to me, but that you . . . you . . .'

'That I what?' she shouted. 'Go on! Say it! Say I killed her. Say I killed Jenny. That's what you want to say. That's what everyone wants to say. So be a man, Lee. And say it!'

He looked at her angrily. 'No, *you* say it. You say it out loud, that you killed her. And then I'll know what to believe.'

She grappled with the handle, swinging the door open. 'I'm not staying here . . .' she said, and she climbed out of the car.

'Where do you think you're going?' Lee said. 'You can't get out here. We're in the middle of nowhere.'

She stood in the road, looking about her. She was wearing the thin shirt and jeans that she had been arrested in. The air was chillingly fresh. She wrapped her arms around her, wondering whether it was possible to walk home from here.

Lee was getting out of the car, rounding the bonnet to talk to her. She began to walk down the road in the direction of Milford.

Lee ran after her. 'Melissa!' He stood in front of her, blocking her way. 'Stop this. Don't be an idiot. Look at the state of you! You can't go running off. Get back in the car.'

She shook her head. 'I don't want to be with you. If you think I did this, if you think for one second that I killed Jenny . . .' She stared up at him. 'How could you? How could you think that?'

He crumpled then. All of the tightness and severity gave way and he was standing there again before her: Lee, with the dent on his nose and his kindly eyes. On his forehead, right in the middle, was a Superman curl that had got stuck with sweat and stress.

'This is crazy,' he said, reaching for her hand, pulling her towards him. She rested her head against his chest. She could hear his heart hammering. There wasn't a noise in the world around them, not that she could hear above the sound of his heart. The trees weren't rustling; there were no passing vehicles. They hadn't seen a soul since they had stopped the car. 'I love you, Mel,' he said. 'No matter what.'

No matter what . . . What did that mean?

No matter if you killed your best friend.

He pulled away from her then. 'Why did you lie about the argument?' he asked.

She looked down at the tarmac on the road that was gleaming in the sunshine, blindingly so in places. 'Because it really wasn't a big deal. We were always arguing, just jokingly. It didn't mean anything. We were like siblings, saying stuff to each other that no one else could get away with. You know that.'

He nodded. 'But then what?'

'Well, she died. And I couldn't say anything about it then because I knew how it would look. But you have to believe me. It happened the way I said it did.'

He gazed at her. What was he thinking? Did he believe her?

'Let's go home,' he said.

She followed him meekly back to the car.

They drove along in a silence for a short way, before she spoke again, just as they passed the welcome sign for Milford.

'I want to go to the funeral,' she said.

He glanced at her. 'I don't think that's such a good idea.'

'I disagree. If the whole town thinks I did this, then—'

'I didn't say that.'

'You didn't have to,' she said. 'It's obvious. I mean, if my own husband thinks I'm guilty—'

'I didn't say that either.'

'Yes, you did.'

'Come on,' he said. 'Let's not go there again. I think you should go home and lay low for a while.'

'Lay low? I'm not doing that. I'm not going to skulk around like some criminal.'

'Stop being so dramatic and just be sensible,' he snapped.

And just like that, angry, rigid Lee was back.

She wondered then whether her former husband was now gone – whether the man she had fallen in love with all those years ago had morphed into someone new, transformed by trauma and worry. Didn't that happen sometimes? Wasn't it why some people woke up with a head of white hair overnight, after sudden life-altering events?

She clenched her hands together, telling herself not to over-inflate things. So, Lee was stressed; he was bound to be. The effects wouldn't be irreversible, though. Not everything was so finite. As soon as her name was cleared and the case was dropped, things would slip back into place.

Wouldn't they?

'What is it that you want, Melissa?' he asked.

'I want you to believe in me again,' she replied. 'And I want to go and pay my respects to my best friend before I lose the chance for ever.'

'Well, I can give you one of those things,' he said.

He didn't have to clarify which one of them it was; she already knew which one it wouldn't – couldn't – be.

⚓

With only minutes to spare, she was feeling nauseous with nerves. Having managed to muster some toiletries together from the glove compartment, they pulled into a parking bay on the high street, fifty metres from the church, in a cloud of deodorant.

It was three minutes to eleven. Everyone else would already be inside. The high street was very still. The shops were closed as a mark of respect. Shutters were pulled down, lights out.

A thin cat was picking its way along the stone wall to the graveyard. Melissa watched it apprehensively. 'I don't think I can do this,' she said.

Lee was already out of the car, getting her pea jacket out of the boot. It would be cold in the church and although the coat was old, it was navy blue so would blend in.

She watched as he shook sand from the coat, before holding it out for her to step into. 'Please, Lee,' she said, as he stooped to button her up. Once again, she felt like a little child. 'I want to go home, just like you said. You were right.'

He shook his head. 'No, I wasn't. You said you wanted to be here for Jenny. So, let's do this. You're Melissa Silk. You don't run from anyone or anything. Right?'

'Right,' she said uncertainly.

It was only as she got to the church gate that she took in the fact that she was wearing her white beaten-down espadrilles. 'Look,' she said, pointing to her feet.

'That's OK,' he said. 'It doesn't matter ... Nothing matters now.'

As they passed through the gate and began the incline up the cracked paving stones, she tugged on his arm. 'I can't do this,' she said. 'Seriously.'

He stopped, looked down at her. 'Yes, you can.'

She shook her head. 'Not like this. Not if you don't believe in me. Not without my Lee.'

'What do you mean? I am your Lee. I'll always be your Lee.' And then he smiled at her, his dimples appearing. And, firmly, he took her hand and led her up the path to the church.

31

After much discussion, they had decided to let Joel and Ned have a normal day at school by not attending the funeral. Had Al been living at home with them, Rachel might not have come to this decision. As it was, she knew that the funeral would exacerbate the boys' misery, and that she alone would be there for them at home afterwards. She didn't feel strong enough to be their crash mat, not on this occasion. And so they had agreed to spare them the needless suffering. After all, Joel's first A level exam was in two weeks' time.

Was Al even aware of that? She hadn't reminded him, lest it should come across as a manipulative move to coerce him into coming home.

And so she found herself pulling up on to the high street on her own, dressed in a new black dress that was too tight on her tummy. She had been dreading the funeral all week, and here it was, minutes away.

She had arranged to meet Al at the opposite end of the high street from the church, outside the Lamb and Lion, in the hope that no one would see them arriving separately.

She sat waiting for him, feeling queasy. The air freshener was still swinging from the motion of the car. She grabbed it, held it still. Then she pulled down the sun visor to look in the mirror, hating what she saw within.

She tried to breathe deeply, but every time she attempted to do so, tears came. She was wearing waterproof mascara and had tissues aplenty, but didn't want to show up with a red nose and puffy eyes. How would she make it through an entire service, if she was already crying three hundred feet away from the church?

It was all such a wretched mess, at the heart of which lay the loss of her dear friend.

How was it possible that Jenny was gone? That was the most brutal side of grief, its finality. One minute someone was there, a vital part of your life, and the next they were gone . . . around the corner of South Rocks.

She pressed a tissue to the corner of her eyes.

Don't cry, not yet.

And what about seeing Melissa? What would they say to each other? There was a chance that she wouldn't be there. That was her only hope.

How cowardly, how contemptible, to be hoping that her friend was detained in a police cell – a cell that she had helped put her in in the first place.

A car pulled up alongside her: Al's black BMW. *You can do this*, she said to herself, before getting out of the car.

'Let's go,' Al said, offering her his arm.

As they walked the length of the high street, so they encountered more parking cars, more people in black heading for the church. Rachel didn't look at anyone, even though she knew them all. She didn't want to say one word more than she had to.

Going through the gates, they had to queue along the path behind the dozens of people awaiting entry.

Rachel squeezed Al's arm. In reply, he patted her hand.

As they passed through the doors, she looked about her, taken aback. The church was crammed full. Al was hesitating, unsure where to go. People were beginning to stand along the side walls. 'I don't want to stand, do you?' he said.

'No,' she said. 'But I don't think we have a choice.'

Someone was gesturing to them. It was the nosy woman from the school office, Gilly Green. She was mouthing something, flapping her order of service at them.

Now she was heading over to them. 'You're at the front, Rachel,' she said.

'Oh,' Rachel said. She hadn't wanted preferential treatment, had imagined slipping into a quiet seat at the back where they could pay their respects unobserved.

'Two pews are reserved for the Sil—Well, the Silkies, on the left-hand side.'

'Thank you,' Al said.

'Pleasure.' And Gilly slipped away.

'Come on then,' Al said. And they made their way to the front, hundreds of eyes tracking their progress.

Sure enough, the second pew, behind Gareth and his family, was empty. They sat down quickly, happy to be out of clear sight, shifting along to the end where the cold wall overshadowed them.

Rachel's hands were trembling. She gazed at the order of service, not taking in a word of it, telling herself not to start crying yet. The church was so full, she felt as though everyone was watching her, curious to see exactly what her grief would look like.

She wanted to motion to Gareth that they were here, behind him, in support of him, but didn't do so for fear that it would make him feel even more spotlighted. He looked very smart in a dark navy suit and was holding himself very still – the whole Davies family were, as though movement would upset their balance.

She looked past Al, at the empty space beside them. If she was spared, their pew would remain empty.

⚓

Gareth sat utterly still at the front of St John's, hands clasped between his knees, his heart pounding as though he were on death row. The more people that came in behind them, filling the church, the more his fear grew. There were voices all around them, low vibrating rumbles rising from the pews to the rafters. The last time he had been this nervous, he had been in this exact same place, he realised – on the day he had married Jenny. There seemed a ghastly symmetry to that and he felt light-headed, pulling at his tie as though it were restricting his air flow.

'It's all right, Dad,' Max said, sitting to his right. Max's face was as white as glue, his lips startlingly red by comparison. His colouring brought to mind the art projects the twins had created as infants – the ones that Jenny had plastered all over the fridge: bright primary colours, contrasts, clashing. What had happened to all that artwork? Would he one day open a case in the attic and there it would be? He hadn't asked Jenny what she had kept over the years. There were so many things he hadn't asked her.

'We can do this, Dad,' Max said, a line of sweat above his mouth.

Gareth turned to his left to look at Olivia. She was sitting with perfect posture, her mouth set determinedly. Her face had the same art-project colouring as Max's. For the first time in years, they looked like twins.

There had been a point that morning where it had looked as though Olivia wouldn't be able to make it. She had been sick with nerves and was refusing to go. It was Max who had thought – with sudden maturity – of how to persuade her otherwise. He had pulled their mum's dark pink coat down from its hook and had told Olivia to wear it. Somehow, it had worked.

Music began to play then and the congregation hushed

behind them. Olivia lost her poise, giving a little gasp and Gareth reached for her hand. Further along the pew, leaning forward to catch his eye, his mother gave him a crooked smile. His father was also looking at him, telling him that he was there for him, that Gareth could manage this, all of which he expressed in the most fleeting of glances.

And then Gareth looked straight ahead of him, clasping his children's hands tightly as though at the top of a rollercoaster about to descend.

Who had chosen this music?

Olivia. He glanced at her. She was looking fearfully at him. On his other side, Max was bouncing his knee up and down. They had all realised their mistake at the same time.

The music had felt like the right fit at the time, one that they had all agreed on. It was Jenny's favourite since childhood: 'Annie's Song' by John Denver.

But it felt like an awful misjudgement now. The song was horrendously sad, in the context of a funeral: full of tenderness, longing, poignancy.

Olivia dared to look behind them and now she was squirming in her seat, wriggling, not knowing what to do with herself.

And then it was upon them: oak, gold handles, flowers, six men in black.

Gareth lost control, pulling his hands away from the twins, covering his face.

Jenny was in the coffin. She was lying in that polished coffin and was being carried by strangers to the front of the church.

His wife was dead. She was gone. His beautiful wife was gone.

Olivia was grabbing at him, trying to bury her face in his jacket. Max was doing the same thing, tugging at him on the other side. Like babies again in that instant, they were wildly grasping for a bigger hand to help them.

He couldn't let them flounder. He placed his arms around

them, holding them as they wept, their tears tapping his trousers before disappearing.

The chords were fading, Denver's voice was fading.

The music had stopped.

Olivia was whispering something to him, her breath juddering. 'Daddy,' she was saying, her mouth touching his ear. 'I'm sorry.'

He didn't know what she was sorry for. He pulled his arms away from the twins and took his handkerchief from his pocket, wiping his eyes. The twins were copying him, drying their faces.

But the moment they all looked forward again, they were presented with the shiny coffin and its perfect frieze of flowers, and the tears began again, forcing them to cover their faces with the handkerchiefs that Grandma had supplied them with that morning.

Everything about death was thorough, meticulous, from the moment you stopped breathing to the high polish on the undertakers' shoes and the sheen on the coffin handles that they lifted. There were no grey areas, no smudges – no smear of a handprint on the coffin, or dark tinge of a wilting flower in the wreath. Death was dealt with deftly with gloved hands, from autopsy to inquest, from last breath to interment.

A silence had fallen. The vicar was making his way towards the pulpit, white robe flapping. Gareth wondered how to compose himself enough to listen to the sermon. Damp all over, his shirt felt cold on his back. Behind him, he could feel hundreds of faces breathing, waiting, watching.

⚓

Rachel couldn't bring herself to look at the coffin, but kept her eyes on Gareth, willing him to get through this, for his suffering to end.

Lifting her eyes upwards, she looked at the dark rafters on the white ceiling, remembering her friend's petrified face, her final plea.

She reached hurriedly into her bag for a tissue. Al placed his hand on her knee. He wasn't crying, was staring ahead of him, grinding his jaw bone. He could have been anywhere – queuing for petrol, chairing a meeting. Knowing him, he would be counting the alphabet backwards in his head. He hated emotional displays in public and would be doing all he could to prevent himself from doing so.

When the music finally stopped, she released her shoulders, wiped her eyes.

There was a hush. Rachel thought that it was because the vicar had moved into the pulpit, but it wasn't that. Something else was happening. Whispers were rippling from the back of the church to the front. People were shifting in their seats, turning to look with ghoulish curiosity.

She knew what it was then, who it was. She gazed ahead, her heart racing.

And then, at the end of their pew, undoing the latch to open the little door, stood Lee. And with him was Melissa.

He entered the pew before her, sitting down with a fair bit of space between himself and them. Al nodded stiffly in greeting, aware that the entire congregation was watching them.

Rachel tried to look at them out of the corner of her eye; Melissa looked thin, sharp featured.

Then Rachel looked away, ashamed for having wished for her friend to remain in police custody. Yet something else was bothering her and she found herself looking at Melissa again.

Lee was clasping Melissa's hand tightly, his chin lifted resolutely. It was a look that said that anyone who wanted to take issue with his wife would have to get past him first. It was a look that would ensure that no one would be taking issue at all.

Every now and then he whispered to Melissa, tucking her hair behind her ear, seemingly oblivious to their large audience.

Rachel felt herself crumble with envy, her heart withering. Lee could not have stood by his wife more convincingly or ardently.

And what did Rachel have? A husband who had walked out on her the moment things got tough.

As the vicar began to speak, Gareth seemed to be in trouble, floundering, looking about him. She watched him in consternation, wondering what she could do to help.

And then, just like that – while Rachel was stalling, weighing up what to do – Melissa shifted impulsively, instinctively, along the pew until she was behind Gareth and then in front of everyone, with no apparent regard for the appropriateness of the action or how it might be received, sat forward, laying both her hands upon one of Gareth's shoulders.

Gareth went still at Melissa's touch, as though her hands were holy, anointed with oil: the biblical laying on of hands.

Rachel could only look on in awe, just like she always had.

The Silkies were still very much in existence, still in operation, still there for each other. Even in the face of Melissa's arrest, she was still at the heart of the group.

It was Rachel who wasn't one of them any more.

32

The light outside the church seemed extraordinarily bright and the air warm when they emerged. Gareth stood gazing about him, loosening his tie. People were starting to make their way to the burial in the graveyard across the road. Gareth and his family, however, were lingering to one side of the doors, debating what to do.

There had already been some discussion last night around the dinner table about who was going to attend the burial. The twins weren't sure that they could handle it.

'Why couldn't she be cremated, Dad, like everyone else?' Olivia said, watching the mourners making their way out of the church and down the path.

'We've already been over this,' Gareth said. 'She wanted to be buried next to her parents, to honour their wishes. They pre-paid for a space for her beside them years ago.'

'But what about our wishes?' she said, squinting up at him.

'I know this isn't easy,' Gareth said. 'But it's what Mum wanted.'

'So, what are we deciding then?' his father said. 'Are we all going? We should make up our minds quickly.'

'I think perhaps the twins have had enough?' his mother said, putting her arm around Olivia.

Max kicked at the small wall marking the pathway. 'I'd like to go,' he said.

'To the burial or home?' Gareth asked.

'The burial.'

'Brave boy,' Gareth's father said.

Olivia didn't move. 'You don't have to do this, Livvie,' Gareth said, taking her hand. It felt so cold, small. 'If it's too much . . .'

Her face creased with indecision, a tear trickling down her face. 'I don't want to regret it if I don't go. But I don't know if I can, like, cope with it.' She gazed at Max, as though expecting him to decide for her. Max shrugged, however, still kicking the pathway.

'I know just how you feel,' Gareth said. 'Why don't you stick with me and we can get through it together?'

'That sounds like a good idea,' his mother said.

So, Gareth held his daughter's hand and led the way, taking his family across the road and into the graveyard.

The majority of onlookers were gathered at a polite distance from where the vicar was standing. Gareth saw in a glance that Melissa and Lee were amongst the crowd, as were Rachel and Al. He didn't know how he felt about any of them. A night's sleep hadn't brought him any clarity about Melissa. The fact that she had apparently been released and had felt it appropriate to lay her hands on him in church changed nothing.

She and the other Silkies were like a patch of gorse or nettles amongst the tombstones. There was no way that he was going near them today.

When the Davieses were gathered in place, in a line at the front again, underneath a yew tree, the vicar began to speak. There was no traffic today in Milford, no passing aeroplanes or birds. The earth felt still, watchful, as the coffin was lowered into the ground.

257

'Goodbye, Jen.'

Gareth hadn't meant to say it out loud. Olivia was distraught, burrowing her face into his chest. Beside him, holding his hand, Max was sobbing silently; Gareth pulled him closer, didn't let go of him.

Then his father stepped forward to throw soil on to the coffin, and his mother did too. Gareth hadn't been expecting this.

'I don't want to. Please, Dad,' Olivia was whispering, digging her heels into the grass, pulling him back. Gareth didn't want to shirk his duty, but nor would Olivia or Max let go of him. And so he had no choice but to step forward with the twins clinging on either side of him as he reached down to the soil, dropped a handful of it on to the coffin, and then recoiled, children in arms.

The vicar was praying. The mourners said an amen that ricocheted through the group.

And then it was over.

They waited for everyone to filter away, for they surely would. No one would disturb the five of them, standing there in the morning light, alongside the open grave.

When all was quiet, Gareth released his grip on the twins. 'Well done,' he said. 'Somehow, we did it, kids. I'm proud of you both.'

'And I'm proud of you,' his father said. 'Hopefully that's the hardest thing you're ever going to have to do ...' He patted him on the back. 'Come on, son. Let's go home.'

⚓

In the sanctuary of the upstairs bathroom, Gareth unscrewed the hip flask and took a long drink. The relief was immediate, immense. Sitting down on the edge of the bath, he took another swig.

The house was very quiet. It turned out that hosting a small crowd was just as difficult as a large one, if not more so, since there was no loud melee to be swallowed up by. Max had taken one look at the gathering and shot upstairs to his bedroom. Olivia was only sitting it out because of Frank.

Gareth had fled just minutes ago, as soon as Melissa and Lee had entered the lounge. It was cowardly of him, offensive even. Yet he hadn't expected them to come. Perhaps it was a statement of innocence on their part. He hoped that it was, for their sakes, but he still couldn't talk to them as though nothing had happened.

Whether Melissa was innocent or not, the police still strongly suspected that Jenny's death wasn't accidental. His father had told him as much after his visit to the station yesterday. The detectives were working round the clock, trying to gather evidence for what they deemed a potential murder investigation.

So, what did that mean? If he ruled out himself, and Melissa perhaps, that only left three other Silkies. Lee hadn't even been there at the time. So, who did that leave: Rachel and Al?

He took another long swig of whisky and shuddered.

Was he seriously going to start suspecting his closest friends of murder, one by one? Less than two weeks ago, in hospital, the day after Jenny had died, he could distinctly remember thinking that he wasn't going to be pointing the finger at anyone.

He had to stick to what he knew for sure, which wasn't very much.

Feeling exhausted, he reached into the bath to check that it was dry, before sitting down in it lengthways, one leg folded over the other. He took another drink from the flask, leant his head back against the wall and closed his eyes.

He would have fallen asleep like that had it not been for the sound of the doorbell ringing. Sitting up with a start, he rubbed his face, gathered his wits.

Woah! The floor rushed as he stood up. He put his hand against the wall to steady himself.

How much had he had? He shook the flask. It was empty. And on an empty stomach too.

Stashing the flask inside the bathroom cabinet, he splashed cold water on his face and cleaned his teeth. Then, after a slap of aftershave to mask the smell of alcohol, he made his way downstairs, telling himself that he owed it to his parents and to Olivia to show his face, since only sixteen-year-old boys were allowed to hide and sadly he was no longer one of those.

⚓

'I don't think I should go,' Al said.

'What? Why?' Rachel said, putting her sunglasses on. It was a calm day with barely a breeze, sunshine glaring on to the bonnets of their cars. Everyone had gone home, departing after the burial, a stream of grief spilling out into the town.

Al turned his mouth down. 'Gareth and I aren't exactly on the best of terms. He won't want to see me.'

'But you were invited. When he rang to invite us, he specifically said for you to come.'

Had he, though?

Looking back, she didn't think that he had.

'It might look rude if you don't go,' she added.

Al detested impropriety. She watched him waver, pursing his lips.

She pressed on. 'And I need you there. I can't go alone.'

She thought once more of Lee's steadfast protection of Melissa in full view of everyone, telling herself that if Al couldn't do this one thing for her then she would . . .

What would she do?

She looked away from him, at her feet.

'OK,' Al said. 'On one condition.' He pointed to the Lamb and Lion. 'We have a drink first. I hate funerals, especially this one.'

'But I'm driving,' she said.

'Just have a spritzer.'

'All right then.'

He smiled. 'Good.' And they went into the pub.

Inside, there was the strangely comforting smell of detergent and yesterday's beer. Rachel sat down at a corner table while Al went to the bar. She felt disquietingly emotionless. After all the build-up to the funeral and her tears during the service, by the time the burial had taken place she had begun to feel empty. It wasn't that her grief had run out, just that it didn't know what to do next.

Al returned, setting the drinks down, taking a sip of Guinness. 'That was bloody awful,' he said.

'It was always going to be,' she said.

'I felt for Gareth.'

'Yes.'

'I was surprised to see Melissa there, though. Has she been released?'

'Looks like it,' Rachel said.

'I wonder what'll happen now,' he said. 'Bit of a disaster all round, isn't it?'

'Yes. Especially us.'

'Don't have a go, Rachel. Not today.'

There was a silence as their mutual irritation hung in the air.

'The boys miss you,' she said.

He frowned at her. 'Look, I didn't come in here to fight.'

'I know,' she said. 'I was just ... talking.' She wanted to cry again then and tapped her pockets for a tissue.

'I'm sorry,' Al said. 'I didn't mean to upset you. We're all ... you know ...'

'I know,' she said, blowing her nose.

'Let's just talk about something nice.'

'OK,' she said.

They spent the rest of the time listening to the radio that was playing out in the kitchen while the staff set up for lunch.

⚓

She wished that they hadn't gone to the Lamb. Not only did they smell of pub, but they were the last to arrive.

The Davies' lounge wasn't exactly alive when Rachel and Al walked in, but any activity ceased the moment they appeared, as though the room were a snow globe in which the last flake had settled. No one seemed to have any intention of shaking things up.

Gareth's affable mum was the first to approach. 'Hello to you both,' she said. 'I didn't get a chance to speak to you earlier. It was all a bit of a blur.'

'Yes,' Rachel agreed. She felt the need to add something. Al was just standing there. 'The flowers were beautiful.'

'Weren't they?' Gareth's mum said. 'Well, come on in and make yourselves comfortable.'

Comfortable. That was one thing they wouldn't be.

They entered the room reticently. Lee was standing at the opposite end of the room with a cup of tea in one hand, his other hand around Melissa's waist.

Once more, Rachel admired Melissa's courage, showing up here, today of all days. No one but Melissa would have done so, although it took a close friend to notice that she was nothing like her usual self. Standing silently in the corner was a first for her.

Over by the patio doors, Gareth's father was talking to an elderly friend of his whom Rachel recognised from town. To her left, Frank and Olivia were sharing a beanbag. Dressed all in black, they looked like long shadows on the carpet.

The dining-room table was laden with food, which no one appeared to have touched. 'Coffee?' Rachel asked Al.

'Please,' he said, as though deeply grateful for the distraction. They moved towards the table, bumping into each other. It was only when they withdrew to the back wall, where they stood, sipping their coffee, that Rachel realised the obvious: Gareth was missing.

Perhaps he hadn't ever intended to attend and would remain upstairs. No one would have blamed him for not wanting to socialise. But Al might perceive it as a slight.

She glanced up at him. Sure enough, he appeared to have drawn the same conclusion and was shuffling his feet.

'I know about the tide table,' he whispered.

'What?' she whispered back.

'The tide table cock-up. The police told me. They let it slip earlier in the week. But I think they did it deliberately, to test my reaction.'

She glanced around the room. Melissa and Lee were looking their way. 'Don't bring this up now. We'll talk about it later.'

'That's why he's not here,' he hissed. 'He's holding me responsible. I told you I shouldn't have come.'

'That's not true,' she whispered. 'Today isn't about you. It's about Jenny.'

She tried to stand tall, despite wanting to hide in the gigantic plant pot beside her. Gareth's parents had been kind enough to set this up. The least they could do in return was be gracious. She would circle the room, pay her respects, and then they would leave.

'I'm going to say hello,' she said.

'Please yourself.'

'Come with me.'

'No,' he said. Then he leant in closer. 'Five minutes,' he whispered. 'I mean it. And then I'm off.'

She set her cup down and made her way over to Olivia and Frank. 'Hello,' she said, stopping before the beanbag, gripping her clutch bag for want of somewhere to put her hands.

Frank looked up at her; Olivia didn't. 'I can't tell you how sorry I am about your mum, Olivia.' Her voice sounded weedy. Her right knee was jerking; could they see that?

It was obvious that Olivia wasn't going to speak to her, for reasons that would be as unclear to her as to Rachel.

Disappointed, she was moving away, when she heard a voice behind her. 'Thank you, Auntie Rachel,' Olivia said.

Rachel turned back, smiled. 'If you ever need anything, just say.' But Olivia had already moved on and was looking down at her phone.

Rachel glanced around the room, wondering whether to soldier on or retreat to Al. Gareth's parents were locked in conversation with the old man. She looked at Al for support, but he was avoiding eye contact. Paying her respects suddenly felt like a reckless mission, standing alone in the middle of the room as she was, without cover.

She had no choice but to make for the Silks.

As soon as they got outside, she would kill Al.

'Hello, Rachel,' Lee said, giving her the most economical of kisses.

'Hello, Lee,' she said, kissing him back equally as meagrely.

She turned to Melissa and was surprised by how gaunt she looked close up. Even her freckles had been knocked from her face, whitewashed away. 'Mel . . . ' she said.

Melissa's movements were slow, with no hint of nervousness. She set her teacup down, then held her arms out to

Rachel for an embrace, as though there were no animosity between them.

Her shoulder blades felt delicately bony and her hair smelt strange – the same scent that a person acquired after coming in from the cold.

They pulled away from each other. Rachel was trying to make sense of what had just happened when Gareth's father approached her. 'Don't suppose I can interest you in a sausage roll?' he said.

'Yes please,' she said, setting her glasses straight, which had been nudged by Melissa's hair.

She wanted to think more about Melissa, perhaps even to talk to her more, but she was being led by the elbow to the buffet table. 'Those are chicken.' Mr Davies handed her a plate and began pointing to various dishes. 'And these here are veggie, so I believe . . . '

'They look delicious. Thank you.' She made a show of selecting two spring rolls and a cocktail sausage.

'Did you like the service?' Mr Davies asked.

How to answer that? No one liked funerals. Stalling, she looked over at Al, hoping that he would join her for food. But he was discreetly tapping his watch, signalling with a flick of his head towards the door that her time was up.

SUE ANDREWS

Senior Stylist, Mon Petit Hair, Milford, Dorset

Sue sat in the window of the salon, feeling the comforting warmth of the sun as it streamed through the pane, on to her face.

It had been a beautiful service. Mr Davies Senior had spoken the eulogy in his melodic Welsh accent, even making a few sweet jokes about Gareth and Jenny first meeting as tiny tots at infant school. The congregation had laughed – a muffled sort of laughter that had rumbled along the pews as though the wind were blowing through.

Sue had spent most of her time watching Melissa Silk, wondering what was going through that woman's mind at such a time. How the entire congregation hadn't gasped out loud when Melissa had put her hands on Gareth Davies' shoulder was anyone's guess. Sue had been gobsmacked. What a nerve!

It was this sort of thing that didn't do Melissa any favours. She was so cocky; it was as though she thought she was above the law. That's what most people were saying, and Sue was inclined to agree.

Like her friend Gilly had said after the service: you didn't get smoke without a fire. Why would the police have arrested Melissa if there wasn't anything in it?

That said, it wasn't a day for judgement, but for remembrance. It was a very sad day for all of Milford.

Shifting position, she looked down at her tote bag anxiously. She'd been meaning to do something about the plastic bag before now, but hadn't been sure what to do with it. Gareth had said to chuck it away and forget all about it.

She hadn't wanted to put it in the wheelie bin at home. What if the police found out about it?

She was being too dramatic. It wasn't a gun, for heaven's sake.

She pulled the plastic bag from her tote and went to the bin in the back area where they mixed bleach and tints. Dropping the bag into the bin, she grabbed a handful of disposable gloves and dumped them on top, together with the contents of the dustpan.

Then she washed her hands and returned to her spot in the window, where she picked up her mug of tea and shuddered.

That was a job well done.

No one would ever dig about in there and find the pregnancy test, not with all those cuttings of human hair on top.

33

'Well done,' Lee whispered into Melissa's hair. 'That couldn't have been easy.'

'It wasn't,' she whispered back, watching Rachel shuffling her way along the buffet table with Gareth's father.

'That was funny, what your brother said about fish,' Lee said.

'Hey?'

'What David said at the burial about everything dying, including fish.'

'Oh,' Melissa said vaguely. 'Yes . . .'

It had been slightly funny. David had said it very loudly. Their mother, holding on to his arm, had looked mortified. Everyone had wanted to laugh; some even did, discreetly, careful not to look as though they were laughing at David, especially at a funeral.

'We don't have to make conversation,' she told Lee. 'We can just stand here.'

He turned his back to the room to talk to her. 'Well, I'm sorry, but I'm finding this really uncomfortable,' he whispered. 'Why are we here again?'

'Because I'm not going into hiding. I'm making a point: that I'm still here for Gareth. Nothing's changed.'

He shook his head. 'You're wrong,' he said. 'Everything's changed.'

'Not for me, it hasn't. Just give me ten more minutes. It's rude to leave yet.'

'In the circumstances, I think you can leave whenever you want. Everyone knows what's happened.'

Mr and Mrs Davies certainly seemed fully up to speed. The elderly couple weren't being frosty – were far too charitable for that – but were watching her guardedly, with questioning eyes.

Lee nudged her. 'Look. Gareth's here,' he said.

So he was. Was it her imagination, or was he swaying? He was holding on to the side of the sofa, as though unable to let go.

'Is he drunk?' Lee whispered.

'Looks like it,' she said, glancing at Gareth's parents, who were preoccupied with hosting and hadn't noticed their son's arrival.

'Well, this'll be interesting,' Lee said.

Gareth was staggering over to Al. Melissa looked quickly at Rachel, who was still talking to Mr Davies at the buffet.

Gareth halted in front of Al, one arm stretched out against the wall, his head hanging forward to talk to him. It looked amicable at first.

And then in an instant it all changed.

Lee handed Melissa his cup as he rushed forward. Melissa didn't react as tea slopped on to her shirt, her eyes drawn to the scene ahead.

Gareth had hold of Al and was pinning him to the wall. 'Tell me! Tell me the truth, you bastard!'

Rachel dropped her plate and went running across the room to Al, skirting around the sofa. 'Stop it! *Stop* it!'

Gareth was lunging at Al's neck. 'That's enough!' Lee shouted, managing to pull them apart, then standing with his arms outstretched, hands pressed to Gareth and Al's chests.

Al was gasping for breath, holding his throat. 'You stupid idiot!'

Gareth was flailing about, punching the air, unable to reach his target. 'I know about the pregnancy test!' he was shouting. 'Was it yours? Tell me!'

'Take it easy, Gareth,' Lee was saying, still trying to keep one hand on Al. It was impossible to restrain them both. Gareth had broken free and was throwing himself at Al again, shoving him against the wall.

Al stared in abhorrence, winded.

'Stop it!' Rachel shouted, grabbing Gareth's jacket to try to wrench him away. Lee had hold of Rachel's waist, was trying to protect her from the punches, pulling her back.

'Leave him alone!' Rachel was screaming. 'What's wrong with you?'

'What's wrong with *me*?' Gareth shouted, stopping suddenly, eyes bulging. 'He screwed my wife!'

Al was trying to straighten his clothes, to muster some sort of dignity. 'I never touched her – not in that way. Jenny deserves better than this, you moron.'

Melissa winced, held her breath. She was still standing there, holding the two teacups, unable to move or react.

Gareth shook his head, incensed. 'You arrogant pompous bastard! You—'

'STOP IT!'

Through the chaos, a scream louder than all the others penetrated through and everyone turned to look.

It was Olivia.

Melissa set the teacups down with a clutter, unable to take her eyes away from the young girl who had commanded their attention and was now looking as though she regretted doing so – as though some estranged part of her had just shouted on her behalf.

Gareth looked stunned. He glanced about him, backing away slightly, as though taking in the wake for the first time:

the food, his parents' hard work, the guests in black who were staring at him in shock. 'Liv, I—'

'It wasn't Mum's test,' she said.

'What?'

'It was mine.'

The room seemed to shrink a little, as everyone inhaled at the same time.

'I was pregnant.'

Olivia remained in the middle of the room, looking painfully vulnerable, alone, covering her face with her hands. There was a swaying motion as everyone went to move to her rescue, but then didn't, for it wasn't clear whose job it was to do so any more.

It would have been her mother's job.

Melissa, only days before, wouldn't have hesitated to act for Jenny. But she no longer knew what her role was here. So she stood, watching, like everyone else.

'What the blazes ...?' said Mrs Davies breathlessly, stepping forward. 'Olivia ...'

'You what?' Gareth was saying, as though finally hearing.

Frank stood up then, his face ashen. 'What do you mean, you *were* pregnant?' he said.

His involvement changed everything for Melissa. She suddenly understood what was happening.

'Frank ...' she said, following him, placing her hand on his arm. 'Did you know about this?'

'Of course I did.' He flicked her off agitatedly. 'What did you mean?' he said to Olivia, more firmly. 'Tell me.'

Olivia gazed up at him. She looked so much younger than her years then. So did Frank. No one spoke; everyone waited.

'I lost it,' she said.

Frank's mouth fell open. 'When?'

'Last week.'

'And you didn't tell me?'

'I couldn't,' she said, beginning to cry. 'I didn't know how to.'

'Oh, Olivia,' Mrs Davies said, drawing her granddaughter into her arms. 'My poor child.'

Child.

They were children.

Everyone was looking at each other now, digesting the information.

'Should she see a doctor?' Mrs Davies was saying.

'I'm fine,' Olivia said. 'I don't need to. I was only a few weeks along. It wasn't . . . '

'You can't be fine.' Mrs Davies turned to address no one in particular, her face turning crimson with distress and concern. 'She can't be fine, can she?'

Frank had returned to the beanbag where he was sitting with his head in his hands. Melissa thought then of the moment outside of school two days ago when she had realised that something was troubling him.

She went to him, crouching down to address him privately. 'I'm sorry,' she said. 'I should have known, should have helped you. I know this must feel—'

'Leave me alone!' Frank shouted. And he pushed her away. Losing her balance, she fell backwards, hitting her bottom on the floor.

She could tell by the look on his face that he hadn't meant for that to happen. But even still, Lee looked furious. He quickly helped her to her feet. 'Don't you dare treat your mum like that,' Lee said angrily, but with control in his voice that wouldn't have been there had it not been for those watching them. 'Say sorry, now. It's been a tough week for—'

'I won't apologise,' Frank said. 'Because no one wanted it.'

'What are you talking about?' Melissa said.

'I knew this would happen,' Frank said, struggling to get up from the squishy beanbag, thrashing about in his angst. 'Jenny didn't want it – didn't want her own grandchild. And now it's gone.'

Frank was at his full height, glaring down at them both. He stood a head and shoulders taller than Lee. She had never seen him look like this – so riled and lost.

'I don't understand,' she said. 'Jenny knew about this?'

'Yes.'

'Oh, my goodness, Frank. Why didn't you tell me then?'

'What was the point? You'd have just taken her side, like you always did.'

'Come on,' she said. 'That's not fair.'

Lee tried to place a calming hand on his son's shoulder, but Frank batted him away.

'Let's not do this here, hey?' Lee said. 'Let's go home and talk about this.'

Mr Davies Senior said something then. They all turned to look at him. The old man looked drained, was walking unsteadily to the sofa where he sat down with some effort. 'I think it's best we call it a day,' he said.

'I'm sorry,' Gareth said then, stumbling towards the door, knocking into the frame. 'I knew I'd cock it up.'

They listened as there was a loud bump as he struggled up the stairs. After a few moments, a door slammed shut.

'We'll make a move,' Lee said to Gareth's parents. 'Thank you for your hospitality. I'm very sorry about all this . . .' He turned to Frank. 'You coming with us?'

Frank shook his head.

At the front door, there was a moment of awkwardness as they found themselves collecting their coats and shoes alongside Rachel and Al.

For an instant, Melissa imagined that they were kids again at Gareth's old childhood home, nudging each other and jostling for space as they left, trying not to wake up Mr Davies, who was sleeping upstairs after his night shift.

Shussshhh!!!

And then they were out of the door, walking away from each other.

No one even said bye.

34

'That was a nightmare,' Lee said, on the drive home.

Melissa kicked her shoes off. Her feet were aching. Everything felt sore, fragile.

'Poor Frank,' she said. 'And poor Olivia. They're just ...'

'Kids,' Lee said. 'Is she even legal?'

'Of course she is,' Melissa said. 'She's seventeen next month.'

'Even so. Did you know they were doing that?'

'Not really.'

He took his eyes off the road to look at her. 'Is that a yes or a no?'

'Neither,' she said. 'I had my suspicions. I mean, Frank's seventeen and they've been together for a while now. Bound to happen eventually. I drummed it into him to be careful and responsible. But I'll admit, I thought Jenny would have forbidden Olivia to do anything.'

'Forbidden?' Lee said. 'Like a chastity belt or something?'

'Don't be daft.'

'Then what?' He put the windscreen wipers on, spots of rain having just appeared. The wipers scraped mournfully back and forth.

'You know how she was about Olivia. She tolerated Frank

for our sake. But it was pretty obvious that she intended her for better things.'

'What's wrong with Frank?' Lee said. 'She could do a lot worse.'

'Don't take it personally. She just wanted Olivia to make the most of her life. I understood that.'

Lee slowed down to turn into their road. 'You and Jenny always were weird.'

She looked at him. 'Weird, how?'

'In your own little world.'

'You've never said so before.'

'Well, I'm saying so now. Besides, I'm not complaining. It's just the way it was.' He eased through the gates of their driveway, bringing the car to a halt in front of the garage doors.

'So, what happens now she's gone?' she asked. 'I'm in my own little world by myself?'

She looked about her, at the house and the garden. The crab apple trees seemed taller than she remembered them. The curtains in the children's rooms were closed, as were the kitchen blinds. Everything looked shut up, awaiting her return.

'No,' Lee said. 'You've got me and the kids. You can't escape us that easily, not even by getting arrested.'

She smiled, despite her low mood, appreciating his effort to lighten the tone.

He unlocked the front door and she stepped into the hallway, inhaling the scent of home: yesterday's sausages, Frank's muddy football boots, Nina's vanilla candles.

'Welcome home,' Lee said. 'I tried to get the place cleaned up, but you know how it is . . . '

'Don't worry,' she said. 'I'm just glad you were there to look after the kids.'

''Course I was,' he said, frowning. 'What else would I have been doing?' He dropped his keys on to the hallway dresser.

'Mel, what I said earlier about everything having changed . . . I didn't mean us.'

'Didn't you?' She gazed up at him, trying to read his expression.

How could he have thought that she was guilty, after all their years together? Prior to her arrest, they couldn't have been a closer couple.

Did he still think that she was capable of murder? Would he admit to it, even if that were the case?

She couldn't interrogate him, felt powerless to do anything about it. She could spend all night persuading him of her innocence, only for the police to knock on the door and take her back there again, maybe for good – away from her home, from her children, from Lee.

Sebastian Smith had admitted that it was a possibility.

'I meant that everything's changed between us and Gareth and Rachel,' Lee said. 'I'm not sure that things will ever be the same again.'

'Well, I'm fine with that,' she said.

'You're not. But give it time and see what happens. We need this bloody police investigation over and done with, that's for sure. No one's going to be offering us any olive branches with that hanging over us.'

They went into the kitchen, which was gloomy, the trapped smell of sausages strong.

'I don't have to get the girls for a couple of hours,' Lee said, putting the kettle on.

'I'll go with you.'

'No, you won't. You're staying here and resting.'

'But I don't want to be on my own.'

'You'll be fine.'

She pulled the blind up and stood watching the rain spotting the water in the bird bath. Polly's skipping rope was lying in the middle of the lawn, looking forlorn and forgotten. 'I can't tell you how much I missed you all,' she said.

'Likewise.' He set two mugs on the counter. 'The girls couldn't sleep. They said you'd never been away from them before.'

'I haven't,' she said sadly.

They sat down at the kitchen table. 'Poor Frank,' she said again.

'Poor Frank?' Lee said, dunking a biscuit in his tea. 'Sounds to me like he had a lucky escape.'

'It won't feel like that to him.'

'That's because it's only just happened. Once he's had a few days to think about it, he'll feel differently. He couldn't possibly have wanted a baby at his age. That's insane.'

'Maybe,' she replied. 'But we've always taught him to be responsible.'

'Yeah, well, looks like he wasn't on this occasion.'

'We don't know that,' she said. 'Accidents happen, even when you're careful.'

'I'm still furious about it, though,' he said, scowling. 'That whole thing back there was embarrassing.'

'More embarrassing than me being arrested and showing up to the funeral in jeans and espadrilles?'

'Well, when you put it like that ...' he said, dunking another biscuit.

That sat in silence, listening to the rain on the windows.

'They said that I tried to make her death look like an accident,' she said, looking at Lee. 'That's why there's been a lot of little things that didn't add up – strange coincidences and cock-ups.'

He pushed the packet of biscuits away. 'They're just trying to get a result, Mel.'

'But they said I did it for the money. They made out that the venue's going under.'

'Idiots,' he said.

'It was as though they'd already decided I'm guilty.' She broke off, frowned at him, her stomach dipping. 'What?'

He was looking at her with a funny expression.

This was it: he was going to ask her to tell him the absolute truth, here and now, just the two of them; just like Sebastian Smith had.

Did you do it?

'I don't know how to say this . . .' he began.

'Just say it,' she said. 'You're scaring me.'

'Well, we've had a few cancellations.'

'A few? How many?'

He grimaced. 'All of them.'

'What? Because of the arrest? I don't believe it!'

He shrugged. 'It's a small town. You know how it is. Things like this don't happen very often around here.'

She stood up abruptly, returned to the window. 'If they don't book with us, we really will go under.'

'The venue might, yes,' he said. 'But the marina won't.'

She turned to look at him. 'How can you be so calm about this?'

'Because it's only money. And we've got other things to worry about right now . . . Come and sit back down. Your tea's getting cold.'

She joined him again, sipping her tea. 'So, what does this mean?' she said. 'Everyone hates me?'

'Not everyone,' he said, patting her hand.

She gazed at his hand – chapped and weather-worn, his wedding band dull and discoloured from years of working out-doors. She longed then for things to go back to the way they had been only days before. She had taken his love for granted, ever since she was a teenager. What if it were no longer there or was distorted in some way, spoilt?

For now, she was going to have to make do with his little

hand pats and reassurances, all the while knowing that there was an invisible barrier between them that felt a lot like doubt.

⚓

After Lee had left to pick up the girls, Melissa was going upstairs to run the bath when the doorbell rang.

What if it was the police, already? She had barely got settled at home.

It could be Frank, though. He might not have taken his key earlier.

She hurried downstairs. Through the glass panel on the door, she could see the caller's outline.

It wasn't Frank.

She stopped, backed away, before realising that she would have been spotted.

She went ahead, opened the door, setting her face to as passive an expression as she could muster.

'Sergeant,' she said. 'Would you like to come in?'

'No, thanks,' he said. 'We're just passing.' He gestured with his thumb over his shoulder to the car. Constable Wilson was sitting in the front seat, the reflection of the crab apple trees dappling his skin like camouflage face paint. 'Thought you'd want to know that the case is being dropped.'

The way he said it – watching her very carefully – felt like a test of some sort.

She remained still, her hand on the door's edge. 'That's good news,' she said.

'Indeed.'

Nothing about his face looked celebratory.

'Just thought you should know,' he said. And he turned away.

That was it? Somehow, she sensed there was more.

Sure enough, he turned back, his bottom lip jutting out

speculatively. 'I've been doing this job a long time, Melissa. I know guilt when I see it.'

Her heart missed a beat. 'What do you mean by that?' she said. 'Why come here and tell me that the case is closed, and then say that?' She looked over at Wilson who was chewing gum, watching her intently.

'Because I don't like this,' the sergeant said. 'Not one bit.' He gazed at her, his brown eyes looking less soft at that moment. 'I know you're guilty of something, but I'm going to have to accept the fact that I'll never know the whole story.'

She stared at him, unable to think of a response.

'I thought you were the key to this very odd case,' he said. 'Maybe I was wrong. Either way, we've drawn a blank.'

'So, that's it then?' she said.

'Pretty much.'

'Do you still think it wasn't an accident?'

'I've always thought that,' he said.

'Then why not keep looking?'

He smiled, jingling the change in his trouser pocket. 'If only it were that easy. We don't have the time or the resources to ponder cases that may or may not be criminal. It doesn't work like that, not any more.'

He seemed miserable. Maybe this was what it was like when a case was left dangling.

'Goodbye, Melissa.'

She watched him walk away, sensing that this was going to be the last time she would ever see him, knowing that all possibility of uncovering the truth about Jenny was leaving with him.

He got into the car and reversed, all the while with Wilson chewing, still watching her.

35

'Mum?'

Melissa opened her eyes. For a moment she thought that she was still under arrest and expected to see blue and white around her and feel the scratchy blanket on her skin.

She put her hand to her head; her hair was wet. She was wrapped in her dressing gown, her skin imprinted with its fluffy towelling. Everything felt damp and achy. She had fallen asleep on the bed after her bath.

'Mummy, are you awake?' Nina and Polly appeared in the bedroom doorway.

Melissa sat up, reached out to them. 'Come here.'

Polly hurtled forward, jumping on to the bed, the mattress bouncing. 'You're back, Mummy! You're back!'

They hugged, Polly smelling of strawberry shampoo and wearing sparkly nightwear. 'You're ready for bed?' Melissa said. 'What time is it?'

'Eight thirty,' Polly said.

'Gosh. I must have been out for the count. Is Frank home?'

'Don't think so,' Nina said, sitting down cross-legged on Melissa's other side. 'Dad said to let you sleep. We wanted to see you, though ... Is that all right?'

'Of course,' Melissa said, smiling at Nina. 'I've missed you so much.' She ran her hand over Nina's hair. 'My beautiful girl. You look prettier than ever.'

Nina sucked her teeth brace bashfully. 'It's only been a few days, Mum.'

'Well, it felt longer. So, tell me what I missed. How's school?'

Nina's eyes darted down to the duvet cover. She began to trace her finger along the floral pattern. 'Not too bad,' she said.

'Are you in trouble, Mummy?' Polly asked.

'No, poppet. At least, I hope not. The police wanted to find out more about how Auntie Jenny died, so they asked me lots of questions, which was why they kept me there. I'm sorry I was away but it won't happen again, I promise you.'

'It wasn't your fault, Mum,' Nina said.

'Charlotte Wilson said you've lost your marbles,' Polly said. 'Your hair's wet, Mummy.'

'Don't tell her that,' Nina said.

'But it *is* wet.'

Nina tutted. 'I meant about Charlotte.'

'But that's what she said,' Polly said, folding her arms and trying to look authoritative in pyjamas that said *Fairies are real*. 'Charlotte said that her mum said it's because of the tragedy.' She set her long-lashed eyes on Melissa. 'What tragedy, Mummy?'

'Well, I . . .'

'You don't have to tell us, Mum,' Nina said, shooting Polly a look. 'Not if you don't want to.'

'I'd rather not at the moment,' she said. 'I'm very tired.'

''Course you are,' Nina said, looking darkly at Polly again. 'Dad said not to say anything to upset you.'

'It's fine,' Melissa said. 'That's what I'm here for. So, what else happened this week?'

Nina looked away, tracing the duvet's pattern with her finger again.

283

'Have you been having trouble at school?' Melissa asked.

Nina shrugged.

'Come on, Nina, sweetie,' Melissa said. 'Tell me what's going on.'

'It's nothing. Just Esme and Eva saying stuff.'

'Like what?'

'They keep whispering and when I go up to them, they stop talking and laugh. And they won't sit by me at lunch or be on my team in PE.'

'That's pathetic,' Melissa said. 'I thought they were supposed to be your friends?'

'It's OK,' Nina said. 'I can handle it.'

'But you shouldn't have to,' Melissa said. 'I'm sorry. It's all because of me.'

'No, it's not,' Nina said. 'We know you haven't done anything wrong.'

'Yes, Mummy,' Polly said, beginning to braid Melissa's hair. 'You're innocent, no matter what Brody in year three says.'

The door opened and Lee came in. 'Frank just rang,' he said. 'He's still at Gareth's. I'll pop over and fetch him.'

'Oh, good,' Melissa said. 'I was worrying about him.'

'Well, now you don't have to.'

Her eyes and head felt suddenly heavy. She shifted further down the bed, underneath the sheets. 'Shall I come with you?' she asked.

'Don't be silly,' Lee replied. 'Go to sleep.'

'Can we sleep with Mummy?' Polly said, turning to look at Lee with Melissa's plaited hair still in her hands, tugging her head.

'No, Pols,' Lee said. 'Let your mum rest. She's shattered.'

'It's fine,' Melissa said, yawning.

Nina knelt up, pressing her hands together. 'Can I sleep here too?'

'Fine by me,' Melissa said.

'Yay!' Polly shouted, tugging Melissa's hair again.

'I'll see you all in the morning. Don't even think about getting up to speak to Frank, Mel,' he said. Then he bent over them, pressing kisses on to their cheeks.

'Have you cleaned your teeth?' Melissa murmured, shutting her eyes.

The last thing she knew, Lee was closing the door and her daughters were lying next to her, their breathing sweet and light, their bodies warm and comforting.

Home.

Saturday 5 May 2018

When she woke, she was aware of something pressing on her, tickling her nose. She opened her eyes. It was daylight. The relief she felt at having made it through the night, at having put yesterday behind her, with the case now closed, was profound. She allowed herself a moment's joy and then turned her attention to Nina, the reason for the tickling sensation. Nina was sprawling over her, hair everywhere.

Quietly, she slipped out of bed. Stepping into her slippers, she was sneaking out of the room, when she heard a voice behind her and a rustle of bedding.

'Mummy?'

'Shush,' Melissa whispered. 'Nina's still asleep.'

Polly was sitting upright, needing no time to go from unconscious to alert. 'Mummy?' she said again, her voice rasping. She wasn't a very good whisperer yet.

'Yes?'

'Who's Hannah?'

Melissa gave a little start.

'No one. Why?'

'You were talking about her last night,' Polly said.

'I must have been dreaming.'

Polly lay back down. 'Like Scarlett.'

'Scarlett?'

'In my class. She's always dreaming about seahorses and—'

'Shuddup,' Nina said, rolling on to her other side.

36

At eight o'clock, Gareth stepped sheepishly into the kitchen. It could easily have been thirty years ago, the morning after he had been caught drunkenly peeing in the daffodil pots, or further back to when he had misfired a catapult, sending a rock through the lounge window.

He hovered behind his mother, who was frying eggs at the stove. He listened to the soothing sound of the eggs spluttering and sizzling. Max was sitting at the table, playing cards opposite Grandpa, who was reading the paper. 'Morning all,' Gareth said.

'Morning, Dad,' Max said.

'Sleep all right?'

'Not too bad.'

'Peckish?' his mother asked.

'A bit,' Gareth said.

'You've been asleep a long time.'

'Comatose, more like,' his father said, then folded his paper up and tossed it on to the table. 'A word, please, Gareth.'

'Perhaps you could keep the eggs warm, Mum …' Gareth said, following his father out of the room.

In the hallway, his father took off his glasses, pressed the corners of his eyes. 'I realise how difficult all this must be for you …'

Gareth hung his head. 'I'm sorry, Dad. I don't know how it

happened. I think it was because I hadn't eaten. It just took my legs away – the burial and then what with everything going on with Melissa . . . '

'It's all right,' his father said. 'Don't apologise. At least, not to me. Maybe you could have a word with your mother, though. She's rather upset about everything.' He frowned. 'Did you know that boy was sleeping with Olivia?'

'No,' Gareth said. 'But then he's Melissa's son. Until recently, we were all close. It felt . . . innocent.'

'Talking of innocence . . . ' His father narrowed his eyes, as though trying to predict Gareth's reaction to what he was about to say. 'I rang the police for an update and they informed me that the case is closed.'

'They didn't have anything on Melissa?' Gareth said.

His father shook his head. 'Not enough to charge her, no.'

'Then who . . . ?' Gareth began.

His father placed his hand on his shoulder. 'No one did. They warned me that it's more than likely going to be put down to an accident. After all that hullabaloo . . . ' He smiled regrettably. 'We've come full circle.'

Gareth contemplated his father's words. It didn't feel like a circle. He wouldn't be picking up where he had left off with the Silkies. Too much had changed.

'What if it was Mel and she got away with it?' he said.

'You won't be the only one thinking that, I can assure you. If she's innocent, then I feel very sorry for her. But if she's guilty, then having this hanging over her for the rest of her life will be a punishment in itself. Look what she's lost: her friends and the good opinion of everyone.'

'I suppose,' Gareth said.

It felt deeply unsatisfactory, though. He would have been all right had they concluded that it was an accident right at the beginning, given that he had been inclined to believe that

288

himself. But why put him through all this turmoil, convincing him otherwise to the extent that he had begun to doubt even his own shadow, just for them to end up back where they had started?

His father interrupted his thoughts with a deep yawn, prompting Gareth to realise that he wasn't the only person who had suffered with recent events. His father was looking frail, depleted, on his way to an earlier grave if something didn't change.

'Dad,' he said gently, 'I think you and Mum should go on home now. It's unfair to expect you to keep your lives on hold any longer. You've done more than enough.'

His father raised his eyebrows. 'And leave you here to cope alone? I don't think so. Poor Olivia was nearly a teenage mother, for Pete's sake.'

'But she isn't ... We're OK, Dad. Really.'

'We're not leaving, son.' His father put his glasses back on, signalling the end of the matter. 'Not until you're settled. And that's final.'

Gareth knew from experience that there was no use arguing with the man.

'Now, if you just go and say sorry to your mother, we can forget all about it.'

'A verbal apology?'

'Of course,' his father said. 'What else?'

'Nothing, Dad. Just fooling.'

At least it wasn't a written apology, like after the daffodil pot debacle.

⚓

'Liv?' He tapped on the door. There was no noise within. He tried the handle; it was locked. 'Olivia? Are you in there? Just answer, please.'

He pressed his ear against the door. He couldn't hear a thing.

He went back downstairs. His father was in the study, doing paperwork for the inquest. 'Have you seen Olivia?' Gareth asked.

'No,' his father replied.

'When did you last see her?'

'I, uh, I'm not sure. Come to think of it, I don't think I've . . . Gareth?'

Gareth was already on his way to the lounge, where his mother was doing her crossword puzzle and Max was playing on his phone. 'Anyone seen Olivia this morning?' he asked.

They shook their heads. 'She never gets up for breakfast now,' Max said.

'But have you seen her today?'

'Don't think so,' his mum said. 'Everything all right?'

He ran back upstairs, panting for breath, looking at his watch. It was nine thirty. She would have got up by now for a glass of orange juice, even if it was just to take it back to her room.

Outside her bedroom, he turned to his side and then ran at the door, putting his shoulder into it. The door didn't give.

'Yowwww!' Barging a door was more difficult than it looked.

His parents were coming up the stairs, Max bounding ahead of them. 'Dad? What are you doing?'

'Her door's locked,' Gareth said.

'So?' Max said.

'Anything could be happening in there.'

He thought of the compass and the cuts on her arm. The pregnancy was the secret that she had been keeping from him. He should have been firmer, taking more of a grip on the situation. He would never forgive himself.

In a panic, he ran at the door again, harder this time.

'Woah!' Max shouted. 'Sick!'

There was a splitting noise as the door gave way and Gareth shot forward, stumbling into the room, the door slamming against the wall. He stood looking about him at the perfectly made bed, the piles of books, the solar sunflower gadget wiggling on the windowsill.

In her armchair, sketching, wearing a pair of headphones, was Olivia. So absorbed in what she was doing she hadn't noticed that her father had just ripped the door off.

His parents appeared behind him. 'What's going on?' his mum said. 'Is she all right?'

'She's fine,' Gareth said, flapping the back of his shirt to get some air to his back. It felt suddenly very hot in the room.

Olivia pulled her headphones down and stared at them. 'What?' she said.

There was a moment's pause and then they all began to laugh.

'What's so funny?' Olivia said, looking at them in turn.

'Notice anything different about your room?' Max said.

She gazed about her, her eyes settling on the hanging door, and then gave a nonchalant shrug. She wasn't going to enter into the joke.

'Never mind,' Gareth's father said, leaving the room. 'We'll soon fix that. I'll go and get my toolbox.'

Max left the room with his grandmother, chuckling to himself.

Gareth waited until he and Olivia were alone. 'Sorry about the drama,' he said. 'I was worried about you. I thought ...'

'What?'

'You know ...' He motioned to her arms. 'Especially after what you told us yesterday.'

'Oh.' She pouted, shifted position. He hadn't meant to bring up the pregnancy so soon. She looked down at her sketch pad; she was in the middle of drawing a heart with

291

elaborate patterns inside it. 'I haven't done that, not since that other time.'

'Well, that's good then,' he said. 'Really good.'

Did he sound patronising? He hoped not.

'And about the other thing . . . The . . . uh . . . miscarriage.' He dared to sit down on the arm of her chair, keeping his arms folded so as not to invade her personal space. 'How are you feeling about that?'

He tried to make his voice sound kindly, void of the turmoil he was feeling. A teenage pregnancy was a father bomb if ever one existed. He couldn't tell her that, though, was going to have to be nothing but supportive and empathetic.

Olivia continued sketching again, as though he wasn't there. But then she began to speak, whilst drawing. 'It was painful,' she said. 'I had a lot of cramps, but it was basically OK. It's hard to know what I'm feeling sad about when there's so much to be sad about, you know?'

He looked at the top of his daughter's head, wanting to stroke her hair as though she were six years old, but not being daft enough to do so.

'I know exactly what you mean,' he said. 'You didn't have to go through it on your own, though. It's a shame that you felt you couldn't come to me.'

She looked up at him then. 'How could I? You've been so upset about Mum. And she didn't exactly react well to the news in the first place.'

He stood up, put his hands in his pockets, stretching his legs. 'I understand. Honestly, I do . . . But why didn't Mum tell me, do you think?'

''Cos she thought you'd be sentimental about it and complicate things.'

'How?'

'By persuading us not to go through with the termination.'

'Would that have been the worst thing in the world, though? I know it's not ideal, but . . . ' What was he saying? It would have been a disaster.

'Mum wanted it dealt with quickly,' she said. 'Before anyone found out.'

'So that was what Frank was talking about when he said no one wanted it.'

'Yes.'

'He didn't want to keep it, though, did he?'

'Not sure. I think he just wanted more time to decide.'

'And what about you?'

'I dunno,' she said. 'I just wanted to go along with whatever Mum said to make it all go away. But Frank thought she was wrong.' She smiled tightly. 'You know what the Silks are like.'

'Oh, yes,' he said.

'Mum was going to pay for a termination and she said if I agreed, she would buy me a flat when I went to university.'

Gareth blew his cheeks out in surprise. 'A flat? Where the heck was she going to get the money from for that?' Then the truth dawned. 'Ah. The marina.'

Olivia looked away, down at the carpet.

'Am I right?' he said.

'Yes. I think so,' she said.

'So that's why she asked Melissa for the money. The police asked me about that and I couldn't think for the life of me why she'd have wanted it back. You know what your mum was like: all heart and no logic.'

'Like my sketch,' she said.

He smiled, looked at the heart on her notepad. 'Just like your sketch.' Sighing, he sat back down on the arm of her chair. 'I have a lot of thinking to do about your mum. There's so much I didn't know.'

Olivia gazed up at him, tears brimming in her eyes. 'I don't think any of it was bad. She was just looking out for me. She wanted me to do well because she never got out of Milford.'

'She said that?'

'Yes.'

He nodded forlornly.

'But she loved you, Dad. I know she did.'

'You don't have to say that.'

'It's true. She said you were her consolation prize.'

'Some prize, eh?' he said. 'Anyway, no use moping. We need to keep going with our plan.'

'What plan?'

He nudged her, trying to lighten the mood. 'We've got to get you and Max all those A grades that your mum wanted you to get. And we've got to prove to your grandparents that we can change a light bulb without killing ourselves, otherwise they'll never leave.'

Olivia laughed. It was nice to see it.

'Also ...' His voice grew serious again. 'I'd like you to go to the doctors. I know you said you're fine, but let's get you properly checked out.'

'OK,' she said.

Encouraged, he pressed on. 'And I want you to carry on with the counselling.'

'OK.'

'Oh. Well ... Good.'

That was easy. He would leave while he was ahead.

But he wanted to give her a little more than that. He couldn't remember the last time she had let him cuddle her. Yet perhaps a kiss was allowed. There was only one way to find out.

Reaching down, he kissed her on the forehead. 'You'll always be my little angel, no matter what,' he said.

'Thanks,' she said.

He smiled, nodded, withdrew.

At the door, he turned back to look at her. 'Liv?'

'Yeah?'

'Maybe don't lock the door from now on.'

37

Sunday 6 May 2018

It was Bank Holiday weekend; they had completely forgotten about it. Melissa would have done the school run on Monday, had she not noticed the calendar at breakfast. The Silkies had always gone camping this Bank Holiday – all thirteen of them, taking over the corner of a Cornish field.

Had someone cancelled the booking? She hoped so. Something told her that they would never be going back there again.

Lee spotted the calendar at the same time, their eyes meeting across the table. The girls were eating toast quite happily, unaware of the gaps opening up all around them. Lee was right: so much had changed. The long weekend stretched ahead, agonisingly blank.

There was a noise out in the hallway and Melissa looked up to see Frank dashing past. She left the table, still holding her toast. 'Are you going out?' she asked Frank.

'Looks like it,' he said.

'To Olivia's?'

'Yep,' he said, his hair flopping forward as he hopped about by the front door, struggling to get his trainers on. He didn't seem to be able to get away from her quickly enough.

'Shouldn't you be revising? I haven't seen you pick up a pen in a while.'

'It's fine,' he said, grabbing his jacket from the peg.

'Good,' she said. 'So, maybe we can sit down this afternoon and look at your exam timetable.'

'Uh . . .'

'Two o'clock sound all right?'

'What?' he said, flicking his hair out of his eyes.

'I know you want to spend time with Olivia. But she's got another year before taking her A levels, whereas yours are in less than two weeks.'

'So?'

'So? It *matters*, Frank. We also need to sit down with Dad and have a talk about responsibility and using protection . . . OK?'

He didn't reply.

'OK, Frank?'

'Whatever.'

She followed him as he pulled open the front door, the fresh air meeting them on the doorstep. Two ravens that had been pecking at the lawn took off in a sudden rush of wings causing her to drop her toast.

Frank stooped to pick it up for her. 'You seem on edge,' he said.

'Sorry. It's . . . I'm . . .'

He nodded, turned away.

'You can ask me about the arrest, you know,' she called after him. 'I can talk about it. It's good to talk about it.'

He didn't reply. She watched as he pulled the garage door down to get his bike. He disappeared for a moment, then reappeared, pushing his bike down the driveway.

'Wait up!' she called, dashing after him, her dressing gown flapping open.

'Mum,' he said, half-jokingly, looking about him. 'You're not even decent. What will the neighbours say?'

'I think that ship has sailed,' she said, tying her dressing-gown belt. 'Frank, I need you to know that I'm always here for you. No matter what.'

'What makes you say that?'

'Because it's not true what you said about my taking Jenny's side. You didn't give me a chance.'

'I know ... I'm sorry.' He turned to go. 'Just forget it.'

'We're OK, though, aren't we? You and I?'

He looked at her, smiled faintly. 'Mum, we'll always be OK.'

'Good.' She stepped back ceremoniously, sweeping her arms in the direction of the front gates. 'You may leave.'

He climbed on to his bike, cycled off. 'See you at two o'clock for The Talk,' she called after him.

Back in the kitchen, Nina and Polly had dispersed. Lee was at the sink, washing up the breakfast things. 'Well done,' he said.

'You heard?'

'Some of it. Needed to be said. He's been sulking around the place all weekend.'

'He's upset. It's a huge thing to go through at his age, or any age. And I think he's fretting about me and the arrest. We should talk to him about that and reassure him. He's got exams right around the corner.'

'He'll be fine, love. We just need some time for things to settle.'

She sat back down, playing with a mauve vase, turning it on the table, looking at her reflection, warped, cloudy.

'What's up?' Lee said, turning to look at her. 'Is there something else wrong?'

'It's nothing,' she said.

He finished washing up and leant back against the sink, arms folded. 'Tell me.'

'Well, it's about Jenny . . . You know I said that Sergeant Lloyd still thinks that it wasn't an accident?'

Lee frowned. 'If this is what I think it is—'

'Just hear me out . . . The sergeant couldn't find what he needed. There was something missing. And what have we just found out? That Olivia was pregnant.'

Lee was looking at her blankly.

'So, maybe that's the missing piece,' she said.

He shook his head. 'I don't believe that for one minute. The case is closed. Jenny's death was an accident. Everyone's known that from the start, except you. And now it's time to accept it and get on with our lives, before we go around the bend.'

'I'm not the only one who feels this way,' she said. 'The sergeant does too.'

'Yeah and you know what else he thought? That you were guilty.'

'You did too,' she said.

He gazed at her steadily. 'That's not fair.'

'I'm sorry,' she said. 'But it's how I feel: as though everyone's doubting me.'

'Well, it's not true. You know I'm on your side. I'm just getting to the stage where I need a bit of normal. And I don't think this is helping, obsessing over Jenny's death. This was what got you arrested in the first place – poking around, digging things up. You've got to let it go.'

'I know but . . .'

'But what?' He sat down in the chair beside her, clasping both her hands. 'You know what I think this is really about?' he said. 'You're trying to fix things, cos that's what you do. But for the first time, you can't make it better.'

'Not for the first time,' she said quietly.

'Hey?' he said.

She hesitated. 'It wasn't the first time I couldn't fix it.'

He gazed at her. 'Oh, Mel, love . . .'

She swallowed awkwardly, her throat feeling too narrow. 'It's OK,' she said. 'I'm fine.'

'No, you're not. You're punishing yourself. You need to stop this.'

'But I couldn't save her. I couldn't—'

There was a creaking noise and Polly entered the room, pushing open the door. 'Mummy?'

'Hey, Polly Pops,' Melissa said. 'Whatcha up to?'

'Nothing,' Polly said, bouncing a small rubber ball on the floor as she approached. 'Could we go and do something outside? I'm bored.'

'What do you fancy doing?'

'I dunno.'

'I know,' Lee said, 'What about Portbridge Aquarium?'

'The one you always say is a huge rip-off?' Polly said.

'That's the one,' Lee said.

'Really?' Polly opened her eyes wide.

'Yep. I think you deserve a treat. You've been a good girl all week. Isn't that right, Mummy?'

'Yes,' Melissa said, smiling.

'Go and clean your teeth,' Lee said. 'And get your big sister. And hurry.'

'You're the best. Thanks, Daddy!' Polly ran from the room and pounded up the stairs.

'Good idea. Well done,' Melissa said, standing up.

'We'll talk again later,' Lee said.

'No,' she said. 'We don't need to talk about it. I'm going to make a real effort to put this behind us, starting now.'

'Great,' he said, kissing her on the tip of her nose. And he left the kitchen, whistling to himself.

She did want to try to move on. Yet if Sergeant Lloyd still

doubted her, and if no other suspect was offered up for public conjecture, and if no one ever really knew what had happened to Jenny, how would she ever be free?

Wouldn't she be forever known around Milford and beyond as the woman who probably, maybe, murdered her best friend?

38

Ned was camping with the scouts; Joel had gone to a friend's house to revise and was staying over the night. This was exactly what Rachel had been afraid of: a silent house.

Bank Holiday weekend and she was all alone.

Being in the Silkies had been an insurance policy against things like this. All of the big things throughout the year had been covered – Christmas, Easter, long weekends. There had been no cracks, no abyss to stare into. The Silkies had covered it all. If one of them couldn't make it, the others had stepped in. A security blanket of friendship, no one ever had to sit in a cinema alone or spend New Year's Eve contemplating the meaning of life.

They had been there for each other, no matter what, not heeding anyone else. Just being part of the Silkies – a gang of thirteen playing cricket on the beach, occupying a large restaurant table with balloons tied to the backs of chairs or walking through the countryside with an array of scooters, bikes, children – had felt intoxicatingly good.

The message to all and sundry had been that this wonderful group of people had made it in life, had succeeded. They had found something special, sacred – a tribe. They were popular, loved, valued, essential, each and every one of them.

Their circle hadn't been selfish, just self-contained.

And now it had cracked open like a coconut and had been laid bare. And on examining the contents, it turned out that the inside of the Silkies had been empty all along.

Some insurance policy.

Sighing, stretching her legs out underneath the kitchen counter, Rachel picked up her phone and scrolled through her contacts, wondering how she hadn't noticed before how dangerously exclusive it was.

The only numbers on her phone that weren't related to the Silkies belonged to the dentist and school. She had been completely myopic; they all had.

The only thing she could do now was rebuild her life, without Al, without Jenny, probably without Melissa, without a plan of any form.

It wasn't clear what was happening about her job at the marina, but she imagined that the atmosphere would be strained between her and the Silks – even with the best will in the world, which none of them would probably even get close to finding.

She reached for her laptop and opened it on the counter, beginning to search for employment websites.

The only listed job opportunity in Milford was for a dog walker. Dogs made her sneeze.

She pushed the laptop away, picked up her phone again, finding Melissa's mobile number. If she didn't make a move soon, any remnant of friendship between them would have dissipated.

For the first time in her life, she wasn't going to mull it over until it had congealed. She was simply going to act.

She dialled Melissa's number and waited, her heart fluttering uncomfortably.

Melissa answered right away. 'Hi, Rachel,' she said. There was a lot of background noise.

'Can you talk?' Rachel asked.

'I'm fine for a minute. Polly ... Pols! That's it. Over there ... Sorry. What were you saying?'

'Nothing. Where are you? Sounds noisy.'

'Outside the aquarium,' Melissa said. 'It's heaving. You wouldn't believe it.'

'I would,' Rachel said.

It was a strained conversation. She would have to execute it quickly.

'I was wondering whether you'd like to meet for coffee?' she said. 'I ... I miss you.' She held her breath.

There was a long pause.

She needed to add something. 'I think Jenny would have wanted us to stay friends.'

Not that, fool.

She closed her eyes, telling herself to speak less.

'I'd like that,' Melissa said.

'Great,' Rachel said. 'When's good for you?'

'Not sure.'

Her spirits sank. 'Would you like to think about it and let me know?' she asked.

'Yes, that would be good. I'm sorry, but I have to go. We're going in now.'

'Go. Be with your family.'

'Bye.'

'Bye.' And they hung up.

Rachel gazed into space, before turning to her phone again, scrolling through the endless photos. The Silkies at the beach. The Silkies camping. The Silkies playing cricket using a stump of wood. Happy Silkies everywhere.

How could it have fallen apart so quickly? How could she and Melissa have gone from the closest of friends to virtual strangers almost overnight?

Perhaps there had been something there all along, a fault in the Silkies that she hadn't seen. Or perhaps this instant dissolution wasn't unique to them, but was the exposed flaw at the heart of friendship – the hidden catch that you chose to ignore in the hope that it would never come to light.

Compared to family, the fact that you could cherry-pick your friends was very attractive, especially in a modern world that valued freedom of choice. There was no need to put up with toxic, dysfunctional or just plain boring family, when you could look elsewhere for company. Given that friendship was entered into voluntarily, you could get into it as quickly as you could get out; unlike suffocating, eternal blood ties. Family was an umbilical cord around the neck, a life sentence. Friends, however, could be dumped, replaced, ghosted, unfriended online. So far, so good.

But what happened when things weren't so good? She recalled an old woman telling her in the supermarket last year that when her husband had been diagnosed with Alzheimer's, her friends had left in droves. The poor woman had ended up joining a support group just to have someone to talk to.

Yet the Silkies hadn't been fickle. They had cared for each other over the years, through good and bad times. True friends stood by each other through life's disasters, especially then. Even so, the bond between the six of them hadn't been strong enough to bear their weight when tested.

People walked away from marriages – after cutting sleeves off shirts, ripping up wedding photos, dividing assets – but the split could never be truly final once there were children involved, once blood ties had been established.

You could ignore your family, disown them, cut them from your life, but genetics forever linked you to them and them to you.

And in the light of tragedy, that eternal, unbreakable cord didn't look so bad.

What tied the Silkies together now? What was left? Sentiment? Duty? Weren't those some of the key components of the glue that bound family together, though? Were old, forced friendships the second cousins of the family tree?

She had been misguided, naïve to believe that they would all be best friends for ever. Not even the Silkies could withstand infidelity, teenage pregnancy, death and a murder inquiry.

Starting to cry, she slid the phone containing all the happy photographs to the end of the counter, where it came to a halt just before falling. Pulling the laptop and the dismal dog-walking opportunity back towards her, she began to fill out the enquiry form, her eyes thick with tears.

She was just going to have to get on with life as best she could, trying to make something of the nothing that she had been left with.

She was about to press send on the enquiry form when the doorbell rang. She looked up at the kitchen window, hoping to see a car in the driveway, but there was no sign of who the caller was.

The bell rang again, petulantly.

Getting up with a sigh, she glanced in the hallway mirror as she passed it, wondering who that dreary pale woman was gawping back at her.

Opening the door, she was surprised to see Al standing there with his suitcase.

'Hi, honey, I'm home!' He held out his hands, smiling, wrinkles creasing around his eyes.

She stared at him. 'What the hell are you doing here?'

'That's quite a welcome,' he said, glancing about him. Public rejection was a recurring nightmare of his.

'Well, I wasn't expecting you,' she said.

'I was hoping we could talk,' he said. 'Can I come in?'

She looked at the suitcase, trying not to read too much into it, even though the message seemed obvious. 'That depends.'

'On . . . ?'

'On what your intentions are.'

He stepped closer. 'Dishonourable . . . Are you home alone, gorgeous?'

She held him away, at arm's length. 'That won't work on me, not any more. You'll have to do a lot better.'

'How about this?' He came closer, leaning in towards her neck.

'Stop it, Al,' she said. 'I mean it. You can't just show up and everything's back to normal. That's not the way it works.'

He stood upright like a chastised child. 'I'm sorry. It's just that I've missed you. And I want to come home. Please. Let me.'

'It's not that simple, I'm afraid,' she said.

'Why isn't it?'

She folded her arms. 'Because you kissed my friend.'

'But that's all it was.'

'No, it wasn't. Because then she died and it became so much more than that.'

'But that's not my fault. I didn't know that was going to happen. It was just a stupid mistake. I've never cheated on you before and it'll never happen again, I promise you. It only happened in the first place because I was drunk and because it was Jenny. I mean, look at what we were like, for heaven's sake – in each other's lives all the time. Maybe we didn't have enough boundaries.'

'Boundaries?' she said. 'Have you been listening to your self-help tapes again?'

He smiled. 'Please, Rachel. I'm sorry I let you down. But I love you. And I have to come home. It's killing me. I can't cope without you.'

He smiled again, but what he was saying was serious, true.

He couldn't cope without her whatsoever. She didn't need him to tell her that.

She gazed at him and at his suitcase, thinking about what she had just concluded about family and friends.

He was Joel and Ned's dad. He had also cheated on her and she would probably never forgive him for that.

But he was her family.

And so she opened the door an inch more and let him in.

39

Tuesday 8 May 2018

It felt like an age since Melissa and Polly had walked to school together. They held hands along the river path, smelling the wild garlic in the air, admiring the abundance of bluebells on the bank. Everything felt daringly hopeful, until Polly mentioned that it was Open Morning.

Melissa's step faltered. 'You want me to come into school?'

'Yes, Mummy. That's what Open Morning is. It wouldn't be called Open otherwise, would it? It would be called Closed. And no one ever has a Closed—'

'OK, Pols, I get it. It's just that . . . '

'What?' Polly said, looking up at her apprehensively. 'Can't you come?'

The timing couldn't have been worse. It had been one thing facing the town at the funeral, where propriety restrained everyone from giving her filthy looks, but primary school playgrounds were the modern equivalent of Roman amphitheatres, where citizens went to watch fights, albeit passive aggressive ones.

She had to be brave for her daughter. She had promised Lee to try to get things back to normal; this was part of that effort.

Facing petty parents was a part of life in Milford. She was fully entitled to attend the open morning.

'It's fine. I'll be there,' she said.

'Yay!' Polly stopped to pick up a snail shell, which she tossed recklessly into the river. And then she plucked a bluebell from the verge and handed it to Melissa. 'Put this in your pocket, Mummy. It'll make you feel brave.'

Kids; just when you thought they had a foot in fairyland, they hit a hole in one.

⚓

The playground was busier than usual because of the open morning. Parents who normally dropped and ran to work were lingering in suits, talking in circles. There was a hush to the air that didn't fit with the volume of people present. Perhaps it was because it was the first day back at school after the funeral, or because there were clandestine matters to discuss. Either way, Melissa, who had previously occupied a space in the coveted spot beside the rose bushes, now found herself standing alone by the wheelie bins.

She stamped her feet, rubbing her hands together, feigning feeling cold so that she wasn't just standing there idle. Hopefully, someone would take pity on her and approach.

Not even Nessa Merry, whose interference Melissa could normally have counted on, was paying any attention to her. Nessa was talking to a group of mums near the water fountain, their heads bent conspiratorially.

Melissa glanced discreetly about her. She didn't want to be seen to be looking for company, but if no one came in the next two minutes, she would resort to the sin of playing on her phone. The unofficial rule was that parents were to be seen making an effort socially when on school grounds, engaging fully with the children and with other parents and staff. Melissa, who had once been an expert at working the playground, was now texting Lee:

I hate this town. :(

She watched Polly, who was hanging from the monkey bars, pants on display, without a care.

Oh, to be nine years old again and upside down.

When the bell rang and the children lined up, Melissa put her phone away and followed the crowd into the school, all the while feeling for Polly's precious bluebell in her pocket.

The parents were being ushered into the main hall while morning register was taken. The hall contained a parent-pleasing explosion of art and science projects. The adults began to circle demurely, pretending to be interested in the displays, whereas in reality they were beginning to take more and more interest in Melissa.

She felt her ears burning as she stopped to look at an impressive papier-mâché frog that no child could ever have created. It seemed overly warm in the room. She unwound her scarf, pushing it into her pocket.

'Well, she's got balls, I'll give her that . . .' Someone said this quite near to her. She turned indignantly to look at the speaker, but the couple beside her were examining the wall display. The mothers on her other side were similarly engaged.

She wouldn't take the bait, nor would she be paranoid and imagine what wasn't there.

She moved away to the science projects. To her relief, the children were beginning to enter the room in a chattering stream of blue jumpers and white socks.

She thought of the blue and white cell.

'Hello, Mummy,' Polly said, appearing at her side. 'This is

mine.' And she dragged Melissa to a table right next to Nessa Merry. 'Look.' She held up a colourful twine bracelet. 'I made it for you, but you can't take it home yet. It's a friendship bracelet. People give them to their best friends.'

Beside her, Nessa gave a very quiet snort.

'It's lovely, Polly,' Melissa said. 'I'll enjoy wearing that. Thank you.'

Polly was taking her to a table now that was covered in papier-mâché lumps and bumps painted grey, blue and green. 'This is Milford, Mummy. It's what it looks like from above, if you were sitting on a cloud and looking down. It's an *air-real* view. Do you think that's what Auntie Jenny can see now?'

Melissa stared at the project, unable to take it in.

'Are you OK?' Polly said, tugging on Melissa's coat sleeve.

'Yes, poppet.'

'Have I upset you?'

'Not at all. I'm sure Auntie Jenny would love it. And I do, too.'

'You don't have to stay, Mummy,' Polly said sincerely, 'if you don't want to.'

Melissa looked longingly at the hall doors, which opened on to the playground. Three steps and she would be away.

She didn't have to stay and take the condemnation that was more on display here than the children's work. She wasn't being paranoid; she could feel it. They were judging her, loathing her for showing up at such a time, in a primary school. Only Polly wanted her here. And Polly would understand if she had to go.

Crouching down, she pulled her daughter towards her. 'I love everything you've shown me. Thank you for asking me to come. Is there anything else you want me to see?'

'No, that's everything.'

'Are you sure?'

Polly nodded.

'Well, then I'll leave you to it.' She kissed her goodbye. 'I'll see you after school, my little pumpkin.'

'Bye, Mummy.' And Polly skipped off to join her friends.

Melissa was halfway up the playground to the main gates before she realised that they were locked and that she would have to return and exit through the school's reception area.

Inside the foyer, she tapped on the glass panel to ask to be let out of the building. The receptionist was laughing with a colleague, but on seeing Melissa, her smile vanished.

It wasn't a brush-off, or even all that rude. It was just a knee-jerk reaction to coming face to face with the woman who had been arrested for murder.

There was a buzzing sound and then the doors clicked open and Melissa was set free into the spring sunshine. There was no traffic about at this time of morning. Her footsteps sounded out loudly as she ran along the river path.

At home, she got into the car and sat gasping for breath behind the wheel.

Starting the engine, she reversed slowly, mindful of the fact that Angela Gould usually came back about this time from the senior school run.

Sure enough, there was Angela's car pulling into the drive-way opposite. Melissa braked, waiting for her neighbour to disappear from view, before leaving, taking off along the road in the direction of the marina.

As she drove, her head was swamped with voices. She turned the radio on, but couldn't find any music – only more voices. She pressed the CD player on and was immersed in the sound of Nina's choral music from drama class: a spiritual piece with soaring sopranos. She went to turn it off, but found herself captivated.

She could hear the sergeant's voice, could see his brown eyes looking at her interrogatively.

I know guilt when I see it.

I know you're guilty of something.

She was driving along a straight stretch of road, doing sixty miles an hour, with forest either side. It was dark, with the light blocked by the trees. She knew the road well – knew that in a moment she would have to slow down to take the steep bend, before turning off for the marina.

She put her foot down, enjoying speeding, when suddenly there was a flash of yellow in front of her and a horrible thud.

She swerved, hit the brakes, the car veering on to the wrong side of the road. Screaming, she swung the wheel and swerved back to the left, before coming to a halt, facing the forest.

The car had stalled. She sat staring in front of her, dazed, looking at the darkness – the straight pine trees that receded for miles.

What just happened?

She looked in her rear-view mirror. She couldn't see anything, bar the trees. With shaking hands, she started the car, reversed and straightened up, before coming to a stop again.

She got out of the car and looked down the way she had just come. Lying in the road was a yellow shape. Her eyes were blurry with panic; she couldn't see it distinctly.

She put her hand to her mouth. The object was coming into focus: it was a deer.

A sudden sound down the road made her turn to look in the opposite direction. A car was approaching. It slowed down, pulling up alongside her.

A silver-haired man called out to her. 'Are you all right?'

'No,' she said. 'I hit a deer.' She pointed up the road.

The man got out of his car. 'Oh gosh,' he said, tucking his shirt into his trousers. 'Nasty feeling, isn't it?' He was inordinately tall, stooping to talk to her. 'I hit one once, twenty years or so ago. Try not to feel too guilty. You didn't mean to do it.'

She was beginning to shiver. 'Why don't you get back in

your car and put the heating on?' he said. 'Keep yourself warm. I'll see what I can do.'

She didn't do as he said. Instead, she watched as he walked the several yards to where the deer was lying, unmoving. She couldn't help but follow him, yet stopped before getting too close. The deer was a baby. She couldn't think what they were called.

'It's a fawn,' the man said, as though reading her mind. 'Bless it.'

Carefully, the man buckled his long frame to bend and pick the fawn up. It was very still. He laid it on the grass verge. Then he brushed himself down and went to his car to pull a roll of paper from the boot and wipe his hands.

'Just as well I came along,' he said.

She nodded.

'Can I do anything else for you? Are you going to be all right?'

'Yes,' she said. 'I don't have far to go.'

'Well, maybe take a moment to gather yourself before setting off.' He smiled at her compassionately. 'And try not to beat yourself up about it. Occupational hazard of driving around here.'

'I should have known that,' she said. 'I've lived here all my life.'

'Catches the best of us out,' he said. 'Well, bye for now. Take care.' And he got into his car and pulled away.

It was only as he disappeared that she realised she hadn't thanked him.

She sat for a long while in the driver's seat, gazing at the road ahead, thinking of the fawn, of the thud as it had hit the car, of what she might have done to stop it from happening, of the flash of yellow before her eyes.

David was sick again, just as they began to play Injuns. She could hear him inside the house calling for Mummy – could hear their mother's footsteps and then the sound of running water in the kitchen.

She turned back to the game again. Jenny was halfway across the garden, lost somewhere in the grass. Hannah, the princess, was also hidden from view, but Melissa knew exactly where she was – near the lavender pot by the laurel hedge. Hannah was guarding the treasure: the beautiful silver apple charm that held the key to all life's secrets and that the pirates were desperate to get their hands on.

Melissa crawled through the long grass, enjoying the sensation of cold grass on her bare legs and the smell of lawn and mud, when there came the sound of their doorbell ringing.

It was a very loud ring. Their mum had rigged it up so that it rang outside. Sometimes it was people wanting to hire kayaks. Business couldn't be missed. So, the whole neighbourhood had to hear their doorbell.

The doorbell was still ringing. Their mum was occupied with David – was calling for her to answer the door.

Tutting, Melissa stood up, picking grass from her knees, looking at the red imprints that the grass had left on her skin.

She ran to the back door, past the grandmother clock and down the hallway to the front door. She never saw who was at the door – never answered it – because now she could hear something else.

Jenny was screaming. Melissa turned around and ran down the hallway, past the grandmother clock, to the back door.

Jenny was standing in the middle of the lawn, screaming hysterically, jumping up and down.

Melissa couldn't understand what was happening at first. Jenny was going crazy. Melissa shouted at her to be quiet.

She ran through the long grass in the direction of where she had left her sister. A crow was cawing above her. The telegraph wires

316

*were humming. It was so quiet, she could hear her blood pumping
in her ears.*

She could see the yellow of her sister's dress in the grass.

Hannah? she said.

She heard something then. A horrifying sound.

And then everything went quiet again.

⚓

Melissa started the car and drove slowly to the marina.

When she arrived at the boat yard, she listened for the sound
of Lee's hammer. On hearing it, she gazed at the estuary, at
the sunlight sparkling and hopping on the water like popping
candy, before unlocking the office and starting work.

ANGELA GOULD

Milford resident, Dorset

Angela had never shown anyone her collection of press cuttings. Given the nature of the subject, they could have been mistaken for morbid curiosity or creepy fixation on her part. She kept them hidden in an envelope at the bottom of a chest of drawers in the spare room. Underneath blankets and pillowcases, no one ever noticed the envelope there.

Lately, since the funeral, she had been drawn to the cuttings. And so, on a quiet morning when she wasn't due to start work at the café for another hour, she found herself slipping into the spare room and taking the envelope from the drawer.

With trepidation, she unfolded the largest of the cuttings. Taken from the *Portbridge Herald*, she had cut it out herself with childlike, zigzagging snips of the scissors. The cutting was now thirty-two years old and was crisp, faded.

There were others, but the *Herald* article was her favourite – not that she liked any of them – because it featured a clear, beautiful photograph.

GIRL NECKLACE DEATH

3-year-old girl choked to death while playing in garden, despite sibling's attempts to save her.

Tragic Hannah Reeve was playing with sister Melissa and friend Jennifer on 13 August in Milford, Dorset, when she started choking on a charm taken from a necklace.

The apple-shaped charm had been given to the toddler as part of the children's game.

Melissa, 10, tried to use basic first-aid training but was unable to save her sister.

Hannah's mother, who was looking after her son inside the house, also administered first aid but the child had already gone into cardiac arrest.

Speaking at the inquest in Portbridge City Hall, Mrs Reeve expressed her immeasurable grief at the loss of her daughter. She also thanked the hospital staff and medical teams who worked hard to try to save Hannah's life.

Coroner Peter Hill said, 'A case like this is rare and distressing for all involved. I wish the family peace and hope that they can move forward from this tragedy.'

He concluded an accidental death.

Angela folded up the cutting again, placing it inside the envelope, which she slid back underneath the blankets in the drawer.

Then she went to the mirror and began to brush her hair in long, careful strokes, telling herself for the umpteenth time that it wasn't her fault, that she had been just a child, that it was a long time ago and someday soon it would begin to feel better.

40

3 months later
Friday 3 August 2018

Rachel was delighted to get the call from Melissa. She hadn't so much as glimpsed her since the wake, and they hadn't spoken since their strained phone conversation outside the aquarium. She had thought many times of being the one to break the silence, but reminded herself of how they had left it: that Melissa was going to think about a suitable date for coffee and get back to her.

She had heard – mostly by listening in to indiscreet conversations at PTA meetings and in the supermarket – that Melissa was turning her back on everyone; Melissa, who had once been so much at the heart of the town that some had called it Melford.

It would be impossible to decipher who exactly was doing the back-turning, given that most people seemed to be holding Melissa responsible for Jenny's death in some way, if only by association and for want of someone else to blame, from what Rachel could gather.

Melissa, innately proud, would be sure to go it alone, given the circumstances. She certainly seemed to be extending herself well beyond the town, so far as the business went. Rachel had noticed that the website had been redesigned, promoting the marina as *the most beautiful wedding venue in the south-west*.

It appeared, from Rachel's long-distance view – since she hadn't gone back to work at the marina since the accident – that the Silks were busy rebuilding their lives. She had concluded that she wouldn't be a part of the new model. And then Melissa had rung out of the blue, suggesting a coffee at the high-street café that Friday.

Rachel arrived early and sat playing nervously with the salt and pepper mills. There were no other customers, save for an elderly lady who was knitting by the empty fireplace.

Rachel glanced at her watch. It was ten to two. She would get a cup of tea, rather than sit here fiddling.

She was standing up, about to place her order, when the doorbell tinkled and in came Melissa.

Rachel stopped still, waiting to see how her friend would react so that she could mirror it. This was an old instinct, one that urged her to let Melissa take the lead.

Yet Melissa wasn't making it easy for her. She was also standing still, the trace of a frown on her forehead. Rachel was going to have to be the one to say or do something. 'Hi, Mel,' she said. And then, finding the formalities unbearable, she hugged her. 'It's so good to see you.'

They drew back from each other. 'Have you missed me?' Melissa said. She was wearing sage-green jeans, a pastel-pink blouse and her trademark espadrilles. Everything about her was intensely familiar – from the twine bracelets on her wrists to the lemony scent of mousse in her hair.

Rachel felt a pang of regret; they shouldn't have left it so long. 'More than you know,' she said, leading Melissa to her table. 'What can I get you?'

Melissa set her satchel bag on a chair and surveyed the board.

'Just tea, please.' And then she sat down, turning her head to look out of the window.

Rachel went to the counter and pressed the bell for service. From the kitchen, there came the sound of footsteps and then Angela Gould, Melissa's neighbour, appeared, wiping her hands on her apron.

On seeing Rachel, Angela immediately looked past her to see who she was with. 'How can I help?' Angela said, not taking her eyes off Melissa.

'Two teas, please.'

When Rachel returned to the table, she glanced back at Angela, who was busying herself with the drinks. 'That woman's odd, if you ask me,' she said.

'No odder than me,' Melissa said. 'I'm like a leper. Half the town cross the road when they see me now.'

Rachel had heard that it was the other way around, but didn't say as much.

'So, how have you been?' Melissa asked.

'OK-ish,' Rachel said. 'I've got a new job, as a receptionist.'

'Really? Where?' Melissa looked hurt, but disguised it well, twisting her hair around her fingers, smiling faintly.

'Don't laugh.'

'Why would I laugh?'

'It's at the donkey sanctuary.'

Melissa kept a straight face. And then she laughed.

The drinks arrived, Angela setting the teapot down rather heavily, slopping tea on to the tablecloth. 'I'm so sorry,' she said, looking appalled. 'I'm such a clot.'

'No you're not,' Melissa said. 'It's fine. It's nothing.'

Angela retreated, muttering as though disappointed in herself.

'Did she seem nervous?' Melissa whispered. 'Is it because of me? No one acts naturally around me any more.'

'I don't think it's got anything to do with you. Like I said, she's just odd.'

'Well, anyway, about the donkeys ... ' Melissa said. 'Do you like it there?'

'Yes, I do,' Rachel said, pouring the tea. 'But it's not for long.'

'Oh? Why's that?'

She put down the teapot, gazed at Melissa. 'I'm glad you called. I wanted to tell you this in person ... It's been difficult, knowing how to say it ... But, we're moving, Mel.'

'Moving?'

'Away.'

She clasped her hands between her knees, feeling mean, underhand. It was better to tell Melissa this face to face, though. It would only have been a matter of time before she had seen the *For Sale* sign outside their house.

'As in, leaving Milford?' Melissa said, astounded.

'Yes.'

'But where are you going?'

'Southfield. It's about twenty miles away, near—'

'I know where Southfield is.' Unsettled, Melissa began to play with the sugar bowl, poking the cubes with the metal tongs. 'What's there?'

'The new head office of Al's company. He's really happy about it.'

'I bet he is,' Melissa said, barely bothering to hide the criticism in her voice. 'He gets to do exactly what he wants. But what about you?' She pushed the sugar bowl away and gazed at Rachel. 'Where are you in all this?'

Rachel hesitated. 'It was my idea.'

Melissa blinked rapidly. 'Your idea? Why?'

Rachel picked up her teacup, took a sip, gathering her words. 'It's a fresh start.'

'You mean running away, more like,' Melissa said.

'No, it's not,' Rachel said. 'It's nearer my parents, and Al's.'

'Your parents?' Melissa said. 'I didn't think you liked them.'

'Of course I do. They're family.'

'But your home's here.'

'It isn't. I've got nothing here. Not any more.'

'You've got me,' Melissa said unhappily.

From the counter, there came the sound of crockery clattering. Rachel glanced over to see that Angela was stacking plates, watching them intensely.

'No, I haven't,' Rachel said, lowering her voice. 'Look what's happened to us ... Have you so much as glimpsed Gareth lately?'

'No, but I've been meaning to call him and—'

'That's what I thought.'

'But leaving isn't going to solve anything. The problems will go with you.'

'What problems?' Rachel said. 'The problems are here, in Milford. Al was right. This happened because we were too inbred and insular.'

'Insular?' Melissa said. 'What are you talking about?'

'Don't you see?' Rachel said, leaning forward to Melissa to whisper. 'Al shouldn't have been close friends with Jenny in the first place, getting drunk with her. She was so pretty and they used to date! It was asking for trouble. We just didn't see it until it was too late ... We didn't have any boundaries.'

'Oh, crikey,' Melissa said, putting her head in her hands. 'Where did Al get that from? Some corporate motivational weekend?'

'It's nothing to do with that. It's the truth. I've given it a lot of thought. I mean, your son got your best friend's daughter pregnant ... Do you see what I mean?'

She hadn't meant that to sound quite so judgemental or critical.

Melissa flushed red. Rachel reached for her hand.

'We're just doing what we need to do to survive, Mel. You of all people should understand that.'

'Me?' Melissa said. 'I've never done anything, other than live in this poxy little town. What do I know about survival?'

'I don't think anyone else sees it that way. You're the strongest person I know. Deep down, everyone admires you, no matter what they might say.'

Melissa shook her head. 'It doesn't feel like that. It feels like I'm an outcast.'

'But you're still here. You're not moving away ... not like us. We don't have what you have.'

'A criminal record?'

Rachel laughed abruptly, then looked at Melissa in dismay. 'Is that true?'

'Yep,' she said. 'Even though I wasn't charged.'

Rachel looked away, down at her teacup. 'I'm so sorry.'

A silence fell.

And then Melissa changed the subject, her tone brightening. 'How are the boys? Are they excited about moving?'

'Yes. It doesn't affect Joel all that much. Hopefully he'll be off to uni soon. But Ned's super excited. We've promised him a hamster.'

'Wow,' Melissa said wryly. 'A hamster. Lucky Ned.' She picked up her tea. 'Sounds like you've got it all worked out then.'

Rachel listened to the sound of Angela tinkling cutlery behind the counter. The elderly knitter had left the café; Rachel and Melissa were the only customers now. There was a loneliness to the afternoon, with no one about on the high street outside.

'Mel ...'

Melissa looked up. With the sunshine on her face, her eyes

325

seemed more yellow than green. She looked tired, as though their meeting had drained her.

'Please don't think I'm stirring up trouble,' Rachel said, 'but did it ever occur to you that Olivia's pregnancy and Jenny's accident were connected?'

Melissa didn't respond right away.

'Mel . . . ?'

Had she upset or offended her?

Melissa picked at one of her bracelets. 'Yes. It did. But I promised Lee to . . . '

'To what?'

She shrugged. 'To let it go. He said that we had to move on.'

'He's right. I'm sorry I brought it up.'

'Then why did you?' Melissa said, a drop of resentment darkening her expression.

'Because . . . ' Rachel put her hand to her face defensively. 'I know that at one stage finding out the truth really mattered to you.'

'Yeah, well, not more than my family or my health. Being arrested for murder tends to do that to you. It puts your priorities in order.'

Rachel didn't miss the accusation, the hurt in Melissa's voice. It would always be there now. It was why they couldn't ever go back to the way they were.

'I hope Joel does well in his A levels,' Melissa said, her voice softer. 'Frank's got no chance. He didn't revise. I tried to make him, but he just wants to work at the marina with his dad — sawing wood, using the old bronze hammer, watching the seagulls fly over the water.'

'Sounds good to me,' Rachel said.

They didn't say much more than that. Bringing up the accident had soured the tone. Melissa kept glancing at her watch. She had to go and pick up Polly.

They brought things to a close, arguing about who was going to pay for the teas, both wanting to do so – to be the one to do something nice.

It made Rachel suspect that this was the last time they would be meeting like this.

In the end, Melissa gave way and Rachel paid at the counter. It occurred to her that she would probably never be in the café again, so she told Angela Gould to keep the change.

⚓

Melissa stopped at her Audi. 'Well, this is me,' she said.

Rachel gestured down the high street. 'I'm parked there, by the salon.'

There was a click as Melissa unlocked the car doors. 'When are you moving?'

'As soon as we've got a buyer. The estate agent thinks it'll sell quickly.'

'Bound to. It's a good house,' Melissa said. 'Have you found a new place yet?'

'Yes. We've had an offer accepted.'

Again, there was the look of hurt on Melissa's face. Perhaps she had been hoping that the moving plans hadn't got that far.

'Well, thanks for the tea,' Melissa said. 'I wish you the best of luck.'

The best of luck. It was the sort of thing that colleagues said at retirement parties.

She pressed a kiss on to Rachel's cheek. 'Take care of yourself,' she said, and got into her car.

Rachel waited. That was it? Melissa was starting the car, looking straight ahead of her.

What did she expect, though? She was leaving Milford. Melissa had every right to protect herself by withdrawing.

Rachel wouldn't interfere with that, not if it helped Melissa deal with things. She tightened the belt on her jacket and walked away, her footsteps sounding oddly disconnected from her.

She wished now that she hadn't parked in front of Mon Petit Hair. Jenny's assistant, Sue, was standing right in the window, cutting someone's hair.

Rachel was waving her keys hastily to open her car when she heard something and turned to look behind her. Melissa was calling out, running down the high street towards her. 'Rachel! Wait!'

Rachel murmured in surprise, then hurried back down the road to her friend.

Outside the florist's, with the scent of lilies and roses thick in the summer air around them, they embraced, Rachel getting some of Melissa's hair in her mouth, which made them laugh.

'I love you,' Melissa said.

'I love you too,' Rachel said. And then Melissa broke away, straightening her pastel blouse before retreating again.

Rachel watched Melissa walk all the way to her car, knowing that she wouldn't look back.

41

Gareth was such a regular fixture at the Lighthouse Centre in Portbridge now that the receptionist no longer had to ask him how he took his coffee.

They always came after school on a Friday. Gareth's boss at the IT firm where he worked had been fantastic, letting him leave early each week for as long as it took. Sometimes, it took tragedy to see the best in people. Prior to this, Gareth had always thought his boss was a bit of a bell end.

It was pleasant, sitting in the centre in August, the sunshine misting up the windows. It seemed a long time ago that he had first brought Olivia in on that bitter day in April. She had changed a lot since then; they all had.

According to Beverley, their inhumanly kind counsellor, Olivia was doing very well. The self-harm had stopped, hopefully for good, and she and Frank had cringed their way through a teenage pregnancy prevention course.

He hadn't seen Melissa, not in a long while. Sometimes, he asked Frank if his mum was all right and when Frank asserted that she was, Gareth left it at that. Maybe this was how it would be until the inquest gave the final ruling. Whether that would change anything, he didn't know. Until then, he was keeping his old friends at a distance.

Time would tell whether it would be a more permanent arrangement.

For now, he had enough to deal with, looking after the twins. They were both excelling at school; Max had even improved his grades. Their organisational system had proved a success, with neither twin missing a single commitment. In that respect alone, Gareth was proud of himself.

But his proudest achievement was the sacred ground he had covered with his daughter, which was nothing short of miraculous.

The solution had come to him shortly after the funeral, on a Saturday afternoon in May whilst watching Max play rugby. Out of nowhere, the father and daughter had reappeared – the same two people he had observed at the game in April, back when he had been berating the loss of Olivia, little realising that he was about to lose his wife.

The father and daughter had reappeared to teach him something, he had felt certain. They were trying to hammer home the point that he had failed to see the first time around.

That very evening, he had suggested to the twins that they supported each other by attending each other's sporting fixtures from then on. Olivia would go to the rugby with them, and they in turn would cheer her on at hockey.

There were grumbles, but he had insisted. And now the twins supported each other, all the while spending time as a family.

Looking back, it was daft that he hadn't thought of it before.

The door to the counsellor's room was opening. Beverley was approaching, with her huge smile. Gareth stood to greet them. 'How did you get on?' he said.

Max smiled at him. 'OK, Dad. It's cool.'

'Cool?' Gareth said. 'Is this the same boy who said that counselling was full of hippies waving incense sticks?'

Beverley laughed. 'You said that?'

Max blushed. 'I was joking. You're all right, Bev.'

'Bev?' Gareth said. 'Bit casual, aren't you, son?'

Beverley smiled, dazzling them. 'He can call me what he likes so long as he keeps coming to see me.' She turned to Gareth. 'Could I have a quick word? Max, would you mind waiting?'

She led Gareth back to her consulting room. They both took a seat on one of the red cubes.

'I have to say, I'm so impressed with Max. He's come on leaps and bounds these past few months.'

'That's great. I'm pleased to hear it. He's a good lad.'

'He certainly is,' she said. 'You don't have anything to worry about. He's coping really well ... That said, I'd recommend that the twins come to the Lighthouse for as long as they can.'

'If you'll have us, then we'll be here. Thank you ... I don't know what I'd have done without this place.'

'I've a feeling you'd have found a way. I think you're stronger than you realise.'

'Well, I don't know about that ...' he said.

'And Olivia just adores you,' she said, standing up. 'Not every father has a relationship like that with his daughter. It's precious.'

At the door, Gareth paused. 'Yes,' he said. 'It is.'

Sunday 19 August 2018

'This is it then,' Gareth said, picking up the suitcase and placing it in the boot of the car.

'Yep,' said his father. 'We don't have to go, though. Just say the word and it can all go back inside the house.'

'No, Dad,' Gareth said, slamming the boot decisively. 'You have to go. It's time. You've been here far too long.'

'Me and your father did discuss moving back here, son,' his mother said, appearing by his side.

'You what?' Gareth said. 'No way. You moved to Pembrokeshire because that's where you wanted to be, and that's where you're staying.'

'But it's so far away,' his mother said. 'Things are different now ...'

'Let's just drop it,' his father said. 'We can discuss this another time.'

'We're never discussing it,' Gareth said, 'because it's not happening.'

'What's not happening?' said Max, coming down the driveway, looking at his phone. He had mastered the art of phone walking, even managing to glide between two plant pots.

'Never you mind,' Gareth said. 'Come on. Let's get you two on the road before the rush.'

'What rush?' said his father.

'You know ... The rush.'

There was no rush in Milford, not on a Sunday in August at seven in the morning. The birds were whistling; the dew was forming mist on the lawn; the sunshine was streaming between the hedges.

His mother was getting into the car, looking at him doubtfully.

'It's fine, Mum,' he told her. 'You've been brilliant. We can manage.'

His father took his hand, shook it. 'I don't doubt it, son. You've made me and your mother proud.'

Gareth felt his eyes tingle as tears threatened. 'Thanks, Dad.'

'We'll give you a bell to say we're back,' said his mum, frantically working the old-fashioned handle to pull the window down. 'But don't expect it to be too early. We'll be stopping off at the Little Chef near Swansea.'

Gareth chuckled. 'I know it well, Mum.'

'Where's Olivia?' his father said, poking his head out of the window to look at the house.

'She's on her way.' Gareth turned to the front door, watching for his daughter. Sure enough, she appeared in her fluffy dressing gown, her eyes bleary from a heavy sleep.

'Do I look beautiful?' she said.

'Never better,' Gareth said.

She looked just like Jenny.

There were parts of his wife that pained him to dwell on – the secretive parts that he would never solve or understand. But he had learnt to focus on the bits that he had been sure of and had loved. Jenny had been beautiful, generous, great fun. What use was it to think otherwise now?

'Bye then, Dad,' Gareth said, twitching his nose to tell his tears to stay back. 'Bye, Mum.'

The car was reversing cautiously, far slower than Gareth ever drove, his dad craning his neck and his mother following suit. She sat beside him like a wing man, taking her responsibility as passenger very seriously.

'Bye, Grandma,' Olivia was shouting, waving. 'Bye, Grandpa.'

Max had pushed his phone in his pocket and was waving too.

Gareth followed after them. Out in the road as they straightened up, he approached the car. 'I'll see you soon.'

'We'll be back for the inquest, son. Sometime in November, it should be.' His father nodded determinedly.

'Thanks, Dad. Thanks for everything.'

'It was our pleasure.'

The way his father said that – earnestly, meaningfully – choked Gareth. He looked down, kicked a stone into the hedgerow.

He remained standing in the lane, watching the car easing away. His mother waved her hand out of the window, and then the car turned the bend and they were out of sight.

Gareth sniffed, rubbed his face. Max joined him, patting his back. 'So, Dad ... it's Sunday. There's nothing on the white-board. What are we going to do?'

'Dunno, son. But we'll think of something.'

They joined Olivia on the doorstep. 'It'll be quiet without them,' she said.

'Yes,' Gareth said. 'It will.'

'Shall I make those cinnamon muffin thingies?' she said. 'Grandma left me her recipe.'

'Sounds good,' Gareth said. 'Put the kettle on while you're at it.'

He stood for a moment at the back door, looking at the early-morning light; at the lawn, which his father had insisted on mowing yesterday before leaving; at the pots of geraniums that his mother had tended to diligently.

His parents had done all that they could for him. He could take it from here.

42

2 months later
Monday 29 October 2018

The text message came through at nine o'clock at night, just as the children were settling down to sleep. It was endlessly dark outside. Nina's Hallowe'en pumpkin was sitting on the step outside the French doors, leering at them, a candle flame dancing in its mouth.

They had just opened a bottle of wine and were talking about their days: Melissa had secured a booking for an international conference at the venue in spring; Lee was renovating a Second World War boat for a rich enthusiast, tearing off the fibreglass deck, treating rotten wood, getting the engine to work.

When her phone beeped, she picked it up, read the text.

We're moving Saturday. Please join us for a farewell drink 7pm Fri. Bring the kids. Let me know if you can come. Rach x

Melissa pushed the phone towards Lee. He read the message. 'That's nice,' he said. 'Are we going?'
She looked at the pumpkin, watching the light flicker inside as though its eyes were winking. 'I suppose we should. It'll be

strange, though. When was the last time we were all in the same room together?'

Neither of them spoke as they tried to think of the answer.

'You should have seen the bees,' Lee said, taking a drink of wine.

'Bees?'

'Yes,' he said. 'There was a massive bees' nest inside the boat.'

She smiled, picked up her phone, texted her response.

We'll be there. M x

Friday 2 November 2018

Rachel had gone to some effort; that much was clear. It wasn't just for them, Melissa realised, since the house had been industrially cleaned and was spotless in preparation for the move. But she had gone all out with the snacks: miniature burgers, pigs in blankets, tempura prawns.

'Are those quail eggs?' Melissa said, pointing.

'Sadly yes. They're from a catering company. Al insisted. It's his way of saying . . .'

Of saying what?

Goodbye? Sorry?

Rachel didn't finish the sentence. Melissa would never know what it was that Al was hoping to achieve. Maybe he didn't even know himself.

So much of what had happened between them had been left dangling, unspoken. Perhaps accidents always did that, creating a troubling silence because something had happened that shouldn't have, leaving everyone to try to make sense of a mistake.

'I'll take your coat,' Rachel said.

'Aren't we going outside?' Melissa said. 'I think Al's got the fire pit going.'

'Yes, good thinking. Keep your coat on.'

'Shall I tell the kids to get a plate and take some food outside?'

'Yes, please,' Rachel said. She seemed nervous, busying herself with arranging plastic cutlery in a basket.

Melissa touched Rachel's hand. 'It's OK,' she said. 'It doesn't have to be perfect. It's only . . . ' She would have said *the Silkies*, but no one ever used that term any more. 'Well, it's just us.'

Rachel stopped what she was doing, looked at Melissa. Her glasses had a little smear across them – butter, perhaps. It saddened Melissa to see it there.

What had happened to them? After their meeting at the café, they had gone months without seeing each other, aside from a few brief run-ins outside the senior school.

Until recently, Melissa had always believed that it would be impossible to hide in Milford. Yet she barely saw anyone, not now that she dashed off at school drop-offs, didn't attend PTA meetings, had stood down from committees and had withdrawn from volunteer teams. It was very easy to become invisible; modern life even seemed to facilitate it.

'I'm sorry if I seem uptight,' Rachel said. 'I wanted everything to be nice.'

'And it is. So now you can relax . . . May I?' She motioned to the unopened bottle of red wine beside them.

Rachel smiled. 'Since when do you ask?'

Since Jenny died.

Since everything changed.

Melissa often had thoughts like this – disconcerting moments that spiked her day. Sometimes, she thought that she would never be able to move past being arrested, even if everyone else around her managed to. It would be forever there, a persistent ghost that frightened as well as shamed her.

She poured two glasses of wine and there was a momentary lull of calm as the two women clinked their glasses together. And then there came the sound of footsteps pummelling down the hallway and the door flung open and in ran Polly, chased by Ned, who was whacking her with a roll of bubble wrap.

'Woah! Slow down!' Rachel said. 'Ned! You'll knock the food over. Everything's been cleaned!'

'Help!' Polly shrieked. 'Mummy!' She grabbed Melissa by the coat and spun her around to deflect Ned, before taking off again, running from the kitchen, Ned thundering after her.

The door slammed shut.

'I'll miss this bedlam,' Rachel said.

'So will I. But I'm sure you'll find bedlam in Southfield. It tends to follow kids wherever they go.'

Melissa sipped her wine and cast her eye nostalgically around the kitchen, knowing that this was the last time she would ever be here.

Rachel was looking at her, about to say something. It always took her such a long time to speak. Melissa waited, trying not to smile at her friend's age-old habit.

'Mel . . . I've been meaning to say this.' Rachel paused, took a breath. 'I'm so very sorry. I never meant to hurt you. If I could replay it, I would.'

'It's OK,' Melissa said. 'I know you—'

They were interrupted by the sound of the doorbell ringing. 'That must be Gareth,' Rachel said.

And it was then that Melissa remembered when they had last been in a room all together: at Jenny's wake.

⚓

Outside, the darkness was thick around them. The next-door neighbours had lit a bonfire, the occasional ember or spark escaping into the night. Some people were doing firework displays tonight. There were crackles and whistles in the sky, echoing through the countryside, lighting up the sea.

You could see Hope Cove from Rachel's garden, although not by night. Every now and then a cold breeze met them from the Atlantic, and Melissa turned to look at the black sheet that lay ahead of them, catching sight of a lone light on a boat or the blink of the lighthouse along the headland.

Al had lit the fire pit. It wasn't for bonfire night, he had assured them, but just something to keep them warm. Melissa glanced along the circle of faces around the flames. The adults were drinking wine, glasses glimmering. The children were toasting marshmallows, apart from Polly who was tired and lying on Melissa's lap.

Melissa hummed a tune, stroking Polly's hair, watching Gareth. He and Al didn't appear to have said very much to each other, yet Gareth had shown up, and Al seemed greatly cheered by that fact alone.

No one had been frosty with her. Gareth had even given her a little peck on the cheek in greeting earlier.

Perhaps all was not lost.

On her lap, Polly gave another big yawn. Melissa was about to suggest calling it a night, when Gareth suddenly stood up. Frank and Olivia were set aside from everyone else on deck-chairs in the middle of the lawn, but even they looked up as Gareth tried to make a chime on his glass with a plastic fork.

'I'd just like to say,' he said, 'that I know things have been very difficult for everyone, but I'm glad that we're all here tonight. Thank you for having us ... Al, Rach, I'm pleased you've found a new home.' He raised his glass to them. 'I hope you'll be happy.'

There was a murmur of assent. 'Aye, aye,' Lee said.

'Aye aye? Who says that any more?' Melissa said.

'Aye aye do.'

Everyone moaned.

'So, here's to us,' Gareth said. 'And here's to Jen … We love you, sweetheart … And here's to the … uh …' His voice wavered. Max quickly stood up, his hand on his father's back. Gareth nodded at his son, then raised his glass higher. 'To the Silkies.'

There was a moment's silence as everyone absorbed his words.

Then there was a shrieking sound as a rocket took off, exploding. From around the neighbourhood, there came the sound of dogs howling, hands clapping, children cheering. There was another screech and they all stood to watch as a cascade of pink light filled the sky.

'To the Silkies,' they said, clinking glasses.

43

Tuesday 20 November 2018

'So, they've gone, then,' Melissa's mother said, filling the kettle. 'I drove by their place the other day and saw a moving van in the driveway.'

'They went over two weeks ago,' Melissa said, head cupped in hands at her mother's kitchen counter. 'Must have been the new people.'

'Well, they'll have big shoes to fill. Everyone knew the Beckinsales.'

'Luckily, it's a big house,' Melissa said flatly.

Her mother turned to look at her. 'What's wrong? You seem down.'

It was always very annoying when her mother asked obvious questions.

'Aside from losing Jenny and now Rachel?'

'You haven't lost Rachel, not in the same way. She's not that far away and I'm sure she'll be back. And in the meantime, you've got your family,' her mother said cheerfully.

What was up with her?

'Speaking of which,' her mother continued, reaching into the cupboard for the coffee jar, 'could you go and check on David?

He's watching that documentary. If I have to see those blessed fish one more time ...'

'No problem,' Melissa replied, relieved to escape. She would take the fish over her mother's simulated bonhomie any time.

The old bungalow felt slower than usual today, as though the second hand on the clock was stuck and kept wobbling. And it wasn't just here; it was the same everywhere. Time had taken on a strange sticky quality in the aftermath of Rachel's departure.

Melissa walked down the hallway, feeling her forehead, wondering if perhaps she were running a temperature or going down with a cold.

Inside the lounge, the air was warm, the radiators emitting waves of warmth that were rippling in front of the windows. David was rocking in pleasure, clapping his hands at the sight of the fish shoals swirling on the screen. There was little light outside, even though the curtains were open. The sun was pale, straw-coloured; there was a frost on the lawn. Christmas was coming, five weeks today, but she couldn't contemplate it yet – couldn't imagine being happy enough to feel festive.

There was the inquest to get through first, which had been delayed and was taking place on 10 December. Only those who had been present at the accident were needed as witnesses. After much consideration, she and Lee had decided not to attend. It would feel inappropriate, as though she were hanging around, hoping for an official pardon.

'How are you doing?' she asked her brother, sitting down next to him.

'Very well, thank you,' he said, not taking his eyes from the screen.

She patted his knee. 'Love you, David,' she said.

'I love you too, Melissa.'

Restless, she stood up and went to the window, looking at

the frozen bird bath and David's tyre, which he had abandoned years ago beside the garage wall.

Behind her, David began to rock gleefully, the sofa creaking. She knew which scene it was without looking. 'Puffins! It's a colony,' he said, stamping his bare feet. He had long, very white feet, with clumps of hair on the toes. It always made her sad to see his feet; she wasn't sure why.

'Yes,' she said. 'It is.'

'Like the one around South Rocks.'

She turned to look at him. 'What?'

He paid no attention, was lost in his documentary again. She went over to him, rooted around for the remote control, which he was sitting on, and paused the TV.

'Hey!' David said, holding his hands up in protest. 'What are you doing?'

She pointed the remote control at him. 'What colony, David?'

He looked confused.

'You just said there's a colony of puffins around South Rocks,' she said.

'Yes,' he said, his face clearing. 'There is. There was.'

'It's not there now?'

'Don't be ridiculous. Puffins arrive at the colony in spring,' he said robotically. 'They leave again in August. Some stay behind in the North Sea for the winter months, and others go further south to—'

'OK,' she said, handing him back the remote control. 'You can put it back on.'

She returned to the window. She was silly to have homed in on South Rocks. It had just been a while since anyone had mentioned that area.

A scraggy-looking sparrow was sitting on David's tyre. She watched it as it hopped about, pecking the frosty rubber with its beak.

David had put the documentary back on. Music was playing – harps and chiming bells, as the fishes swam. The music and the heat in the room made her feel light, as though she were spinning in a tumble dryer.

'It was there in April,' David said. 'It was a surprise.'

She turned again to look at him. 'Hey?'

'A surprise,' he said, nodding.

'For who?' Her scalp suddenly felt very tight.

David was ignoring her, staring at the screen.

'For who, David?' she said. She stood in front of the TV, blocking it. 'Jenny?'

David was trying to look past her, swivelling his head to do so. 'No.'

She thought again. 'Was it Jenny's surprise for someone else?'

'Yes, that's right,' he said.

'But how did she know about it?'

He frowned. 'I don't know,' he said, glancing at her nervously.

She paused the programme again and sat down beside him, taking his hand. 'Please think about this, David,' she said gently. 'It's really important.'

He did as he was told, just like he always did. He was thinking about her question, was even looking away from the paused screen and down at the carpet.

'I told her. I saw her in town,' he said. 'Is that bad?'

'No,' she said. 'Of course not. You did nothing wrong. But what exactly did you say to Jenny?'

He tapped his head, trying to concentrate. 'I told her that it was a good idea to take her friends around South Rocks as a surprise, to see the new colony. No one else knew about it.'

She could hear her mother's footsteps approaching down the hallway. She spoke quickly, her voice low. 'So how did you know about it, David?'

He gazed at her with his beautiful summer-green eyes.

'Mum told me.'

The door opened then and their mother appeared, carrying a tray. 'Sorry that took so long,' she said. 'I forgot to put the kettle on. I was standing there stupidly waiting for it to boil.' She looked at Melissa and then David. 'What on earth's wrong?'

44

'What's this all about, Melissa? You drag me in here, interrogating me . . .'

They were standing in the kitchen, with the door closed, facing each other over the central island. 'Tell me the truth,' Melissa said. 'About the colony.'

'Oh, enough about the colony! This is nonsense. Our drinks are getting cold. What's got into you?'

'I want to know why you told David to tell Jenny about the puffins. She wasn't exactly a bird enthusiast, was she?'

'Which is why I didn't say that,' her mother said. 'He's making it up.'

'And why would he do that?'

'Because he's David. He gets confused.'

'Well, I don't think he seemed confused about this. In fact, he seemed pretty clear about it to me.'

'Either way, it's nonsense. Let's go back to the—'

'Stop it, Mum!' Melissa shouted, bringing her fist down on the counter. 'I can tell that you're lying. I just want to know why.'

Her mother leant across the counter towards her, her dark eyes glinting threateningly. 'Keep your voice down, young lady,' she hissed. 'I've already told you: I am not going to discuss this. I need to get back to David. He's my priority.'

'And don't I know it.'

Her mother, halfway towards the door, stopped, turned around. 'I beg your pardon?'

'It's OK, Mum. I know how it is. David comes first. I always just had to get on with things, didn't I? Good old Melissa. No wonder I ended up like this.'

'Like what?' her mother said, cocking her head in curiosity. She genuinely didn't seem to think that there was anything wrong with her daughter.

'Well, let me see,' Melissa said, holding out her fingers, checking them off. 'So far this year, I've been called hot-headed, interfering, controlling; I've been arrested on suspicion of the murder of my best friend; and half the town – if not more – can't stand the sight of me.'

Her mother flapped her hand dismissively. 'Oh, that's a load of tosh. Since when have you cared what people think?'

Melissa stepped towards her. 'Since forever, Mum. I've always cared. You just didn't know it. You've never really seen me.'

'Never seen you?' Her mother laughed. 'Oh, please! This conversation is ridiculous.' She folded her arms. 'I know everything there is to know about you. I know that you're strong and resilient and that until recently – until you started feeling sorry for yourself – you were the most formidable woman in this town. I didn't have to mollycoddle you. You'd have hated that. People looked up to you. That's who you are, Melissa. That's who I raised you to be.'

Melissa gazed at her mother, who was gesticulating with her hands as she spoke, her curly hair flapping about, and for the first time, despite their differences, saw herself.

'So what if I made mistakes?' her mother was saying. 'I was doing my best as a single parent, raising a child with special needs and a headstrong young missy, with another child in the grave and a divorce, not to mention a mountain of debt.

So, pardon me if I didn't raise you as beautifully as you might have liked.'

Her mother broke off, glancing back at the closed door, ever mindful of David.

'What mountain of debt?' Melissa said. 'I didn't know anything about that.'

Her mother snorted. 'Of course you didn't. You were too busy making a list of all my faults, by the sounds of things. But just so you're clear: when your father left, the kayak academy was bleeding money left, right and centre. It wasn't my dream; it was his. Yet I had no choice but to get the place up and running and keep it in the black.' She prodded her chest with her thumb. 'That was muggins, here. Keeping it all together. And it wasn't easy, I'm telling you. If you want to know where you get your hard-nosed resilience from, then look no further.'

'I'm sorry,' Melissa said. 'I didn't know ...'

'Well, now you do. So, if it's all right with you, I'm going to sit down with my son before my coffee gets cold.'

'No,' Melissa said. 'It's not all right.'

Her mother clenched her hands, stamped her foot. 'For crying out loud, Melissa! What do you want from me?'

Melissa pulled out the stool, sat down at the counter. 'I'm not leaving here until you tell me.'

'Tell you what?'

'The truth ... You planted the idea with David about going around South Rocks, didn't you?'

Her mother laughed, throwing her head back. 'That's absurd! I have no idea what you're talking about. It's all getting on top of you. You've been working too hard at the marina and—'

'You told him to tell Jenny, but to keep it a secret. Did he know how dangerous it was around there? I'm guessing not. He wouldn't send someone to their death. He's too sweet for that. But ... how about you? Would you?'

348

'I don't need to answer that. How dare you? This whole thing has got out of hand,' her mother said, adjusting her waist scarf agitatedly. She had recently dyed her hair, which looked brassy under the kitchen lights. Melissa sometimes thought of telling her that her hair shade was too dark for her age, yet never had the courage to do so.

If her mother thought she was all balls and resilience, she was wrong – again.

'The police knew everything, Mum,' she said. 'They knew how it was done. They accused me of it – said that I predicted the storm, deleted the booking, didn't update the weather, tampered with the kayak. It didn't occur to me that the only other person who could have done all that ... was you.'

'Don't be so stupid,' her mother said, still fiddling with the scarf.

'Why?' Melissa said. 'Why would you do that to Jenny? Have you any idea what this has done to her family? And what about me? This has almost destroyed me and my marriage. Poor Lee! How could you put us through all that? I'm your daughter! I'd never do that to Nina or Polly, ever.'

'Well, aren't you the perfect parent, Melissa?' her mother said bitterly, turning away.

Melissa stood up, went to her. 'How could you?'

'I knew they wouldn't press charges – that they wouldn't have any evidence.'

'But how could you have known that, unless you knew the truth? Is that why you were being so nice – the invitation to lunch ...?'

'Lunch?' her mother said, confused.

'It all makes sense now.'

'What does?'

'The only thing I don't know is why. What did Jenny ever do to you?'

She hadn't thought the question through, hadn't thought

349

anything through since coming into the kitchen. She realised then where they were standing: at the window, overlooking the garden, all the way across the grass to the laurel hedge.

'Oh,' Melissa said, clasping her hand to her mouth. 'Hannah.'

Returning to the counter, she sat back down, feeling faint. The floor was rushing up at her, her ears hissing. 'What have you done?' She began to cry.

Her mother approached her, gripped both Melissa's arms, shaking her. 'This has gone too far. That's enough!'

But Melissa wasn't listening to her mother, was wriggling to break free, panicking. 'You killed Jenny. You killed her!'

She was just about to jump down from the stool when she felt a blinding smack against her cheek and stopped still.

'I'm sorry,' her mother gushed, her hand frozen mid-air. 'I didn't mean to hit you.'

Melissa stared at her mother in shock, touching her fingers lightly to her cheek.

'Melissa . . .'

'Get away from me!' she said, holding her hand up in defence as she climbed down from the stool.

'Please. This has all gone wrong. I didn't mean to hurt you. I just wanted you to stop shouting and calm down. David's in the other room. He'll hear.'

'You're worried about David?' Melissa said. 'What about Jenny? What about Gareth and the twins? What about me?'

Her mother held the counter edge, her voice trembling. 'And what about Hannah? She'd be thirty-five years old now. A grown woman with children of her own.'

'This was revenge?' Melissa said. 'But Jenny was just a little girl too at the time. She was ten!'

Her mother looked up then in anger, her mouth a network of lines. 'Old enough to know better. And she was about to do it all again too, to your own son.'

'What are you talking about? What's Frank got to do with—'

'Jenny was going to abort his child – your grandchild – my great-grandchild.'

'How did you know about that?' She looked at her mother in bewilderment. 'This was about the termination?'

'That wretched woman had already caused the death of one of our family,' her mother said, turning away again. 'I wasn't going to stand by and let her do it again. She'd already got the private clinic booked, and was bribing the children. Olivia was promised a flat for university, amongst other things.'

'Bribing them? That's insane! She was just looking out for her daughter. That's what good parents do, Mother, not that you'd know anything about that!'

'Stop it!' her mother said, turning on her heel to snarl at her. 'Stop defending her! Stop attacking me! That's the way it's always been with you. Well, I've just about had enough of it. If you weren't going to do anything about the situation, then I was.'

'But I didn't even know about it! How could I have done anything? I don't understand how *you* knew about it.'

'Because Frank came to me,' her mother retorted quickly, proudly. 'We're family, Melissa. We help each other out.'

'Frank ... came to you?' Melissa said. 'You barely know each other!'

'He still came to me, though. And not to you. He didn't think you'd take his side. He thought you'd side with Jenny. And he was right, listening to you now.'

'And he wanted to keep it?' Melissa said. 'At his age? He was sure of that?'

'No,' her mother said, scowling. 'He wasn't sure of anything. He just wanted more time. He was confused and frightened, poor boy. But Jenny didn't want them to get attached to the idea. She just wanted it gone as quickly as possible. She was pushing them too fast. Which is why they came to me. I saw reason and asked Jenny to—'

'You went to her?'

'Absolutely. And she had the nerve to send me away, practically slamming the door in my face.'

'That doesn't sound like her.'

'Well, I can assure you that's what happened.'

'Then maybe she felt she had good reason. You were attacking her decision, undermining her.'

'Oh, for crying out loud!' her mother said. 'You're *still* defending her!'

'That's because,' Melissa shouted, 'she was my best friend!'

'Some friend,' her mother said, her voice low, full of malice. 'She killed your little sister.'

'I'm sorry, Mother, but that's where you're wrong.'

For the first time, her mother looked wrong-footed. She stared at Melissa. 'What do you mean?'

Melissa felt her cheek again; it was throbbing. Sitting back down, she tried to gather the words but they wouldn't come, even though she had practised this conversation often enough, going over the lines at night. Her mouth felt dry, her mind empty.

'It wasn't Jenny,' she said.

'What are you talking about?'

'Jenny didn't give Hannah the charm.'

'Then who did?'

Melissa spoke quietly, trying not to betray the tremble in her voice. 'It was me.'

'What?' Her mother was looking at her in disbelief, her eyes angry little dots. 'I don't believe you. You're bluffing.'

'Why would I do that? It's true. I made Jenny take the charm off her necklace. She didn't want to because it was brand new. But I got my way, and I gave it to Hannah. It was me. All me.'

Her mother had gone white in the face. 'Then why did she say it was her? When the ambulance men were here and the police ... She said so, in front of everyone. Why would you have let her tell us that?'

Melissa hesitated, wondering whether to tell the truth. She had to, though; she had already waited too long.

'At the time, I just went along with it. I didn't know what else to do. But afterwards ...'

'Yes?'

'Afterwards ...' she said falteringly, '... she said that she knew you wouldn't take it out on her ... But that if it had been me ...'

'What are you saying, Melissa? She was protecting you from me? What am I? Some sort of monster?'

'No. You were just always very hard on me, compared to her.'

'Because she wasn't my child. That's only natural!'

'Yes,' Melissa said. 'But she wasn't close to her parents and she knew how painful that was ... And years later, when we were in our teens, she told me that it hadn't mattered what you had thought of her. But that she had done it to protect our relationship.'

'Whose relationship?'

'Ours, Mum,' Melissa said. 'You and me.'

'Oh.'

'So, you see,' Melissa said, 'she really was the best friend I ever had.'

A silence fell. She strained to listen for the sound of David's programme, wondering whether he was still watching it, but she couldn't hear anything.

'That's remarkable,' her mother said, picking up a tea towel from the counter and folding it neatly, as though that mattered. 'Quite a sacrifice. But it still stands that she was going to abort the baby. And besides, it wasn't guaranteed that the South

353

Rocks trip would be fatal. That was in the lap of the gods. It was simply a lesson in how precious life is — how it shouldn't be trifled with.'

Melissa felt her heart shrink, retreat. She didn't want to fight any more.

'Jenny was the last person who needed that lesson, after everything she and I had been through,' she said.

'I beg to differ.'

'You're not going to admit what you did?'

Her mother smiled tautly. 'I think we both know that's never going to happen.'

'So, what now?' Melissa asked.

'Well, it seems to me that you have a choice to make.'

'What choice?'

Her mother patted the folded tea towel. 'If you go to the police with this, David will go into care. And take it from me, I know what happens when adults are put into care after a lifetime of being looked after at home. The effects can be devastating.'

'That won't be a problem. I'll look after him.'

'Alongside the marina and three children? I'd like to see that. Plus, if anything scandalous happens to me, he won't cope. The trauma will kill him. He'll need professional help.'

'I'll work something out.'

'Well, let me know when you do. I'll be interested to hear. After all, this is the perfect decision for you.'

'What does that mean?'

With the shadow of a smile, her mother walked away. At the door, she said, 'It's friends or family, Melissa.'

Melissa picked up her bag, followed her mother. 'That's easy,' she said. 'Barely a decision at all.'

'Oh?'

'I choose Jenny.'

Her mother looked stunned. 'You're going to the police?'

Melissa didn't reply, left the room, making her way down the hallway.

'Melissa! Where are you going? You can't just walk away!'

'Tell David I'm sorry to go without saying goodbye. Give him my love,' she said, closing the front door behind her.

Outside, she remembered how cold it was. The sun was sinking low in the sky, illuminating the last of the red leaves that were clinging to the trees. Flies were circling lazily, their wings aglow in the sunshine. She took in the long grass, the place by the laurel hedge, before getting into her car and driving away.

ANGELA GOULD

Milford resident, Dorset

Angela had always wanted to be a Silkie. Had she had a bucket list – had such a thing existed back then – she would have put *be a Silkie* right at the top, ahead of having kids or getting married; and she hadn't been the only one.

Not that anyone would have dared to suggest such a thing to Melissa Silk. She had been too intimidating. But that was before Jennifer's accident, and the arrest. She hadn't been herself since then. Word about town was that she was softer, more accessible, less sure of herself. Ironically, the scandal had levelled her social status, making her one of them, which in turn made her appealing.

It seemed that Melissa would always find popularity, or rather, it would find her. Even Nessa said so, and she had always been one of Melissa's harshest critics, and her biggest fan, truth told.

It would be easier for Angela to approach Melissa now, as soon as she had summoned the courage.

It was thirty-two years since she had last done so.

On that day, 13 August 1986, she had washed her hair especially and had worn the cornflower-blue dress that her mother had made her for Sunday school. She had opted to make Tollhouse Cookies for the occasion. She wasn't sure what they were exactly, but they had chocolate chips in and she had taken the recipe from a library book.

She was carrying the cookies in a Tupperware box, which she set down on the porch while she rang the doorbell. She didn't live far away, but it was a hot walk along the lane and she felt damp and sticky; she flapped her dress as she waited.

Someone was coming. But then she heard a horrible screaming sound, rising over the rooftop of the bungalow, piercing the sky.

She could hear Melissa shouting, then Melissa's mother. Something terrible was happening. Petrified, she picked up the Tupperware box and ran all the way home.

Sometimes, she wondered what she had set in motion by calling around that day, drawing Melissa away from the person she had been charged with looking after. Had she not done so, perhaps sweet little Hannah Reeve would have still been alive today.

Would Melissa see it that way? There was only one way to find out.

She would have to be brave and knock on her door again.

EPILOGUE

Monday 10 December 2018

On the day of the inquest, Melissa and Lee went down to Hope Cove.

It was still a beautiful spot, even in winter. Her mother's academy was closed for December, as it always was. Melissa didn't spare it much thought as she and Lee passed it by, holding hands on their way down to the beach. She tried not to think of the last time she had been here, standing underneath the hawthorn trees at twilight, retrieving her friends' bags on the day of the accident.

That was all behind them; almost.

They had brought biscuits and a flask of hot chocolate laced with brandy. Together, on a blanket, they sat side by side, gazing at the shifting sea.

Every so often, she checked her phone. Rachel had said she would text them the outcome.

They had been texting each other a lot lately, far more than they had when Rachel had still been living here. The distance between them had helped. The Beckinsales were settled in their new home and were thriving, by all accounts. Melissa was pleased for them, in a roundabout sort of way. Eventually, her pleasure wouldn't have any kinks or misgivings.

'No matter what happens today,' Lee said, 'this is the end. Agreed?'

'Agreed,' she said.

They looked at the sea, sipping the hot chocolate, the brandy warming her stomach. She tried not to look at South Rocks, but inevitably her eye was drawn there; Lee was doing the same thing.

'She was a good person,' he said.

'Yes,' she said.

'What she did for you . . . '

Melissa nodded. 'My mother used the word "remarkable". But I don't think that's strong enough. More like heroic.'

'I'm still your number-one hero, though, right?'

'Always.' She leant into him for cover from the wind, pressing her face into his jacket. 'Do you think I did the right thing?'

'Yes. It's what Jenny would have wanted.'

'Even if it meant hiding the truth?'

'Even then,' he said. 'She took a bullet for you when you were kids so that you could still have a relationship with your mum. Family was precious to her.'

'Not precious enough, though, in my mother's eyes. Jenny wanted to abort the baby.'

'Because she thought that was what was best for Olivia.'

Melissa took another sip of hot chocolate. 'And this is what's best for David. He's the innocent party here.'

'Exactly. If you feel yourself wavering, think of him.'

Stretching out her legs, she pushed her boots into the sand, watching the sand hoppers bouncing high into the air.

She hooked her hand through Lee's arm 'She completely misunderstood when I told her I was choosing Jenny,' she said. 'She thought that meant going to the police.'

'Yep,' Lee said, reaching into the bag for the biscuits.

'But it meant standing by family.' She bit her lip pensively. 'When should I put her straight?'

He gazed at the sea, taking in the outline of South Rocks, the breaking waves, the sunshine lighting the horizon. 'No rush,' he said.

'I'll never forgive her.'

'Then don't think about it ... But speaking of forgiveness ...' he said.

She looked at him. 'What?'

'I'm sorry I doubted you. I never truly believed you were guilty.'

'It's OK,' she said. 'But it is frustrating that I can't clear my name.'

'That's the price you pay for protecting your brother,' he said. 'People move on quickly, mind you. It'll be old news soon.'

Her phone beeped then. She picked it up, looked at it. 'Here goes nothing,' she said.

He bent his head to read the message with her.

All over. Verdict = tragic accident. Going home. Will phone at Christmas. Rach xox

'So that's it,' Lee said.

'Yes.'

And they stayed a little longer, until they had drunk all the hot chocolate and the sun had dipped low, almost into the sea.

Saturday 22 December 2018

Three days before Christmas, there was a knock at the door. Melissa wondered who would be calling this early on a Saturday morning. She was in the middle of making mince pies with the girls. Polly had signed her up for the town's Christmas

360

fete cake stall, saying that she had always run it in the past so why not now?

To her surprise, it was Angela Gould. She seemed dressed up, wearing a bright lipstick and a long blue woollen coat.

'Oh, hello, Angela,' Melissa said, trying not to make her greeting sound like a question.

'Hello, Melissa,' Angela said. 'Is this a bad time? I wanted to catch you before you went out … in case you were going out … because you sometimes go out …'

'I'm just making mince pies.'

'Mummy?' Polly called. 'Can you hurry up? Nina's doing it wrong.'

'No I'm not,' Nina shouted.

'I *have* come at a bad time,' Angela said.

'No, I'm OK for a minute. What can I help you with?'

Angela hesitated. 'I was hoping to have a quick word.'

'Oh. Well, come on in. You can talk to me whilst I roll pastry.'

'Actually,' Angela said, following Melissa down the hallway, 'it's quite a personal matter.'

Melissa turned to look at her neighbour in curiosity. Angela seemed flustered, her eyes darting about nervously. 'In that case, we'd better go in here.' And she led Angela into the dining room, closing the door behind them.

Angela sat down at the table. Melissa, however, remained standing, leaning against the radiator for warmth. 'I mustn't be too long,' she said. 'Kids can make a lot of mess with flour and eggs.'

'Yes,' Angela said.

The atmosphere felt awkward, tense.

'I like your coat,' Melissa said, to break the silence. 'It's a pretty colour on you.'

'Thank you,' Angela said. 'Cornflower blue.'

Angela had such a strange look on her face then that Melissa suddenly felt apprehensive.

'What's this about?' she asked.

Angela closed her eyes and spoke quickly, as though fearful that she might change her mind and stop talking. 'Thirty-two years ago, the day that your little sister died ... I was there. I called to your door. I was coming around to see you ... It was me who knocked on the door.'

Melissa stared at her. 'What?'

Angela opened her eyes. 'I've carried this burden all these years. Please don't hate me.'

Melissa didn't know what to say. She gazed at the woman sitting before her, with her watery eyes and lipstick that bled into the cracks around her mouth. And in an instant, her anger rose.

If it weren't for her, Hannah would still be alive; and if that were so, then Jenny would still be here too. And Melissa would never have been arrested.

She thought of her mother and what she had done – a toxic chain of events that would never have taken place had this inane woman not knocked on their door.

Polly called to her then, from the kitchen. 'Mummy? Where are you?'

Melissa came to, feeling ashamed. What was she thinking? Angela had only been a child too – just ten years old, a year older than Polly was now. She was no more guilty of causing what had happened than Melissa or Jenny were.

'Who else knows about this?' she asked.

'No one,' Angela said, pulling a tissue from her pocket and holding it to her eyes. 'I was so upset about it, I kept it to myself.'

Melissa thought about that, imagining Angela holding such a troubling secret deep inside her for so long.

She knew exactly how that felt. She also knew how it felt to be judged and vilified.

'It wasn't your fault,' she said. 'It was brave of you to come here today. But I think we should keep this to ourselves and say no more of it.'

'OK.' Angela blew her nose, trembling pitifully. 'I'm so very sorry.' She looked up at Melissa then and the two women locked eyes for a moment.

'I know you are,' Melissa said. She glanced at the closed door. 'I should get back to the kitchen.'

Angela rose immediately. They went down the hallway in silence.

At the front door, as Angela stepped off the porch, Melissa suddenly thought of something. 'Angela?'

Angela stopped. 'Yes?'

'What did you want?'

'I'm sorry?'

'The day you called round. What did you want? You didn't say.'

Angela looked away. When she spoke again, her voice was steeped in sadness. 'To be your friend.'

Melissa gazed at her in surprise. And then Angela turned away and left.

'Maybe give me some time . . . ' Melissa called after her.

Once again, Angela stopped, her head cocked hopefully. 'Not a problem,' she said. 'I've already waited thirty years . . . Merry Christmas, Melissa.'

'Merry Christmas to you, too.'

She watched her neighbour leave, glimpses of blue flashing through the hedge as Angela went along the road, before disappearing. And then she closed the door and went back to the kitchen to join her girls.

ACKNOWLEDGEMENTS

I would like to thank both my formidable agent, Nelle Andrew and my talented editor, Emma Beswetherick for believing in me and always pushing me to excel. Thank you also to junior editor, Ellie Russell for being so diligent and supportive throughout the process of bringing this book to life. I would also like to give special thanks to my publicist, Clara Diaz. Big thank yous also to marketeer, Laura Vile; to editorial assistant, Sarah Murphy; to the cover designers Hannah Wood and Design by Sim; to Abby Marshall in production; to the copyeditor, Alison Tulett; to the proofreader, Sandra Ferguson and last but not least, audio editor, Sarah Shrubb. You have each played a part in the creation of this book and I'm indebted to you all.

A hearty slap on the back to my brother, Rob Weeks, for helping me with the nautical aspects of this book on a very hot day last year in June. Thank you also to my dad, Trevor Weeks, for taking me onto the Atlantic in an inflatable canoe as a child, which in no way inspired the nightmare kayaking scene in this story... Finally, thank you to Lisa Gannaway, Bec Vaughan, Ali Carter, Sally Pasche, Anita Rowden and Lisa Parker for your friendship and encouragement; and to my dearest mum, my loving husband, Nick, and my two beautiful sons, Wilfie and Alex. I couldn't do it without you, nor would I want to.

Friends Don't Lie

READING GROUP QUESTIONS

⚓ Who is your favourite character and why?

⚓ Can you talk about the theme of marriage in the story? Are each of the Silkies in the appropriate relationship?

⚓ How well do you think the author handles the subject of grief?

⚓ Did you guess any of the Silkies' secrets along the way?

⚓ Can you discuss the gradual unravelling of the Silkies' friendship in the story?

⚓ Blood is thicker than water. How does this well-known phrase inform the story?

⚓ Can you explore the theme of parenthood? Do you think the main characters behave well as parents?

⚓ How well do the gossipy extracts punctuating the narrative work in adding a framework to the storyline? Did you enjoy them?

⚓ Do you think people in friendship groups always take on 'roles', such as leader, follower, pacifier etc.? What roles would you give to each of the Silkies?

⚓ Were you happy with the way the story ended, or would you have ended it in any other way?

BEHIND THE BOOK: A
CONVERSATION WITH CATH WEEKS

What inspired you to write the story of *Friends Don't Lie*?

We were on holiday in Dorset when the idea came. I spent a lot of time in Dorset as a child on family days out, as I grew up not far away in Somerset, so I always find myself feeling relaxed and inspired there. My husband, Nick, and I were sitting on the beach, gazing at the sea, when Nick said – you should write about a big group of friends that live here... And from that one little comment, a book was born!

This is your fourth novel. Does writing get easier with each book?

Yes and no. My confidence grows with each book and it becomes easier to write in my personal style and voice. But the writing process never gets easy and nor should it. I try to keep my reader in mind at all times and I know the high standards that they will hold me to (not to mention my agent and my editor!). If I ever got to the stage where I found it a cinch, I probably wouldn't be doing my job properly.

Who is your favourite of the Silkies and why?

Melissa. I really enjoyed creating her character. She's so well-meaning but things often backfire for her because she's the victim of her emotions, as well as her tendency to be rash. Plus, she likes to be the one in control. I think there's a bit of Melissa in all of us, especially if you're a mum in charge of a young, frenetic family!

Do you think the Silkies have a healthy or unhealthy relationship? Can you talk a little about friendship in the story?

When I first got to know them, everything seemed gorgeous with the Silkies and I envied their intimacy. After all, the chances of your childhood friends staying local and close to hand is less likely these days, so the Silkies were a fantasy at best. But the longer I spent with them, the more I found myself thinking that perhaps there's a reason why friendship groups disperse once we leave school and go out into the world. In a way, the Silkies hadn't evolved and as soon as tragedy hit them, the cracks appeared. That said, I think there was a genuine love between them that endured. I deliberately left it open at the end for Melissa and Rachel in particular to find each other again.

The theme of grief appeared in your previous novel, *The Wife's Shadow*, yet the grief you write about in this book is raw and very real. Did you find this difficult to write?

Grief often pops up in my stories because it's such a strong emotion to explore as a writer. But I also find myself shying away from it for all the same reasons that we generally do as a society: for fear of seeming morbid or gloomy. I did find the grief scenes in this story difficult to write because Jenny died suddenly and there's always a shock element to an untimely death that's hard to capture. Gareth's grief was so intense, I found myself having to dial it up and dial it down, fiddling with it like a temperature gauge until I hit the right level.

Marriage is another theme explored in each of your stories. Why do you think this makes for such interesting subject matter in women's fiction?

I suspect that the subject will always be of interest because marriage can't help but reflect the times that we live in. I read recently that divorce rates are beginning to go down and that this is being partly attributed to the more even distribution of roles in the home. Marriage is a barometer for how we're doing personally in our lives, as well as generally as a society. I think it's always going to be something that women like to take a peek at, going behind the curtains to see how other people are going about it.

Can you talk about any other themes in the story?

One of the themes that I was most aware of whilst writing was that of family versus friends, and the old adage about blood being thicker than water. I never used to think that this was remotely true but the older you get, the more you begin to see where this phrase is coming from. When my first son was born very ill, it was only family who visited us in the neonatal unit. That's not to say that my friends weren't supportive; they really were. But when things become vital, critical, it's like there's an invisible line which friends hesitate to cross, and which family – even those whom you may not even think you're close to – are able to step over without a thought. If you've ever been in this situation, you'll know what I mean. People say *I'm family* in hospitals all the time; it's like flashing an ID badge that gives instant access.

Was it difficult writing the story from so many different points of view?

Sometimes, I find it easier to dart between characters than limit myself to one viewpoint because it keeps things moving and I also like to be able to get everyone's opinion. But the main challenge in doing so is making sure that I keep the thread between all the characters very strong so that it doesn't feel like a series of independent stories, rather than a smooth patchwork quilt, which is what I'm aiming for . . .

371

Could you have ended the story in any other way?

I'm not sure. I can't start writing a book without seeing the end in sight. I always know where I'm going and what I have in store for the characters. Melissa, ghastly mother aside, was always going to be OK because she has such a strong marriage. The only real dilemma that I had was whether she would let her mother off the hook. But by this point I had already worked through the family versus friends debate and felt that Melissa wouldn't ever hurt her brother, David, not even for her best friend, Jenny.

What are you working on now?

I'm at the fun brain-storming stage of my next book. I enjoyed the friendship elements of *Friends Don't Lie* so much that I'd like to explore this further, this time focusing on the power of female friendship. My characters are beginning to creep forward and introduce themselves to me, which is always a good sign. I just haven't ironed out the plot details yet. All I can say is that I won't be going to the Dorset coastline for inspiration any time soon because I've had my fill of kayaking disasters for now!

If you enjoyed reading *Friends Don't Lie*, then look out for Cath Weeks' gripping novel *The Wife's Shadow*

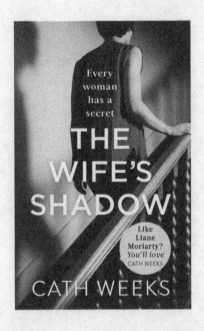

'If you enjoyed BBC's *Doctor Foster*, then you will happily devour this novel about a woman hiding a dark past'
Woman and Home

An emotional and suspenseful family drama of
secrets, betrayal and intrigue ...

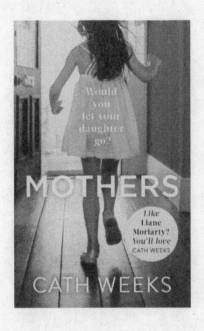

Available now from